A

Ship

Empire Rising Book 2

D. J. Holmes

https://www.facebook.com/Author.D.J.Holmes

d.j.holmess@hotmail.com

Comments welcome!

Cover art by Ivo Brankovikj

Contents

Prologue

11th Karack, 210 AC (After Contact), Vestar, two hundred years before the Void War.

Commander Agri'gar was inspecting the latest military checkpoints he had ordered set up to protect the newly constructed government buildings in the city of Amack. As he was walking around one of the inner courtyards a colossal boom erupted in the sky above him. While his subordinates dived to the ground he merely ducked down and peered up to see what was happening. Gaping up at the sky he saw a giant fireball passing over the central towers in the center of the city. It took several seconds to pass out of sight, heading in the direction of the Kal'dar Mountains.

Instinctively, Agri'gar lifted two of his four hands to his ears to shield them from the noise of the explosion the asteroid would make when it impacted with Vestar's surface. He waited for over thirty seconds but no sound reached them.

"That was no asteroid," one of his officers said.

"Is it an Omen?" another asked.

"Yes," Agri'gar said, removing his hands. "Something strange has happened. I believe it may well be the Omen we have been looking for." *One that I hope signals the end of this ridiculous Kulrean experiment in democracy,* he thought. "Prepare four of our armored transports, we're going to see where this thing crashed," he added.

*

Two days later and Agri'gar let out a long breath as he crested the top of another large hill. They had been forced to leave the transports behind several hours ago and the muscles in his four legs were burning with the strain of climbing over several mountains.

As his eyes took in the sight before him he almost choked on his next breath. There were scorch marks running along the middle of the next valley that could only have been caused by the fireball he had seen two days ago. The marks ran all the way to a large cliff at the other side of the valley. At the bottom of the cliff there was a large hole that looked like a cave. There was no sign of damage to the rocks or debris from an explosion so the fireball couldn't have caused the cave. *It flew into the cave,* he thought bewildered.

"This way," he shouted to the rest of the team. Without bothering to wait for them, he took off down the hill towards the cave. When he reached its entrance he pulled a torch out of his backpack. Seeing that the scorch marks continued along the floor he didn't hesitate to head in. About three hundred meters in, his light began to reflect off something metallic. Try as he might he couldn't make out its shape with his small torch.

His curiosity was satisfied a couple of minutes later when the rest of his team caught up and shone their torches on different parts of the structure.

"It's a ship," Agri'gar said in amazement.

"Welcome Vestarian," a voice said from within the ship, "I am a Kragorian warship, I have permission to share some of my military technology with you."

"You are a ship?" Agri'gar asked confused.

"Yes, I am the ship's artificial intelligence. I have been programmed with your language and given permission to dialogue with you," the voice said.

"Why are you here?" Agri'gar asked still confused.

"My makers are an ancient race of space explorers. They know of the Kulreans. They thought your people might like to have the means to free yourselves from the manipulation of your society," the ship explained.

"Yes," Agri'gar said, as his confusion slowly gave way to excitement. "I would like that very much."

"Then let's begin," the AI said. At the same time, it sent a message back into space confirming it had made contact with a suitable alien.

*

In a cloaked ship in orbit around Vestar the message from the artificial intelligence was received by Commander Shurlang. "Break us out of orbit," he said to his bridge crew. "Our scout drones have identified another three species suitable for our purposes. Take us to our next target at full speed. I want to get home before my claws fall off from lack of use!"

Haven Colony, present time.

First Councilor Graham Maximilian stood to address the assembled councilors of the Haven Collective. It was rare for all the councilors to meet together; their constitution ensured bureaucracy was kept to a minimum. As a rule, they tried to keep full meetings of the Council down to two or three a year. Only when something really important needed their immediate attention did they all meet together. The day to day running of their world was handled by smaller sub committees made up of some of the councilors. Even then, when there was an important issue to be decided it went to a general vote by the entire population. The result was a clean and efficient system that kept bureaucracy to a minimum.

Before speaking Maximilian paused for effect. It was a trick he had learnt from watching holovids of his great grandfather. As he paused he surveyed the room. The councilors all sat in their assigned booths in a semi-circle facing the First Councilor's podium. They were arranged in three layers, each on top of the other. Any one of the booths could extend into the center of the room. Despite there only being one hundred councilors, the council chamber housing the booths was an impressive building. Built in their capital city, Liberty, by his father, the chamber could have housed double the number of booths. Along the walls there were magnificent paintings and sculptures, some of which were even originals from Earth. The roof of the chamber comprised of a stunning series of mosaics depicting the construction, launch and landing of the colony ship that had brought everyone's ancestors to Haven two hundred years ago. The whole chamber had been meant as a display of his father's wealth, the only real measure of power on Haven.

As Maximilian eyed each of the councilors in turn he noticed there were several new faces. That was to be expected. The founders of the colony had been sick of the bureaucrats and career politicians of Earth. Such people had driven them to head to the stars in the first place. When setting up their own governing council, they had ensured that councilors could only serve for a maximum of six years. Without the pressure of having to campaign for reelection, the councilors were able to focus on championing the needs of those who elected them.

Finally Maximilian spoke, "Ladies and gentlemen of the Council. I welcome you and I hope we can conclude our business quickly. You have all been briefed on the petition that has been set before us. Is there anyone who wishes to speak on the issue?"

Three lights lit up on his podium to indicate that three councilors were requesting to speak. As the First Councilor, Maximilian couldn't actually present his opinion on any given matter. He was meant to remain impartial. Yet, he did control who spoke when and that in itself was a powerful tool.

Councilor Young had been one of the most outspoken isolationists since he had been appointed to the council three years ago. Maximilian let him speak first.

"I should think our decision on this issue is obvious. No human from Earth has set foot on our planet since our forefathers founded Haven. Even though the Earth nations now know of our existence, it will likely take them decades to find us. I see no benefit from accepting this petition. We have no idea what consequences may come of letting even one person from Earth into the Haven system. We could destroy everything we have been building for the last hundred years. This Council has been elected because our people think we can wisely make decisions on such important matters. We must not let them down. Our forefathers left Earth for a reason. We have been thriving on our own; there is no need for us to risk this. We need nothing from this Earthling or any other!" Pouring as much disgust into the pronouncement of Earthling as he could Young finished by flicking his hand in dismissal towards the space above that somewhere out there held Earth.

As his booth retracted to its original position the booth of Councilor Farks extended into the middle of the chamber.

Farks was a young firebrand but he was very popular among the younger populace on Haven. Everyone took what he had to say seriously; he had a large backing and was generally thought to reflect the views of the next generation of Havenites.

"My esteemed colleague is correct. Our isolation has served us well these last two hundred years. We have built a civilization our forefathers would be proud of. However, our forefathers were not idealists. They knew one day we would make contact with Earth again. That day has already come and passed. Earth knows we exist. They may not have found Haven yet, but they will. We need to be prepared. If we cannot face the Earth nations as equals, they will try to absorb us into one of their colonial empires. We cannot allow that. Already we have increased our military spending twice in the last year. I have no doubt we will do so again. Yet all our efforts may prove worthless. The Earth nations have been fighting each other for the last two hundred years. While our forefathers travelled across the stars in cryostasis, the Earth nations were developing weapons of war. When our grandfathers and fathers were building our beautiful colony, the Earth nations were developing weapons of war. We can spend as much money as we have on building new ships, however, if we don't have the weapon technologies with which to arm them, they will be no better than defenseless freighters. If the Earth nations decide to send warships our way, our fleet will disintegrate before them. We need to accept this petition. If we don't, then we won't just be risking everything we have built here, we will be guaranteeing our eventual demise."

Satisfied he had got his point across, Fark's podium began to retract. Maximilian had left Councilor Pennington to the last. They were old friends and they had already discussed the issue in depth. She was seen by most of the councilors as the elder stateswoman of Haven. Pennington was the longest serving CEO of any industrial enterprise on Haven. The fact that it was the largest on Haven made it all the more impressive. So even though she had only recently been elected to the council, every councilor knew her and many counted her among their close personal advisors.

"As I see it we have little choice," she began. "The Earth nations will discover us sooner rather than later. None of us want to enter into open conflict with them. That will only be prevented if we meet them as equals. We can only do that if we have the technology being offered to us. The logical decision is therefore to accept the petition. There are risks involved. We all know this. Yet we will not get a better opportunity than this. I therefore advise every one of you to vote in favor of accepting." As she finished she bowed to the gathered councilors and then hit the button that would return her booth to its place.

Maximilian was about to call for a vote when another light lit up. With a sigh he accepted, there was nothing else he could do.

Though as her booth began to extend he addressed the chamber; "Councilor Rodriguez will address us now and then we will proceed to a vote." He didn't want to drag this debate out any longer.

Once her booth came to rest in the middle of the chamber Rodriguez slowly turned in a circle to gaze at the councilors around her. "Today's actions have brought shame on this council. You all know me, you know my family, we have done as much as anyone to build up this planet, our home. Yet if we accept this petition we will be bringing shame on all our forefathers and everything we have built here. They left Earth to get away from its politics, its infighting and its wars. Have none of you thought about who this individual is? About what he has done? He has been declared a war criminal. If no one else will say it, I will. If we accept this petition, we will be bringing everything to Haven that our forefathers tried to leave behind. I will not vote in favor of this, and I ask each of you to carefully consider not just the political implications of this decision, but the moral ones as well. If we go forward with this, we will be beginning down a path that will take us back towards what our forefathers escaped. This decision should not be taken lightly."

"Thank you," Maximilian said through a forced smile. She was not an isolationist but she still opposed every effort he and his allies on the council tried to make to prepare Haven to meet the human nations. She seemed to think that if they revealed themselves to the Earthlings, Haven would be recognized as a separate political entity. That, he knew, was a mistake. If there was one thing he had learnt from his great grandfather's writings it was that Earthlings would never leave a source of profit untouched. As long as Maximilian and his allies held sway in the council, Rodriguez would never find out if her theories were correct. The risks of her being wrong were simply too great.

"We will now hold a vote on the petition that has been presented to us. Each councilor has five minutes to vote, you may confer with your aides before you make your decision. I will start the timer now," he said.

As muted discussions broke out around the chamber Maximilian sat down in the First Councilor's chair behind his podium. Apart from the paintings and carvings from Earth, the chair was the only other thing in the room not from Haven. It was the command chair from the colony ship which had brought his people here. His great grandfather, Harold Maximilian, who had funded the construction of the colony ship, had had the chair removed when they landed on Haven as a keepsake. His father had then placed it in the council chamber when he had constructed the impressive building. Even though the populace elected the position of First Councilor, his father had hoped that generations of Maximilian's would continue to sit in the seat. So far things were working out nicely in that respect.

When the timer reached zero he stood to address the chamber. "Your time is up. Any votes that have not been cast will be counted as abstentions." Looking down, Maximilian smiled as he saw the result of the vote. "The petition has passed," he announced, "by a vote of seventy five to twenty three."

The silence in the chamber was broken as a number of discussions broke out from the various booths. A couple of councilors actually began to shout at each other across the room. As Maximilian opened his mouth to intervene he was distracted by a beep from one of his COM units. He activated it, hoping to dismiss whoever had disturbed him and regain order on the chamber floor. "Yes, what is it?" he demanded.

"My apologies for disturbing you First Councilor," one of his aides said. "I have Admiral Harris on a COM channel for you. He said it was urgent."

"Put him through," Maximilian said irritably.

"First Chancellor, I'm afraid I need to be quick, there is no time for pleasantries," Admiral Harris said as his faced appeared on a holo screen at Maximilian's arm.

"Go on," Maximilian said, nodding.

"Our system defenses just picked up a large gravimetric pulse at the edge of the system. My analysts have never seen anything quite like it. It appears to have been produced by a ship exiting shift space. Yet the size of the pulse is off the charts. It is either from an extremely powerful shift drive that has brought something massive into our system, or an extremely crude one that makes a fluctuating gravimetric anomaly to enter shift space. It wasn't produced by one of our ships and from the data we have gathered on the human nations they have built nothing that could produce such a pulse either. We believe it may have been constructed by someone else."

"Someone else?" Maximilian said confused. "You mean you think this might be a first contact situation?" he continued with incredulity.

"As farfetched as it seems, that's our best guess at the moment," Harris answered. "I contacted you to get your permission to put our defenses on high alert and to send out two destroyers to intercept the ship."

"Right," Maximilian said as he paused to gather his thoughts. Suddenly his desire to keep Haven secret and isolated from the rest of the human nations seemed like wishful thinking. If mankind was not alone in space, then everything was about to change.

"You have my permission to bring our military to full alert. Though don't send any military ships. I want you to commandeer an unarmed civilian freighter and send out a team to make contact with the ship. If it isn't human I don't want to antagonize it."

"Yes Sir, I'll see to it immediately," Harris responded.

As the COM channel closed Maximilian stood and called for order from the councilors. When there was silence he spoke, "I'm afraid we are not yet done today. I have just been made aware of another situation that may need our attention."

*

Maximilian was still sitting nervously at his podium several hours later. Every councilor had stayed in their booth; they were all frantically discussing the latest development with their aides and others outside the chamber. Maximilian had been monitoring the Haven newscasts. Already there was panic in many of the main cities and it would soon spread to the outlying towns and villages. He had left the chamber to make a brief appearance on the news but it had produced little effect. The fact was that he didn't yet have enough information to appease himself, never mind the public.

Finally his chair alerted him that Admiral Harris was requesting a COM link. "Yes Admiral, what has your team found out?"

"It's confirmed, they are aliens," Harris said. "They call themselves the Vestarians."

For a long moment Maximilian was left speechless. *First contact? How can this be?* he thought. Shaking himself he blurted out the first question that came to his mind, "Your people have been able to speak to them?"

"Of course they have," Maximilian corrected himself, already angry that the shock of the situation was affecting his thinking. "How else could you know their name?"

"That is correct Sir, or at least, they have been able to speak to us and can understand us. I have been getting mixed reports. Some of their technology seems to be more advanced than ours. For instance, their ability to translate our language so quickly. Yet their ship seems to be decades or even centuries behind ours. They don't appear to have access to valstronium and whatever drive system they are using is much slower than our impulse drives."

"What do they want?" Maximilian asked.

"Technology. They say they have come to our system in the hopes of trading for military technology. Supposedly their planet is under the control of another alien species and they want help overthrowing them and gaining their freedom."

"Supposedly?" Maximilian said.

"Well Sir, if you wanted to trade military technology with someone wouldn't you make up some kind of sob story to gain their trust? It may be true, but how are we to know they won't just turn round and use our technology against us? The report from my men was clear on one thing. These aliens aren't very good at diplomacy. They are practically demanding that we hand over everything we have, and as far as my analysts can tell, they aren't really offering us much in return. Apart from their translation technology, I'm not even sure they have anything we would want."

Whether they have anything of value or not is irrelevant, Maximilian thought to himself. *There is no way I am giving an unknown alien species any military technology. What am I going to do now?*

"Stand by Admiral," he began, "I need to address the council. We will have to take a vote on this. Alert your team on the freighter that we will be sending a diplomatic response to this request for technology. Tell them to prepare for the aliens to be disappointed. There will be no trading today."

Once the COM channel closed Maximilian turned to address the gathered councilors once more. "Ladies and gentlemen, we have another vote to take, this one may be the most important in the history of our colony. Yet there is only one choice before us." *Impartiality be dammed,* he thought as he laid out the alien's request.

Chapter 1 – HMS Endeavour

Throughout the First Interstellar Expansion Era warships got ever larger and larger, yet many historians believe it was the exploration ships that proved to be the most important.

-Except from Empire Rising, 3002 AD

20th January, 2466 AD, HMS *Vulcan*, Earth Orbit

Captain James Somerville, Duke of Beaufort, sat behind his desk in his briefing room. Fighting back a yawn he reached for another datafile. Glancing at his holo clock he was startled to see he had come on board HMS *Endeavour* over eight hours ago. After going through the official procedure of taking command, he had settled into his office and reviewed every piece of information he could find on his new ship.

Officially classed as an exploration cruiser, she was still more powerful than his last command, the destroyer HMS *Raptor*. *Endeavour* boasted two extra missile tubes in each of her broadsides and she had three plasma cannon turrets that were a caliber heavier than *Raptor's*. He had also been happy to see *Endeavour* had been outfitted with two flak cannons. When she had begun construction flak cannons had not been a part of her armament. Yet the success of the flak cannons in the war with China had led to a hasty design change for all new Royal Space Navy construction. Having just left the RSN shipyard *Vulcan* two months ago, *Endeavour* had benefited from this new design policy.

Despite his tiredness James was determined to continue working his way through the files and familiarizing himself with the crew of his ship. If he stopped his mind would only turn to Christine. It had been six days since her wedding to Na and it was still all over the news outlets. The new Emperor and Empress of China were causing a sensation not just in Britain and China but all across the globe. Yet James wanted nothing to do with the whole affair, his emotions were still too raw. After spending months in the Void fighting the Chinese fleet he had dreamt of coming home to Christine. In the war he had won glory for himself and redeemed his family name. At last he had been in a position where he would have been considered worthy to make a proposal to the Princess of England. Instead, Christine had found herself with a choice between her heart and her duty and James had lost out. He knew she had made the right decision. It was the only decision she could have made as a British princess. Nevertheless, it didn't ease his pain and the sooner he was able to take *Endeavour* out on her maiden voyage the better.

With a stretch and another yawn he reached over and tapped a button on his desk. Outside his office a chime rang, alerting the waiting officer that she could enter. After reviewing the files on *Endeavour* he had scheduled an interview with each of his senior officers. On his first command, the exploration ship *Drake,* he had made a bad start with his officers, something that had taken almost two years to remedy. He was determined to do things differently on *Endeavour.*

The exploration cruiser had four commissioned officers to oversee the crew. Only three were currently on board and James had not known any of them. He hoped the informal interviews would speed up the process of breaking down the barriers that always existed between a captain and his officers.

Thankfully he wouldn't need one with his Fourth Lieutenant when she came on board. The most junior lieutenant position had been vacant when James had taken command and he had been delighted to see a file from *Vulcan* that included a request from Lieutenant Becket to be assigned to *Endeavour*. She had been a Sub Lieutenant on board his last two commands, *Drake* and *Raptor*. When James had been off enjoying some rest and relaxation in the South Pacific, she had taken her Lieutenant's exam. James hadn't been surprised to see she had passed with flying colors. He had immediately approved the request and was looking forward to greeting her when she came on board.

For now though, he switched his focus to another female officer, one he didn't know what to make of. After the discovery of the Void, the Admiralty had decided to make a new position on all their exploration ships. Among the science community there were all sorts of weird and wonderful theories about what was out there in the dark of space. Up until a year ago, a dark matter bubble – what the Void was, had just been another one of these theories. James' discovery of one had sent the theorists into overdrive. Everyone was now wondering what else was out there. Presently humans had only explored less than one one-hundredth of a percent of the galaxy. The possibilities were endless. In response to all this hype the Admiralty had decided to appoint a Science Officer to each of their survey ships. The Science Officers would command a small team of astrophysicists and analyze all the sensor data the ship collected. Yet they would remain outside the official chain of command, meaning the officer wouldn't hold any authority over the rest of the crew. As a result James wasn't sure what he thought of the new position.

As the door to his office alerted him that someone was about to enter, he stood to greet Lieutenant Rachael Scott. He had already seen a picture of her from her personnel file, but as she walked in he was still taken aback. She had long, thick blonde hair and bright green eyes that sparkled. Even though she looked nervous to be meeting her captain for the first time she still gave off that air of confidence that reminded James how nervous he got when in the presence of a beautiful woman.

As she came close, James held out his hand. "It's good to meet you Lieutenant," he said with a smile. "There's no need to be nervous, this is just an informal meet and greet."

"Thank you Sir," Rachael responded. "As you no doubt know this is my first ship so I'm still a little green."

"That's ok," James said. "You'll pick things up quickly. So sit down, I want you to tell me a little about yourself." As he spoke James sat himself and waved at a chair for Rachael to take.

"Well, I don't know if you know this Sir, but we actually shared some classes together back at the academy."

Surprised, James blurted out, "Really, which ones?" before he realized he was admitting he didn't remember her.

"That's alright Sir, I didn't expect you to recognize me," Rachael said when she saw the embarrassment on her captain's face. "We only shared some of the basic classes. I entered the academy because I wanted to join the Navy's astrophysics department. After taking first year I pursued my degree and doctoral studies back on Earth."

"Yes, I saw your degrees listed in your file," James said, "You seem to have done very well for yourself. May I ask, how did you end up aboard *Endeavour*? Forgive me for thinking this, but I would imagine someone with your skills would be more useful back on Earth, not spending months at a time on the outer edges of space."

"Actually, I chose this assignment," Rachael replied. "To be honest, I always wanted to serve on a navy ship. It was my father who pushed me into studying astrophysics. That's not to say I don't love my field of study. But I love space too. *Endeavour* will allow me to pursue both my loves. You maybe don't realize it, but *Endeavour* is kitted out with some high tech labs and a state of the art central computer. I can continue to work on my theoretical models aboard *Endeavour*."

"And they won't get in the way of your duties?" James asked with a little concern. He had encountered enough scientists in the past to know that when they got caught up in their studies, the rest of the world seemed to fade away.

"I hope not Sir. I realize that I have duties aboard *Endeavour*, they come first of course. Though I'm sure you've been wondering what a science officer will be doing with themselves during extended cruises. Even when *Endeavour* is out mapping the unexplored dark matter, the majority of our sensor data will be of no interest scientifically. As I understand it, these science officer posts were designed to give young researchers field experience that will benefit them in the future while also giving them the space to pursue their scientific studies. In fact, as part of my request to join *Endeavour*, I had to present a proposal on what areas of astrophysics I will be researching."

James wasn't sure he liked this answer any better. It was sounding more and more like Rachael was just going to be a passenger he or one of his officers would have to babysit. A navy ship came with enough responsibilities for its officers without adding babysitting inexperienced officers to the list.

To her credit Rachael seemed to sense his concern. "If you don't mind me asking Sir," she began, "but I get the impression you don't approve of the Admiralty's decision to post science officers to survey ships?"

James paused before he answered, he choose his words carefully as he didn't want to start off on the wrong foot with Rachael, "I wouldn't say I don't approve. It's just; I've spent more than two years aboard a survey frigate. I know how monotonous the daily routine can be. There is almost never anything of significance that comes up, especially something that would interest someone of your intellect. I'm just afraid you will get bored and have wasted your time aboard my ship."

Rachael smiled, and when she did James saw something else in her. Her initial nervousness had been genuine; he was sure of that. Yet now, behind this new smile, he saw a more confident woman, a woman who knew how to get what she wanted. "It's funny you say that," she began, "because I actually wanted to make a request. You already know how I wanted to join the navy and serve in a ship, but what I didn't tell my father was that I want to command one someday."

James almost laughed but the earnestness in her voice caused him to forcibly suppress any such notion. "Command? But you only studied a year at the academy, how do you expect the Admiralty to change you from the science track to the command track?" he asked instead.

Rachael smiled that smile again, and James knew he would have to watch her closely. He trusted her motives, but she was obviously skilled in getting what she wanted.

"Actually, that is where you come in. I know the Admiralty will never consider me for a command post without any experience. I was hoping to convince you to allow me to command the occasional watch. I could relieve you or the First Lieutenant, maybe once or twice a week. Of course, it would only be during watches when there is no potential danger. When we would be traveling through known shift passages. But over time, especially if we are assigned to a long survey mission, I could build up some command experience. In a few years, I could then request a transfer to a survey frigate as a second lieutenant. In time I might be promoted to command one. I'm not deluded. I don't have any aspirations of commanding a warship, but maybe one day I could have my own survey frigate."

James was taken aback. This wasn't exactly how he had expected this interview to go. He had been worried that he would have to babysit an untrained officer. Instead, he thought with a chuckle, he might have to watch his back in case she tried to steal his command from him.

He was pleased though; she obviously felt comfortable enough to open up with him. That was something James had noticed more and more since he had returned to Earth just over a week ago. Almost everyone in Britain had grown up knowing his family name and by association with his father, he knew that he had become almost notorious. Yet after the discovery of the Void, especially the events that surrounded the Chinese attack on the

Swedish colony ship, he had found himself a public figure in his own right. His brief association with the now Empress of China had added to that of course. Since his return to Earth, he had found that many people already felt they knew him and so were much more open.

Turning his mind back to the problem at hand, James knew Rachael's request would fit in well with his plans. Yet he also saw one major problem.

"Your aspirations are praiseworthy, but there is likely to be one issue that may stand in your way. The Royal Space Navy is designed for war. Even our survey frigates are designed to have a role in times of war. My first command, *Drake,* demonstrated that. Even with all the command experience you could get here on *Endeavour,* I'm not sure the Admiralty will see you as command material. You will still lack the tactical training cadets at the academy get."

Rachael looked deflated by his comments and so James held up a finger to halt her thoughts, "However, I think I can help start you in the right direction. You may not like it but it is the best I can do for you. Once we leave Earth I plan to introduce a secondary watch using the auxiliary bridge. The secondary watch will be solely for training purposes. The idea is that the Sub Lieutenants who are off duty can take it in turns manning the auxiliary bridge, as if they are running their own watch. Some can man the command consoles while one of them acts as the officer of the watch commanding the ship. I also plan to make up some training scenarios for them to go through.

"I can't put you right in as the officer who commands the watch as almost all the Sub Lieutenants have more experience than you. However, I can put you into the rotation. You will have to take your turn manning the command consoles but you will also get to command the watch. I'm sure you'll quickly pick up the necessary skills and in time, depending on how you do, I'll be able to consider allowing you to take some real watches on the bridge. In the meantime you can review the tactical training cadets get at the academy and develop your skills as you man the tactical console on the mock bridge. How does that sound?"

Rachael hesitated for a second. James wasn't surprised. Joining the Sub Lieutenants would be potentially embarrassing. She was older than them all and at least technically her rank of science officer made her more senior than them. Joining them would cause everyone on board to think less of her rank. A look of resolve settled on her face.

"I'll do it," she said, "Thank you for the opportunity Captain, I hope I won't let you down."

"I hope so too," James replied.

As he was about to change the subject and ask Rachael about her studies an alert from his desk notified him that someone on the bridge was trying to contact him. Opening a COM channel he said, "Yes, this is the Captain?"

"Captain," Seamus Mallory, the Second Lieutenant began, "Orders have just arrived from *Vulcan* Sir. An encrypted data file is awaiting you at your command chair."

"Thank you Lieutenant," James replied. "I will be up presently."

Looking over at the Science Officer, James stood and shook her hand again. "I'm afraid we will have to continue this another time. I'm sure it will be a pleasure having you on board."

"Thank you Sir," she responded, "and can I say that it is exciting to be serving under you. I hope we can make a discovery as important as the Void with *Endeavour*."

James laughed and then answered, "Me too, but you should be careful what you wish for, discovering the Void led us to a war."

After watching her leave James took a moment to compose himself. A shiver of excitement ran down his spine. This was the first time he would be entering the bridge. After going through the protocol for taking command when he had come aboard he had come straight to his office to read up on *Endeavour*. Now he was about to enter the place that would be his home for the foreseeable future. *Endeavour* was his third command and he knew from experience that he would be spending long hours in his command chair. From there he could direct the three hundred men and women on board, as well as control all of *Endeavour's* weapons.

A few years ago the thought of commanding another survey ship would have filled him with dread. His first command, the survey frigate HMS *Drake*, had been a punishment rather than a reward. Giving him the ship had been a ploy to keep him away from Earth and the British princess. Yet, over time he had come to love the navy and his first command. Now command was all he had left. The idea of an extended survey mission into outer space actually excited him. Or at least, it was better than the thought of staying on Earth.

Before heading to the bridge he went into his personal quarters to retrieve his captain's jacket. His steward from *Raptor* had accompanied him to *Endeavour* and Fox already had all his things unpacked and stowed away. With a glance at one of the reflective screens in his quarters he straightened his uniform, patted down his thick blond hair and headed for the bridge.

As he entered and every eye looked at him, James suddenly felt a little self-conscious. *Endeavour's* bridge was much bigger than *Raptor's* and there were many more people about. Before he had a chance to take everyone in, Lieutenant Mallory stood to vacate the command chair.

"The bridge is yours Captain," he said as he saluted.

"Thank you Lieutenant," James said as he approached his chair. "You can continue the watch, I will be reviewing our orders."

As Mallory walked over to sit in the Officer of the Watch's command chair, James slowly lowered himself into his home aboard *Endeavour*. The seat was identical to the one onboard *Raptor* and he immediately felt at ease. Before opening his orders he looked around the bridge again. Everyone was still staring at him. "At ease, back to work," he said with a wave of his hand.

When all the eyes in the room turned back to their duties James took the opportunity to assess his bridge crew. There were five Sub Lieutenants manning the ship's command consoles, Navigation, Sensors, Tactical, Defense and Communications. To either side of him there were secondary command chairs, both of which were a new addition for James. Lieutenant Mallory sat in one while the other was vacant. To one side the Science Officer sat, looking over her shoulder James could see she was reviewing some sophisticated looking graphical image. He quickly moved on, knowing that whatever she was doing was way beyond his comprehension. As well as the usual Sub Lieutenants there were also a number of Ensigns on the bridge. Their job was to assist their seniors and take over in the event one was injured during combat. Finally there were the two marine guards standing at ease by the door to the bridge. After Major Johnston's successful boarding of a Chinese destroyer during the Void War, the RSN had instigated some new protocols to prevent the same thing happening to a British warship. One of which meant there was a marine guard on every ship's bridge.

Happy that everyone was working efficiently, James turned his attention to his command chair. The data chip containing his orders had already been placed in a slot on his chair and a screen was flashing, demanding his password. After he typed it in and pressed his finger to the scanner to confirm his DNA, a file appeared on the screen. His orders were simple. He was to take *Endeavour* through the shift passage to the Alpha system and then onto Chester, the furthest British colony from Earth. In times of peace *Endeavour* was designed to be a survey ship. As the first survey cruiser the British had built, she was designed for prolonged periods of space travel in unexplored space. His orders were to carry-out a survey cruise of up to nine months beyond Chester.

Having already met with his uncle, Admiral Somerville, the First Space Lord of the Admiralty, James knew his orders were only for show. Sure enough as he scanned through them he found a set of coordinates in his objectives. To anyone else who looked at the orders it would look as if someone back at the Admiralty had made a mistake for they made no sense. Yet, they were his real objective. He didn't want to put them into a computer to project them until they left Earth, just in case someone was watching what he did. His uncle had impressed on him the importance of secrecy. Still, from the look of the coordinates it appeared *Endeavour* would be rendezvousing with a ship somewhere near the New Edinburgh system. There he would get his real orders, along with all the information the Royal Space Navy Intelligence had managed to obtain on Chang. For now, it was important that everyone, including his crew, thought *Endeavour* was about to set off on a long exploration mission, for the duration of which they would be out of contact with Earth.

Alongside his orders another file was flashing to get his attention. It was the report from the Master Engineer aboard *Vulcan*. He was responsible for overseeing every ship constructed by *Vulcan*. *Endeavour* had left space dock just over two months ago. From that time the First Lieutenant had been putting her through her space trials. Her final act had been a stealth run through the Sol system to test her capabilities. She had passed with flying colors and a week ago she had docked with *Vulcan* for the engineers to give her a once over to ensure she was still space worthy. As the first of her class, every caution was being taken to ensure she was performing as expected. James was happy to see the Master Engineer's report cleared *Endeavour* to take up her duties among the fleet.

As he closed the report he turned to the Second Lieutenant, "How long until we finish taking on our stores and ammunition?"

Lieutenant Mallory took a moment to answer as he brought up the relevant file, "six more hours Sir. After that we will have everything we need on board to operate independently for up to a year."

"Very good," James said. If he had wanted to look up the file he would have done it himself. Mallory should have known how things were progressing without having to check.

Turning back to his command chair he opened a ship wide COM channel. "Attention, this is your Captain speaking. I have just received our orders. We are heading to the Chester system and from there we will begin exploring the unmapped shift passages in the area. *Endeavour* has been given a clean bill of health by the engineers from *Vulcan* and as soon as we have replenished our stores, we will be breaking orbit. I suggest any of you that want to contact loved ones and say your goodbyes do so now. That is all."

Comfortable in his command chair, James brought up a number of files that he hadn't had time to review yet. He was so engrossed in reading them that he lost track of time. His thoughts were broken when his First Lieutenant, Stephen Ferguson, sat down beside him in the vacant command chair and spoke, "Sir, I'm pleased to report that we have just stored the last penetrator missile. *Endeavour* is ready to leave."

"Very good Ferguson," James said, "you have been commanding *Endeavour* for the last two months. I think you have earned the privilege of taking her out on her maiden voyage. You have the bridge Lieutenant, set course for the Alpha system."

As Ferguson barked orders to the rest of the bridge James watched his ship come alive. The Sub Lieutenants were all chatting frantically with one another and even the senior Lieutenants looked excited to be off on an adventure of discovery. James knew that wasn't where they were headed. He was excited nonetheless. The Void War had cost him his future with Christine. He couldn't get that back. But he could get some revenge on the Politburo member who had started it all. *Chang, I'm coming for you,* James thought as *Endeavour* disengaged her docking clamps and climbed out of Earth orbit.

Chapter 2 – Innocence

In those days piracy was almost unheard of.

-Excerpt from Empire Rising, 3002 AD

11th February 2466 AD, New Edinburgh System

Three weeks later James was on the bridge as *Endeavour* dropped out of shift space into the New Edinburgh System. They had passed through the system on their way to Chester just over a week ago with all the ship's equipment fully powered up, ensuring that *Endeavour* had been visible for all to see. They did the same in Chester. James had even entered the inner system and had a lengthy conversation with the system commander in order to discuss the latest survey findings from around Chester. From there James had jumped *Endeavour* out of the Chester system towards unexplored space. To anyone who was keeping tabs on his ship it would look like she had been sent out on an exploration mission.

To his crew's bewilderment, instead of beginning to map out the dark matter, James had ordered *Endeavour* into stealth mode and jumped back to Chester. For over a week they then slowly worked their way back through British space to New Edinburgh. It was here that they were to meet their contact and get the final update on their real orders. The coordinates that James had indicated they were to head towards was that of the shift passage that linked New Edinburgh with French colonial space. Thus, James suspected they would be heading in that direction, possibly they would be going all the way to the New France system itself. James had never seen it, but he had read a lot about the system, it had been the place of the biggest space battle in human history, up until the Void War at least.

"Navigation," James said once the holo plot had updated to show nothing unusual in the New Edinburgh system. "I have just sent some new coordinates to you, plot us a course to take us there."

"Aye Sir," Sub Lieutenant Jennings responded. James had been impressed with the Sub Lieutenant's skill in their stealth runs through the British systems on their way back to New Edinburgh. A number of his Sub Lieutenants were newly promoted and were still very inexperienced. He and the First Lieutenant had been forced to keep a close eye on them. No doubt it would take a few months for them to settle into their roles. James had assigned them all extra shifts in the auxiliary bridge to hone their skills, but Jennings hadn't been among them. She was already well on her way to earning her promotion to full lieutenant.

"Lieutenant Ferguson, can I see you in my briefing room?" James asked as he rose from his command chair and strode from the bridge. Ferguson nodded and got up to follow his captain.

As he entered the briefing room James called out to his steward, "Arthur, can you bring us both black coffees, please."

Without waiting for a reply, he turned back to Ferguson and motioned for him to sit. As the First Lieutenant followed his direction James took a moment to study him. At six foot two inches Ferguson was impressively built, yet James had already noticed that he seemed very light on his feet. Coming from

Ireland he had a strange accent and James wondered if, in stereotypical fashion, he had stowed some alcoholic beverages on board. Ferguson's record was notable so he was happy to overlook both issues in any case. After serving on board a survey frigate he had been promoted to a Lieutenant and posted to one of the RSN's battlecruisers. Then, just before the outbreak of war with the Chinese, he had been promoted to Second Lieutenant and transferred to a destroyer. The destroyer in question had spent the first half of the war on patrol in the Oxford system but when the Admiralty had decided to send raiders into Chinese space, his ship had been sent up the Beta shift passage to harass the Chinese. Both his Captain and the crew had performed well and Ferguson's reward had been another promotion. James had been delighted to see another raider on board *Endeavour*. Alongside Captain Lightfoot, James had caused the Chinese a number of headaches behind their frontlines in the last war. Yet having to carrying out such missions had been unexpected and the Royal Navy was still relearning the skill of operating behind enemy lines. Whilst Endeavour was officially classed as an exploration ship she was designed to also operate behind enemy lines in times of war. In fact *Endeavour* was the first ship purpose built for just such a mission and it was good to have an officer on board who knew what he was doing. His record was certainly impressive and everything James had seen of Ferguson only served to confirm that he was a very competent officer.

"We'll be having a briefing with all the senior command crew but I think you deserve to know what we're about first," James began.

"Thank you Sir," Ferguson said. "It will be good to know what is going on. Your orders so far have been strange. I assume our mission won't involve too much exploration in the immediate future?"

"Call me James in private please," James said, smiling, "And you could say that. There's a reason the Admiralty picked a Captain and First Lieutenant for *Endeavour* who were involved in the raids into Chinese space. You've heard of the Chinese Minister Chang of course. Well, we're going after him. The UN wants him arrested for war crimes and our government is keen to see him punished for starting the war."

"That sounds like a real mission," Ferguson said with a widening grin. "Do we have any intel on his whereabouts?"

"No, but we are meeting a contact at the coordinates I gave Jennings. Whoever they are, they will be giving us the information we need. I also suspect we will be taking on board some passengers. I can't imagine RSN Intelligence will let us go tearing after Chang without some form of assistance or oversight."

"In that case I look forward to meeting our contact," Ferguson replied. "I lost some good friends in the final battle with the Chinese at Wi Xiang. It would be a real pleasure to be one of the ones who brings Chang to justice."

"Indeed," James said, "my sentiments exactly. We'll brief the rest of the command staff once we have met with the contact and have more information but I wanted you to know what we are about first. We're going to be working together very closely over the next few months and there is likely to be information I can only share with you, so I wanted us to get off on the right foot."

"I understand Sir, I mean James," Ferguson said with a nod.

"Good, well in that case there is another issue I want to bring up." Before progressing any further James paused and took a deep breath. He hesitated as he thought again about bringing up the next issue; it was not something he had faced before. "It's about Second Lieutenant Mallory. I have been observing him, as I have all my Lieutenants over the last three weeks. On paper he seems like a good Lieutenant, he meets all his efficiency targets. Yet he doesn't seem to get on well with the crew and he meets his efficiency targets too well; he never does more than he has to. Is my assessment fair or have I misjudged him?"

This time Ferguson hesitated. James understood. Ferguson had only known James for a few weeks. It was a First Lieutenant's duty to oversee the other Lieutenants and only come to the Captain whenever something happened that demanded his attention. If he started telling on his junior lieutenants now, he could lose their respect and confidence.

Before he closed down and refused to speak, James prodded Ferguson some more. "Ordinarily I wouldn't bring this up so soon but reading between the lines, there were some concerning comments in his personnel file. I know I shouldn't be sharing this with you but we need to trust each other completely. Both his previous captains commented that Mallory was an efficient officer, but lacked leadership experience. I think they were trying to say something. At the start of the Void War he was a fifth lieutenant. His promotion to second came about because of deaths among those higher up, not because he was deemed worthy of promotion on merit alone. If we were just going on a routine survey mission I would let it slide and try to work on him. However, our mission to find Chang is a sensitive one – I need to know who I can trust and depend on. If my guess is right, we'll be heading into French colonial space and who knows where from there. If Mallory is going to prove a liability, I need to know now."

As James had been speaking Ferguson had been staring at the deck. He brought up one hand and began to rub his jaw. "Alright," he began after another pause. "I'll be honest, so far my assessment of him has come close to yours. In dry dock at *Vulcan* and then during our space trials he did everything that was expected of him. Yet there was something about him that didn't sit right. I did some digging before we left Earth. I'm sure you didn't recognize the name but his family owns a large stake in the Chester colony. As a result, they have a lot of influence over the Members of Parliament that come from Chester and have some clout in the Commons."

James considered Ferguson's information. Since the British expansion into space the parliamentary system had undergone an extensive revision. No one wanted to see an interstellar repeat of the American War of Independence. Therefore, every new colony was able to elect a number of Members of Parliament who would be sent to London to act as their representatives in the House of Commons. In addition, as the colony developed both the King and the sitting Prime Minister had the ability to grant noble status to individuals who had excelled in developing the colony. They could then take up a seat in the House of Lords or appoint a representative who attended in their place when they were not in the Sol system. Chester wasn't the largest or most influential colony but its position at the edge of British space meant it was a key strategic system and got a lot of attention.

"When he first came on board," Ferguson continued, "he was

boasting about already knowing where our first mission would be to. Supposedly a lot of the tax revenue from Chester went towards the construction of *Endeavour* and her sister ships. The Chester MP's have been pushing for the RSN to focus more of its exploration efforts in their direction. As I understand it, the pay back for the investment was a promise that *Endeavour* would be assigned to explore beyond the Chester system. I suspect Mallory's assignment to the ship wasn't an accident either.

"I was also able to look into some of the records from Mallory's previous ships while we were still in Sol, records we don't have access to here. In both his previous ships a number of crew members were brought up on disciplinary charges for gambling. There was one report that implicated Mallory, but it was quashed from higher up. Even without the sway his family holds over their MP's his father is a rich man in his own right and has some influential contacts in the RSN, so if he was involved, it's no surprise he walked away scot-free.

"I haven't found any proof yet but I am suspicious he has already started to set up gambling sessions on *Endeavour*. A large percentage of the crew hail from the Chester system, so it's likely he already had some contacts when he came on board."

James could easily believe it. Gambling was banned on RSN ships. It always led to resentment or even fights. Men and women stuck on board the same ship for months at a time always found ways to resent each other. The RSN felt that falling out over gambling debts or accusations of cheating didn't need to be one of them. Plus, if an officer was involved, it always got worse. The officer in question could use their position of authority to bully the others involved or threaten exposure and punishment if they didn't get their way.

Yet for a child of a wealthy businessman or noble, gambling could be a powerful temptation. For someone who grew up having it all, what excitement was there in owning more things? But the risk of losing it all, or of taking it all from someone else, that was alluring. James knew this first hand. His elder brother was an irredeemable drunk and gambler. That was one of the reasons his father had left James the family's Dukedom. The other, James strongly suspected, was that his father had taken a perverse pleasure in knowing that his least favorite son would inherit a Dukedom in financial meltdown and covered in public shame. If Mallory was involved in gambling, James resolved to put an end to it, even if it ended the young Lieutenant's career. The RSN had a proud tradition to live up to. James had decided to try his best to honor those who had died forging that tradition; he would be damned if he allowed anyone else to tarnish it.

"Thank you for being so open with me," James said in response to Ferguson's revelations. "I want you to keep an eye open for any gambling, whether it involves Mallory or anyone else. As for the Lieutenant himself, you can leave him in my hands. If he gives me any reason to confront him, I intend to set him straight. If he doesn't show more of a willingness to develop into a complete King's officer, his career will end at the lofty height of Second Lieutenant."

As James spoke he looked at the plot of *Endeavour's* progress into the New Edinburgh system. "We'll end our conversation here Lieutenant. We're almost two hours away from the rendezvous point. I want to go back to the bridge and see what there is to see."

"Aye Sir," Ferguson replied, "I hope I don't let you down on this mission."

"Don't worry about that," James answered smiling. "You're forgetting, I have read your files too. I'm sure you will perform your duties admirably."

As Ferguson walked out James couldn't help but analyze his own self-doubts. If one was to read all the news reports of his feats in the recent war with the Chinese they couldn't help coming to the conclusion that he was some sort of tactical genius. However, James knew the truth, some of his victories had been down to sheer luck and when he had saved the Swedish colony ship he had almost ran from combat. Still, he knew that the experience had changed him. He wasn't going to run away from a fight again, not if the stakes were so high.

One thing the Void War had taught him was that it took a lot to be a competent naval commander. He had served closely with Captain Lightfoot and Rear Admiral Jensen. Both of them had been expert tacticians and leaders. James knew he didn't yet live up to their standards. Yet he was determined to try.

It helped that his uncle had confidence in him. James knew Admiral of the Red Jonathan Somerville wouldn't trust just anyone with the latest class of ship to come off the British naval construction lines. Despite his self-doubts, James knew he needed to prove his uncle's confidence was well placed. This mission and *Endeavour* would certainly give him the opportunity to see just what sort of Captain he was becoming.

*

Ten minutes later James was once more sitting in his command chair on the bridge.

"Possible contact," Sub Lieutenant Malik called out.

"At the coordinates I gave you?" James asked.

"Yes sir," Malik answered. "We're picking up some faint radiation, enough for us to be able to determine that it's likely to be leakage from a small to medium ship with most of its systems powered down. I have been viewing some visuals of the area but as yet we haven't been able to identify anything. The computer thinks there is something there but it can't get enough of a resolution to accurately estimate what it is," he added.

"I see," James answered. To the bridge at large he added, "I'm expecting to meet a RSN or a RSNI contact at the location. We will then be getting new orders."

He couldn't help but smile as he saw the Sub Lieutenants looking at each other, thinking they were being sneaky enough to avoid his noticing. A secret rendezvous with new orders. Their imaginations were no doubt running wild. Up to now the crew had no doubt been a little concerned with his actions. Once his latest revelation spread around the ship things would start to make sense.

After another twenty minutes the computer was finally able to make out what was waiting for them at their destination. As Sub Lieutenant Malik brought up the visual on the main holo display, he talked the bridge through the computer's findings. "It's a Hauler class freighter. They are one of the most popular freighter designs among the smaller independent traders. From the markings it appears to be registered to an Indian shipping company. As far as our ship's records indicate, there is no such ship owned by the RSN."

"And there's not likely to be any official records if the ship is operated by the Royal Space Navy Intelligence," James concluded, which only served to send another series of looks between the Sub Lieutenants. "I want one of our plasma cannons charged and targeted on that freighter. As far as we know they are friendlies but I don't want to take any chances."

When *Endeavour* got close enough to the freighter, James sent out the prearranged signal, a series of beeps and dots using the laser communication relay. The freighter replied with its own beeps and dots.

"Communications, I'm sending you a data file now. Check to see if the freighter's signal matches the one in the file." James said to the Sub Lieutenant manning the communication console.

"The signal is a match Sir," she quickly replied, "wait," she said as she paused to peer over her console. "We're getting a laser COM link from the freighter."

"Put the channel on the main holo display," James ordered.

When a face appeared in front of his bridge crew James was momentarily startled. The beaming white smile, accentuated by the black hair, brown eyes and dark skin of Georgia Gupta, clearly indicated that she had been looking forward to her surprise. "Welcome to New Edinburgh Captain Somerville," she said by way of greeting.

"Lieut... Err... I mean, Commander Gupta," James began, still a little taken aback. "It's good to see you. I thought you were being given your own command?"

"I was," she replied, "You are looking at her. *Innocence* was commissioned into the RSN two years ago. She's a Q ship. You've heard about the strange disappearances that have been going on in this area of space over the last decade. Well, *Innocence* was designed to get to the source of the problem. She has been cruising about between Indian, French, Canadian and British colonial space trying to get herself into trouble. At least she had been. When I was promoted to Commander I was given her and put on special assignment. It seems the Admiralty wants us to continue to work together. I can't say I'm too disappointed. Things are never boring when you are around," she concluded with another beaming smile.

James nodded in understanding. A Q ship was a freighter armed with military grade weapons. The idea was that an attacker would approach in the hope of boarding the helpless freighter, only to find themselves staring down the barrel of a pair of plasma cannons. Piracy was a rare thing in human space. It was simply too expensive to build and maintain a spaceship without a large industrial base. Nevertheless, a number of ships had been going missing in and around the areas Gupta had mentioned. Not enough to cause any major concern, but enough that the Admiralty had decided to do something.

James now understood how he was to overcome the obvious problem he had seen in the Admiralty's plan. Sneaking *Endeavour* into foreign space in the hunt for Chang made little sense. If he wanted to actually find Chang on a planet he would have to land a party from his ship and doing so would reveal *Endeavour's* presence. With *Innocence* joining the hunt, they would have the perfect cover. The freighter could enter any system without causing a stir. She was already well known in these parts.

"Well I'm glad to have you with us," James said in response to Gupta's last comment. "I presume you want to come aboard and brief my officers on our updated orders?"

"Yes Sir, I'll come over right away if that is ok."

"Certainly, I'll see you shortly," James answered with a nod. It was going to be good working with Gupta again.

Chapter 3 – Old Friends

In many ways the Royal Space Navy was like one big family, almost everyone knew each other and many got on well. Of course that also meant there was more than one fierce rivalry that threatened to tear the family apart from time to time. Now those days are long gone, the Empire's navy is simply too vast.

-Excerpt from Empire Rising, 3002 AD

11th February 2466 AD, New Edinburgh System

James and Commander Gupta walked into *Endeavour's* conference room and stood facing the assembled officers. Along with the senior officers from *Endeavour* and the Sub Lieutenants who weren't on duty, RSNI Agent Julia Bell and Major Johnston were also crowded into the room.

The last two members of Gupta's team had been as much of a shock for James as Gupta's presence. He had met Major Johnston during one of the first acts of the Void war. He had come on board James' first command with a group of Special Forces marines to attempt a daring boarding action on a Chinese destroyer. After that the Major had been assigned to command the marine detachment aboard the destroyer *Ghost*. A ship James had worked closely with. When James met him for the second time aboard *Ghost* he had changed. In the intervening time Johnston had lost his wife. She had been killed during a Chinese attack on one of the British colonies. As a result he had become a blood thirsty killer. There was no other way to describe it. As James thought about it, it wasn't a surprise to find him on this mission. The Major's success and efficiency in the war with China was beyond doubt but as James had read his battle reports he had observed the change in the man. To someone who hadn't known him before he would look like the perfect soldier, cold, detached and methodical. Yet to James it was obvious the Major was broken, he had pushed down his grief and focused all his efforts on getting revenge. *He might become a problem*, Jams thought to himself.

Agent Bell was another matter. He had also met her during the war with the Chinese. She had proven herself a very talented spy and a proficient warrior. James had been very glad to see her. His team would need her undercover skills if they were to stand a chance of finding Chang.

"I hope you have already made the necessary introductions," James said to the gathered officers. "We are all going to be working closely together over the next several months.

"Commander Gupta and I have reviewed our orders closely and we think it appropriate we fully brief you all at this time as we may not get a chance to all be in the same room again." James moved to one end of the conference room so that everyone had a clear view to the main holo display that dominated the front of the room. With a few touches on one of the command consoles he brought up an image.

"I'm sure many of you recognize this man. Chang Lei is the former Chinese Minister of Intelligence. He led the Politburo when China began hostilities with us almost two years ago. After Emperor Na's uprising he fled Earth. Initially it was thought that he fled to one of his facilities in the Chinese colonies but when the infighting between the various Chinese factions settled down he was nowhere to be found. Both our government and the UN have arrest warrants out on him and we have been given the mission of bringing him home to face trial.

"Now," James said as he switched the view of the holo display to show colonial space around the New Edinburgh System. From New Edinburgh a shift passage led off into French colonial space. New France itself was only two weeks travel away. From there it was possible to travel either into Indian colonial space, towards the single Canadian colony, Quebec, or if one wanted, to the Rostov system. The latter destination would be certain suicide for *Innocence* and a very dangerous journey for *Endeavour*. Rostov was the only Russian colonial world that had a shift passage connecting it to the rest of human space. The Russians hadn't opened communications with any Earth nation for over twenty years. Occasionally the Earth nations would send in a stealth ship to see what the Russians were up to. Those that returned showed a constant buildup of military ships. Everyone on Earth was more than a little nervous about the Russians' actions, yet no one wanted to take any pre-emptive measures. They were all hoping the Russians would remain content in their own colonial space.

"You'll be glad to know we don't think he has passed through Rostov into Russian space. Rather, RSNI has intercepted some information that suggests that Chang is hiding out on one of the Indian colonies. Though we don't know which. Our best guess is that he is trying to barter or bribe his way to being hidden somewhere where he can live in peace. I'm afraid we're going to burst his bubble.

"The data RSNI intercepted linking Chang to India was a money transfer. We believe Chang is trying to move as many assets to

India as he feels he safely can. *Innocence's* Commander Gupta and Agent Bell are going to be our doorway into Indian space and Chang. Agent Bell spent several years undercover in the Chinese colonies and can pass for a Chinese national with ease. She will be posing as an ex-intelligence agent Chang has hired to smuggle some of his wealth out of China. Gupta is obviously of Indian origin – her grandparents actually come from New Delhi. She will be posing as an independent freighter owner hired by Agent Bell to transport Chang's possessions. With a bit of luck they will be able to move around freely on the Indian worlds and sniff out where Chang is.

"*Endeavour's* job will be to provide heavy fire support. We will follow *Innocence* through Indian space in stealth, ready to come to her aid if and when she needs us. Major Johnston has been appointed to command *Endeavour's* marines. He didn't come on board *Endeavour* at Earth in case his presence raised some suspicions about the nature of *Endeavour's* mission. For the moment he will remain on board *Innocence* to command a squad of marines. Their job will be to retrieve Chang once Agent Bell locates him.

"Are there any questions at this point?" James finished.

A number of hands shot up and James worked his way down them in order of seniority. When it came to Sub Lieutenant Davies, James was asked a question that hit on his main concern with the whole mission.

"What happens if the Indian authorities capture some of the people we send down to a planet? Or worse yet, they impound *Innocence*. What will we do from *Endeavour*?" Davis asked.

James knew what his gut reaction would be. He would bring *Endeavour* into orbit and land enough marines to break into whatever building his people were being held in. Especially if Gupta was involved, they had grown close after they had settled their differences back on *Drake*. Yet as a Captain in the Royal Space Navy he couldn't. His mission parameters were very clear. *Endeavour* was not to reveal her presence at any time unless it would secure the capture of Chang.

Relations between Britain and India had been souring over the last two decades. After the war with Russia the French colonies had been devastated. Both Britain and the US had poured trillions of credits into rebuilding the colonies and helping France develop her empire. If the Russians decided they wanted to have another go at taking New France, Britain and the US wanted to make it as difficult for them as possible. Yet India and France were direct competitors. Their colonial empires shared a border and so they were both trying to outdo one another as they continued to expand into space. The limited planets that could be reached by the shift drive ensured that for every credit of support Britain gave France, India's chance of increasing her wealth, power and prestige diminished. The Indian rulers had been making a fuss about the support for years. Both in the UN and through Earth's news outlets, they did everything they could to disrupt Britain and portray her as a villain.

There was no doubt that if they found a British officer and RSNI agent operating in their space they would be quick to go public and cry foul. If they were caught, Bell and Gupta knew the British government would disown them. They would then look like common pirates who had stolen and armed their own freighter. Certainly there would be no way *Innocence* could be traced back to the Royal Space Navy, RSNI had made sure of that.

As those thoughts raced through James' head an awkward silence enveloped the conference room. Recognizing that this was a question she should answer Agent Bell jumped to her feet. "That is a risk we are aware of. Everyone on board *Innocence* is a volunteer. If we get caught we are on our own. We all know this. The solution however is rather simple," she said with a dazzling smile. "We won't get caught."

The chuckles that echoed around the room dissipated the tension that had crept into the meeting. Using the distraction to shake himself James addressed the meeting again. "If there are no further questions you may leave. Those of you who have updated assignments will find them on your personal datapad." When no one raised their hand James closed the meeting, "you're dismissed."

*

Fourth Lieutenant Becket was making her way back from *Endeavour's* Marine Barracks when her COM chirped. When she answered it the Captain's voice addressed her, "Lieutenant, can I see you in my briefing room?"

"Yes Sir," she replied.

"Have a seat," James said as she entered the Captain's conference room.

Commander Gupta was seated beside the Captain and as she sat Becket gave her a nod. "We want to discuss *Innocence* with you," James began.

"Officially Agent Bell is her Second Lieutenant but she has no command experience so Gupta is going to need assistance running the freighter. Seeing as you two already know each other I thought you would be ideal. You were at the briefing though, you know the risks if *Innocence* or any of you get caught. I can't come to your aid.

"What do you think?" James asked after a pause.

Becket took a second to consider the risks her Captain had mentioned. Then it hit her, Gupta would have to join the landing parties that would go down to the colonies they visited to ensure their ruse of being an independent Indian freighter held up. That meant she would be the one left in command, something that would look good on her record! "I would be delighted to join *Innocence*," she said hastily.

"Very good," Gupta said with a smile. "We're also going to need a few extra crew members to make sure the freighter is fully manned when we send down a landing party. We're going to need to be ready for anything. I want you to liaise with First Lieutenant Ferguson and organize ten crew members to transfer across with you."

"Yes Sir," Becket responded.

"Great," Gupta said as she stood. Stretching out her hand to Becket she continued, "it will be a pleasure to work together again."

"Thank you," Becket said as she shook her superior's hand.

As both women turned to leave his office James waved Becket

back, "not so fast Lieutenant, I have one more thing for you."

"Yes Sir?" she asked.

James made a point of waiting until Gupta left the office. As she went through the automatic doors she turned and raised a quizzical eyebrow at James but he only winked at her and motioned her to keep moving.

When the doors closed he turned his attention back to Becket. "I have one more request for you. You remember Major Johnston from his time on board *Drake*?"

"Certainly Sir," Becket began, "the Major and his marines beat me black and blue as I trained with them for the boarding mission against that Chinese destroyer. I'm not going to forget any of them in a hurry."

"Good," James said, "I hope he hasn't forgotten you either. I'm sure you know his wife was killed during the Chinese attack on the Cook system. To be frank, he hasn't been the same since. Professionally, he is one mean marine. His record in the war was impeccable. In fact, his efficiency ratings improved after his wife's death. But emotionally he seems to have switched off. He is cold, distant. In the long term he could be a liability. Especially as we're going after Chang, the very man responsible for the war and for the attack on Cook.

"Our mission is to bring Chang home alive so that he can stand trial publicly. Given the anger and rage Johnston is dealing with I'm not sure he is operating under the same rules."

As James was talking Becket kept nodding prompting James to

ask, "You've noticed all this then?"

"Yes Sir," she answered, "it's hard to miss. I've only bumped into Major Johnston a couple of times since he was on board *Drake* but the change is unmistakable."

"Good, then we're in agreement. I'm actually surprised his superiors haven't picked up on it," James said. "In any case, the problem has now fallen on our shoulders to remedy, or I should say, on your shoulders."

"Mine?" Becket said, raising her voice in surprise.

"Yes yours," James said with a smile. "He took a liking to you during your combat training onboard *Drake*. I think he looked at you as a kind of daughter. I want you to try and rekindle those feelings. Ask him to continue to train you in hand-to-hand combat while you are both on the freighter. Talk to him, befriend him, get him to feel again. We need him at his best, especially if things go south during one of the landing missions. We can't have Johnston putting his personal vendetta above the lives of those under his command. Do you think you can do that?"

Becket hesitated. She liked Major Johnston and she wanted to help him but she wasn't sure she could break through the Major's defenses and she didn't want to let the Captain down.

James could sense Becket hesitate, but he didn't have time to try to persuade her nicely. Johnston had him worried, in his current state he could very easily undo any plan they put into motion. "I'm making this suggestion because I want to help Johnston, but if you aren't on board with this I will involve Gupta. She will have to monitor Johnston and remove him from command if she thinks he is a risk. I know neither of us wants that. If we can get the Major we met on *Drake* back, then it will be good for all of us. What do you say?"

Becket felt trapped, she didn't know if she could get through to the Major but she didn't want to ruin his career either. "I'll try," she said with an obvious lack of enthusiasm.

"Thank you," James said with a touch more energy. "In that case you can go talk to Lieutenant Ferguson about those extra crewmen for the freighter."

"Yes Sir," Becket said as she rose to leave.

"And good luck Lieutenant," James called after her, "I know you will continue to do me proud."

Once the door slid shut James leaned back in his office chair and sighed. The thought of having to leave Gupta and Becket behind was not a pleasant one. Yet if they were caught he would have no choice. Britain couldn't afford to get into another shooting war so soon after the war with the Chinese. Many of the fleet's heavy warships were still undergoing repairs. Ordinarily the Indian navy was only a mild concern for the Admiralty but if the Indian government wanted to make a point, their fleet could cause a real headache.

There was nothing he could do other than make sure everyone was as prepared as they could be. That wasn't much of a comfort though. They would plan and run simulation after simulation on their way to Indian space, but when it came down to it, there would be no way to predict all the variables.

To distract himself he brought up the proposed route to New Delhi. Agent Bell believed India's largest colony and she hoped there would be a trail there she could pick up. Yet it was over four weeks travel away and she had planned a number of stops. It would look suspicious if a trading freighter didn't actually call into some of the ports it passed through to trade.

At New France they would be stopping to unload some mining equipment Bell had brought from Earth. Then the freighter would make a stop at Cartier to unload some fresh fruit for the fleets stationed there. That would be exciting James knew. Outside of the Sol system Cartier had the greatest concentration of warships in the entire Human Sphere.

Cartier was the only French colony that had a shift passage connecting French colonial space with the colonies owned by the Russian Star Federation. After the Russians had tried to invade and conquer the French colonies twenty years ago it was now heavily defended. The French stationed more than half of their fleet in the system and there were a number of flotillas from other nations as well.

James was especially looking forward to getting a glimpse of the American battleship stationed there. Boasting fifty eight missiles in each of her broadsides the Americans claimed the USS *Freedom* was the most powerful ship ever constructed. After seeing the British fleet go toe to toe with two smaller Chinese battleships he didn't doubt it – at least as far as the rest of the other Earth nations went. No one quite knew what the Russians had been building for the last twenty years.

After their fleet had been beaten back in the last war the Russian government had abandoned Earth and fled to their colonies. At the time there hadn't been the political will to invade their space and so they had been left alone. Very quickly relations had soured to the point that all communication had ceased. Now the Russians had become a great unknown and both America and Britain felt they needed to station some ships in the Cartier system to deter the Russians from any rash moves.

The combined fleets in Cartier were constantly on high alert and regularly carried out live fire mock fleet engagements. For a moment James entertained an idea that had popped into his head. It didn't exactly fall in line with the spirit of the orders he had been given. Yet it wasn't specifically forbidden.

With a nod he made up his mind. He was going to get as close a look at the *American* battleship as he could. *Endeavour* was meant to be the stealthiest ship the Admiralty had ever constructed. It would do his crew good to get some real experience avoiding detection. Plus it would be fun testing out the effectiveness of the American's detection capabilities. They could take some close up visuals of the battleship and when they got back to Earth, they could send them to the US Space Navy headquarters as a gift. No doubt their intelligence division would love to know the British had snuck a ship close enough to picture the worn paint on their prized possession.

With a bit more excitement for this second leg of their journey he set down his datapad. Gupta would be heading back to the freighter soon and he wanted to go over a few ideas with her face to face. They probably wouldn't get another chance to talk in person until they found Chang. After that he needed to tour the ship with Ferguson. Being fresh out of the shipyard meant there was always something needing their attention.

Chapter 4 – Childhood Memories

In the first Interstellar Expansion Era terraforming technologies were just in their infancy and so mankind was largely limited to Earth like worlds. Nevertheless, in the desperate race to claim new territory the human nations did settle some planets that today's citizens wouldn't even consider.

- Excerpt from Empire Rising, 3002 AD

15th March 2466, HMS *Innocence*, New Delhi System

Five weeks later Commander Gupta stood adjacent to the main docking hatch awaiting the freight inspectors. *Innocence* had entered the New Delhi System over eight hours ago and had slowly made her way to the colony of New Delhi itself. They had been ordered by the planet's orbital traffic control to dock with one of the main trading stations in orbit over the colony. Now they were just waiting for the freight inspectors to give the go ahead for *Innocence's* crew to begin unloading the cargo she had to trade.

Already Gupta had endured two such inspections in French colonial space but she doubted the procedures would be much different here. Thankfully their mission didn't require the freighter to carry any illicit cargo and the inspection should be routine.

With a groan of frustration she checked the time again. The inspectors were almost twenty minutes late. This wasn't something new either. It seemed the inspectors at New Delhi, as well as those in the French colonies, liked to make sure independent freighter captains knew who was in charge. Already they were a week behind schedule. The larger trading companies would never stand for these kinds of repeated delays for their ships. Independent captains didn't have the same clout so Gupta had to work to their schedule.

Her frustration wasn't helped by the fact that she knew James and the others on *Endeavour* had been having a much more stimulating cruise. While she had been enduring inspections and overseeing cargo manifests James had been testing *Endeavour's* stealth technologies.

A combination of the latest stealth coating and improved heat sinks allowed the ship designers at HMS *Vulcan* to claim *Endeavour* was the stealthiest ship yet produced by the RSN. When her reactors and all non-essential systems were powered down, *Endeavour* became a dark hole in space. She couldn't maintain it for more than a few hours but even then she had the same technologies all RSN ships had. By incorporating heat vents RSN ships could vent their waste electromagnetic radiation out into space along specific vectors. This allowed them to remain in stealth mode for prolonged periods of time. The vents weren't nearly as effective as *Endeavour's* heat sinks but the combination of the two put *Endeavour* in a class of her own.

James had certainly shown *Endeavour* was a new breed of warship. While she had been unloading a cargo of fruit for the warships in the Cartier system, James had snuck up on a flotilla of American ships carrying out some war simulations. Gupta had already seen the images James had taken and she knew that if they were ever shown to the Americans they would be less than happy. The level of detail was impressive; whoever had been manipulating the optical sensors had been able to find a small two-meter scrape in the armor of one of USS *Freedom's* heavy plasma cannons. No doubt the Americans would think the image doctored but if they analyzed it they wouldn't find any signs of manipulation.

At first Gupta had thought James was pulling her leg, there was no way *Endeavour* could have gotten so close. Granted, the Americans hadn't been using their active sensors to scan the area of space *Endeavour* had used to approach them. Even so, their passive sensors should have been good enough to alert them to something unusual. That they hadn't only served to bolster Gupta's view of the scientists and engineers who had worked on *Endeavour's* design.

As footsteps echoed down the trading station's metallic floor her mind was brought back to the present. *Finally*, she thought, *the inspectors are here.*

Without waiting for permission to enter, four Indians in grey uniforms walked through the docking hatch. Gupta nodded to the tallest of the four, the decorations on his uniform seemed to suggest he was the senior inspector. Without showing any expression in return he stepped forward. "I presume you are the captain of this freighter?" he asked.

"Yes, this is my pride and joy," Gupta answered as she tried her best to actually sound pleased about having to command a slow pondering freighter.

"Name and registration details," the inspector said almost before Gupta finished speaking.

Frowning, Gupta answered him as she handed over a datapad with *Innocence's* registration details and documents identifying her as the owner and captain, "Neysa Avvari."

"I see your ship has been to New Delhi a number of times before. Yet I don't have any record of you having been here," the inspector said with an air of disdain.

"That's right," Gupta said, "I bought her a few months ago. My family owns a number of factories back on Earth that produce items for the Bharati Cooperation. I didn't want to take a role on the firm's board so I bought *Innocence* and set off to make my own fortune."

She had to hide a smile as the inspector's demeanor changed. The Bharati Cooperation was one of the largest Indian manufacturing companies on Earth and they controlled a lot of the industrial operations on New Delhi along with those in the other Indian colonies. RSNI had worked up her cover carefully. Having family connections to the Bharati cooperation was obscure enough that no one would be surprised that they hadn't heard of her or her father. Yet, at the same time it suggested she might have enough influence to make life difficult for anyone who caused her any trouble.

With a bit more respect the inspector handed back her datapad and said, "Everything seems to be in order here. If you are ready we can begin the inspection."

"My crew are waiting for you, if you'll follow me," Gupta said as she turned and walked deeper into the freighter. With her back to the inspectors she let out the smile she had been restraining. *I could get used to having connections,* she thought to herself.

*

Forty five minutes later Gupta was at the docking hatch watching the inspectors leave. As far as she could tell they had completed their inspection in record time. Finally, it was time for the real mission to begin.

Once they left the ship she keyed her COM unit, "Agent Bell, the inspectors have left, they have granted us permission to send trading teams to the surface. Our mission is a go."

"Affirmative," Bell replied. "We'll meet you at the docking hatch."

Gupta switched the channel on her COM unit, "Becket, I'm heading down to the surface with Agent Bell. You have command of *Innocence*. Make sure the crew aren't too efficient at unloading our cargo; we might need an excuse to stay docked longer than necessary. Oh and see to it that no one else comes on board the freighter. Some traders might try to come here and make deals, just tell them you can't authorize any trades without me present."

"Ok Commander," Becket responded, "I'll keep the freighter on standby in case we need to make a quick exit. Good luck down there."

"Thank you Lieutenant, see you when we get back," Gupta said as she keyed off her COM.

A few moments later Agent Bell and her team arrived. Five marines including Major Johnston accompanied her. Only two of them openly carried small side arms for protection. Heavy weapons were banned on New Delhi and they didn't want to draw too much attention to themselves. Gupta knew that each marine could easily take care of themselves in hand to hand combat and no doubt many of them had more than one concealed weapon of one type or another.

"All ready?" Bell asked when she joined Gupta.

"Yes, I'm good to go," Gupta replied.

"Good," Bell responded as she gave Gupta a light punch on the shoulder. "This is going to be fun. You spacer types need to learn to spend a bit more time on solid ground."

"I'm not sure about your definition of fun," Gupta said with a snort, "but it will be good to stretch my legs."

"Of course it will," Johnston said gruffly, "I've spent more than enough time cooped up on this freighter for several life times. Let's get this mission started. The sooner we find Chang the better."

"Agreed," Gupta said in an understanding tone. She knew it couldn't have been easy for the marines to spend so much time in so small a ship. "Thankfully the main shuttle hanger isn't too far away so we will be on the surface soon."

Gupta brought out her datapad and opened up the schematics for the trading station. It wasn't the largest in orbit around New Delhi but it was still impressive. With a diameter of over three kilometers it had docking stations for over fifty freighters. She had already checked and found that thirty six of the berths were taken by ships from the other naval powers. New Delhi was certainly attracting a lot of foreign trade, suggesting the colony was developing at an impressive rate.

No doubt as a money making scheme, freighters docked at the station were not allowed to launch their own shuttles. The station's regulations said it was to avoid any collisions with incoming freighters. In reality it was to ensure all the freighter crews had to pay for the station's shuttles to take them to the colony if they wanted to enjoy some leave. Gupta wasn't too concerned though, the Admiralty was footing the bill for all their expenses.

With the schematics open in front of her she set off at what she thought was a brisk walk towards the main shuttle bay. Five minutes later they arrived and as Gupta paused to look around at the various shuttles and catch her breath Bell gave her a poke in the ribs. "I see we might have to factor slow walking naval officers into the timing of our plans for future missions," she said in a whisper so none of the shuttle crews could overhear.

Gupta stuck her tongue out at the intelligence agent and pointed at one of the smaller shuttles. "That should do us, we don't want to book a flight with one of the larger shuttles and end up waiting around for it to fill up before departing."

"Very well," Bell said, "I'll do the haggling, and everyone else can get themselves on board."

Five minutes later Gupta stared out of the shuttle window at the approaching planet, deep in thought. The planet looked beautiful. Over ninety percent of the planet's surface was water and the cloud cover was much thicker than on Earth where she had grown up. There was obviously a storm passing over the capital city of Bhopal as there was a maelstrom of swirling and twisting clouds. Through the occasional breaks in the clouds she could see the deep blue of the sea and the thin green of the peninsula Bhopal was built on. Despite the storm the city looked peaceful and tranquil and not at all what Gupta had expected.

Her grandparents had left New Delhi over seventy years ago. Her grandfather had been a shop assistant for a small equipment shop that supplied a number of rural mining operations on one of the south continents. They had spent years eking out a living and saving enough for one-way tickets back to Earth. They had been seeking to escape the dreaded caste system that had been exported from India to her colonies.

Her family was from the Sudra caste and her grandparent's grandparents had been forcibly moved from India to New Delhi. There they had made up just two of the hundreds of thousands of migrants the Indian government had thrown onto the planet to help jump start its economy. Of course, being from the Sudra caste they hadn't been allowed to use the many opportunities a new colony presented to colonists to make their fortune. Instead they had been forced into mind-numbing menial jobs.

When her grandparents had finally managed to escape and return to Earth they had stayed well clear of India. Instead Britain had offered them all they wanted, freedom from the caste system and an opportunity to better themselves through their own merit. Thanks to the hard work of her grandparents and parents, Gupta had been able to afford the education that had led her to the naval academy and space.

Now she was at New Delhi and though her grandparents were

dead she knew her parents wouldn't be pleased to hear she had visited the colony. Despite everything she had heard about the colony she still had to admit that it was beautiful. It was no wonder the Indian government had managed to convince so many people to move away from the slums of India to such a pristine world a few generations ago. Even the city was something to behold, Gupta thought as the shuttle broke through the clouds. Surrounded by ocean on three sides and sprawling the entire length of the peninsula that reached back to the main continent, it almost conjured images of the lost city of Atlantis. Its largest spires were also impressive; some reached up almost two kilometers into the sky and were beautifully matched by their reflections in the glistening ocean.

However, once they got down into the midst of the city the beauty began to wear off. It looked just like one of the many cities Gupta had visited before. Here and there were obvious signs that some sectors of the city were less cared for. Half demolished buildings stood beside others that looked like they had been abandoned years before. Such sites plagued almost all of the human colonies. With space no longer at a premium it was far cheaper to just build on new land than spend the time and effort to demolish and clean up an old building before erecting another.

When the shuttle set down and kicked up a large dust cloud within a poorly kept landing platform the allure of New Delhi had already worn off. Gupta was ready to get the mission completed and get off the planet that had haunted her nightmares as a child.

After disembarking the shuttle, Bell took the lead. She had been to New Delhi before and had a basic working knowledge of its layout. She was also the only one who knew the contact they were going to meet so all Gupta had to do was look like a freighter captain on the hunt for a good trade opportunity.

Thirty minutes and two maglev trains later they arrived at their destination, a downscale looking restaurant. "You six go in and order yourself some food, I'm going to have a drink at the bar," Bell said.

Without any further explanation she walked on into the restaurant, leaving Gupta to assume that Bell had already arranged to meet the contact at the bar.

For any civilian the meal that followed would have been less than appetizing but for five marines and a naval officer used to naval meals it wasn't the worst they had ever had. The ordeal was made worse however by the stares her companions got from the locals. Gupta fit in with her Indian complexion but in this part of the city foreigners stood out like a sore thumb and everyone who entered the restaurant took a few moments to stare at them. Thankfully at least, no one sat too close to their table. If they had, their interest might have been pricked even more for each of the marines simply sat in silence as they ate, constantly checking their surroundings. Even Major Johnston, someone she knew from her time as the First Lieutenant of *Drake*, didn't try to strike up a conversation with her.

Just when Gupta was reaching the end of her patience she saw a young man enter the restaurant, walk over to Bell and take a seat beside her at the bar. After briefly trying to start up a conversation with her he got up and moved further down the bar, looking upset at having his advances rebuffed. Gupta had been studying the exchange closely to see if their contact had passed off anything to Bell. Either he had nothing for them or his field craft was very good for Gupta had seen nothing. She guessed he was a highly trained British operative permanently based here. Something like what Bell had been doing at Wi Li when Gupta had first met her during the Void War. He certainly had the Indian complexion to fit in.

Despite the quick exchange Bell must have got what she wanted for she soon stood up and made her way out of the restaurant. As she paused to wait for the automatic door Gupta could have sworn she looked back and gave her a quick wink.

As she made to get up and follow after Bell, Johnston's hand reached out for hers, "hold on a minute Captain, its best we aren't seen leaving together. Give it a few minutes and we can pay the bill and make our way out.

"Of course," Gupta said, scolding herself for being so naive. Obviously she had a lot to learn about this spy business.

Once out on the street again there was no sign of Bell. Johnston didn't look concerned and, shrugging his shoulders to the rest of the team, he led them off in a seemingly random direction. Sure enough it didn't take Bell long to fall in beside them.

"Did you get everything we need?" Gupta asked as soon as she could.

"I hope so, we'll not know until we get somewhere more private to look over the data file he gave me," Bell answered.

"Back to the freighter then?" Gupta continued.

"No, I think it would be better if we looked for some rooms in a hotel nearby. There we can look over the data and make a plan of action for tomorrow. If this data confirms our suspicions we'll be making a visit to the Varun shipping company's headquarters here in Bhopal. There's no point going back to the freighter. We can all enjoy a more luxurious night's sleep," Bell answered with a smile.

"You can't do all this spy work without a good night's rest after all," she added with a wink for Gupta.

Chapter 5 – Mr. Banik

Once the interstellar trade companies and corporations were just small competing entities. It would take many hundreds of years for them to come to dominate our society and large swaths of the galaxy in the way they do now.

- Excerpt from Empire Rising, 3002 AD

16th March 2466, Bhopal, New Delhi

The next morning Gupta woke early and got dressed in her best civilian uniform. She was going to an important meeting and she needed to look her part. Bell was already waiting for her. The rest of the marines would be following behind them as at this meeting they would have to keep their distance.

Instead of riding the maglev trains around the city they opted for an air taxi to take them to the headquarters of the Varun Shipping Company. Their RSNI contact in Bhopal had come through for them. He had tracked the payments from one of Chang's shell companies to the Varun Shipping Company and one of the mid-level managers based in Bhopal. The data strongly suggested Chang had bribed a division within the Varun Company to smuggle him out of Chinese space and provide him with a safe place to hide. The financial trail led to a certain Rahul Banik. He was only a mid-level bureaucrat and Bell believed he was taking orders from higher up. Their current plan was to rattle Rahul and see where it led them.

When they arrived at the headquarters they had to go through a security check before they were allowed in. Once through they approached the reception desk.

"May I help you," a young Indian woman asked politely.

"Yes," Gupta said stepping forward. "My name is Neysa Avvari, I would like to request a meeting with Rahul Banik, I believe he is a shipping coordinator here."

The Indian receptionist took a moment to look over Gupta's attire. Without a company insignia on her uniform she obviously came to the conclusion that she didn't work for any of the other big shipping companies. "I'm sorry but none of our coordinators take meetings that haven't been arranged in advance. If you are looking for a shipping contract we have many listed on the planet's data net you would be welcome to apply for," she said.

"I'm afraid I have other business with Mr. Banik," Gupta began, hoping the receptionist would be able to read between the lines. "If you can tell him I'm carrying cargo from the Chinese colonies that one of his clients requested be transported out of China then I think he will make an exception."

There was no way the receptionist knew of Chang but if she guessed Gupta had been hired to transport something illegal for Varun then she would likely contact Banik directly, the Chinese connection would do the rest.

"Ok," the receptionist said, "if you would have a seat in our waiting area I will contact Mr. Banik and get back to you."

"Thank you very much," Gupta said with a half bow before

turning around and heading towards the seats they had been directed to.

Barely a couple of minutes passed before a security guard appeared in the reception area and approached them. Gupta felt a shiver of disappointment pass through her as she saw him walking directly for them but to her surprise instead of asking them to leave he said, "If you ladies will follow me, Mr. Banik will see you now."

After following the guard to one of the top levels of the building they were ushered into a large room. In front of them an ageing, slightly overweight Indian sat in an oversized chair. "Come in," he said nervously. "This wasn't a meeting I was expecting. Do you mind telling me who you are exactly? I don't have time to be wasting on unnecessary meetings."

"Of course Mr. Banik," Gupta said in a conciliatory tone. "We won't take up much of your time. My name is Neysa Avvari, I have to apologize though. I'm afraid I wasn't the one who wanted this meeting with you. I'm simply an independent trader, it is Ms. Qu-Shin who hired me."

With that Gupta stood back and Bell stepped forward. "I must apologize too Mr. Banik. I'm sorry for the deception but I didn't want my name on any official record of our meeting. Qu-shin is just a cover; my real name is Li Bai, formally of Chinese Naval Intelligence.

"I believe we have a mutual friend. Before he left China he tasked me with gathering a number of his prized possessions and transporting them into Indian space. He gave me your name as his contact so I'm here presenting myself to you. Ms. Avvari has a freighter in orbit awaiting your directions. We're ready to take the cargo to our mutual friend on your say so."

As she had been speaking she had been watching Banik's face closely. At the mention of a 'mutual friend' his face had flattened into an emotionless disinterested stare. She knew she had the right man.

"I'm sorry young woman," Banik said in a flat tone that reflected his face, "but I quite simply don't have a clue what you are talking about. If you want to give me the name of your client then I can look up our records but as far as I know, Varun hasn't had any dealings with Chinese colonial space since the war broke out."

Bell let out an exaggerated sigh, "Come now Mr. Banik, I don't think our mutual friend would want us brandishing his name about indiscriminately. He spoke to me personally before he left Chinese space and he gave me your name as his contact. This isn't my first time doing something like this you know. You don't have to play dumb."

At the last sentence Mr. Banik jumped to his feet. "Look here young lady. I don't know who you work for or who this mutual friend is. I've already told you so. Now, I've had enough of these allegations, it's time for you to leave. The security guard who escorted you up here will see you out."

With that he sat down again and pushed a button on his desk. The large double doors they had entered through swung open and Bell turned to see the security guard standing there with two of his comrades for backup.

Waving them in with his hand Banik shouted angrily, "Escort them out please, and don't let them talk to anyone else. They have already caused enough trouble."

Before leaving Bell couldn't help turning back to the coordinator, "You're making a mistake, the Minister won't be pleased if he doesn't receive his possessions."

If she had any doubts Banik's reaction settled them. "Out," he shouted in anger though his look of alarm was clearly visible at the mention of Chang's former position as the Chinese Minister for Intelligence.

Their escorts were more than a little rough showing them out and once they were back on the street Bell led Gupta towards a bar. This early in the morning it was deserted but the privacy gave them the opportunity to speak openly.

"Well, what did you think?" Bell asked Gupta.

"I'm no expert at reading facial expressions but he had guilty written all over him," she replied.

"Exactly," Bell said, "now all we have to do is wait. Did you manage to plant the bug?"

"Yes, I slipped it under his desk when he was focused on you," Gupta answered.

"Ok," Bell said as she flipped open her datapad "now let's see who Banik calls."

It only took a matter of seconds for the datapad to alert her that the bug was picking up an outgoing COM channel from Banik's office.

"Damn," Bell swore.

"What's the matter?" Gupta asked.

"My datapad can't decode the security encryption, they must not be using one of the standard encryptions the RSNI provided me with. If we want to figure out who Banik is speaking with we're going to have to return to the ship and use its computers to decode the encryption."

"We still have audio from the bug right?" Gupta queried.

"Yes, maybe Banik will let a name slip. Let me play the call from the start," Bell replied as she switched on the volume of the datapad to play Banik's conversation."

"I'm sorry for contacting you Sir."
......

"Yes I know I need a good reason to use this COM channel."
......

"It's just, I had some visitors in my office just now. One of them claimed to be an ex Chinese intelligence officer. They said they were working for a certain Chinese Minister and had a freighter full of the Minister's cargo."
......

"No, everything we had of his has already been transported on.

I've never been informed of any additional cargo."

......

"Yes Sir, I'll get on it right away. Thank you Sir," Banik finished with obvious relief in his voice.

"Well," began Gupta, "that seems to confirm our suspicions, though we're none the wiser as to who organized all this. What do we do from here?"

Bell didn't answer for two men had just entered the bar. Immediately they surveyed the room and for a spilt second their gaze fell on Gupta and Bell before passing on. Both men found seats that allowed them to watch the door and the two women. That was all Bell needed to tell her that they were up to no good. "Now we do nothing, we have just made a couple of new friends. I think we might need a little help from our marines," Bell said.

Gupta turned to stare at the two men but Bell quickly kicked her under the table. "Eyes on me, come on, we're leaving," she said as she rose and pulled Gupta with her.

Outside she caught the eye of the marine who had been lounging about in the street outside Varun's headquarters and flashed him a few hand signals before their two new friends followed them out of the bar. Taking Gupta by the hand she began to walk briskly down the street. With an occasional glance behind her she led the two men on a complex trail, twisting through the streets of the city. When they found a street market taking up one of the city's open squares Gupta thought for sure that they would lose their followers but they turned out to be better than she thought for a couple of streets after the market they reappeared.

Increasing her pace again Bell continued to follow a random path through the city. Eventually she passed an alleyway where one of the marines lazily leant against a wall. When he caught her eye he retreated back into it.

"This way," Bell said as she turned Gupta towards the alleyway. As they walked down the narrower street they passed a section that was in almost complete darkness, the sunlight being blocked out by one of Bhopal's lofty towers. "Good luck," she said into the darkness.

As they reached the end of the alleyway they heard a number of grunts from behind them. Nodding in satisfaction Bell turned them onto one of the city's main streets. "Now we get back to the ship," she said, "and see if we can figure out a plan to get the information we need. Today hasn't exactly gone to plan."

*

That night Bell, Gupta, Becket and Major Johnston all sat in the Captain's quarters of the freighter.

"Were the ship's computers able to decode the COM data from your bug?" Becket asked Bell.

"No, their encryption is extremely good, it must be military grade. Without a dedicated decryption computer there is no way we will be able to crack it," Bell answered.

"Well that's suspicious in itself, our intel suggested they would only be using civilian grade encryption," Johnston complained, "where do we go from here then? It's time we got our hands on this Chang bastard."

"I'm not sure," Bell began, "there's no doubt Banik had a hand in smuggling Chang out of China but he's too junior, I think it highly unlikely he knows where Varun have placed Chang."

"Still, he's our only real lead, surely he will have some information that we could use," Becket interjected.

"True," Bell agreed, "but there is no way he will take another meeting with us and short of kidnapping him we have no other way of getting face to face with him."

"Exactly," said Gupta, "that's what we need to do."

"What?" Bell asked with concern.

"Well, I don't mean we kidnap him exactly. But we can break into his house, confront him face to face and force him to tell us what he knows about Chang," Gupta explained. It was clear from Bell's face that she wasn't convinced but Gupta pushed on with her idea. "Look, it's Friday today. Tonight Banik will go home and no one will expect to see him back at work until Monday. We can break in, confront him and then leave him restrained. No one will come looking for him until Monday at the earliest. By then we will have high tailed it out of New Delhi and onto wherever Banik's information leads us. I don't see that we have any other option, does anyone else?"

"Sounds good to me," Johnston said, "I'll be happy to interrogate this Banik fellow."

"I'm not sure," Becket countered. "If we do this there will be no turning back. If we can't get to Chang in time, Varun will be on to us and if they move him again we will be back to square one. This seems like an all or nothing plan."

Johnston waved his had dismissively at Becket. "Of course it's all or nothing Lieutenant. Our boarding of the Chinese destroyer, Admiral Cunningham's battle with the Chinese fleet at Wi Xiang, they were both all or nothing plays. When we don't have any other options that's what we always do, we go for it."

Becket made to respond but Gupta cut her off. She didn't want Becket riling Johnston up; he had a short enough temper as it was. "What do you think Bell?" she asked, "ultimately it's your decision."

Bell didn't reply immediately. Instead she carefully thought over a few different options. After almost a minute she looked up at the rest of the group. "I don't see that we have any other choice. Whoever is pulling the strings at Varun already knows someone is poking around their operation. If they haven't already they'll soon decide they need to take more steps to protect Chang and cover their own tracks. We need to move fast and confronting Banik is the only option we have on the table that will let us accomplish that. Unless anyone has a plan to get us the information we need any faster I'm going to go with it."

Everyone else remained silent as she eyed them, making her decision for her, "ok then, Major Johnston put together a number of operational plans to get us access to Banik. I'll start working up the questions we need to ask him. Once we're ready we'll take another shuttle down to the surface and get into place."

*

That evening Gupta stood down a darkened alley not unlike the one her and Bell had led the two Varun agents into. This time she was the one waiting. Banik was obviously a dedicated worker for it wasn't until after 8pm local time that he appeared walking along one of the routes Bell had identified Banik would likely take home. The late hour suited their plan fine though for the sun had already set ensuring most of the streets in the financial district were deserted. When she saw him she keyed her COM unit, alerting the rest of the team.

After reviewing the security to Banik's home Johnston had decided against breaking into it. Instead he had found a cheap hotel near the Varun headquarters that didn't ask too many questions. He had booked a suite for the entire weekend and asked not to be disturbed. That way they could get what they wanted from Banik and leave him there to be found by the cleaning staff on Monday.

After Banik had travelled down the street for a while Gupta stepped out from the alleyway and began to head after him. The other marines had been spaced out watching a number of other routes Banik may have taken. A few minutes later two clicks from the COM channel informed her they were now ahead of Banik and in place.

Immediately she broke into a light jog. When she was sure she was in ear shot she called out, "Mr. Banik, Mr. Banik, excuse me Sir."

Instinctively Banik turned around to see who was calling his name. As Gupta jogged up to him he looked confused. "Do I know you?" he asked.

Some impression I left, Gupta thought to herself. Obviously Banik had gone away from their earlier meeting with Agent Bell engrained on his mind. The fact that she wasn't in her trader uniform anymore probably threw him off too.

"It's Neysa Avvari from earlier." Gupta began after catching her breath. "I met you with a colleague of mine, Ms. Li Bai. I wanted to talk to you about my cargo."

"Now listen here," Banik began but before he could say anymore one of the marines who had been sneaking up on him jabbed him in the neck with an auto-injector filled with a potent tranquilizer. As he fell to the ground the other marine caught him and propped him up. The first sent two more clicks through his Com unit.

On cue Major Johnston brought the rented aircar he had been circling overhead in to land. As soon as it landed Bell and another marine opened the door and jumped out. Together the four of them and Gupta bundled Banik into the aircar and once Gupta was aboard Johnston lifted off. In all, it had taken less than a minute to abduct Banik.

"Good job everyone," Bell encouraged. "Now, when you take him out of the aircar make sure it looks like two of you are supporting him on his feet. There should be no one around the back entrance to the hotel. Our Major picked one well out of the way. But just in case make it look like you are just helping your drunk mate back to his bed."

"Aye, Aye Mam," one of the marines acknowledged with a grin, "I think I have had enough practice with that to make it look believable," he finished, eliciting some chuckles from the other two marines.

Turning back to look at the limp Banik, Bell gently kicked his rather large backside, "you better have something good for us when   you   come   to!"

Chapter 6 – Intimidation

17th March 2466, Bhopal, New Delhi

Banik awoke with a start. With a throbbing head he groggily tried to open his eyes. Light pierced the slightly opened slits and he recoiled at the pain it caused. Suddenly it felt like one of the elephants that had been imported to New Delhi was rampaging around inside his head. *Where am I?* He struggled to think. *I don't remember getting home last night, all I remember is... that woman!* In alarm he tried to open his eyes again and the shooting pain made him groan.

Alerted to the fact that her charge was waking up, Bell strolled across the hotel room into Banik's field of view. "Good morning Mr. Banik, it's good to see you again."

"You," he growled. "What have you done to me?"

"Done?" Bell asked innocently. "Why we haven't done very much. We just thought you might be more talkative if we organized another meeting. We thought something more informal would allow us to come to better terms."

As she finished she swiveled round the chair they had Banik tied to, to let him see the rest of the hotel room. The presence of four bulky men who looked less than pleased wasn't lost on Banik.

"What do you plan to do with me?" he asked worriedly. "I already told you I don't know this Minister of yours. There is nothing more I can do for you."

"Now, now Mr. Banik. There is no point telling us any lies. We already know you know all about former Minister Chang," Bell said. Holding up her datapad she began the recording of Banik's conversation with his superior.

As the recording finished Banik's head slumped in defeat. "Now that we have cleared the air," Bell began, "you are going to tell us everything we need to know about the whereabouts of Chang Lei. If you cooperate we'll leave you in this hotel room and come Monday morning the cleaning staff will find you none the worse for wear. If you refuse, I'm going to hand you over to these marine friends of mine.

"I'm not Chinese intelligence. We're Royal Space Navy and we're here to bring Chang to justice. Each of these men served in the war against the Chinese. They all lost friends. As I'm sure you can imagine, they are all highly motivated to locate and apprehend Chang. If you want to stand in their way you're going to regret it."

Once again Bell swung Banik's chair around so he could see the marines. Major Johnston gave the Indian a small smile, fury radiating off him. It was so strong that Bell was taken aback; the Major was clearly a better actor than she thought.

"There now," she said swinging him back so that he was facing her. "Do we understand each other?"

"Yes, I suppose we do," Banik conceded. "What do you want?"

"That's very simple. Tell me everything you know about where and how Varun smuggled Chang out of Chinese space," Bell answered.

Banik spoke in short sentences but as Gupta listened on from the sidelines it all became clear. Whoever had organized the escape had been ballsy, that was for sure. Through contacts Varun had on Earth they had actually bribed a British freighter to take Chang out of Chinese space. As part of the peace settlement with China, Britain had enforced a strict free trade policy. A large portion of the Chinese freighter fleet had been destroyed in the war and many of the British freighters had rushed to fill the demand. It would have been easy for one to evade the patrols the RSN and the remnants of the Chinese navy had hastily tried to implement.

According to Banik, Chang had been kept well-hidden from the freighter crew so they didn't know who they were transporting. Nevertheless, Gupta knew that whoever the luckless freighter Captain turned out to be there would be hell to pay. Once in the Sol system, Chang had been transferred to a Varun freighter and then taken to New Delhi. There he had been transferred to a local mining freighter that toured the outlying Indian mining colonies picking up their processed ore and taking it back to New Delhi for use in its ever expanding industries. Banik knew the first stop the freighter made on its journey was the colony of Kerala. However, as it was an independent freighter hired out of the Varun offices on Kerala, he didn't have access to the rest of its route.

After asking him about the freighter's schedule for a third time and getting the same answer Bell cursed. "Another dead end!" she shouted in frustration.

"Let me have a few minutes alone with him," Johnston asked,

"I'm sure I can squeeze a few more details out of him."

"No, no please. I've told you the truth. I can't tell you anymore," Banik pleaded. "I don't know, I don't," he continued as Johnston stood up and approached him.

"That will be enough," Bell said as she jumped in between Johnston and the Indian, noting the fury in Johnston's eyes. *Maybe he wasn't acting before*, she thought. "There will be no need for any squeezing, torture won't get us anywhere, he'll just tell us anything to get us to stop and then we'll be running around on a wild goose chase."

"This is our only source of information," Johnston almost shouted. "If you're not willing to do what is necessary I am! You don't have to stay for this, I can contact you when we have what we need."

Bell held her ground and Gupta was afraid things were about to come to blows. "Wait," she shouted. "Maybe there is another option."

"Banik?" she asked, "won't the Varun offices on Kerala have information on the freighter's schedule?"

"Well... yes," he said after a moment's hesitation, "but that won't help you. There is no way to access them from New Delhi."

"No," Gupta agreed, "but you could access them if you were on Kerala couldn't you?"

Banik looked horrified at Gupta's suggestion. "Leave New Delhi? You promised to let me go if I cooperated. Varun will fire me for sure."

Bell jumped on the idea. "We promised to let you go if you helped us locate Chang, you haven't done that yet. But look," she followed up before Banik could interrupt, "we are not unreasonable. We know that if we abduct you and take you to Kerala you'll lose your job and your home. But we can compensate you. I have been given permission to be very generous to anyone we can persuade to help us find Chang. How does five million credits sound?"

At that Banik's face lit up. Bell had done her research; she knew that even as a mid-level manager in the Varun shipping company it would take him twenty years to see five million credits pass through his accounts. "In addition, I can offer you a full pardon for any crimes my government may have deemed you to be a part of and we can offer you asylum within our colonies. We could give you a new identity and make sure Varun and the Indian government can't track you."

"What do you say?" Gupta asked.

Despite the generosity of the offer Banik hesitated. He had built a life on New Delhi, he had friends and a sister who had her own family. *But if I lose my job where would I be? No one will want to see me; they will be ashamed of me.*

Sensing his dilemma Bell gave him her final ultimatum. "Listen, you have two choices before you. We're taking you to Kerala, either we force you at gunpoint to do what we want and then leave you on Kerala or you cooperate and get a new life in British space. You need to decide now."

"Ok," Banik said reluctantly. "I'll do it."

"Right," Bell said swinging into action. "Johnston, you and your marines gather up your things. Gupta and I will get Mr. Banik to the aircar. We should be able to take a shuttle back to the trade station in orbit. No one should suspect anything. Let's get moving everyone. The sooner we get out of here the better chance we will have of getting to Chang before Varun move him because as soon as they realize Banik is missing, that's the first thing they will do."

*

25th March 2466, *HMS Endeavour*, edge of the Kerala system.

A week later, after a mad dash to the Kerala system, James asked Gupta the same question for the third time, "are you sure you are up for this Commander? You'll be without any back up."

"I know Captain, but if it is what needs to be done then it is what I will do," Gupta answered.

"We'll have your back Commander." Major Johnston assured her from his seat in *Endeavour's* conference room. "We may not be going in with you but at the first sign of trouble we'll have you out in no time."

James nodded in agreement. "I want you to take a full squad of marines from *Endeavour*, you can shuttle them down in two loads from the freighter if you have to but I want a full squad ready to go at a moment's notice."

"Don't worry Captain," Bell said reassuringly. "I have debriefed

Banik fully, we now have a fair idea of the security guarding the Varun offices on Kerala, I'll be with Johnston and his men and we'll be ready for any eventuality."

"Very well," James said, "the mission is a go. Just remember if any of you are caught you are on your own. Don't take anything that can identify you and whatever you do, if you get the information we need make sure it is transmitted to *Endeavour* immediately. We can't fail in this matter."

"Yes Sir," Bell said. "We'll head back to *Innocence* now and prepare to jump on into the system with your permission?"

"You have it," James said.

As the crew of *Innocence* filed out James was left with his First and Second Lieutenants. "This has been my hardest mission yet," he confided in them. "All this waiting and watching. Knowing there is nothing we can do."

"You're right Sir of course," Second Lieutenant Malory began, "but at least we have used the time wisely. All the drills with the crew have improved our efficiency ratings dramatically. That will please the Admiralty. And for our maiden voyage we have aptly demonstrated *Endeavour's* stealth capabilities. We've been in unfriendly space for almost two months and no one has come close to spotting us."

"That's not the point," First Lieutenant Ferguson said. "We could go anywhere and do as many drills as we wanted. It's the fact that while we sit up here in safety others, even our fellow crewmembers, are risking their lives. Doesn't it leave a sour taste in your mouth?"

"Well yes, I know what you mean, it isn't easy for any of us," Malory answered.

James rather suspected he didn't, as far as he could tell all Malory was interested in was his own efficiency reports and whatever illicit activities he managed to get away with. James was now sure Malory had set up at least one gambling ring on *Endeavour*, all he needed was some proof.

Knowing he wasn't going to get any today he switched the topic. "How are the crew holding up?" he asked.

"Their fine Sir, the extra drills and simulations have been helping everyone take their minds off the monotony. Plus the extra rec time you approved has helped a lot," Malory answered.

"That's correct Sir," Ferguson added. "But I think they are still being affected by how surreal this feels. Everyone is extremely motivated to get Chang and bring him to justice. But as we've said, just sitting around while others take the risks sits uneasy with most of the crew. I think that's why our efficiency ratings are so high, guilt is a strong motivator."

"I see," James said. "Well there is nothing else for it at the moment. Everyone will just have to keep going as is. Hopefully once we get a firm location on Chang we can play a more direct role in his apprehension."

*

26th March 2466, Kerala.

—

Gupta stood in front of the main doors to the Varun offices on Kerala. The building wasn't nearly as impressive as the lofty tower back on New Delhi but that reflected Kerala's status. The planet had only been colonized eighty years ago and as it was a barren rocky world there wasn't much there to attract new colonists. Nevertheless, its mineral deposits and strategic location meant the Indians had set up more than just a military outpost and now the planet's single city boasted a population of more than one hundred thousand. Most of them served the military base or the growing mining industry.

Taking a deep breath, she prodded Banik towards the automatic doors. "Don't forget what I'm carrying with me, one wrong move," she warned him.

"Yes, yes. I know, one wrong move and I'm history. Your Chinese friend has drilled that into me a thousand times. Let's just get this over with," Banik responded.

Gupta was just making sure. It was a bluff but she needed Banik to believe it. Bell had drummed it into him that RSNI had developed an auto injector that would get past any security scans. They had told him that Gupta was carrying one filled with a deadly poison. At the first sign of betrayal she would make sure he received the full dose.

"Here we go then," Gupta said as the automatic doors opened.

Banik smiled at the receptionist and set his identity card on the desk. "Good morning, I'm a senior shipping coordinator from New Delhi. I've been sent here to follow up on a few old shipping contracts we need to tidy up for our records. Headquarters back in India have requested a full review of all civilian contracts."

"Good morning Sir," the receptionist responded as she picked up his identity card and ran it through her scanner. "May I have your hand for a DNA scan as well?"

"Certainly," Banik said as he reached out his hand.

"Thank you Sir," your identity is confirmed. "Who shall I inform that you have arrived?"

"Well actually. Mr. Shankar and I go way back. We worked together for Varun on Earth for a number of years. Back in our youth of course," Banik chuckled.

"I was kind of hoping to surprise him," he said as he slipped a hundred credit bill to the receptionist. "If you don't mind I'd like to go up to his offices unannounced and just pop in."

"Don't worry," Banik added when the receptionist looked a bit uncertain. "I will tell him I snuck past reception, no one will know you let me in," he said as he slipped her another hundred credit bill.

"Ok," the receptionist said a bit more happily as she entered a few details into her datapad. "You can go on through, your identity card will give you access to Mr. Shankar's office."

"Well we're in," Banik said as they walked through the main security doors.

"Yes, now let's do what we came to do and get out of here," Gupta responded.

"Right, just follow me and look relaxed. We'll find a free computer terminal, get your information and we'll be out of here in no time," Banik said confidently.

Gupta just nodded and followed Banik into a turbo lift. It took them up three floors before stopping. According to the plans for the building the third floor was the manager's floor. They had timed their arrival to coincide with lunch and they hoped to find at least one of the offices empty. Sure enough the place looked deserted.

"Right, let's get to work," Gupta said. "Here will do just fine," she added as she walked through the door into the nearest office.

As Banik sat down in the desk chair and switched on the terminal he paused and looked up at Gupta. "As soon as I log in as a guest my details will be in the system. Varun will know I have betrayed them. Can I really trust you?"

Gupta had been expecting this would come. She slowly reached for one of her pockets and said, "you don't have to trust me, you just have to want to live. There's no turning back now."

Sighing, Banik looked back at the terminal and punched in the final part of his password to unlock the computer. He brought up the flight schedule for the independent traders hired by Varun, then he focused on the freighter in question. "I have the *Dawon's* schedule, data chip please?" he asked when he found what he was after.

Gupta pulled out a data chip. Banik placed it in the terminal and downloaded the data they needed.

"Job done," he said as he handed the data chip back to her with a smile, "now you can get me out of here if you please. I have a nice five million credits waiting for me."

Chapter 7 – Evac

26th March 2466, Varun offices, Kerala.

"What are you doing in my office?" a voice shouted from just outside the door, making Banik and Gupta jump.

They stared at the man blankly for a few vital seconds before Banik cleared his throat and began to speak. "Eh... hello there, my name is Rahul Banik. I'm visiting from the New Delhi offices. I just needed to use a terminal to check some data about a proposal I'm bringing to Overseer Shankar. I hope we haven't caused any offence."

Whoever the newcomer was it didn't look like he bought Banik's excuse. He raised his COM link. "Reception, I have a Mr. Banik snooping around in my office. Does he have permission to be on the eighth floor?"

"A Mr. Banik? He came to visit the Overseer but he didn't have an appointment. He was supposed to go directly to the Overseer's office," came the reply over the COM channel.

"Right, get secur..."

Gupta pounced on him and knocked him to the ground at the mention of security. "Quick, let's get out of here," she called.

Banik did what he was told and followed Gupta as he stepped over the unconscious man on the floor. They both ran to the turbolift and got in. Gupta hit the button for the ground floor. As the lift began to go down she pulled out her datapad and inserted the data chip. It automatically began to transmit to the freighter in orbit. At the same time, she keyed her COM unit. "Major, we've got the flight schedule but our cover has been blown."

Before the Major could respond the lift ground to a halt. "Shit," Banik shouted.

Gupta reached out and hit the emergency button to open the turbolift door. It began to open the doors but stopped as someone cut the power to the turbolift. "What's going on?" Johnston asked over the COM channel.

"Security has shut down the turbolifts. We're able to get out but we'll be stuck on the second floor. I'm sure they have sealed off the ground floor already. We're going to need some help," Gupta answered.

"Ok, we're ready," Johnston said calmly. "The schematics of the building show an emergency stairwell to the south west of the building. We'll breach the building at the front entrance and secure the stairwell. If you can make it there we'll take you the rest of the way out. Good luck Commander."

Leaving the COM link open, Gupta reached through the partially opened lift doors and heaved on the second floor doors that were almost at her head height. Thankfully it didn't require much strength to force them open. Turning to Banik she said, "Are you coming with me? Our offer of protection still stands."

"I don't have much choice at this point," he answered. "You're going to have to boost me up there though."

"I guessed as much," Gupta said as she knelt down and put her hands together to provide a foothold for Banik to step up from. As she lifted him towards the opening she swore to herself. *That's the last time I make a deal with an overweight Indian on a ground mission.*

*

Outside the Varun buildings Bell, Johnston and twelve marines approached the main doors. As they did the doors automatically opened and everyone rushed in.

The receptionist's eyes widened in alarm when she saw fourteen people stampeding into her building. She opened her mouth to scream but a bolt of electricity hit her and she crumpled to the floor.

There were two armed security guards standing in front of the turbolifts and another off to the side. All three fell to similar bolts of electricity from other marines. The stunners weren't very accurate as the electricity didn't shoot through the air in a linear path but in close quarters they were accurate enough for the marines.

"Right, first fire team hold reception. I'll take second and secure the guard station and the rest of the ground floor, Bell you take third and get to the stairwell, secure it up to the second floor. Gupta should be there waiting for you."

Without waiting for a response he moved out, leading the second squad. The guard station was close to the entrance and he only had to round two corners to get to it. When they got there the door was locked. It was clear that whoever was inside had already seen the marines enter the building. Peering through the window Johnston saw two Indians staring back with a mixture of anger and fear. One of them gestured rudely at him. He smiled back and shot a few bolts of electricity at the door. Instinctively, they ducked. There was no need though for the door easily absorbed the shot.

"Samuels, Jones, you two watch this door. If they try to get out blast them. The rest of you with me," Johnston ordered as he moved off to secure the rest of the ground floor.

Meanwhile, Bell had found the stairwell and was making her way to the second floor. When she got to the second floor she keyed her COM channel. "Stairwell secure. You can come out now."

Gupta prodded Banik to his feet. They had been hiding in a corner office beside the stairwell waiting for the all clear. "Time to make a run for it," she told Banik.

As they ran out of the office a voice called from behind them. "Stop or I'll shoot."

Ignoring it they both rushed on.

Bell crouched as the doors from the second floor whooshed open. Gupta and Banik ran through followed by three loud pops. Rather than being armed with plasma, the rifles that most militaries used, Varun security seemed to be armed with chemical propellant weapons. Banik cried out in pain as a bullet ripped through his leg. He stumbled down the stairs into a waiting marine. Two more bullets tore into the permacrete of the stairwell wall.

Once Gupta passed her position, Bell jumped up and sent a stream of stunner blasts down the corridor towards the approaching guard. None of them hit but he dived into cover.

As if from nowhere more pops sounded from above and bullets crashed into the stairwell around Bell. Before she had time to focus on a target she fired a stream of electric bolts up the stairwell towards the third floor where more security guards had appeared.

That gave one of the marines time to grab Banik and help him down the stairs. The other three marines followed Bell's lead and continued to pour fire up the stairwell at the security guards, keeping them pinned down. Bell and Gupta got up and followed Banik.

At the bottom of the stairs Johnston was already waiting for them. "Everyone in one piece?" he asked.

"More or less," Bell answered. Pointing to Banik she said, "Our friend has nicked himself but it's nothing that won't heal."

"Ok then, we need to keep moving," Johnston ordered. "We have the Varun security guards under control but they will have alerted the local police. They will be here any minute."

He spun and began to bark orders into his COM unit. "Fire team two fall back, fire team one prepare to evac, we're coming your way."

Once they were on the street Johnston broke the team into a fast jog. Two marines carried Banik while Gupta struggled to keep up. In the distance a distinctive siren sounded. Quickly, they rounded the corner and were out of sight of the Varun buildings.

"Good job everyone," Bell said as she opened her COM. "Lieutenant, what's the status on our pick up?"

"The two shuttles are already on their way," Becket answered from orbit. "They will be at the extraction point in two minutes."

"Look alive everyone. The extraction point is a five minute sprint from here. The sooner we get there the sooner we get out of here. We'll stop for a thirty second break half way to swap Banik over to two fresh marines. Everyone ready to go?"

After a chorus of 'yes Sir' Bell broke into a sprint as she held her datapad out in front of her so she could see the route they needed to take.

When they got to the halfway point the two marines carrying Banik efficiently passed him off to two others. Overhead two sonic booms announced the arrival of the rapidly decelerating shuttles. No doubt they had broken all the local laws for shuttles coming down from orbit.

There were sirens from the local police all around them. If the police forces didn't know where they were, the two shuttles would surely give away where they were headed. "This is it everyone, let's double time it. If you see any of those police aircars don't hesitate to put a few stunner rounds into them," Bell said.

They quickly covered the ground to the open square that was their extraction point. As they rounded the final corner the shuttles were just setting down. Off to the side two police aircars looped around a twenty story tower and descended.

"Stunners," Bell called. She lifted her weapon and poured fire into one of them. As the first bolts of electricity began to hit the police aircars two ports on each craft opened, revealing a small plasma cannon. To Bell they didn't look any bigger than the standard plasma rifles marines were usually equipped with but they would still shred her men.

"Take cover," she shouted.

The next moments seemed to happen at once. Three stunner bolts hit one of the aircars, overloaded its navigational systems and caused it to dive towards the ground. This threw its aim off and a number of plasma bolts ripped up a section of the square between them and the shuttles.

The other police aircar fired off six plasma bolts. The first two tore up the ground in front of them, sending up a shower of permacrete. Even before the permacrete hit them, the next four plasma bolts rained down into the middle of the group. Those who hadn't already hit the ground were thrown there by the force of the plasma bolts impacting right at their feet.

Head ringing, Bell waited until she heard the police aircar whizz past overhead to lift herself back to her feet. It would take them a few vital seconds to turn and come back; her team needed every one of them.

"On your feet everyone," she shouted. She couldn't help pausing to survey the damage. One marine still lay on the ground, a large hole blown right through his chest. Another marine had taken a grazing plasma bolt to his leg but two of his buddies were already helping him onto his feet.

"Leave Samuels," Johnston shouted. "Get to the shuttle."

Bell had to push two of the marines away from Samuels' body and force them into a run. It went against all their training to leave a comrade behind. Yet they couldn't afford to be captured. Samuels' body couldn't tell the Indians anything about who they were. If they managed to capture some of the team however, eventually the Indians would be able to get some information out of them.

The shuttles were only four hundred meters ahead. *Nearly there,* Bell thought. Just then she heard the whine of the police siren. "Spread out," Johnston ordered.

Looking around she wasn't sure if it was going to be enough. Everyone had given up trying to shoot the aircar down and they were just sprinting for the shuttle. A few of the marines let out a cheer. Spinning round, Bell saw one of the shuttles taking off again; two of its weapons ports were open with their plasma cannons extended. It fired a stream of bolts towards the police aircar, spinning again she saw they all missed. It must have been intentional, for no shuttle gunner could have that bad an aim, he would have been reassigned a long time ago. It seemed to work, for the police aircar swerved erratically and gunned its engines, lifting off into the atmosphere.

"Get Banik, Gupta and our injured into the first shuttle," Johnston ordered as they approached the landing site. "It can take off and cover us while the second shuttle lands."

When they reached the shuttle everyone was bundled in. Before Bell knew it Johnston had pushed her up the shuttle's landing ramp. "Up you go agent, there's room in there for you too."

Before she could protest he reached in and hit the button to close the landing ramp and jumped back. "See you on *Innocence*," he said with a wave.

Once the ramp closed she made her way to the cockpit. As she passed Gupta she gave her a reassuring smile. "We're still in once piece," Gupta said as Bell patted her on the shoulder.

"Pilot," Bell called loud enough for the pilot to hear through his flight helmet. Instead of responding he pointed at a rack with two spare helmets. She donned one and switched on its mike. "Take off," she ordered, "but circle round the landing site. You need to keep any police aircars away long enough for the other shuttle to land and pick the rest of our men up."

"Yes sir," the pilot responded.

As the shuttle lifted off and circled the square there was no sign of any further police presence. Bell wanted to take that as a good sign but she knew it probably meant they had been ordered to fall back. That could only mean that whoever was in charge of the planet's security had called in some heavier support.

"Ma'am, the other shuttle is lifting off," the pilot informed her.

"Take us out of here," she ordered. "And ignore any of the planet's flight regulations, get us to the freighter as quickly as possible."

*

On board *Innocence* Becket had already powered up the freighter's main reactor and was boosting out of orbit. The smaller shuttles would easily be able to catch the slower freighter.

"Lieutenant, we're being hailed by one of the system patrol frigates," Sub Lieutenant McClure said.

"Put it on the holo display," she ordered.

A small woman with brown hair, brown eyes and a tight fitting Indian naval uniform appeared on the holo display. The look on her face said she wasn't in the mood to suffer fools. "With whom am I speaking?" she demanded.

"My name is Lisa Jones," Becket lied. "I am currently commanding this freighter."

"You look rather young to be captaining your own freighter," the middle aged Indian naval Captain said in contempt.

"I am the Chief Mate, my captain is indisposed at the moment but she is on her way. How may I help you in the meantime?" Becket answered as politely as she could.

"You are ordered to bring your ship to a halt and prepare for a customs inspection," the Indian naval officer said in a tone that expected to be obeyed.

"I'm afraid I don't understand," Becket said. "We were inspected yesterday and we haven't loaded any cargo from the surface or any of the trading stations in orbit. Why do we need to be inspected again?"

"I have my orders straight from the planetary governor. Whoever is on those two shuttles approaching your freighter is not allowed to leave the system. Let me say this again real slowly for you young woman. Heave to now and cut your reactors or I will open fire."

"Hold on, I'm in way over my head, let me think this through," Becket said playing on the naval officer's obvious contempt for her.

"There is nothing to think about," the officer snapped, "you have my orders."

"But I have orders too, we have a very time sensitive cargo. If we don't leave Kerala now we will incur heavy fines on our contract. As I understand it some of my people on those shuttles got into a fistfight in a local bar. You have our registration details, if there have been any damages you can forward them to my company and we will reimburse whoever needs payment. There is no need to carry out another customs inspection."

"Freighter, understand this," the officer almost shouted over the COM channel. "Your crew have been placed under investigation by the planet's governor. If you do not cut your engines now we will have to open fire. You are not leaving this system."

"The frigate has opened one of its missile ports," one of the Sub Lieutenants called.

"You have thirty seconds then I open fire," the Indian naval officer said with a feral smile.

"You can't do this," Becket said in anger. "You're going to ruin my career," she added as she slammed her fist down on the command chair, hitting the button to cut the transmission.

Immediately she was fully composed again. "How long until the shuttles dock?" she asked.

"One minute."

"And if the frigate opens fire in thirty seconds how long until the missile will strike us?"

"It will take it five minutes to catch us," the same Sub Lieutenant answered.

"Ok, here's the plan. We're going to let them open fire and wait until the missile gets to within two minutes. Then I want all our hidden point defenses activated. We should be able to handle one missile. At the same time I want to open fire with our plasma cannon. We may not be able to hit them at this range but it will give them something to think about and hopefully keep them off our backs long enough for us to engage the shift drive. Are the capacitors fully charged?"

"Yes Sir, we are ready to jump as soon as we get out of Kerala's mass shadow."

Becket only nodded. The shift drive had revolutionized human space travel but it had some major drawbacks. It needed a lot of power to activate and its capacitors had to be charged for a long time between jumps. It also couldn't be activated too close to the gravitational field of other objects. Things like stars, planets, asteroids and the dark matter strewn about in space between the stars severely limited where ships could go.

That meant they had to play a game of cat and mouse with the pursuing frigate. The frigate knew where the edge of the mass shadow was and knew that if they let the freighter reach it their quarry would escape. Yet Becket had to trick the frigate into allowing them to reach the mass shadow anyway. Thankfully, the freighter's hidden weapons meant she had a few tricks up her sleeve.

"Missile launch," McClure reported.

"Get those shuttles landed," Becket ordered.

Knowing that the Sub Lieutenant could handle it, she focused her attention on the incoming Indian missile. It was the first time a British ship had seen an Indian warship fire one of its missiles in anger in decades. She hoped they didn't have any surprises for her.

The plot updated to show that the missile was closing with them slower than expected. The computer updated its information on the missile to estimate that it was one of the Indian navy's earlier missile designs. Becket wasn't too surprised; the Indian navy's patrol craft were probably the last ships to receive new technology.

"Shuttles have landed," McClure informed her.

"Ok, tactical," she said to the Sub Lieutenant manning the weapons terminal on the bridge. "Prepare to bring the point defenses online. As soon as you have them powered up and tracking the incoming missile you can open fire on the frigate with the main plasma cannon. At this range it isn't likely to do any damage but it will let that frigate know we have teeth.

"McClure, once we bring up the point defenses take us to full acceleration. We need to make it to the mass shadow before they can hit us with a full broadside," Becket ordered.

Innocence was a Q ship. Built to look and act like a freighter, she also had enough weapons to take on any pirates that tried to attack her. That meant she carried a lot of point defense weapons and had military grade engines. Offensively she had a single missile tube on her port and starboard bows but as the freighter was fleeing from the frigate they couldn't be brought to bear on it. Instead they would have to rely on their single heavy plasma. It was a powerful weapon at close range, able to punch right through the valstronium armor of most warships. However, over long ranges the plasma containment field on each of its bolts disintegrated, robbing each shot of much of its force. In the Void War Becket had seen James use the heavy plasma cannons at range to distract his opponents and she planned to do the same here.

"Now," Becket ordered once the missile got to within two minutes of hitting *Innocence*.

The main radar array powered up and began tracking the missile more accurately. As soon as the targeting computer obtained a firm lock the small point defense plasma cannons fired tens and then hundreds of plasma bolts at the missile. Sensing the targeting radar the missile had already begun evasive maneuvers and it successfully dodged the first wave of plasma bolts.

The familiar thump, thump of anti-missile missiles erupting from their launchers meant the holo display filled with more plots as it tracked the short lived missiles' attempts to intercept their larger brother.

"I got it," the tactical officer called out as an AM missile managed to detonate close enough to the Indian missile to damage it and throw it off course.

"What is the frigate doing?" Becket called to McClure.

"They have gone to full military power. The heavy plasma bolts don't seem to be having any impact at this range," he answered.

Becket looked at the plot on the holo display, the frigate had been slow in trying to match their speed, caught by surprise. The extra acceleration *Innocence* had put on meant they would get to the mass shadow before any missile fired from the frigate reached them.

As if they couldn't see what she was looking at the frigate fired two more missiles at the freighter. *Innocence* had been designed to defend herself against two incoming missiles but Becket was thankful that they wouldn't have to put it to the test. In war things never worked as they were expected to. Just relying on being able to shoot down one missile had been enough stress for one day.

She was distracted from the holo display when the turbolift opened and Gupta, Bell and Major Johnston stepped onto the bridge. "Status report," Gupta asked.

"We managed to shoot down the frigate's missile. They have fired two more but we should be able to jump out before they reach us," Becket said, vacating the captain's chair.

"Good work," Gupta said as she surveyed the plot on the holo display, confirming the information for herself.

"Commander, we have passed through the mass shadow," McClure called.

Becket looked at Gupta who nodded at her. "Jump us out of here," Becket ordered.

With a bright flash and a release of electromagnetic radiation *Innocence* disappeared from the pursuing frigate's sensors into safety.

Chapter 8 – In Chang's Footsteps

The Haven colony started off as an attempt to escape from the politics of Earth yet in the end it would come to play a significant role in the establishment of the Empire.

- Excerpt from Empire Rising, 3002 AD

4th April 2466 AD, HMS *Endeavour*, Andaman system

James was excited. Finally *Endeavour* was going to play her role in apprehending Chang. They were cruising into the Andaman system under stealth. *Innocence* was lying back in the outer system with her systems powered down. They didn't want any sign of their presence to get back to the Indian gas mining station that was their target.

Andaman was a bare system. It only had four planets, one of which was the gas giant they were approaching. None of the other planets had anything of value on them so the Indians had only established a gas mining station in the system.

After reviewing the data Gupta and Banik had recovered on the *Dawon's* schedule, Andaman had jumped out as the most likely location Chang was hiding. *Dawon* was an ore freighter and had no business going out of its way to visit a gas mining station. On top of that, it was only scheduled to stop at the station for several hours. Long enough to offload an important passenger and some cargo but not long enough to do anything else.

Agent Bell, Major Johnston, Gupta and James had concluded that Chang had to be on the gas mining station. *Endeavour* was now on her way to prove their theory.

"What are our passive sensors picking up?" James asked the Sub Lieutenant manning the sensor terminal.

"It looks like there are currently two freighters docked with the station. Neither of them looks like the *Dawon*." Malik answered.

"Ok, pass on the information to Major Johnston, he will have to detail some marines to commandeer the two freighters," James ordered.

"Ferguson, I want you to take over tactical," James said turning to the First Lieutenant. "I want you to use the passive sensors to identify any point defense weapons the station has. Once we're close enough we will bring up the active sensors to get a firm lock on your targets. As soon as you get a lock I want them destroyed. Our point defense plasma cannons should be more than powerful enough to take out their defenses at close range. I don't want the station to have anything left that can shoot at our shuttles. And make sure our plasma bolts are not strong enough to punch through the hull of the station. We don't want to kill Chang by depressurizing a part of the station he is in."

"Understood Sir," Ferguson answered as he vacated the First Lieutenant's chair and moved over to tactical.

Now all they had to do was wait. *Endeavour* had already proven the effectiveness of her stealth capabilities on this cruise and so James had no doubt they could sneak up on the station. Major

Johnston had his Marines ready to go and by the time they got in range Ferguson would be prepared to neutralize the station's defenses. For four more hours James sat in almost silence as he watched the station grow ever closer on the holo display.

When it was time he opened a channel to the shuttle bay, "Ready to go Major?"

"Ready when you are Captain, my boys are looking forward to getting our hands on this Chang bastard," the Marine replied.

"Just remember," James began in his best Captain's voice, "we want Chang alive. He is no use to us dead. Make sure your men understand that."

"I'll do my best Sir but shit happens in war," Johnston said without much concern.

"I expect nothing less than your best, and Major, cut the swearing on official ship communications," James said as he closed the COM channel.

"Are you confident you have identified all the point defenses?" he asked the First Lieutenant.

"Yes Sir," Ferguson replied, "a few seconds with the active sensors will confirm but we're as confident as we can be just using the passives."

"Ok then, on my mark you can deploy the active sensors, engage your targets as soon as you have a lock. Communications," James said turning to the COM officer. "Ten seconds after we activate the sensors give the go ahead to the marines."

"Acknowledged," the Sub Lieutenant said.

"On my mark then, three, two, one, Mark!" James announced.

Endeavour's main radar array powered up and fired over five terawatts of energy at the station. James had managed to get his ship to within a light second of their target and Ferguson had almost instantaneous readings on it. Three seconds after the radar was switched on the battle computer alerted Ferguson that it had a firm lock on all of the targets he had identified. With a single tap on the tactical terminal over fifty of *Endeavour's* small point defense plasma cannons fired low powered shots at the station, causing a wave of explosions to ripple across its surface. Before the command crew aboard the station even knew what was happening, *Endeavour's* battle computer analyzed the first shots, identified a number of point defense instillations that were still functional and targeted them again. The First Lieutenant took a couple of seconds to review the readings before he approved a second volley of plasma bolts. Eight seconds after the first volley, another fifteen explosions erupted around the station. Meanwhile, Major Johnston's four shuttles, fully loaded with marines in combat armor, left *Endeavour* and charged for the station.

In a rush to identify the source of the incoming attack and get over their initial shock when *Endeavour* powered up from stealth, the command crew on the station didn't even detect the shuttles' launch.

"Hail that ship," Station Commander Chowdhury demanded.

When James' face appeared on screen Chowdhury was taken

aback to be facing a military officer from another naval power. His anger soon won out, "How dare you fire on an Indian station! This is an act of war. I demand you turn your ship around and leave this system immediately."

"Now, now. No need to lose your temper," James said calmly. "Let me introduce myself, eh... Commander is it?"

Without waiting for a response he continued, "I have reason to believe you are harboring a war criminal, former politburo Minister Chang. On behalf of the UN and the British Government I am here to take him into custody. If you turn him over immediately no further damage will befall your station."

"Listen to me Captain," Chowdhury said, pouring as much scorn into the title as he could. "Britain holds no power in India, you British might think you can just bully whoever you want but not India and not me. If you make one more act of aggression I promise you I will see you taken before a UN court on charges of war crimes."

"So be it," James said with a smile, "prepare to be boarded."

"What?" Chowdhury said, half to James and half to his command crew. "Quick, close all the external doors to the shuttle bays," he ordered.

"Too late," one of his staff called. "I'm detecting shuttles entering bays two and four."

"Alert our security teams," Chowdhury ordered. "Tell them to prepare to repel boarders!"

*

Finally, Johnston thought to himself as he stepped out of the shuttle onto the deck of the gas mining station.

His marines had already secured the shuttle bay he had landed in and one of his Lieutenants approached him when he stepped out, "We're ready to move out," she informed him.

Keying his COM unit to address the marines who had landed on the station he said, "Listen up marines, whichever squad finds me Chang first gets free drinks all night the next time we're in port. Happy hunting, and remember," he added for Somerville's sake, "stunners only, but if you encounter some hard resistance you have my permission to switch to your side arms."

Typically marines were equipped with heavy plasma rifles when they were on operations along with a chemical propellant side arm. Captain Somerville had ordered them equipped with stunners instead of plasma rifles as the station was a civilian operation but Johnston had allowed them to take their side arms. They would follow Somerville's instructions at first but if his men's lives were at risk they would switch.

"First two cargo bays have been secured Sir," another of his Lieutenant's reported.

"Acknowledged," he replied.

Confident that his subordinates had the systematic search of the station in hand he opened the schematics of the station on his combat armor's HUD. Chang was most likely to be in the crew's quarters and that was where he wanted to be.

"Sergeant Harken, I'm coming to join you in your search," he said over the COM to the marine overseeing the search of the crew quarters.

Once he identified the quickest route to the Sergeant he set off at a run. The fire team designated to protect him took up positions around him.

"I hope you are ready to see one of the most powerful men in the galexy grovel at your feet," Johnston said to Fourth Lieutenant Becket who was keeping pace beside him in her own battle armor. Somerville had sent her to accompany him in case he needed any technical assistance controlling the station. He was ok with that, Becket had been training with him on board *Innocence* and although she wasn't a marine, she continued to impress him.

"Ready when you are," she replied with a grin. "Let's just make sure he is alive long enough to do some groveling before the UN too, it would be a shame for the entire world not to see it."

"Humph," Johnston said, not so sure he agreed.

"We're encountering resistance from the station security force," a Lieutenant reported over the COM. "There were three of them. Two are down, the other has fallen back. They were armed with chemical propellant weapons."

"Keep pushing them back," Johnston ordered, "don't be afraid to use some live rounds yourself to scare them off. They have no business standing up to combat armor."

Brave fellows, Johnston thought as he neared the crew quarters, *or stupid.* Nothing but a high explosive round or a bolt from a plasma rifle would penetrate the marine's armor.

"We've got five or six security guards who have barricaded themselves into a section of the crew quarters, at least one of them has a plasma rifle," Harken reported. "We can take them but if we stick to our stunners we're going to take casualities."

"Use your side arms," Johnston approved, "but stay behind cover. Mark their position on the schematics and we'll see if we can flank them."

As the information on his HUD updated it became clear that there were two or three routes they could take to flank the defenders. Whoever had designed the station hadn't been thinking about defending from boarders.

"I guess all your extra training is going to be put to use," Johnston said to Becket, "come on, follow me."

"Side arms out," he said to the rest of his marines.

This is what I have been afraid of, Becket thought to herself. Using lethal weapons could very quickly lead to an 'incident' when they found Chang, of course it would be an 'accident' according to Johnston's official report but Becket knew he wouldn't lose any sleep over the war criminal's death. There was nothing for it but to keep going though so she gritted her teeth and increased her pace to keep up with the Major.

Two corridors away from their targets Johnston came to a dead stop as the distinct sound of chemical propellant shots being fired could be heard. The marine in front of him peeked his head around the corner. Becket was able to read most of the marine's basic hand signals and she moved forward with the rest of the marines when he signaled it was all clear.

They stopped at the next corner. By now the low thrum of a plasma rifle firing out multiple shots was clear through the louder cracks of the other weapons. This time when the marine poked his head around the corner it was met with a number of hardened tungsten rounds bouncing off the durasteel walls of the station. "Contact," the marine signaled.

"Harken, we're in position to the east of the security forces. They have line of sight on us but if we rush them together we'll be able to take them," Johnston said over the COM. Every station had its own internal geographic layout to help humans navigate it and the marines were using one of the schematics for the station they had been able to retrieve from the RSNI data files.

"Acknowledged Sir," Harken responded.

"Stun grenades in five, four, three," Johnston began but Becket didn't hear anymore as she dialed her audio output on her armor way down. Stun grenades had hardly been upgraded in the last three hundred years but they still proved to be potent weapons against unsuspecting opponents. They were actually more harmful to soldiers in combat armor in closed spaces as the armor greatly increased a soldier's hearing.

Even with the gain way down, she heard three distinct thuds as the grenades went off in the adjoining corridor. She upped her audio and charged around the corner with the rest of the marines. All of them had their side arms out and were firing a hail of bullets into the barricade the security guards had set up. Momentarily embarrassed that she had forgot to pull hers out she nevertheless added a flurry of electric bolts to the ordinance that was raining down on the defenders.

As they got closer she could see two guards were already down injured. The others tried to pop out of their cover to return fire. A number of bullets rattled off a nearby marine's combat armor and a single plasma bolt struck a marine on the leg. He went down with a grunt, his armor pumping him with meds to reduce the pain.

Before the guards could get any more shots off, the marines with Major Johnston and the marines with Sergeant Harkin zeroed in on them with their weapons. In a blink of an eye, all of them hit the deck as multiple bullets hit their mark.

Harkin was the first to reach the barricade and he hurdled it in one jump and spun around with his weapon pointing at the injured security guards. Coming face to face with a marine in combat armor was a fearful thing and they threw away their weapons.

"Good job Sergeant," Johnston said, "let's help our wounded and finish searching this section of the station."

Five minutes later Becket entered the last room in the crew's quarters to find it empty. "Damn," Johnston shouted as he punched the room's durasteel wall with his power armor.

"Report," he said into his COM unit. "Any sign of Chang on the station?"

"Negative," came back the replies from his two Lieutenants. The Sergeant who was leading a search team came on the COM channel, "Sir I have found something you might want to see. There are a number of Chinese artifacts in cargo bay seven. They look packed up and ready to ship out but I haven't seen anything remotely like them in the rest of the cargo bays."

"Thank you Sergeant, I'll come right away," Johnston replied with a bit more excitement.

"Agent Bell, can you meet me in cargo bay seven?" he said.

When they got to the cargo bay Becket understood what had drawn the Sergeant's attention. There were a number of large crates filled with ancient pots, vases, rugs and art. Many of the designs looked Chinese to her but she wasn't sure.

She turned as Bell entered the cargo bay and let out a long whistle. "Well, well, this is a find. It looks like we have half the Chinese national museum here. I'd say we are on the right track as far finding Chang is concerned," she said as she lifted a few of the items the marines had already unpacked from one of the crates.

"No sign of Chang himself then?" Bell asked as she turned to face Johnston.

"No," he replied. "But he was here. And I bet our Station Commander knows where he is!"

"Lieutenant Adams, have you secured the bridge?" Johnston asked over the COM.

"Yes Sir," the bridge is secured, "we're moving all the crew to one of the cargo holds so we can watch them."

"Hold the Commander, I want a word with him," Johnston ordered.

As he stomped off towards the bridge Becket knew there was about to be trouble. Still, Johnston hadn't done anything wrong so she didn't know what else she could do but follow along.

Once they got to the bridge they found the Station Commander on the ground with a large red welt developing on his cheek and a marine standing over him.

"He tried to reach for my side arm Sir," the marine reported when he saw Major Johnston heading straight for him.

"Nothing he didn't deserve I'm sure," the Major said with a wave of his hand.

"Now Mr.," Johnston said to Commander Chowdhury. As the Indian began to open his mouth Johnston cut him off with a raised fist. "I don't want to know your name. I only want to know one thing. Where has Chang gone?" Again before Chowdhury could speak he was cut off. "Ah, Ah, think carefully before you answer, I'm in no mood for games."

"Go to hell," Chowdhury shouted when he got his chance. "You are here illegally, you will all be strung up for this."

"That is not the answer I wanted to hear," Johnston said as he whipped out his side arm. "One more time, where is Chang?"

This time Chowdhury simply spat at Johnston's armor.

A loud crack echoed around the station's control room as Johnston fired a round that just missed his target's head.

Still on his knees Chowdhury spun around in shock and tried to scurry away but the marine guarding him grabbed him and threw him at the Major's feet.

"One last time," Johnston said as he leveled his gun right at the Indian's head. "Where has Chang gone?"

"No," Bell shouted but she was too far away to do anything.

Becket saw no alternative, she was closest to the Major so she took two quick steps and shoulder charged him out of the way. There was another crack as the Major's side arm went off.

"Damn you Lieutenant," Johnston growled as he heaved Becket off him. "What do you think you are doing?"

"I'm sorry Sir, I slipped," she replied sheepishly

Johnston grunted and then shoved her out of his way as he approached the Indian Commander again, gun already raised. Thankfully Bell was already at his side leaning over him, shielding him from Johnston's line of sight.

"Listen to me," Bell was saying to him. "I can't protect you from him. You either tell me what we want to know or I let him at you again."

As Bell moved back slightly Becket could see a nasty gash along the Commander's cheek; Johnston's second shot had grazed him. He looked shocked and bewildered from the sudden realization that he might not get through this ordeal alive.

"Fine, just leave me alone. I didn't want him here anyway," Chowdhury said.

"Want who here? Chang?" Bell asked.

"Yes, yes. He was here," Chowdhury admitted.

"And where is he now?" Bell followed up.

"Two freighters came for him four days ago. He left on the first one yesterday. The other is here taking on the cargo Chang brought with him," Chowdhury informed Bell.

Becket spun round to access one of the stations control panels, searching its logs. Quickly, she found what she was looking for. "Two freighters did enter the system four days ago, one of them left yesterday. The other is the freighter docked in bay five."

"Major, you stay here until you have calmed down," Bell said. "If you try to follow us I will be forced to report what happened here. Becket, you're with me."

On their way through the station Bell contacted the marines who had boarded the freighter and ordered them to make sure no one on the freighter touched anything. She didn't want them to purge their computers.

When they arrived at the freighter a marine escorted them straight to the bridge. "Let me introduce myself," Bell said to the

Captain, "I am Special Agent Julia Bell of the Royal Space Naval Intelligence. We're here looking for former minister Chang. There's no point beating around the bush, we know he left yesterday on another of your freighters. We want to know where it was headed."

"Let me introduce myself," the freighter captain said in a strange accent Becket couldn't place. "I am Captain Stockport of the Haven freighter *Carmen*. As our two governments haven't signed any official political treaties and we're not a member of the UN, I'm afraid you have no legal right to detain us. I demand you release my ship immediately."

Oh crap, Becket thought, *things just got interesting.*

Turning out of earshot Bell opened her COM unit, "Captain, we may have a problem. We believe Chang left on a Haven freighter yesterday. I'm speaking with the Captain of another Haven freighter at the moment. He wants us to release his ship."

James took a few minutes to reply. A ship from Haven was the last thing he expected to find here. Only a few of them had ventured into the colonial space of the Earth nations. Whatever happened now would be a diplomatic incident. *In for a penny, in for a pound,* James said to himself. "See what you can find out from the Captain Agent Bell, I'm sending over Science Officer Scott to look at the freighter's computers. We are here to find Chang, the political ramifications will have to sort themselves out later."

*

Several hours later James gathered his Lieutenants, Sub

Lieutenants, *Endeavour's* Chief Engineer, Agent Bell, Major Johnston and Commander Gupta in *Endeavour's* briefing room.

Lieutenant Scott stood to begin her briefing. As she looked at everyone she couldn't help being nervous. Giving a scientific lecture to peers who knew you were an expert in the field was one thing. Addressing Lieutenants and the Captain who all had far more experience in space than her was another. *Still*, she told herself, *you have to start somewhere.*

With a deep breath she began, "The colony ship *Haven* left Earth over two hundred and sixty years ago. As you know the French first made contact with a Haven ship in the Mauritius system two years ago.

"Before the discovery of the shift drive almost one hundred sub light colony ships left Earth. Since then we have made contact with several of the colonies that were established, however, it seems the vast majority of them set out for planets that are not accessible through the shift drive. As a result, the last colony we made contact with was over a hundred years ago. Until two years ago we weren't expecting to ever hear from the rest again – unless someone volunteered for a very long sub light voyage to visit one.

"Well, as you all know our first contact with the Haven ship came as a big surprise. What's even stranger though is that we still haven't located the Haven colony itself. Given that their colony ship didn't have shift drive technology it couldn't have travelled further than here from Earth." As she spoke Scott manipulated the holo display in the briefing room to show a red sphere projected around Earth. Outside the sphere was the system of Mauritius where the French had first made contact with the

Havenites.

"Now of course," Scott continued growing in confidence, "the chances of the Haven colony being anywhere near the outskirts of this sphere are very slim. If they have had the time to build up their colony to the extent where they can build orbital construction yards and freighters, then they must have founded their colony at least one hundred years ago. This means their colony is likely to be somewhere within this sphere."

As she manipulated the holo display again the sphere shrunk to less than half its original volume. "Now here is the strange part. The Havenites on our freighter tried to purge their computers but their tech is not nearly as sophisticated as ours and I was able to retrieve most of their data, including their flight data. Here is the flight path the freighter used to get to the Andaman system."

Again the holo display changed and this time what it displayed caused a number of gasps to escape from the on lookers. "Almost unbelievable I know," Scott said, "current Admiralty projections predict either us or the Indians will have surveyed out that far in another fifty years or so. Yet the Havenites seem to know shift passages that lead out there already."

The holo display had changed again, zooming out from Earth and the projected position of the Havenite colony to show British, French, Canadian and Indian colonial space. From the Indian system of Andaman, a series of dotted lines jutted off into unexplored space, showing the shift passages the freighter had used to get to Andaman.

These shift passages were the only way ships could traverse the great distances between stars, for although the shift drive allowed faster than light travel, it was severely limited by the dark matter strewn between the stars. The dark matter prevented the shift drive from engaging and humanity had to map out a safe passage through the dark matter if they were to use the shift drive to reach another solar system. Often the dark matter completely surrounded systems, or caused shift passages to abruptly end, making it impossible to travel to them. On a map the shift passages often looked like the roots of a tree with many smaller and smaller roots breaking off, almost all of which ended in dead ends. As a result, all the space powers were involved in an exploration race, seeking out new shift passages and new solar systems as they competed for the limited galactic real estate that the shift drive had made accessible.

"How can this be?" Second Lieutenant Mallory asked. "The Indians and us have been exploring this section of space for over two hundred years, there is no way the Havenites should be out here."

Evidently no one had an answer and First Lieutenant Ferguson asked another question to break the silence, "What are their shift drives like?"

"Chief," James prompted.

"Primitive," Chief Driscoll answered, "they're basically the same design we use but they resemble shift drives from about eighty years ago. I'd guess if these Havenites have any military ships they would be a bit more impressive but not by much."

"So they have no other type of drive system? Nothing to explain this data," James asked.

"Not as far as I can tell," Driscoll said. "It's a mystery to me."

"So what do we do?" Gupta asked. "We've come too far to turn back now."

Instead of a general discussion breaking out like James had come to expect from such meetings aboard his previous ships, everyone looked to him. They had all been working together for over three months but it hadn't been enough time to break down the barriers of rank that usually prevented junior officers from venturing their own opinions.

"I brought you all here to see what you think," James said, "I want to hear some options."

Silence descended on the meeting until Becket spoke up. She had served as a Sub Lieutenant on his first two commands and she knew he welcomed everyone's opinion. "We are here to find Chang, I don't see why we don't continue?" she asked.

Her question broke the silence and an energetic debate raged over whether *Endeavour* should return and leave the political decisions up to the Admiralty or push on and see where these new shift passages led.

Surprisingly, Ferguson was leading the argument for returning home and he was making a strong case. Already, they could be in trouble for commandeering a Havenite ship, never mind aggressively boarding an Indian gas mining station. Partly because of the weight of his arguments and partly because none of the Sub Lieutenants wanted to contradict their First Lieutenant, the debate died down.

James was pleased to see the fourth Lieutenant wasn't so intimidated. "Let's be realistic," Becket began. "We have already seen that however Chang is orchestrating this, he is very good. He got himself out of Chinese space, snuck through the Sol system under everyone's noses, passed through French and now Indian colonial space. And, somehow, he has gotten himself tied up with this Haven colony. I don't think there's any doubt. If we don't follow him now, his trail will be long since cold by the time the Admiralty decides what to do and sends another ship out this way. If we really want Chang, we have to act now."

One or two of the other officers looked like they were about to offer their own arguments against Becket but James held up his hand to hold them off. "I have heard enough. I have made my decision. Scott, load your data into the navigational computer. We're going after Chang."

Chapter 9 – Burden of Command

But at the time everyone thought we were alone in the universe, who could have guessed what would be discovered.

- Excerpt from Empire Rising, 3002 AD

1st May 2466 AD, HMS *Endeavour*, unknown system.

Four weeks after leaving the Andaman system, James sat in his command chair on *Endeavour's* bridge waiting for his ship to jump out of shift space at their destination. For the first week they had carefully made their way up the shift passages the freighters had used to get to Andaman. They had taken small jumps along each shift passage to survey the dark matter and make sure the passages really were passages. Any ship that was unexpectedly pulled out of shift space by a gravimetric anomaly could be torn apart and jumping up an unexplored shift passage would usually be suicide. After a week though, James had run out of patience and the freighter's data had continued to prove 100% accurate. He had decided to jump *Innocence* the full length of the shift passage they were in. Her crew had been replaced by a couple of volunteers and they had made the jump. Just as the data from the freighter's computer had suggested, they had come out in an unexplored star system. After receiving the good news James had taken *Endeavour* to the new star system.

Instead of surveying it, he headed straight to the next shift passage the freighters had used and on towards their final destination. Now at last they were about to enter the system the freighters had begun their journey from. Despite their best efforts to question the captain of the Havenite freighter on the Indian mining station James and his subordinates were none the wiser about what they should expect. Everything they understood about the Haven expedition and the potential of the shift drive said it was impossible for anything to be this far from Earth. Yet here they were.

"We will exit shift space in thirty seconds," Sub Lieutenant Jennings announced from the navigation terminal.

"Passives only," James said to the Sensor officer.

As usual the bridge crew only felt a slight wobble run through the ship to alert them that they had exited shift space.

"What have we got Sensors?" James asked as the sensors began to update the plot on the main holo display.

'The star is a class M," Sub Lieutenant King reported.

"I'm also picking up seven other planets in orbit around the star. Wait," King said dramatically and bent over his terminal. Everyone turned to look at him and his prolonged silence only served to raise the tension.

"The computer has identified a number of electromagnetic disturbances," he finally said. "It is estimating that they were caused by thermo nuclear explosions. It looks like there has been a battle in the system recently. Very recently in fact, they can't be more than a day old."

"Not quite what we were expecting," James said to help break the tension. "Chang certainly likes to keep life interesting for us. Are the passive sensors picking up any signs of infrastructure on any of the planets King?"

"Yes Sir, there is a lot of electromagnetic radiation coming from the fifth planet. It is consistent with a heavily industrialized world," King answered.

"Sir, we're not alone," Sub Lieutenant Jackson, who was manning the tactical station, called out over his college, "the gravimetric sensors are picking up a large fleet moving towards the fifth planet."

"He's right Sir," King added. "I'm detecting two smaller fleets. One is maneuvering into what looks like a defensive position around the fifth planet while the other is angling towards the larger fleet."

James nodded and watched the drama play out on the main holo display. He could already guess how it was going to go. When they got closer to the large fleet the smaller group of ships suddenly veered away. At the same time the gravimetric plot showed a new group of contacts accelerating rapidly towards the large fleet.

"Missiles," Ferguson said, "the battle isn't over yet."

"No," James said. "What information have we got on those ships?" he asked to give himself time to think. They had stumbled into a major battle, one that looked like it was going very badly for the defenders. *Endeavour* was no ship of the line. She wasn't designed to take her place amongst the heavier ships of the RSN and fight in major fleet actions. If he took her towards the planet that had likely been Chang's destination he would be risking his ship and his crew. Yet he needed to find out more about what was happening. *There shouldn't be an industrialized world out here, never mind two war fleets engaging each other,* he thought.

"The two smaller groups of ships appear to have the same acceleration profiles," Sub Lieutenant King reported. "They appear to be using impulse drives, though they don't seem to be as powerful as ours. The larger fleet is a lot slower. I'm detecting a trail of ionized particles from them but I can't make out what they are. It doesn't look like they are using any drives I'm familiar with."

"Send the data over to Lieutenant Scott, see what she can make of it," James ordered. "I'm designating the two small fleets as Havenite warships. The third fleet are unknowns for the present. As impossible as it sounds I think we have just discovered the elusive Haven colony. I don't know how they got here, or what they have been up to, but it seems like they may need our assistance.

"Navigation, take us in towards the fifth planet, full military power. Once we get up to our maximum velocity we'll reenter stealth mode."

"Yes Captain," Jennings acknowledged.

*

Aboard the Havenite cruiser *Solitude,* Admiral Harris watched the approaching alien armada. The last week had been one long nightmare. After refusing to trade weapons technology with the alien race their ship had departed only to be replaced by a number of warships that had raided the mining outposts in the outer system. In response he had dispatched his fastest ships to the outer rim of the system to fend off the attacks.

Being beyond the mass shadow of Haven's star, the aliens had proceeded to simply jump out of the system every time his ships got near. That had continued for almost a month. Eventually he had succeeded in predicting one of their targets and managed to get two frigates into a blocking position. The ensuing battle had set his mind somewhat at rest but now he knew it might be their doom.

Before the battle he had been calling on the councilors of the Havenite Collective to send diplomats to Earth to request aide. He thought he had been winning them over but after the success of the first real battle with the aliens the councilors didn't want to risk telling the Earth nations where they were. Now it was too late.

The small skirmish at the edge of the system had gone in his ship's favor. The two frigates had managed to get into missile range and fire four missiles at the single alien ship that had jumped into the system. Its point defenses had destroyed three of the missiles but the fourth had hit the alien vessel damaging it enough that it immediately jumped out of the system.

Everyone on Haven had thought it was all over. The aliens had been shown that Haven could defend themselves and would therefore leave them alone. They had been wrong. A week ago an alien armada had jumped into the system with over fifty ships. They had demanded the colony with all its technology and orbital industries be surrendered to them. After the Council refused, the alien fleet had attacked a number of mining stations and slowly made its way to Haven itself.

Harris suspected the first attacks on the stations had been to test Haven's defenses to make sure they had no surprises. Now they were coming in for the kill.

"Sir, we've just lost the *Valiant*," one of his officers reported, bringing his mind back to the battle.

"What? Show me a replay of the sensor feed," he ordered.

As he watched the replay, *Valiant* fell out of formation with the rest of the small fleet that was attacking the alien armada. *Solitude's* infrared sensor's showed the *Valiant* flaring up before it exploded.

"It looks like whatever they were hit with burnt the valstronium armor right off their ship before it tore its way into their hull," the sensor officer commented.

"Some kind of directed energy weapon," Harris concluded. "Inform our attacking ships not to get any closer to the alien fleet than *Valiant* did."

He had eight, *no seven now*, he reminded himself in anger, ships attacking the incoming armada. They were his smallest and fastest ships, which allowed them to charge into range with their missiles and fire off a volley before the enemy could return fire with whatever weapons they had. At least that had been the plan. They weren't having it all their own way with the loss of *Valiant*.

As he stared at the plot he knew his tactic wouldn't work. The small ships weren't doing enough damage to stop the aliens. At this rate they would get into range of the planet and be able to engage the rest of the Havenite fleet. If they managed to destroy his ships in orbit, the colony would be at their mercy. They could bombard it from space or land ground troops to take whatever they wanted.

He was determined that it wouldn't be a one sided fight. Fear of the Earth nations had driven the councilors to fund the construction of two defense stations around the planet. They weren't very impressive by the standards of the other human powers but each one was almost twice as powerful as his flagship. More importantly, they were disguised to look like the other industrial stations in orbit and should come as a surprise to the approaching aliens.

Around them he had gathered the rest of the Haven fleet. In formation with his cruiser *Solitude,* he had three light cruisers, eight destroyers, and another eight frigates. They were ready to go down fighting.

"Sir, I'm getting an incoming transmission from a ship designating itself as HMS *Endeavour.* Her captain wants to speak to you," the COM officer announced, sounding as if he didn't believe his own report.

"Put the transmission on the main holo screen," Harris ordered, wondering what on earth was going on.

Earth indeed, he thought to himself as the image of a warship's bridge appeared with what was clearly a British Captain sitting in the command chair.

"Hello," James said, "I am Captain Somerville of his Majesty's ship *Endeavour*, with whom am I speaking?"

"Welcome Captain," Harris said already running the tactical possibilities through his head, "I am Admiral Harris, the commanding officer of the Havenite fleet, I hope you're here to offer your assistance. As you can see we are in a little bit of trouble."

"Greetings Admiral," James answered, though it took just over five minutes for his reply to reach Harris. "I wish we were meeting under different circumstances. Can I ask who these hostiles are that are attacking your world?"

"Aliens, Captain," Harris' reply came back five minutes later. "I know I know, it's almost impossible to believe but we have had the last few months to get our head around it. They showed up in our system and demanded we trade weapons technology with them. When we refused they began attacking our mining stations and a week ago this fleet showed up. It looks like they intend to take our planet and our technology by force," Harris said and then waited patiently for Somerville's response.

"I see," James said, careful not to show any emotion. He wasn't sure if he trusted Harris, aliens were a far-fetched explanation. Sure, the scientists insisted that humans would come across sentient alien life eventually. After all, most of the habitable planets they had discovered had some form of life on them. Yet they had been exploring the stars for over two hundred years and found nothing smarter than a dolphin.

"I'm going to need you to send me everything you have got on these ships and whoever is controlling them," James said guardedly.

"It's already being sent," Harris answered. "May I ask, where is your ship? We can't pick it up on our sensors. Are you close enough to help us before their fleet gets in range of our planet?"

James didn't answer immediately. Instead he waited for Ferguson and Scott to go over the data they had been sent.

"I don't see any other explanation Sir," Scott began, "the particles from their drives and the readings we're getting from their ships do not match anything humans have built nor any experimental technology I'm aware of."

"I concur Sir," Ferguson added. "Their ship designs are like nothing the RSNI has data on and the residual electromagnetic radiation from the outer system is consistent with Harris's story about being attacked."

James nodded before taking a moment to let the gravity of the situation sink in. Humans were not alone in the galaxy. Worse, already they seemed to be at war. Yet the British weren't at war. Maybe the Havenites did something to start this fight and maybe the aliens would be happy to open peaceful relations with the other human nations. There were just too many unknowns. *And then*, he thought, what help can *Endeavour be*? It looked like their technology was more advanced than the Havenites and these aliens, *but is it enough?* He didn't know the answer to that question; nevertheless, he had to make a decision, that was the burden of command.

Taking a deep breath, he faced the recorder that would transmit his words back to Admiral Harris. "Ok, we're in," he said, "*Endeavour* is an exploration cruiser but we have some teeth. We're currently closing in on the alien fleet from behind. We entered the system over six hours ago and accelerated up to our maximum speed. Now we're in stealth mode closing on the aliens. What is the tactical situation?"

When he got the transmission Harris almost shouted for joy. *Plasma cannons,* he thought as he controlled himself. *Maybe we can win this.*

When the Haven colony ship had left Earth over two hundred and fifty years ago Harold Maximilian had ensured that some of the best scientists on Earth came with the colonists. They had brought with them theoretical designs of the shift drive and although it had taken them nearly one hundred and fifty years to develop it, they had managed it.

When the first Haven ships had made contact with French vessels from Earth they had been surprised to find out that Earth had developed the shift drive over a century before them. Just as surprising had been the revelation that Earth warships were equipped with plasma cannons.

As Haven had begun to develop warships they had also come to the conclusion that long-range missiles were the way forward. However, they had also known that a shorter-range energy weapon would be very effective against warships. Lasers had been rejected for their effective range was severely limited by the diffraction of the laser and the current technical limitations on reducing the wavelength of the beam. Plasma cannons on the other hand were known to be theoretically possible and would have made ideal weapons, but their scientists hadn't yet managed to crack stabilizing the containment fields for each bolt.

Since they had made contact with the Earth nations they had managed to procure a few working examples of hand held plasma rifles through the black market to reverse engineer, but as yet they didn't have a working prototype to begin to equip their ships with. For the last week Harris had been cursing their failure to prioritize this for he knew they would have made a big difference in the coming battle.

Now at least we have some, he thought.

"You can no doubt see their fleet with your own scanners," Harris began. "They have forty nine ships. Twenty of their larger ones, and twenty nine smaller ones. We've designated the larger class of ships as cruisers and the smaller ones as frigates. The smaller ships carry four missile tubes on each of their bows. We haven't seen what their cruisers carry but we suspect they will have at least ten missiles to each broadside. Their missiles seem to have an effective range of half a light minute so we have a slight range advantage but not enough to make a difference.

"Under my command I have a cruiser, three light cruisers, eight destroyers, and eight frigates. There are another seven frigates currently harassing the alien fleet. They have managed to destroy two of the alien frigates. Their point defenses are good but our missile ECM is able to penetrate them.

"We also have two defense stations disguised as industrial nodes. My current plan is to wait for the alien fleet to get into optimal range of our missiles and fire everything we have at them. We don't have any plasma cannons so my only play is to hope we can overwhelm their defenses and cause them enough damage that they break off."

As James listened to the tactical situation he kept an eye on the sensor feed of the alien fleet. It was an impressive armada. He knew the Havenite weapons technology was at least two decades behind the other Earth nations, probably more like three or four behind *Endeavour's* state of the art tech. The aliens appeared to be slightly behind the Havenites. Yet what they lacked in quality their fleet appeared to make up for in quantity. Even as he watched the seven attacking Havenite frigates veered into missile range and fired off a volley of fourteen missiles at the nearest alien cruiser. When the missiles entered point defense range hundreds of AM missiles shot from the alien ships and they took out all but one of the missiles. It managed to get a proximity hit on the large alien ship but the ship continued on, apparently able to shrug off the hit.

"There's one more thing, Harris added. "The aliens have some form of directed energy weapon. You should have been sent the sensor feed of *Valiant's* destruction; it will show you their effective range. My scientists believe it is some form of x-ray laser but they can't understand how they have enough power output on their ships to be able to fire it over such long distances."

"Thank you," James said, "give us a few minutes to formulate a plan. I don't think we have time to join you in orbit. We'll have to engage the alien fleet separately and hope we can whittle them down enough for you to be able to manage them when they get to Haven."

"Very well Captain, we'll take whatever help you can give us," Harris said.

After James watched the Admiral's last message he opened up the small holo projector on his command chair and projected the current sensor feeds. James had seen more combat than he had ever imagined he would when he signed up to the RSN. Yet he knew he still had a lot to learn when it came to leading a ship into battle. The Void War had taught him that. *If we're going to survive this and help the Havenites we need to use all of Endeavour's strengths*, he thought to himself. Slowly, a plan began to formulate. When he was happy with it he sent it over to Lieutenant Ferguson's command chair. "What do you think?" James asked Ferguson.

It was five minutes before James and Ferguson were happy that they had worked out all the details of the plan. When they were satisfied, James contacted Harris again, "I'm sending you our plan, please make sure your frigates are made aware of our approach. We will need them to coordinate their fire."

"You will have our support," Harris replied after the five minute delay in transmission.

Cutting the COM channel James then opened one to *Innocence*, "your mission is a go Commander. Once you have your target don't wait around for us."

"Aye Sir," Gupta acknowledged. "Happy hunting Sir. I wish I was on the bridge with you."

"Me too Commander, but you have your own hunting to do. Good luck" he added with a smile as he cut the transmission.

"Open a channel to the whole ship," James commanded the COM

officer. When she nodded at him to let him know it was open he addressed the crew.

"Men and women of *Endeavour*, I'm sure you've all heard by now that we are facing alien warships. They are headed straight for a human colony and it seems that their intention is to invade or bombard it. It may not be a British colony but those are our fellow human beings down there. We have a duty to protect them and who knows, if these aliens aren't stopped here, it may well be a British colony they attack next. The Havenites have no tradition of warfare but they stand ready to fight these aliens. We know how to fight, so let's show these aliens that Humans aren't as easy prey as they seem to think!"

Nodding to the COM officer to cut the transmission, James turned to the navigation officer and said, "Power up the engines, let get this battle started."

Chapter 10 – All or Nothing

It's an old saying, yet one that the history of space warfare has proven true; no battle plan ever survives contact with the enemy.

- Excerpt from Empire Rising, 3002 AD

1st May 2466 AD, HMS *Endeavour*, Haven system.

As soon as *Endeavour's* four fusion reactors powered up and funneled energy into her impulse engines she became visible to everyone in the vicinity of the Haven colony. While the two fleets battling each other had been too busy to notice her first acceleration burn into the system she was now operating in an area that was being heavily monitored. Ignorant of the surprise on both the Havenite and alien warships at seeing a new ship appear so close to them, James was focused on his immediate goal.

"Ferguson, take command of the main plasma cannons, target one of their cruisers and hammer it until it's destroyed. Tactical, wait until the Haven missile salvo passes us and then add our own. They should be targeting the two alien frigates on the edge of their formation."

"Aye, Sir" Julius, the Third Lieutenant called from the tactical terminal. Ferguson didn't bother answering; the bolts of super-heated plasma that shot towards the alien fleet spoke for him.

The first four bolts tore through the armor of the alien warship like it didn't exist. There wasn't any immediate sign that the bolts had done any serious damage but thirty seconds later, when another four bolts crashed into the ship, it tore apart and disappeared in a colossal explosion.

Satisfied that their plasma cannons were able to destroy whatever the alien ships were made from, James switched his attention to the Havenite flotilla of frigates. The seven small warships were once again angling towards the much slower alien fleet. They unleashed a volley of twelve missiles at the aliens. Becket timed her launch perfectly and *Endeavour* added eight of her own to the volley.

When the missiles got into range of the alien's point defenses hundreds of AM missiles began to pour out of the alien ships, trying to intercept the larger ship killer missiles. Sensing the incoming AM missiles, the Haven and British missiles switched on their ECM and randomly altered their flight path, making themselves harder to track.

"Two missiles have been taken out," Julius called. "Now three."

"Penetrator missiles activating now," she said several seconds later.

On the screen, James could see that ten more missiles had sprung into existence to confuse the alien's point defenses. The penetrator missiles were ECM missiles that exchanged their thermonuclear warheads for the ability to fool even the most sophisticated human sensors. They had been one of the main reasons that the smaller British warships had managed to go toe to toe with the Chinese navy in the recent war. For the alien fleet with their apparently inferior sensors, the missiles played havoc with their point defenses. Only two more missiles were destroyed and fifteen locked in on the two alien frigates. Nine of them managed to get direct hits and two alien ships disappeared off the holo display in a haze of electromagnetic radiation from the explosions. When the sensors burned through the radiation they showed both ships tumbling out of formation, venting atmosphere from numerous holes.

"Very good tactical," James said, "line up another broadside with those frigates, hit them again!"

"Damage report," Second Lieutenant Mallory called over the open COM channel to the auxiliary bridge. His job in the auxiliary bridge was to oversee the internal systems and be ready to take command in case the bridge was damaged. "I'm getting reports that several of our point defense plasma cannons and AM launchers are damaged. No sign of any missile strikes, I'm not sure what happened."

"Evasive maneuvers Navigation," James called.

"Check the sensor logs," he said to Mallory. "We believe the aliens destroyed one of the Havenite frigates with some sort of laser. Their range may be greater than we thought."

"I'm on it Sir," the Second Lieutenant replied.

"Any more damage?" James asked the bridge.

"Nothing yet," Sub Lieutenant King at Sensors called out. "Lieutenant Mallory and I are reviewing the sensor data. There were several heat blooms on the outer hull just before the automatic damage reports began coming in. It looks like the

Havenites were right, they must have some kind of directed energy weapon. Likely a laser."

"Sub Lieutenant King is right," Mallory confirmed over the COM channel. "I don't think their weapons have the power to penetrate our armor at this range but they can take out the point defense and sensor blisters on the outer hull."

"Very well," James said, "we will have to keep up our evasive maneuvers."

"Glancing hit Sir," Becket called out, "We just got another heat bloom across our aft armor. It was only for a split second. No damage reported."

"Third alien cruiser destroyed," Ferguson shouted over the noise of the bridge. "The rest of their fleet is taking evasive maneuvers, it's going to be harder to get hits from this range.

As he had come to expect from his previous combat experience James was beginning to lose track of the minor details of the battle. Drowning out some of the information being shared between the bridge crew he focused on the holo display to keep track of the big picture.

The alien fleet was still headed for Haven. Despite the impressive damage *Endeavour* was doing to them they were determined. The larger Haven fleet was in position around the two stations that Admiral Harris had identified as their concealed battlestations. The alien fleet had been reduced to forty four ships but James wasn't sure they were doing enough damage. The alien fleet would be in range of the Haven ships' missiles in another ten minutes and the aliens would be able to fire off their own shorter ranged missiles two minutes after that.

As he watched the main holo plot another of the cruisers fell out of formation, showing that Ferguson was still using the plasma cannons to deadly effect. Several seconds after the ship blew up completely a large section of the alien fleet slowly began to turn. Immediately James checked their projected course.

Seeing the same thing Sub Lieutenant King, manning the sensors station, called out, "Captain, the alien ships are reorienting, they are bringing their broadsides to bear on us."

"I see it," James acknowledged. "Navigation, you know what to do, pull us back.

The Havenite frigates had fired a second salvo and as *Endeavour* turned Julius fired another eight missiles to join them as they sped towards the aliens.

The alien ships that had turned responded with thirty missiles of their own. As the missiles were projected on the holo display James cringed. *Endeavour* was designed to be able to defend herself against ten modern missiles. Even if Haven's data was correct and these alien variants weren't as effective as British tech, thirty was a lot of targets for her point defenses to take out. Thankfully *Endeavour* was equipped with two flak cannons, without them she wouldn't have a chance.

Even as he thought of them, both flak cannons fired off hundreds of high explosive shells that detonated in front of the incoming missiles. They threw up a wall of shrapnel that the missiles had to fly through. At relativistic speeds it only took a glancing blow from a piece of shrapnel for the quickly accelerating missiles to be damaged or thrown off course. Space was a big place though and the flak cannons couldn't hope to hit all the missiles. Twenty of the thirty missiles made it through the first storm of shrapnel and thirteen came through the second.

The flak cannons powered down as the missiles entered the range of the small point defense plasma cannons. Space between *Endeavour* and the incoming missiles was filled with green plasma bolts as the point defense gunners tried to hit their targets. Soon AM missiles launched from *Endeavour's* racks to intercept the incoming missiles. Thirteen were reduced to eleven, then eight.

It's still not enough James thought as he watched helplessly. Everyone else had a job to do to defend the ship but all he had to focus on was the holo plot tracking the missiles getting closer and closer.

"Here they come," Julius shouted. Before James could ask her what she meant, the plot around *Endeavour* lit up with over a hundred new contacts.

As soon as they appeared they shot towards the incoming missiles and nine became three. *Endeavour's* point defenses concentrated on the remaining targets and the sheer weight of fire blew them out of space.

Havenite AM missiles, James realized as he scanned the holo plot to see the Havenite frigates had decelerated hard to fall into a defensive formation around *Endeavour*.

"We're clear," Ferguson announced, "we're beyond the missile range of the alien ships. It doesn't look like they are turning to pursue us."

"Good work everyone," James said to the bridge and the Havenite frigates.

"Thanks," a voice said from one of the small holo displays on James' command chair. "We were just in time it seems. Admiral Harris sent us to give you a hand."

"Indeed you were," James said looking down at the frigate captain whose face had appeared on the small holo display of his command chair. "Your AM missiles are quite effective."

"Not half as effective as your flak cannons," the Haven Captain replied. "When I saw they had launched thirty missiles I thought your ship was history. I'd heard reports from your war with the Chinese but I didn't think they were that effective."

"Yes, they came as a surprise to the Chinese too," James said with a smile. "I owe you a drink later Captain but for now let's get back to business."

"Agreed," the Haven Captain said.

Lifting his voice, James addressed the bridge crew and the Haven Captain. "Ok, we're out of plasma cannon range but we can still hammer them with our missiles. Julius, coordinate with the Haven Captain and take out as many of the alien frigates as you can before they engage the main Haven fleet."

"Yes Sir," she answered.

"I've sent some information to your datapad," Julius added. "I think we might be able to pull off an old trick."

"I'll have a look," James replied.

He grabbed his datapad and scanned the information Julius had sent him, pausing to watch as the next salvo of missiles launched towards the alien fleet. When he got to the end of the data he knew Julius was onto something.

"Communication, can you open a COM channel to Admiral Harris for me?" James asked.

"Yes Sir, channel is open," came the response.

"Good work Captain," Harris said when James's image appeared before him. "You guys are giving them hell – I just hope it's enough. They'll be in range of our missiles in four minutes."

"Thank you Admiral," James began. "I may have something for you. Have you been able to study the history of naval warfare since your people have made contact with the other human nations?"

"To a certain extent. We've only been able to get information on specific wars and battles that were made publicly available at the time. I'm probably missing more than a few vital details," Harris confessed.

"No problem, I can fill you in. I'm sending you over our sensor data from the alien ships," James said. "If your tech guys look it over they'll see the alien AM missiles use the same radar wavelength as their main search radars. We used to do the same before the Russians used it against us in the war over the French colonies. You'll probably only get one shot at it but if you alter your missile's ECM to detect the wavelength of the alien's main search radar you will be able to predict their AM missiles' seeker radar as well. If you can alter your missiles in time you can get them to project their own radar signals back at the AM missiles and confuse them."

Harris wasn't looking at James, he had his head buried in his own datapad and was nodding as James spoke. "Ah, I see," he said. "I think it might work. We only have a few minutes until contact; I need to pass this on immediately. I hope to see you on the other side Captain," he said as he looked up at James before cutting the transmission.

"Me too," James said to an empty screen.

Looking back at the main holo display he requested a status update from the bridge.

"Thirty seconds until our next missile salvo reaches their outer point defenses," Ferguson informed him. "The Haven frigates are keeping station with us. So far we've taken out four of their cruisers and five frigates."

James looked at the state of *Endeavour's* missile tubes; they would be ready to fire again in two minutes. By then the aliens would almost be able to engage Harris' fleet defending the colony. They were decelerating and it looked like they planned to enter a high orbit over Haven and sit there until they blasted Harris out of their way. *Endeavour,* on the other hand, was still tearing towards the planet at full speed and her momentum would soon take her away from the battle. That had been the plan all along. It was her speed that had allowed her to swoop into plasma range of the enemy fleet. Now though, it was a hindrance.

"Navigation, I'm sending you an updated course," James said as he input some flight information into his command chair.

"Received Sir," the navigation officer acknowledged, "I think it will work but it might get a little hot in here. We'll be pushing *Endeavour* right to her limits."

"I know," James said, "but we can't leave anything on the table. It's all or nothing now."

"COM send a message to the frigates following us," James ordered next. "Tell them thanks for the escort but they won't be able to follow us on our next move. They can engage as they see fit."

"And Julius," James added, "if you can, fire off our last broadside before we go behind the planet. Aim everything at one of their frigates."

*

Admiral Harris sat in his own command chair on board his flagship *Solitude*. He had been mightily impressed by the display of the British warship. He knew now that his fleet wouldn't have stood a chance if the British fleet had discovered Haven and come claiming the system for themselves. That was all but irrelevant now however. Even if his ships survived the coming battle they would not be in any state to stop anyone from doing what they wanted with Haven.

That assumed there would be anything of Haven left. The British ship had done all it could. Now it was up to his ships. His smaller fleet of frigates and *Endeavour* had been using their speed to harass the aliens without having to worry about return fire. Now they were traveling too fast to break and enter orbit. They would get one more salvo at the alien fleet before they had to break off.

"The alien ships will enter missile range in thirty seconds," one of the bridge officers called out.

"Signal the fleet to fire with the flagship," Harris ordered.

When the alien ships crossed the red line displayed on the bridge's main holo display, *Solitude* and the rest of his ships and the two battlestations opened fire. Ninety three missiles shot towards the forty remaining alien ships.

It took the missiles five minutes to accelerate out of Haven's orbit and reach the point defense envelope of the approaching alien ships. Before they got there the aliens had opened fire themselves and over one hundred and fifty missiles were homing in on Harris' fleet.

Hundreds of AM missiles shot from the alien ships to try and knock out the Haven missiles intent on destroying them. Initially they had some success taking out twenty, but by then the Haven missiles had been able to analyze the radar being beamed out by the alien ships, altered their own ECM emitters and bombarded the AM missiles with the exact wavelength of electromagnetic radiation their seeker heads were following. The AM missiles had been using the radar signals from their parent ships along with their own limited radar as it bounced off the approaching missiles to track them. Suddenly they began to get numerous false readings and many of the AM missiles lost lock on their targets all-together. Only twenty five managed to take out incoming missiles, leaving forty eight ship killers to explode among the startled alien ships.

Harris pumped his fists as the holo display projected multiple explosions among the alien fleet. "How many did we get?" he called out.

"Six of the alien ships are dropping out of formation, our sensors have lost track of another three. I think they have been destroyed outright. Other ships are showing signs of damage but they are holding formation," one of the sensor officers reported.

"Good, get ready to hit them again. Only equip half our missiles to try the same trick this time. If they catch on to what we did it'll not work a second time so I want to hedge our bets," Harris ordered.

"Enemy missiles being engaged by point defenses," someone on the bridge called out.

Without plasma weapon technology Harris' fleet depended solely on AM missiles to fend off incoming ship killer missiles. His technicians were still dumbfounded over how the aliens managed to effectively project laser beams over such long distances but at least their previous skirmishes with the aliens had shown their ECM technology was primitive compared to Haven tech.

The alien's hundred and fifty missiles were reduced to ninety, then forty, then twelve which made it through to their targets. Nevertheless, they still caused colossal damage as they exploded among the Haven ships.

"We've lost the frigates *Hawk* and *Sealion*," the sensor officer called after the explosions stopped, "the destroyer Lightening has also taken a direct hit. She's reporting only one of her missile tubes is functioning."

"What about the battlestations?" one of the Lieutenants asked.

"Both have taken direct hits but are still fully functional."

"Return fire," Harris snapped.

At his request eighty five missiles rocketed out of their tubes towards their targets. On their way they passed another one hundred and thirty alien missiles heading the opposite direction.

It's about to get real hairy! Harris thought.

A second series of explosions ripped through his fleet and Harris was thrown about in his seat as *Solitude* took a proximity hit. "Damage report," he called out.

"Two missile tubes are down, sections three, four and five are open to space and venting atmosphere," someone shouted.

"Damn," Harris swore. "And the rest of the fleet?" he asked.

"I'm not sure," his first officer called. "Our sensors aren't functioning properly, I'm getting unconfirmed reports that one of the battlestations is down and a number of ships aren't reporting in."

"The aliens have launched a third salvo," someone else called out. "It will enter point defense range in sixty seconds."

Before Harris could swear again the sensor officer interrupted him. "Sir," he called in excitement. "There's a ship rounding the planet, it's lighting up the infra-red sensors like a miniature sun!"

*

James had gripped his command chair with white fists as he was forced to watch the battle unfold between the two fleets. The images had been relayed to *Endeavour* from one of Haven's ground bases. After firing their final salvo he had gunned *Endeavour's* engines up to one hundred and ten percent of their normal operating limit and plunged his ship into the planet's atmosphere. The combination of the breaking from the engines, the friction from the upper atmosphere and the planet's gravity had allowed him to swing around the planet and come up behind Harris's ships.

The maneuver had burned off a couple of millimeters of the valstronium armor and the internal heat sinks were threatening to overload and boil his crew alive in their own ship. The bean counters back at the admiralty would be mad, valstronium was the most expensive commodity known to mankind and the heat sinks would no doubt need replacing. Yet it had been worth it. The maneuver meant he was coming up from under what was left of Harris' fleet just as the third salvo from the alien ships was coming into attack range.

As the battle came into view of *Endeavour's* sensors it was clear the Havenites were losing. One of the battlestations was an expanding ball of debris and Harris only had his flagship, one light cruiser and two destroyers left. The aliens had taken some serious losses too; it looked like they had less than thirty ships left, but they had fired a third salvo that was sure to end Harris' fleet.

"Fire all point defenses," James ordered.

Even before he finished speaking the flak cannons had flung their shells into space. The one hundred missiles in the alien's third salvo were all aimed at the two remaining destroyers and the battlestation and were closely packed together. The flak cannons devastated their numbers and only fifty made it through the wall of shrapnel.

On the holo display James saw numerous plasma bolts and AM missiles from *Endeavour* and the remaining defenders reach out to pluck the rest from the plot. What had looked like certain destruction for Harris' fleet was staved off, but there were still too many missiles for the ships to get them all. Three struck the remaining battle station. One flew into a gash caused by an earlier hit and penetrated three decks before it exploded, tearing the station apart.

Another two missiles struck the last light cruiser. To this point she had managed to survive the battle completely unscathed but as both missiles hit her hull they exploded twenty meters apart and split the cruiser in two. Both ends quickly began to be pulled into Haven's gravity, spewing atmosphere and bodies into the cold of space.

"A missile has locked onto us," Julius called out.

"Taking evasive maneuvers," the navigation officer called as he threw *Endeavour* into a tight turn and roll.

The missile wasn't fooled and it adjusted its course to match *Endeavour* but a last second twist caused the missile to overshoot its target. Sensing it would no longer achieve a direct hit the missile detonated only fifty meters off the bow. Everyone on the bridge was thrown about in their seats as the force of the explosion rocked the ship.

"Proximity hit," Mallory called from the auxiliary bridge after he got his wits back. "We've lost most of the bow point defenses and missile tube seven is down."

"Acknowledged," James said. "Return fire."

As soon as the sensors burned through the dissipating electromagnetic radiation from the thermonuclear explosions Ferguson opened up with the plasma cannons. One of the cruisers took hits from four bolts that tore through the ship, turning it into a brief ball of fire.

Julius added to the carnage as she launched seven missiles at the aliens. The distance had closed enough that it only took them one minute to reach their targets and in the confusion five hit their mark, taking out another two cruisers.

"They're accelerating," the sensor officer called out excitedly. "It looks like they are trying to break orbit.

"Missile launches," Julius called out. "No wait, they are from behind us. Those Haven frigates followed us into Haven's atmosphere. They're firing their own missiles at the aliens."

James checked the holo plot himself, there were indeed six more Haven ships swinging round the colony. It didn't look as if they had ventured as close to Haven's atmosphere as *Endeavour* had but then there were only six frigates. There should have been seven. He suspected one hadn't made it. "Match our missiles to their trajectory and fire when ready. We need to make sure those aliens don't come back in a hurry."

"They're out of plasma range," Julius reported. "I managed to get another of their frigates. Should we pursue?"

James checked *Endeavour's* damage reports and the holo display again before answering. All of the Haven ships except the newly arrived frigates were reporting serious damage and his ship wasn't in any state to be pursuing a superior force. "Negative, we need to help our friends. We'll fire one more salvo and let them go."

"Captain, they're turning again!" Julius called out.

"What?" James asked, confused. It made no sense for them to turn back now. They had lost their earlier advantage. Then he saw the alien commander's plan.

"Cancel that last fire order." James shouted. "Julius detonate our missiles in front of their incoming salvo. We need to take out as many of those missiles as we can. They are going for the orbital industries."

Even as he spoke a final salvo of missiles erupted from the alien ships. Alongside their main ship killer missiles there were over three hundred of their smaller AM missiles.

"It's worse Sir," Ferguson called out. "Those AM missiles will have to go ballistic long before they reach their targets but our sensors are estimating that some of them are aimed at the planet, not the orbital stations. It looks like the aliens have targeted Haven's major cities!"

"Navigation, put us directly in front of their missile salvo. We need to bring every point defense weapon we have to bear on those missiles. Communications, signal the rest of the Haven ships that can to follow us.

"Make every shot count," James said to the bridge. "Lives are counting on us."

Orders given, James had nothing to do but watch events unfold. Julius's missile salvo exploded right in front of the oncoming alien missiles. A number of the ship killers wavered and then shot off in random directions, indicating that their targeting computers had been taken out by the radiation from the nuclear explosions. The holo plot updated to show that a number of the smaller unarmored AM missiles had been destroyed.

Next the flak cannons opened up, followed by the point defense plasma cannons and *Endeavour's* AM missiles. All the surviving Haven frigates had followed *Endeavour* and Admiral Harris had managed to get his flagship into position to fire off his AM missiles as well.

The alien missiles began to fall off the plot but as they rushed past the defending ships there were simply too many.

"Captain, Admiral Harris is signaling the orbital stations and the planetary leaders to expect incoming fire," the COMs officer reported.

"Acknowledged," James said. As the alien missiles tore into the orbital industries and detonated among them he knew it was probably too late for many of the men and women who worked on them. Worse, *Endeavour's* infrared sensors lit up as a number of missiles entered the atmosphere. Some exploded from the excess heat but a number survived reentry and fell towards their targets on ballistic trajectories.

"Signal Gupta," James ordered. "Tell her that things are about to get a little hot for her landing party!"

Chapter 11 – A Warm Welcome

Orbital bombardments are now largely a thing of the past. Yet the firsthand accounts of those who lived through such experiences make for terrifying reading.

- Excerpt from Empire Rising, 3002 AD

1st May, HMS *Innocence*, approaching Haven

Commander Gupta had forced herself to watch the unfolding battle between *Endeavour* and the alien fleet. She knew James wouldn't hold back and she had been silently praying for his safety. When the first alien salvo of thirty missiles had been launched at his ship she had nearly broken cover and tried to come to his aid. *Innocence's* point defenses were meager compared to *Endeavour's* but they would have provided some help.

James had impressed on her the importance of her mission though. In the grand scheme of things her ship wouldn't make any difference to the outcome of this battle. She had been reluctant to admit that as she was coming to love her first real command, even if it was a freighter. Nevertheless, she knew James was right. Whatever happened today around Haven, she and James had been given a mission from the Admiralty and it was her job so see it through. Even more important, if things didn't go their way news of these aliens had to get back to Earth.

As *Endeavour's* impressive show against the aliens had captured everyone's attention she had slipped *Innocence* into orbit around Haven – making sure she was a long way from the fighting.

Now she was on the bridge of her freighter, watching a shuttle carrying Major Johnston, Agent Bell, Lieutenant Becket and a squad of marines head down to the colony's surface.

Since entering the system they had been monitoring Haven's communications and although their tech base was impressive, there were some things that the British, and the rest of the human nations for that matter, were just way ahead of them on. Being out of contact with the rest of human society for so long meant they had missed out on a lot of inventions. One area the Havenites didn't yet realize they were outclassed in was communication encryption and decryption. *Innocence* was able to listen to every transmission in the system – at least every human transmission.

The vast majority of the COM chatter coming from the planet had been about the approaching aliens but the attack had left the Havenites in disarray. More than once a low level ground commander had requested orders on what to do with a certain guest called Chang. It seemed Chang had been undergoing a debriefing with Haven intelligence and was providing them with all the political and technical information he could. With the approaching aliens the officer in charge of the debriefing had been requesting updated orders. Eventually they had come through and he had been ordered to move Chang to a secure government safe house on the edge of their capital. Very helpfully the communication had included coordinates for the safe house. Major Johnston and Agent Bell were on their way to pick up Chang before anyone knew they were there.

"Oh no," Gupta said not realizing she had spoken aloud when James' communication came through along with an updated sensor feed. She relayed the information to the shuttle and sat back in her command chair to say another prayer.

*

"It looks like things are about to get a little dicey," Johnston said over the shuttle COM. "We have incoming missiles from the alien fleet and there will be a lot of debris falling from orbit. At least some of it will be coming in near the city."

"Great," Bell said.

"I hope everyone aboard *Endeavour* is ok," she added giving Becket's shoulder a squeeze. The Lieutenant had been very quiet during the mission so far. No doubt she felt guilty for not being at her station on board *Endeavour*. Yet James had insisted she accompany the landing party. Bell was glad the Lieutenant was with them; she had proven useful on their previous missions.

"I'll be landing you about a klick away from our target," the shuttle pilot said. "Our target building is right on the edge of the city. It's a four story apartment complex. There is some pretty dense forest that runs right up to the edge of the city so I'm setting you down in the nearest clearing I can find."

"Just get us there in one piece," Johnston said.

"Hold on," the pilot interrupted, "we're being hailed by ground flight control."

"Let me speak to them," Bell said as she moved forward and sat beside the pilot. She put on one of the spare flight helmets, activating its audio.

With the expertise of a stage actor she put on a very panicked and shaky voice, "This is the shuttle *Delivery,* we're fleeing the orbital bombardment, I repeat, we're fleeing the orbital bombardment. Our station was destroyed; we've got nowhere to go. We're just trying to land."

"You are entering a restricted area," the voice said again over the COM channel. "You need to turn around, you can't land there."

"We just want to land and get our feet on solid ground before something else goes wrong," Bell said, sounding even more hysterical. "I'm sorry, we're landing here. I don't want to go into space ever again!"

Before the ground controller could say anything more, Bell cut the transmission and took off the flight helmet. "That should buy us enough time," she said.

"Remind me never to play poker with you Agent," Johnston said with a grunt of respect.

"We're touching down," the pilot informed them as two heavy bumps alerted them that they had landed.

"Everyone out," Johnston ordered as he led the way down the descending ramp at the back of the shuttle.

When Becket stepped out onto the alien planet she was immediately struck by the strange vegetation. In the past she had always spent her time in the cities of the colonies she had visited. She hadn't really seen any alien fauna before except in zoos on Earth. Even then she had been more interested in the wild animals.

Haven had what passed for trees on Earth except that they were covered in thick branches all the way down to where their trunks met the ground. Their leaves were much wider and thicker than any Becket had seen and they sparkled with shades of pink, red and violet. They would have been beautiful if they didn't have to trek through them.

"This is going to be tough going," she said to the marines.

"Nonsense," Sergeant Harkin said, grinning as he jumped out of the shuttle. "I knew it was a good idea to bring this baby," he added as he hefted a large device that looked like an oversized hilt of a sword.

"A plasma lance," Bell said, stepping forward with interest.

"Not for you lady," Harkin said, waving his finger at her. "I had the foresight to bring one and so I'm going to be the one that gets to use it."

"We don't have time for this," Johnston said, "Harkin, you take point. The rest of us will follow you."

Grinning, Harkin pushed his way past the jealous marines towards the densely packed trees. With the flick of a finger he ignited the plasma lance. A long green stream of plasma stretched out of the hilt, forming what looked like a sword of plasma mimicking something out of an old science fiction movie. With ease, Harkin swung the plasma lance back and forth, cutting a path through the thick foliage.

Initially it was hard going and Harkin's heavy panting could be heard over the COM channel but two minutes after they set out Becket heard a strange snap-hiss that she guessed was the plasma lance being switched off.

"I think I have found a path," Harkin said confirming her guess.

"O'Brian, you take point, double time it," Johnston said to one of the marines.

With a hand signal acknowledging the order she set off at a jog along the path with her eyes and plasma rifle constantly scanning back and forth. A couple of minutes later they came to the end of the path. O'Brian ducked down and signaled for the rest of the team to do the same.

Johnston and Bell shuffled forward to take a look at their target. Becket moved up too and peered over their shoulders. It was the sky that caught her attention first. Through a clearing in the thick foliage what looked like a scene out of a sci-fi movie depicting the end of the world greeted her

Hundreds of pieces of debris were streaking across the sky, tumbling towards the ground. It almost looked like the entire sky was on fire. As she was watching, one of the pieces ignited and accelerated towards the ground. It impacted a significant distance away from the city and a bright flash erupted from the impact zone. Her combat suit's visor darkened her vision to protect her from the blinding light.

"That was a nuke," Bell said as everyone felt the vibration of the shockwave under their feet.

"Yes," Johnson agreed, "there'll be more where that one came from. Let's just hope *Endeavour* is still up there taking out the ones aimed at the city."

"There's our target," he said, returning everyone's attention to the mission.

The apartment complex was at the end of a series of large buildings that pushed out into the forest. A permacrete road led away from the complex back towards the heart of the city. Parked outside were two Armored Personnel Carriers. It didn't look like there was anyone inside but there were at least two guards standing outside the complex.

"They have plasma rifles," Harkin said, "I wonder where they got those from."

"The black market," Bell said. "Or Chang brought them with him as a bargaining chip."

"Either way it doesn't look like they are going to give up Chang without a fight," Johnston said, "we might be fighting for these bastards up in space but they still chose to take in a war criminal and hide him from our government. That means they are going down, we can deal with the political ramifications later.

"Here's the plan," he continued. "Bell, Harkin and I are going to circle around the complex through the forest. O'Brian and Hastings, you two are our best shots. When I give the signal take out those two guards. Once they're down we will rush the main doors. You provide covering fire and join us once we are in.

Clear?"

Everyone signaled that they understood and Johnston and his team ducked under the nearest branch and headed off, circling the complex.

As she waited, Becket couldn't help but be distracted by the display overhead. Every second seemed to add more burning debris to the already packed sky. She ducked as another object ignited and rapidly accelerated towards the ground. This time there was no explosion and when she opened her eyes to look she saw that the missile had impacted with one of the pieces of debris. It had blown it into hundreds of smaller pieces that were burning up in the atmosphere. She hoped that was a sign that some friendly ships were still in orbit trying to limit the damage to the colony. If it was the aliens trying to limit the damage to their new prize, getting Chang would soon become the least of their worries.

That turned her mind back to the situation at hand. The irony wasn't lost on her. In orbit *Endeavour* was fighting with everything she had to protect the Haven colony yet on the ground they were about to attack a Haven intelligence safe house. If they all survived today the political fallout would take years to sort out.

A click over the COM channel brought Becket back to reality.

"Three, two..." O'Brian said before two plasma bolts shot out from where she and Hastings were lying in the thick foliage.

Both bolts struck their marks and without combat armor both targets went down with large holes burnt right through their bodies. Immediately, the other two marines in their group were up and as Becket followed they sprinted towards the apartment complex.

A Haven intelligence officer burst out of the complex's main doors, plasma rifle up as he scanned for targets. His rifle began to track the approaching marines but before he could fire off a shot Johnston rounded the building and gunned him down.

As if from nowhere plasma bolts rained down on her small group. The two marines dived to the ground and Becket followed suit but not before she saw a plasma bolt strike the marine beside her in the leg. A grunt escaped from the marine's lips before she swore, "I'm hit."

"Target on the roof," O'Brian called over the COM. Before anyone acknowledged a plasma bolt flew from the trees and took out the man raining shots down on the marines. "Got him," O'Brian informed everyone.

"Get moving," Johnston ordered Becket and the two marines with her. Without waiting for them he and Bell pushed their way into the complex.

Becket helped the injured marine to her feet and they half ran, half limped towards the building. When they got there O'Brian and Hastings had already caught up with them and they entered to see Johnston standing over a dead Havenite.

"Search the building," Johnston said, "Chang has to be here somewhere."

Bell waved Becket over and together they searched the ground floor while the marines spread out to cover the rest of the building.

The first five rooms they checked were empty but when they turned into a corridor with two more doors there was a dead Havenite lying against one of the walls. Bell approached one of the doors and pointed Becket towards the other. With a kick of her power armor she busted the door down and peeked in, Becket followed her lead.

"In here," Becket shouted ducking out of the room. As she had poked her head around the doorframe she had seen Chang. He had been descending a set of steps that looked like they were cut into the foundations of the building. He must have paused to see what had happened to the door for he had been looking right at her when she looked in. Immediately, he had raised the plasma rifle and fired a quick burst of bolts at her.

"He's in here," Becket said again over the COM. "There were dead intelligence officers. I think he has escaped from them."

Before she could say any more a massive boom shook the building and an unstoppable force picked Becket up and threw her across the corridor into the room Chang had been in. Before she knew what had happened an enormous weight descended on her legs and she let out a piercing scream before she blacked out.

*

The same shockwave threw Johnston to the ground on the second floor and when he managed to get back to his feet and look around he found himself staring out across the forest they had used to hide their approach. The wall, room and corridor he had just searched no longer existed. Outside he could see a large chunk of space station that had buried itself in the ground. The resulting shockwave must have blown half the apartment complex away.

As his mind cleared, he remembered what had made him dash out of the room that no longer existed. *Becket saw him*, he thought. He dashed towards the staircase that had been his target before the explosion. It was no longer there. *Screw this*, he thought before jumping into the hole where two flights of stairs had been.

He landed with a crunch and despite the combat suit he knew his knees would be hurting for a few days. Sprinting through what was left of the building he came to where Becket and Bell had been. Half the corridor was still intact but the explosion had blown the other half away. Bell was lying on her side in the corridor. A quick look at her combat suit's display of her vital signs showed that she was ok, she had just blacked out from the concussive force.

Pushing on, Johnston entered the room that must have held Chang. On the ground there were two dead Havenites with plasma rifles at their feet. In one corner Johnston saw Becket under a great pile of rubble. Only her head poked out and something must have smashed her visor for her face was cut up and scratched. In the other corner of the room there were stairs descending to the basement of the building. Johnston rushed over to them and peered down. It looked like they led to a tunnel that ran out under the apartment complex to who knew where.

As he was about to dive down the stairs after Chang he looked back at Becket and stopped in his tracks. She looked innocent and helpless, just as he knew his wife had looked when she died.

Johnston closed his eyes, he had been dreaming of his chance to look Chang in the face for over a year. Every day he woke up and swore to himself he would make the Chinese murderer scream for mercy as he told him of how his wife had died. He had dreamed of crushing every bone in Chang's hands then his feet and then finally his legs before squeezing the life out of the bastard and watching with pleasure as his eyes bulged and his mouth gasped for air. Only then would he know the memory of his wife would be able to rest.

And yet as he opened his eyes and looked at Becket crushed under the durasteel beams and permacrete rubble he imagined her screaming out in pain as he saw his wife scream out in fear in his dreams every night. She had been visiting family in a small fishing village on Cook when the Chinese attacked the colony, blowing up the orbital shipyard. Large sections of the station had plummeted through the atmosphere and impacted on the planet. One had caused a massive tsunami that had killed his wife and everyone else in the village before any warning had got to them. Every day he woke up in a sweat with the image of his wife standing before a massive wave as she screamed out his name in fear.

The fiery trails streaking across the sky above him and the rumbling and tremors caused by the debris impacting on the ground only made things worse as they mimicked the nightmares where he would see the falling debris and the approaching tsunami through his wife's eyes.

With a shake he brought himself back to reality. He was torn, he wanted to avenge his wife's death. Yet he knew that if he didn't act this image would haunt him for the rest of his life. Becket had almost become a daughter to him. From the first day she had showed up at his house to recruit him to the hours they had spent on the freighter training together, he had come to think of her as family. In all his rage and anger he had pushed his feelings to the side but now, seeing her like this, they came rushing back.

With a deep groan of frustration, he threw down his plasma rifle and ran to Becket's side. Using the strength his combat armor gave him he threw large chunks of rubble off Becket's lifeless form. Finally, he dug down to a large durasteel beam that was crushing her legs. He lifted with all his might. Nothing happened at first but then, slowly, the beam began to move. With his knee and one hand Johnston propped the beam up and used his free hand to pull Becket out from under it.

With a gasp he released the beam, allowing it to crash to the floor. He checked Becket's vital signs. She was alive but her legs were broken. Johnston hefted her over his right shoulder. He turned and approached the stairs to the underground passage. With his free hand he reached for one of the devices he carried. A couple of twists and it was armed. Crouching down to get a better angle he looked to check what direction the tunnel headed in. Satisfied it headed out towards the forest and not towards a nearby building he hurled the device down the passage with all his might.

"If anyone is still left in the building you need to get out now," Johnston shouted over the COM. "I've just set a concussion grenade at full yield to go off in sixty seconds. Evac back to the shuttle ASAP."

Johnston leaped out of the room, pausing only to put the still unconscious Bell over his other shoulder before he sprinted out of the building and towards the forest.

He was still sprinting when the grenade went off and the force threw him to the ground. As he fell he was careful not to injure his two charges. Rolling over he looked back at the apartment complex. What was left of the building had been thrown over a hundred feet into the air before it fell back in on itself, forming a crater over three hundred meters wide.

Checking the sensors on his combat suit Johnston saw that it had only been three minutes since Becket had spotted Chang. There was no way he could have got far enough away to escape the explosion. The underground passageway would have directed the force of the explosion for at least a couple of miles along its length, assuming it was that long.

As he turned back to look at Bell and Becket he was satisfied he had made the right choice. "Sit rep," he said over the COM channel.

"This is O'Brian Sir," the marine said. "Harkin and Hastings are with me, we're almost at the shuttle. Jones has taken a plasma bolt to the leg but he should be ok. I'm afraid there is no sign of private Henning. I think he was searching a part of the building that got blown away by the debris."

"Thanks private," Johnston replied.

When he got back to the shuttle the rest were already aboard. He handed Becket and Bell up to the other marines before stepping into the shuttle himself. "Take us out of here," he commanded the pilot.

Opening a channel to the frigate he spoke to Gupta. "Chang is dead, or as near to it as I can be sure. That was the best we could do."

"I understand Major," Gupta replied. "Good job."

*

On the bridge of *Endeavour*, James was trying to coordinate the rescue of the hundreds of survivors stuck on the damaged orbital stations when his command chair beeped to inform him he had an encrypted message waiting for him. It was from Gupta and was simply two letters MA.

With a smile of satisfaction, he uploaded all of *Endeavour's* sensor logs from the battle and sent them to Gupta with his own text message. *Au revoir.*

*

Ten minutes later the shuttle docked with *Innocence* and Gupta took the freighter out of orbit. With all the confusion going on no one had challenged her ship and with luck she would make it back to Earth without the Havenites even knowing she had been here.

Chapter 12 – Pirates

What the Havenites called The Gift would eventually be one of the main reasons the human race survived the War of Doom. Yet in the beginning it only caused war and strife.

-Excerpt from Empire Rising, 3002 AD

8th May 2466 AD, HMS *Endeavour*, Haven system.

A week after the battle for Haven, *Endeavour* was still in orbit around the colony. James and his crew had been rushed off their feet. After intercepting most of the Vestarian's final missile salvo and staving off total disaster, they had thrown themselves into helping Haven recover from the alien bombardment. In response the Havenites had been more than generous in assisting the crew in getting *Endeavour* repaired and fully operational.

"The final checks on missile tube seven have been completed," First Lieutenant Ferguson reported to the senior officers James had assembled in *Endeavour's* conference room. "It is now fully repaired and functional again. We have also loaded fifty of the Haven navy's most modern anti-ship missiles. We will have to carry out some minor modifications but we should be able to use them if we run out of our own. Their range and firepower is substantially less than ours though."

"Thank you Ferguson," James said, "you have done a stellar job in overseeing the repairs. *Endeavour* is almost as good as new thanks to you."

"Just doing my duty Captain," Ferguson said with a wave of his hand as if he wanted to swat the praise away. "It was really the Havenite engineers who made it all possible. Even with a large part of their orbital industry destroyed they were still able to provide us with all the parts we didn't have ourselves. It really is a miracle what they have managed to accomplish here."

"Indeed," James acknowledged. "In fact, that is why I called this meeting. We have been invited to a formal reception that the Haven Council is hosting on our behalf. We are the first Earth ship that has come to their colony and they want to officially welcome us, and thank us for our aid in fighting off the Vestarian attack. So we're going to get a chance to enjoy ourselves. You have all earned it over the last week."

Smiles broke out among the senior officers and James was pleased they were all going to get a chance to unwind. Everyone had been pushed beyond their limits. It didn't help that Lieutenant Becket was still in the medical bay. As *Innocence* didn't have the medical facilities to look after her Gupta had sent her over on a shuttle before she had taken the freighter out of the system. *Endeavour's* doctor had fixed Becket's broken legs and she was well on the way to full health, all she needed was more rest.

Major Johnston had also returned with Becket to take command of *Endeavour's* marines and James hadn't been surprised to see Agent Bell also coming on board. She wasn't going to miss the political intrigue of Haven and the on-going drama of humanity's first contact with an alien race.

"However," James said before the senior officers got too excited. "I don't want you having too much fun. Haven is still a great mystery. We don't know how they managed to establish a colony so far away from Earth without a working shift drive. Nor do we know how they built up their industrial base so fast. We're also totally dependent on their version of events for how the first contact with the Vestarians went. For all we know they could have started the hostilities. To that end each of you will have a mission during your time on the surface. We need to find out how the Havenites got here and how they managed to build their colony up so fast. Ferguson is right, what they have accomplished here is a minor miracle.

"Every other human colony established before the shift drive was failing miserably by the time we made contact with them. Something different happened here and we need to know what it was. To that end I tasked Lieutenant Scott with investigating Haven through whatever means she was able to gain over the last week. While the rest of us have been helping them and repairing *Endeavour,* her science team have been sifting through the reams of data Haven has given us on the aliens and all the sensor data and communication data we have picked up from the planet.

"Lieutenant Scott, if you could present your findings so far?" James asked as he stepped away from the center of the room and took a seat.

Scott nodded at James and got to her feet. The last time she had given a briefing to the assembled command officers she had been very nervous. Now her nerves had all but vanished. She suspected that the battle had had something to do with that.

As *Endeavour* had flown into battle she had almost been beside herself. Having spent many hours with the Sub Lieutenants running training simulations in the auxiliary bridge she had thought herself ready for combat. Reality had proven her wrong. While the command crew on the bridge had shown themselves able to handle the suspense of flying into battle Scott had been a nervous wreck.

It had taken *Endeavour* a number of hours to get into range of the Vestarian fleet. In that time Scott had found herself questioning her abilities and her decision to join *Endeavour*. She had convinced herself that she had no business being in the middle of a battle.

Yet when the first missiles had been fired something had changed within her. Her instincts had taken over and she had found herself doing what she did best, analyzing everything. The aliens had a number of unknown systems and weapons and it had fallen to her to figure them out and provide tactical advice to the other officers. At the time she hadn't thought of the responsibility, she had just been doing what was asked of her. Afterwards she had reflected on the whole ordeal and it had given her a new measure of self-confidence. She knew from all the simulations she had run that she had the skills to serve on a King's ship. Now she knew that when it came to real combat she had the strength and ability to do her duty.

"As our Captain said," she began confidently, "there are still many unknowns. Nevertheless, my team has been able to fill in a few details.

"First, let me say that our sensor scans of the system supports the account Haven has given of their dealings with the

Vestarians. There are a number of electromagnetic sources in the outer rim of the system consistent with small battles. There are also a number of debris fields supporting the idea that the aliens attacked the outer mining stations.

"What's more interesting is that the alien's technology seems to be an odd mixture of advanced and primitive technology. We obtained a clear scan of their jump into shift space as they retreated and their shift drive appears to be highly inefficient. What's more, their shift drives emit a massive amount of waste electromagnetic energy when they are activated. As a result, we have been able to confirm a number of recent jumps that the alien ships have made within the system. Some were over two months old and yet we were able to detect the residual electromagnetic energy. As far as we can tell, all this activity correlates with what the Havenites have told us.

"And yet, despite being more than a century behind us in shift drive technology," she said as she brought up a short series of images on the holo display, "the Vestarians were able to take out the frigate from an extreme range with a directed energy weapon.

"We have analyzed the smaller hits *Endeavour* took from the same weapons and it appears that they use some form of x-ray laser. Our own scientists have been working on directed energy weapons but when it comes to laser technology they have reached an impasse. The effective range of a laser is determined by the energy supplied to it and the laser's rate of diffraction. We have theoretically had the ability to produce ships with similar x-ray lasers but at present it would take a ship the size of the Chinese battleship we captured at the end of the Void War stuffed full of fusion reactors to power one laser with enough range to compete with our plasma cannons. So either they are way ahead of us on energy production or they have found a way to significantly reduce a laser's diffraction rate, or both. Added to that, the aliens must have some pretty impressive targeting computers if they can hit ships at such long ranges.

"However, they do not appear to have incorporated their laser technology into their point defense network and the only reason I can imagine for this is that they haven't been able to miniaturize their larger lasers. Yet given the technical skills required to build the things in the first place it shouldn't have been too hard to do this.

"Certainly this strange mix of technology suggests the Vestarian's story, of looking for weapons technology to help overthrow some other alien civilization that has enslaved them is legitimate. Haven has many technologies that are way ahead of the alien's, particularly their sub light drives and missile tech. However, the Vestarian's subsequent actions suggests that their request was a front."

Taking a break to have a sip of water Scott asked, "Are there any questions so far? My team have put together a fuller brief on our best guess of the aliens' technological abilities for you all to look over later."

She took another sip as she waited to see if there were any questions. When no one spoke up she changed the image on the holo display to show the Haven system.

"Let's move on to Haven itself then," she said. "The system still has a number of functioning asteroid mining facilities along its outer rim, ones the Vestarians didn't touch. The Havenites have also established a significant presence on the system's seventh planet. They call it Athena. It seems they have found rather large deposits of valstronium on the planet and they have built up an impressive extraction and refinement operation. Alongside the development on Athena there are two gas mining stations around the two gas giants in the system. Both orbital structures are significantly larger than any similar gas mining stations we have, suggesting they are used for other purposes as well.

"If we turn to Haven itself. A large part of their orbital industries have been destroyed but at least forty percent survived. Groundside, our best estimate is that there is a population of at least twenty million. Almost a quarter live in Haven's capital but the rest are spread out all over the planet. Their news organizations are reporting that upwards of twenty thousand were killed in the orbital bombardment. Most were killed by the debris that fell from orbit. The two nuclear missiles that managed to detonate on the planet's surface didn't hit any population centers and only killed a few thousand each.

"Putting all that information together with what we know the Havenites brought with them on their colony ship, we have an approximate date of founding.

"2250," Scott announced and then paused to take in everyone's reaction.

"Impossible," Driscoll the Chief Engineer shouted, "there's no way they could have gotten out here that fast. When did they leave Earth?"

"Our records indicate they left in 2198," Scott answered.

"You see, impossible," Driscoll repeated.

"Impossible, but clearly undeniable," Ferguson said. "We have seen what they have accomplished with our own two eyes."

"There must be some other explanation," Bell added as she jumped into the conversation. "There is always a plausible explanation. In this case, one I think we're all going to find very interesting when we figure it out."

"What have you managed to get from their communications?" Mallory asked. "Surely there is lots of information out there about their history?"

"Yes and no," Scott answered. "The Haven authorities have flat out refused every request my team has made to gain access to their datanet. For the first two days after the battle we were able to break the limited encryption on many of their COM channels but then everything went dark. We believe their government issued a strict ban on all non-essential COM chatter.

"That being said, we were able to get enough information from casual conversations about grandparents and great grandparents as well as from a number of discussions about business deals that dated back decades. They all support our estimate that Haven was founded approximately two hundred years ago. The real mystery then, is how they got here so quickly after leaving Earth?

"We do have one clue," Scott continued before anyone jumped in. "There were a few references to something called the Gift. As far as we can tell Haven isn't a particularly religious colony, everyone is free to believe whatever they want. Though when it comes to the Gift, it is spoken of as if it was a gift from the gods or a god. There were a few phrases like; 'the Gift brought us here' or 'this is all thanks to Maximilian's Gift.'

"Like I said, this is just a clue. As to what this gift is, I have no idea. Though it is a starting place. Whatever it is, it appears to have helped the colonists get this far from Earth as quickly as they did."

"So the impossible is possible," Ferguson said looking at the Chief Engineer.

"Maybe," Driscoll conceded. "But I'll tell you one thing. They didn't do it using the shift drive. Remember, I had a look at the drive in that freighter, and there is no way they had the tech to get from Earth to here two hundred years ago. However they did it, they have me intrigued."

"There is one more thing we found," Scott said as she changed the holo display again. "Does anyone recognize any of these ships?"

"That's a Webb class interstellar freighter," Third Lieutenant Julius said, "it's a British built freighter, where are these images from?"

"It is a Webb," Scott said as she gave Julius a smile. "In fact all of these eight freighters are British, French or Indian design. From the markings on the hull we have identified this freighter as the *Rosemary.*

"These images were taken by our optical sensors as we rounded Haven before our final attack on the alien fleet. Our focus at the time was elsewhere and so no one noticed them, but one of my team spotted them as they were reviewing the battle sensor logs."

"How did they get all the way out here?" Julius asked

"Piracy," Scott answered and she was shocked to see the change that came across the naval officers faces. Major Johnston and Bell didn't look best pleased but that was nothing compared to the rest of the officers.

"Explain," James ordered in a carefully controlled tone.

"The *Rosemary* was reported missing five years ago," Scott began. "She was actually one of the missing ships that prompted the Admiralty to build *Innocence*. We weren't able to identify any of the other freighters but their type and class are consistent with other freighters that have been reported missing in the last seven years.

"The only reasonable conclusion is that the Havenites captured these freighters themselves or they bought them off whoever did."

"Sir, we can't let this stand," Mallory said in indignation. "Even if they just bought these freighters from pirates, they are complicit in their crimes."

"And let's not forget they intentionally took in Chang, a wanted war criminal," Johnston said. "I think we may have been a little too nice to our new friends," he added, pouring sarcasm into his last word.

"Yes," James said. "But we need to tread carefully. We already knew they had intentionally given Chang safe passage. From the limited political reports I have been able to access it seems as if they have been playing hard ball with the Earth nations ever since they first met that French cruiser two years ago. Despite repeated attempts they have been flat out refusing to reveal the location of their homeworld. Their impressive military buildup suggests they have been paranoid about the Earth powers for a very long time.

"I'm guessing they made contact with us long before we knew about it. At least eight years ago if the missing freighters were all stolen by them. That means they have been planning for when we would find them for some time. They probably wanted our freighters to get a look at our tech.

"If you think about it, they probably feared one of the main powers would just claim their world and annex it into their territory. Certainly the Indians would love to get their hands on a fully developed colony.

"All in all, I think that means we need to take a measured approach. Haven is going to cause Earth problems in the future. The presence of the Vestarians only complicates things. If we go in gung-ho now we might drive Haven into the arms of the Indians or the Canadians for protection.

"However," James said as he paused to let what he had just said sink in. "That doesn't excuse their actions. Let me assure you. They will be held accountable. Nevertheless, for now we need to be a bit more circumspect. We need to treat the next few days as a fact finding mission. We need to bring as much information as possible back to the Admiralty, ultimately they and our political leaders will have to decide what to do with Haven. Our job is to give them as much detail as possible.

"So, I don't want any mention of Chang or these freighters at the reception. As hard as that may be," James added, waving down the looks of protest that appeared on his officer's faces.

"We need to know how they got here, and how they built up their tech base so quickly. And, most importantly, we need to know all we can about these aliens. Whatever the Havenites have done in the past, these Vestarians are the real threat. We don't know where their systems are nor how many ships they have. What we fought a week ago could just have been a scouting force."

The room went quiet as everyone contemplated James' last statement. More than one officer suddenly realized that even as they sat, other alien fleets could be leaving a line of devastated human systems in their wake as they sought to attack Earth.

"Cheer up," James said, "we don't know anything for sure. There's no sense in worrying about unknowns. Let's just focus on this reception. Try to make friends, get people to open up. And remember, you are permitted to have fun at the reception. The last week has been intense, so relax, unwind, but don't give away any state secrets!" he said to a few chuckles.

"Ok then, the reception is in six hours," James added as he stood. "You may hand off your duties to your Sub Lieutenants and go prepare. I want you all in your dress uniforms. The more we impress the Havenites the easier our future with them will be.

"You are all dismissed," James said as everyone got to their feet and made their way out of the briefing room. Before James left he approached Third Lieutenant Julius and asked, "Can you join me in my office Lieutenant?"

"Yes Sir," Julius replied.

As they both stepped through the adjoining door to James' office he turned to the Lieutenant. "I'm afraid you'll have to stay behind to command the ship. With Becket in sickbay I want at least one senior officer still on board. I do have a task for you though."

"I understand Sir," Julius said with obvious disappointment. "What do you want me to do?"

"Our sensors only got a short glimpse of the captured freighters. Since then the Havenites have been keeping them at the opposite end of the planet to *Endeavour*. It's possible not all of the Haven government know about them. While we are at the reception I want you to take *Endeavour* out on a short cruise. See if you can loop around the planet and get a better sensor sweep of the freighters. If we can identify the rest of them, it may give us some useful information. If Haven ground control asks, tell them you are testing the repairs. I'm sure they will get a little nervous. If they do, remind them of who saved their colony and push on. If ground control gets nervous enough they will send a message to whoever oversees the freighters. I'll be keeping an eye on their leaders, their response may just give something away."

"I understand Sir," Julius said. "I'll give them something to worry about."

"Very good," James said as he clasped the Lieutenant on the shoulder, "just don't let them know what you are after."

"Aye Sir," she said grinning. "I know how to keep my cards close to my chest."

"Very well, go get ready to take over the watch then," James said, ending the conversation.

Chapter 13 – Introductions

8th May, 2466 AD, Liberty, capital of the Haven Collective

As James stepped off the maglev train that brought his officers from Liberty's main landing port to the Collective's Council Chamber, he couldn't help being impressed. The Council Chamber wasn't the largest building in the city but it was by far the most decorative. Whereas the rest of the colony was built purely for function, no doubt a necessity for a fledging colony, the council chambers were ornately decorated and clearly modelled after government buildings back on Earth. The whole building was made out of some local white stone. Along its front a flight of twenty steps led up to a series of what looked like marble colonnades. The shape of the building had been designed to reflect the images James had seen of the colony ship that had brought the colonists to Haven.

As he went up the steps, James saw the First Councilor, Graham Maximilian, standing between the two largest colonnades with his back to the doors that led into the chambers. "Welcome Captain," he said as he stepped forward, taking James' hand. "It's a pleasure to get the chance to honor the man of the hour."

"James, please," James said, "and the honor is all mine. My crew have been very impressed with everything you and your ancestors have been able to do here in Haven."

"We have worked hard," Maximilian said and then spoke up as he addressed the officers James had brought with him. "You all performed admirably, both in the battle with the Vestarians and dealing with the aftermath. I will be sending a message to your Admiralty praising every one of you.

"Now come, come," Maximilian said, shooing everyone up the stairs towards the main doors. "It's time you all got a chance to enjoy yourselves. We have prepared a feast for you."

At the mention of food the pace of the group picked up and James found his mouth watering. Whilst the food on board naval vessels was usually pretty good, the frozen rations couldn't live up to a freshly prepared meal.

As they stepped through the main door it was obvious that whoever had designed the council chambers had spent as much time on the inside as the outside. "This is a very impressive building," James said to Maximilian.

"Yes, my Father took great pride in constructing this building. He said it represented everything we have accomplished here."

"Your Father was the First Councilor too?" James asked.

"Indeed, and his before him and his before him starting with Harold Maximilian, the founder of the colony," Maximilian replied. "The First Councilor is elected every ten years but so far our people have been happy to see Harold's vision for our colony continue to rest in the hands of his descendants. We all still look up to him."

"You are a direct descendant of Harold Maximilian?" James asked.

"Yes, he is my great grandfather," Maximilian replied. "After being taken out of cryosleep he spent the rest of his life building this colony. My family have been dedicated to his vision ever since."

"Then you have done extremely well in just four generations," James commented.

"Thank you," Maximilian said, "though for most of the population I can assure you it has been more than four. We have a lot of incentives to help our population grow. I already have over fifteen great grandchildren and no doubt there will be many more before I step down as First Chancellor. My eldest son is eager to take over but he will have a few years to wait yet."

"That's very interesting, James said, "I'm sure I will have lots more questions for you."

"I'm sure," Maximilian said with a wry smile. "As I do for you. For now though, let's enjoy our meal. If you would step into this room," he added as he stood aside and gestured to the door in front of him.

As James stepped through a loud round of applause greeted him. The room was over one hundred feet long and a single table stretched its length. Seated along the table were over eighty people, all of them standing, applauding *Endeavour's* officers as they entered.

"We like to show our appreciation," Maximilian shouted over the noise before he turned to the crowd and waved for them to bring their clapping to an end.

As the noise died down a number of servants appeared and

directed the naval officers to their arranged seats. Maximilian directed James to a seat beside the head of the table and then sat at the head himself. As James sat he shook hands with Admiral Harris who was seated to his right, "Good to meet you face to face Admiral," he said.

"And you," Harris replied, "For a while I didn't think I'd be meeting anyone again. Your stunt with Haven's gravity saved our bacon."

"I was just doing my duty," James said as the servants brought out the first course of the meal, "a British naval officer is expected to put his life on the line for others. I'm just glad we were able to get here in time."

"About that, how exactly did you manage to get here?" Harris asked.

At that James noticed Maximilian pause mid-sentence in his conversation with the councilor who sat opposite James and turn to hear his answer.

"Well," he began choosing his words carefully. "You have probably noticed that *Endeavour* isn't your typical cruiser. She may be the size of a medium cruiser but she doesn't have the armaments of one. Instead she is equipped with extra cargo space and a few other things even I don't have clearance to know about. She is designed to be able to carry out long survey missions. *Endeavour* is an exploration cruiser you see, the first of her class. We had been testing her long range survey capabilities when we stumbled across your system."

"An interesting concept. Even so," Harris said just as carefully, "you are still a long way from British space. We expected to bump into an Indian or a French ship sooner or later. Not a British one."

"That I can understand," James said, "but as you know, we are in direct competition with the Indians for new colonial systems. My mission was to go beyond Indian space and see if we could beat them to a new system. It seems I have succeeded."

"That you did," Harris said. "And I bet you found far more than you were expecting."

"Certainly," James chuckled without having to fake anything. "That brings me to a few questions of my own. You know it has been more than a hundred years since any Earth power made contact with a pre-shift drive colony? You certainly gave us a surprise finding you all the way out here."

Before Harris could formulate an answer Maximilian interrupted the verbal sparring. "Come now Captain, there will be plenty of time later for discussing all that stuff. You are here to enjoy a good meal. Let me introduce you to Councilor Pennington. She is one of the most powerful people on Haven."

Sensing that he would get nowhere if he pressed the issue James turned to smile at the councilor. "My pleasure Councilwoman," he said.

In what followed the Councilwoman sought to impress him with the extent of her family's businesses and her own personal wealth. Certainly the various industries her family owned and run were significant but to James they were just possessions, not overly important in the grand scheme of things. Growing up he had been surrounded by wealth and fame. His father, now dead, had been the Duke of Beaufort and one of the wealthiest Lords in the British Star Kingdom. He could have bought everything in the Haven system combined and still had plenty of credits left over.

Despite his youth James had learnt the fleeting nature of such things for his father had committed suicide and in the aftershocks it had been revealed that he had lost most of the family fortune in bad business deals and gambling. As the younger of two sons James had always known his brother would take over the family Dukedom and business. James had been enrolled in the RSN by his father instead. Initially hating it, he had slowly come to love the navy, but in a cruel twist of fate his father had left the Dukedom to him rather than his drunk of a brother. James had always suspected his father had done it out of spite. Being landed with an almost bankrupt Dukedom hadn't done James' career or social life any favors. Yet, with the help of a friend from the naval academy and some good investments in the Void, his finances were starting to look very healthy. James wasn't sure as he didn't check such things regularly but he suspected he could give Pennington a run for her money if it came to comparing assets.

Not that he was going to tell her that. He wanted Haven's council dealing with him as a naval captain, not as a Duke with potential political connections and clout. Things were complicated enough as it was, *besides*, he thought, *it is not as if I have any sway with the King or parliament.*

The meal and conversation continued on for over an hour before the servants removed the last course and two large doors were opened at the far end of the room. Taking it as a signal, the guests got up and made their way into a large reception room. A jazz band was playing and the group split as some made their way to the bar, others went to the tables that lined the room, and a few made their way onto the dance floor.

As James paused to watch he saw Major Johnston and Agent Bell were mingling like experts with a number of the military personnel who had been invited to the reception. Johnston was actually laughing and James was delighted at seeing the change that was slowly coming over the Major. It seemed that whatever had happened with Chang on the planet had broken the anger and self-recrimination Johnston had been dealing with. James had been disappointed they hadn't been able to recover Chang, or at least his body. Yet events had taken on a life of their own and Chang had become the least of his worries.

With a wave of his hand he motioned Mallory and Ferguson away, both had been about to come to his side after the meal but James wanted them to continue to mingle. Whilst Mallory came from an important family in Chester it appeared that neither of the Lieutenants were comfortable among such distinguished guests. So far James had only met a few of them but it seemed everybody who was anyone had been invited to meet the British officers.

Sighing, he stepped away from the wall and began to mingle. After sharing pleasantries with a number of people a stunningly beautiful woman in a fiery red dress stepped in front of him.

"Hello there Captain," she began, "or should I say Duke," she added with a mischievous smile as she held up her hand for James to kiss in the tradition of the British aristocracy. As he lent in James took a moment to take in her beauty. Sparkling brown eyes sat wonderfully against her lightly browned skin and long dark hair flowed over her shoulders and down her back. Her red dress accentuated the rest of her body in all the right places without being too revealing. James couldn't help it and, despite his alarm at being recognized, as he kissed the back of her hand he inhaled deeply, drinking in her perfume.

"Don't worry," she whispered, waggling a finger at the look of concern that had crossed James' face. "Your secret is safe with me. Though if I can do my homework properly it is only a matter of time before others figure it out."

"I guess you have me at an impasse, may I ask who you are?" James said.

"Of course you can," she said resting a hand on James arm. "I am Councilor Suzanna Rodriguez, I have been serving on the council for the last five years. And I might add, doing everything I can to keep this colony from falling into the hands of an aggressive Earth nation."

"I wonder," she said as she linked her arm through James' and directed him to the side of the room. "May I pick the brains of one of the heroes of the Void War and an ex-consort of a princess of Britain?"

"Of course you can, that is why I'm here," James began. "Although I think hero is going too far, and if you know my background you'll know I don't exactly have much sway in British politics. I'm out here after all, as far as the Admiralty is concerned, in the middle of nowhere. That being said, I'd be happy to help you any way I can. Though I might want something in return," he hastily added, trying to stay on top of the situation.

"I'm sure we can come to a satisfactory arrangement," Suzanna said with a smile. "Let me be honest though. I am a business woman first and a politician second. Councilors are only allowed to remain in office for one term. Then we have to return to public life. I stood for election because I thought the council needed a different voice in their debates, not because I love all the political maneuvering. There may be some here who love to play the game of politics but I like to say it straight and come to the point.

"And my point for the last five years has been this. We on Haven need to reveal ourselves to the Earth nations and the UN. We settled this colony without any help from any Earth government and we have built it up for the last two hundred years."

"And yes, I know," Suzanna said, "I'm sharing details with you that we have been forbidden to share with you, but you will figure it out eventually, as will the rest of mankind now that you have discovered our home.

"So answer me this," she pressed on, "if we were to return to Earth with you, officially reveal ourselves, open full political dialogue and request that the UN recognize our planet and the surrounding space as a sovereign state. How do you think it would go?"

James was taken aback by Suzanna's openness. She meant it when she said she liked straight talking. Already she had confirmed a number of Lieutenant Scott's guesses.

"I'm not sure I have the experience to answer that. Though I can make a few educated guesses," he began. "The UN Interplanetary Committee are the ones you would have to convince. They would have the power to recognize your planet as an independent planet. Yet nothing gets through the Committee without multinational support. From time to time the majority of the representatives overrules the wishes of the minority but the Earth powers are so fractured it rarely happens. No one wants to give an advantage to one of their competitors and so even if one or two nations sided with you, they would be outnumbered.

"But even that is unlikely, if you do go to the UN, you will be going alone, without any backers. In such a scenario I'm not sure how you would get your way. Even if you had not just been attacked by an alien fleet.

"You want me to be honest," James said. "Well your government will have to face facts. Your defenses have been decimated. There is nothing stopping the Indians, the French or even the Canadians from coming here and forcing their wishes on you. And you know I can't speak for my government either. Once they find out about Haven they might set their sights on you as well."

"So you are saying our position is hopeless," Suzanna said in frustration. "Even if we had of come to you five years ago?"

"Not hopeless," James corrected, noting she had admitted that Haven had learnt of the Earth powers before the contact with the French cruiser two years ago. "Just difficult. If you had of come to the Earth powers on your own, when you rediscovered us, things might have been different. You could have made friends and alliances and worked the system until you were ready to play your cards and make a bid for independence. Now, with no navy and no defenses, you don't have many cards left."

"Damn that Maximilian," Suzanna said and James got a glimpse through her outward exterior to the inner frustration and weariness she carried around with her. "He has been so terrified that the Earth powers would come and steal his little kingdom that he has endangered our future."

"Maybe," James said, not wanting to totally disagree with her. "But your First Councilor isn't completely wrong. There are many Earth powers who would jump at the chance to add another colony to their empires. Even if it came with twenty million unruly colonists."

There is one other problem with your plan," James added as it came to him. "At the moment there are no independent colonies. Every colonized planet is ruled from Earth. If Haven were allowed to keep its independence it would set a precedent. Other colonies may begin to think they can rule themselves too. I don't think Britain would be too worried by the idea but others would. They would stop at nothing to prevent you from keeping your independence.

"Did I hear my name being mentioned," Maximilian said as he approached James and Suzanna.

"Yes Sir," James said, "but I was only speaking of how impressed I am at the job you have done here."

"Good, good. I must be doing something right if I can impress a naval captain with your experience. I'm sure you have visited colonies all over the Human Sphere," Maximilian said as he rested a hand on James shoulder and gently turned him away from Suzanna.

"I have some people I want you to meet," he added as he beckoned the two people who had followed him over to step forward. "This is councilor Farks and my youngest daughter, Elena. Farks is one of the newest councilors elected to our planetary council and my daughter and he are engaged."

"Congratulations," James said as he shook their hands.

As he stood back Maximilian leaned in to whisper in his ear. "I wouldn't waste your time with Ms. Rodriguez. Her family own the smaller gas mining station I'm sure your sensors picked out. They made a lot of important contributions to our colony in the past but now they have fallen back in the pecking order. If you want to make some friends with influence in the council, I suggest you get to know my soon to be son in law."

Raising his voice slightly so everyone could hear him Maximilian said, "He was elected with the highest majority in fifty years," as he clasped the younger man on the back.

James took the opportunity to glance back at Suzanna and tried to make his disappointment at being interrupted evident. Before Maximilian stepped over to block his view she simply shrugged at him and mouthed one word, *politics*.

With an inward sigh James turned his attention back to Farks and his fiancée, "And what are your responsibilities in the council?" he asked.

He was thrown into another meaningless conversation and it took all of his patience and limited acting skills to feign interest as both Farks and Maximilian alternated from trying to impress him and catching him off guard with a sensitive question.

Finally, he thought as his COM unit buzzed. Julius was letting him know that she was beginning *Endeavour's* maneuvers. For five more minutes the conversation dragged on but then, out of the corner of his eye, James saw three men in military uniforms walk into the reception. They made their way over to Admiral Harris who came over to the group that had surrounded James.

"If you don't mind Captain, I need to borrow the First Councilor," Harris said as he broke into the conversation.

"Certainly," James said as he looked at the Admiral with a lot less respect than he had earlier in the evening. As they both walked away James saw Suzanna stalk off after them. He felt more than a little disappointed at the prospect that she too was involved in the pirated freighters.

*

Suzanna had stomped her feet a number of times as she had waited to get another chance to talk to James but each time an opening came Maximilian brought in another guest to introduce. More than once he had given her a very dirty look. She knew in no uncertain terms that the First Councilor didn't want her anywhere near the British Captain.

When Admiral Harris had suddenly interrupted them and taken Maximilian away she followed to see what all the commotion was about. When the three military personnel approached Maximilian and the Admiral she carefully latched herself onto a nearby conversation in a way that allowed her to keep an ear on Maximilian.

"We may have an issue developing Sir," one of the naval officers said. "The British Warship has broken orbit and is circling the planet. I have ordered the freighters to keep their distance from *Endeavour* but her acceleration profile is just too great. Sooner or later she is likely to come across them."

"Did you ask them what they are doing?" Maximilian asked with concern. "They are supposed to be staying put in orbit."

"They said they are testing some repairs they just completed. We asked them to return to their assigned orbit but they refused," the officer answered. "I think whoever was left in charge up there is a bit of a hot head. She told me that if I didn't like it I could go invite the Vestarians back."

"I see," Maximilian said, trying to control his anger. "Admiral, what do you suggest?"

Harris took a moment to respond as he thought through his options. "We still have a few frigates fully functional. I suggest we hold an impromptu training exercise. We can fly the frigates into *Endeavour's* path and request that they alter course. That should give the freighters some time to get out of their sensor range. They will know we are up to something but they won't know exactly what."

"Very well, I want you to see to it personally. If the British learn that we were the ones who captured their freighters they will not be pleased."

Captured their freighters? Suzanna thought to herself. *Captured their freighters?* Then it hit her. For more than a year now a question had been niggling at the back of her mind. Her family's company specialized in inner system trade and owned one of the gas mining stations. For the last few years a couple of her competitors had been making a remarkable number of breakthroughs in freighter design and propulsion. It was now obvious, the discoveries hadn't been made by Haven scientists at all.

"This is outrageous," she almost shouted as she stalked over to Maximilian who was now on his own. "You actually sanctioned piracy? Your actions could end up starting a war!"

"Shut up," Maximilian said, his anger overflowing. "You stupid bitch, what do you know! If you had your way, we would already be slaves to some Earth power. Get out of my reception before I call security. And don't talk to any of the British officers again do you hear me? I can break your political career and your family's business if I want!"

Suzanna was too stunned to respond. She thought Maximilian was a fool but she had always thought he was a kind fool. She had never seen this side of him before. He looked ready to kill. Worse, he was prepared to use his position to get his way. That was something the First Councilor was never supposed to do.

As she walked away she began to reevaluate everything. *Has Maximilian been manipulating things from the beginning?* she asked herself, deeply concerned.

*

James had been contemplating how best to make his escape from the reception. He had spoken to just about everyone present and he knew he wasn't going to get any more useful information out of them. Suzanna seemed to be the only one who was willing to talk openly and James was eager to discuss things further with her.

Across the room he heard a loud shout and before he could get a clear view through the crowd he saw Suzanna rushing from the room, her red dress flowing out behind her.

As quickly as he could without making a scene he gave chase and when he got out of the main reception room he called after her, "Suzanna, hold on."

As she turned he saw that she was blinking back tears. "Is everything ok?" he asked when he finally caught up.

"Yes, I mean no," she said, unsure of herself. "What do you want?"

"I was hoping to talk further, I think we both have a lot of information that could help each other," James said.

Suzanna took a deep breath to compose herself. "Yes... yes, you're right," she said as she placed a hand on James' arm. "Maybe you would like to come visit me at my family's gas mining station. We would have more privacy there."

"Eh, I don't know if that would be proper," James said, feeling a little flustered at how the conversation had turned.

Suzanna couldn't help chuckling. "Listen Captain, I like you, maybe even in that way. But there are more important things going on. Come to my gas mining station. There we can talk freely and get better acquainted if you like."

"That sounds like a plan," James said, not entirely knowing what he was agreeing to.

The sound of footsteps made them both turn to look down the corridor they were in. Two security guards were approaching them. "I can't talk anymore now," Suzanna said. "I need to leave."

"Come to my station," she said as she turned in the opposite direction to the guards and took off at a brisk walk.

James was left staring after her, wondering what exactly was going on. *Why is a Haven councilor running away from her own security guards?* he asked himself.

Before he could think through what was going on Maximilian appeared. "Ah, there you are Captain. We were beginning to think we had lost you. What are you doing out here?"

"Just getting some air," James lied. "I'm used to being stuck in a cramped ship, not surround by all these high and powerful people. I needed a few moments to myself."

"Understandable my boy," Maximilian said. "But I must take you back with me. You are the center of the party after all. There are more people who want to meet you.

James suppressed a groan. "Lead on," he said instead.

*

It took another two hours for the reception to fizzle out but when it did James eagerly made his way back to *Endeavour* and his quarters. When he got there, there was a private message waiting for him.

Don't make it obvious

There was no name attached to it but James knew who it was from.

Chapter 14 – Ms. Rodriguez

All stories of political intrigue involve tumultuous love affairs and that which gave rise to the Empire was no different.

-Excerpt from Empire Rising, 3002 AD

12th May, 2466 AD, HMS *Endeavour*, Haven System

"We will be docking in ten minutes," Sub Lieutenant Malik said from the navigation station on *Endeavour's* bridge.

"At last," James thought. The day after the reception James had requested permission to take *Endeavour* on a tour of the system to see all that the Havenites had accomplished on their own. He had said he wanted to make sure *Endeavour* was fully functional and ready to face the Vestarians if they returned. Maximilian had agreed but only under the condition that Captain Denning accompanied him. Denning had commanded the frigate that had come to *Endeavour's* aid in the first half of the battle with the Vestarians and convinced the other frigates to follow *Endeavour* into Haven's atmosphere in order to come to Harris' aide.

Denning's frigate *Dauntless* was currently undergoing repairs in one of the surviving repair yards in orbit around Haven. He had therefore been free to show James around the system and supervise what James did and didn't see. So far they had visited the small colony on Athena along with a number of the bigger mining stations and the gas mining station in orbit around Selene. Now they had come to James' real target. Suzanna's gas mining station.

"I'm going to the docking access hatch. COMs let the station know I'll be coming aboard. Becket, you have the bridge," James said.

"Aye, Sir," Becket answered.

It was good to see Becket on her feet again. The doctor was still advising her to take it easy. Certainly she wasn't allowed to resume her training with the marines. But she was ready to stand watch. James had been glad for both Ferguson and Mallory, along with some of the other senior officers, were still on Haven. They had made a number of contacts at the reception and were spending time with them, offering their help whilst secretly trying to find out more about Haven.

As he got up to leave Denning got out of the adjacent command chair and followed him into the corridor. Before they got to the turbolift that would take them down to the docking hatch James turned and said, "If you don't mind, I would like to tour this station alone."

"I'm not sure that's possible Captain," Denning said. "My orders are to accompany you everywhere."

"And you have," James said, "I have enjoyed your company. Your observations have been very informative. But you see I'm hoping this isn't just a business call. I met Councilor Rodriguez at Maximilian's reception and I was hoping this would be more pleasure than business, if you get what I mean."

"You sly dog," Denning said with a grin. "You certainly move fast.

I guess I can cut you come slack. I'll give you half an hour with her, but after that I must insist I accompany you. If Harris or Maximilian hear about this, they won't be pleased."

"I'm not so sure," James said coyly. "Don't they want closer relations between our two governments?"

"Ha," Denning said, he slapped James on the back, "that they do. I'm going to my quarters to call my wife. You have half an hour. After that I'm coming to find you so we can take a tour of the rest of the station. That is why you are supposed to be here."

"Got it," James said, "I owe you one."

Denning dispatched, James turned to the task at hand. He needed to get as much information out of Suzanna as possible. When he got to the docking hatch he only had to wait a couple of minutes before *Endeavour* docked with the gas mining station. When he stepped through a man in a tight fitting uniform with the logo of Suzanna's company over his heart greeted him.

"Welcome Captain," he said, "I am the manager of this station. Councilwoman Rodriguez is waiting for you, if you will follow me."

"Lead on," James said, falling in behind the manager.

As they walked through a number of corridors to a turbolift, James couldn't help noticing that everything looked identical to the other stations he had visited. It seemed that the Havenites constructed everything from the same schematics.

"Councilwoman Rodriquez is waiting for you just through this door," the manager said when he paused before a door that didn't automatically open for him.

As James approached it he reached over and allowed the door to scan his DNA, it swished open and James stepped forward.

"Captain," Suzanna said, jumping to her feet from the couch she was sitting on. "A pleasure to meet you again," she continued as she approached him, smiling and offering her hand.

As James kissed it he noticed that she had another perfume on, equally as intoxicating as the one from the reception.

"The pleasure is all mine," James said. "We don't have long I'm afraid. Maximilian sent Captain Denning to accompany me on my sightseeing tour. He will be joining us in about thirty minutes. He thinks I wanted to meet you in private to get to know you better."

"Get to know me better. Is that what it is called on Earth these days?" Suzanna asked with a smirk.

Before James could answer her face changed and she became serious. "I jest Captain," she said as she reached out and touched his arm. "Let's get down to business then if our time is limited, come join me on the couch. Would you like anything to drink?"

"No thank you," James answered as he sat down beside her, aware of how close they were.

"If we don't have long let us lay our cards on the table," Suzanna said. "I want to find a way that my people can keep their freedom and not have to live in fear of an Earth power stealing everything we have built up here. Our forefathers left Earth to get away from the politics and the bureaucracy. We don't want to go back."

"And my duty is to find out how your forefathers managed to get so far from Earth in such a short time and how they managed to build such a successful colony," James said. "If you want my help, for whatever it is worth. You are going to have to tell me everything. If your people hold anything back then the Admiralty and our government will treat you as rivals to be crushed, not as potential allies. For the last two hundred years our Star Kingdom has been in a constant battle not to be outdone and hemmed in by the other Earth powers. Niceties are no longer a factor in our foreign policy."

"I understand," Suzanna said, "much has changed on Earth since our colony ship left. The shift drive saw to that."

"Indeed it did," James agreed. "So how do you purpose we proceed?"

"I know you have nothing to lose from simply walking away. I am the one putting everything on the line. If Maximilian finds out I am meeting with you he could end my political career. So I guess I will go first."

After a deep breath Suzanna plunged in. "I know why you are really here. You were following Chang. My station's sensors picked up the freighter that jumped into the system with you. I also managed to access Haven's orbital sensor logs from the battle. No one else has noticed it yet but your freighter entered orbit around our planet and sent down a landing shuttle. Seeing as I haven't heard anything about Chang since, I presume your people found him?"

"Yes," James said, impressed at her honesty. "Do you care to tell me why your government chose to harbor a war criminal? My government could see it as an act of war and grounds for seizing your entire colony."

"Fear," Suzanna said. "I argued against it but the council voted to accept his petition for asylum. They thought the military tech and political connections he would bring would be a step towards guaranteeing our freedom."

"And what about the piracy your government has participated in? Was that out of fear too?" James asked, cutting to his main concern.

A look of surprise came over Suzanna's face and then her head dropped. "I hope you believe me when I say that I only learnt of the stolen freighters at the reception. That is why I left so early."

As she looked back up James saw anger in her eyes. "The council had nothing to do with that. We would never vote for such a thing. It was an act of war."

"Then who?" James asked, pleased that she didn't have anything to do with it.

"Maximilian and Admiral Harris and maybe a few other councilors working with Maximilian," Suzanna said. "You have to understand, they fear Earth taking over as much as I do. I don't agree with their tactics but from their perspective they are doing everything they can to keep our people free. We needed to be able to meet you as technological equals."

"I have to be honest," James responded, "harboring Chang could have been forgiven, perhaps. But attacking our shipping, the Admiralty will never forget it and if it gets out to the public, there will be an outcry. Even if the government was willing to let it slide for political reasons, if it got out they would be forced to come down hard on you."

"So we have sealed our fate?" Suzanna asked.

"Not entirely, I have been giving this a great deal of thought. There is one option I can see working but you won't like it," James replied.

"What is it?" Suzanna asked.

"I need some more information first," James responded. "How long has Haven known about the other Earth powers?"

"Our first exploration ship happened across an Indian colony seven years ago." Suzanna replied. "The Council voted not to reveal ourselves until we knew more about how Earth's history had progressed. We didn't know if the Indians ruled all of human space or only their own sector. When that French cruiser stumbled across another one of our exploration vessels it was unexpected. It threw all our plans off."

"How many systems have you discovered so far?" James followed up intrigued by the mention of exploration ships.

"I'm not entirely sure, twenty at least," Suzanna informed him. "We have established mining colonies on some of them and on the one habitable planet we found we have set up a small colony.

At the moment there are no more than thirty thousand colonists there."

James sat back and let out a long sigh. Things were getting more and more complicated. "Twenty systems, two habitable planets. You know this is going to get everyone's attention back on Earth. This is a game changer. If the Indians or the French get their hands on your discoveries, they will dominate this area of space. You realize the Void War was fought over just such a discovery."

"We know," Suzanna said. "This is why we have been so secretive. We know what this means to the Earth nations."

"Well I can tell you this," James said. "There is no way you will be able to keep all your discoveries. Maybe some of the systems you have established mining colonies on, but the rest will likely be divided up according the UN border rules."

"We can give up most of those systems," Suzanna replied. "We just want to retain our sovereignty."

"Tell me this then," James said, changing tack now that he was sure that he was going to get all the information he needed. "When was your colony founded?

"2256," Suzanna answered.

"And how have you managed to produce such an impressive colony by yourselves? Every other colony ship that left in the Sub-light Expansion Era we have made contact with was struggling badly."

"I don't know if I have an answer for that," Suzanna said. "We founded our colony in 2256, things were very hard for the first colonists but they prioritized developing a space industry. Once we had access to the resources of our solar system the colony took off in leaps and bounds. Everyone in the first generation was highly motivated. They knew what they had left and they were eager to start something new. I don't know if you know but Harold Maximilian, the colony's founder, brought a number of scientists with him who had been working on the shift drive. Everyone knew that sooner or later the Earth nations would be coming and they impressed on their children the importance of meeting them as equals."

"I have one more question," James said but before he could ask it Suzanna held up her hands.

"I cannot tell you, at least not yet. I need more of a guarantee than just the word of a naval captain. If your government can provide some assurances then I would be willing to reveal how our colony ship got to Haven so fast."

"You are talking about the Gift?" James asked.

"Yes," Suzanna said a little surprised. "Where did you hear it referred to as that?"

"Your interplanetary COM systems aren't as secure as you might think," James said. "I understand you are reluctant to reveal anything about it but I need to know. Is it repeatable? Could another ship make the same journey just as fast?"

"Yes," Suzanna said. "In fact, with the shift drive, much faster. I cannot tell you the details, but you will think it even more important than the twenty systems we have discovered."

"I see," James said, retreating into his own thoughts as his mind raced with the possibilities.

"No more questions?" Suzanna asked a minute later, bringing James back to reality.

"No, I don't think so," he answered.

"Then what options do we have? How can you help us? I hope you realize I'm putting a lot of trust in you."

"Yes," James said resting his hand on Suzanna's. "You have my word I will do whatever I can to help you, but as I have said. I don't have much influence back on Earth."

"Nonsense," Suzanna interrupted, "don't forget I know who you are Captain. You are the Duke of Beaufort, discoverer of the Void and hero of the Void War. Some of the news reports our spies have brought back say that you singlehandedly beat the Chinese fleet. Besides, I have seen your ship in action personally; there is no hiding your skill. I rather suspect you have a lot of influence back home."

James looked at the floor embarrassed. "You shouldn't believe everything you read."

"So you didn't save a colony ship full of helpless civilians from certain destruction against a far more powerful warship?" Suzanna pushed.

"My crew did," James said. "I just got lucky. Truth be told, I almost ran away." He wasn't sure why he was sharing this with her but he didn't want her to put all her faith in him.

"My ship was in stealth when the Chinese attacked. They didn't know we were there. I almost ran away and allowed the colony ship to be destroyed. I was only thinking of myself. Even when I came to the colony ship's aid it was because I didn't want to live with the shame of being called a coward," he continued as he brought his eyes back up to meet Suzanna's, "so don't think I am going to be your knight in shining armor who can fix all your problems."

To James' surprise Suzanna burst out laughing. "Don't worry Captain, I'm not looking for any Knight to sweep me off my feet."

Before James could interject and tell her that is not what he meant she went on, "And don't forget that I have read all the reports about you. A coward wouldn't have gone on to win the victories you did in *Raptor*. Nor would he have fought so valiantly to protect my people here on Haven. You may once have been a coward, but I think you are something more now.

"And so if I chose to put my trust in you, then that is just something you are going to have to live with Captain," she finished sternly. "Now, tell me about your plan," she said as she reached across and gave his hand a squeeze.

James had to pause for a moment to take in all Suzanna had said, she seemed to jump around a lot and he couldn't tell what she thought of him. "I think there is one option that may work," he began to say. "Though I'm not sure that you're going to like it."

"Go on," Suzanna said.

"Your main problem is the Indians, for the last few decades they have been growing more and more upset as our colonial empire eclipsed theirs. If they think they can take your system and your discoveries without repercussions they will. They know our fleet is severely weakened by our war with the Chinese. Most of our largest warships are still undergoing repairs and refits. Apart from the French, there is no one else in this sector of space with the power to stand up to them."

"And the French are too worried about the Russians to openly risk their fleet," Suzanna guessed.

"Exactly," James said. "If they could benefit from your discoveries they would jump at the chance but I can't see that happening without committing military resources, something they won't risk. The Indians are your main concern.

"Your second problem are the Earth powers who rule their colonies exclusively from Earth. I don't think the US or the Germans would have any problem supporting your independence in the UN council. They have given full voting rights to their colonies and they are on the other side of the Human Sphere. However, other powers like Brazil and China will vehemently oppose any move to give a colony its independence. It will start to give their own colonies ideas."

"So you're saying keeping our freedom will be blocked in the UN no matter what the Indians or French do?" Suzanna asked.

"I think so," James answered. "That is where my option comes in. What do you know about the Bradford colony?"

"Nothing really," Suzanna answered.

"It was a colony established by a sub-light colony ship. In 2184 the then Lord Bradford, with aid from the British government, financed his own colony ship and set off with four thousand colonists for an inhabitable planet twenty light years from Earth.

"One of our shift drive exploration ships finally made contact with the colony in 2290. Their colony ship had only arrived fifty years previously but they had set up their own government and whilst they weren't flourishing, they were eking out a living for themselves.

"When they were discovered, the British government wanted to integrate them into our small colonial empire but the populace was reluctant to come completely under our political control. They had forged an identity on their new colony and they wanted to keep it.

"After a lot of political wrangling it was agreed that the colony would become a British protectorate. They had to sign up to certain fundamental British laws concerning human rights and trade policies but apart from that they were free to make their own decisions. The only other requirement was that they had to contribute to the upkeep of the RSN and the warships that protected their borders.

"Once the details were worked out the population voted on the proposal and it was accepted. Because everything was done above board and democratically, the UN Interplanetary Committee was forced to recognize the people's decision."

"And you think that would work here?" Suzanna asked, not sure she liked James' idea.

"Yes, it kills a number of birds with one stone." James said, trying to reassure her. "You get to keep your internal sovereignty. You would only have to agree to a number of laws, laws I think your people already agree with. Technically you wouldn't be an independent colony which should appease the other Earth powers. If your people voted to become a protectorate then the UN couldn't complain and with British warships parked in orbit over Haven, the Indians would think twice about making any moves."

"What about our Planetary Council? Will it be able to remain in power?" Suzanna said.

"That may be a little trickier," James replied. "After becoming a protectorate parliament appointed a governor over the Bradford colony who holds ultimate responsibility for its governance. The day to day running of the planet is carried out by a planetary committee who are democratically elected but parliament insisted they appoint a governor who had veto powers over anything the planetary committee proposed.

"Given what your council has already done and the actions of your First Councilor, I'm not sure how my government will want to proceed. They may subsume your council under the authority of a governor or they may wish to disband it all together and replace it with something else."

"I don't know," Suzanna said. "I'm not sure I would even accept such a proposal, never mind our people. We are fiercely independent."

"I understand," James replied in a conciliatory tone. "But you may not have any choice. If you don't agree to join us you could have the Indians knocking on your door in just a matter of months. That is nowhere near enough time for you to rebuild your fleet and defenses, even if some of the other Earth powers helped you. What's more, if my government felt the Indians were going to make a move they may make one of their own. We dealt with the Chinese threat to our expansion. The last thing anyone in London would want to see is the Indians taking their place."

"I'm going to have to think about this," Suzanna said. "If we were to head down this road Maximilian would have to be removed for he would never agree to it. We would then need to get enough support in the council to overthrow him. I don't even know if that is possible."

"It will not be easy," James agreed. "May I make a request to help us get the ball rolling?"

"Sure," Suzanna said, "whatever I can do to help I will."

"I need to get word back to the Admiralty. *Innocence*, that's the freighter you saw, is on her way back to Earth now with the sensor feed from the battle. It will cause a storm on Earth but the Admiralty will be acting on old information. They need to know that at least a part of your council is willing to work with us. And they need to know about the possibility of incorporating you as a protectorate. If they don't get this information they may come in with all guns blazing.

"If my analysts were able to pick up the stolen freighters from reviewing the sensor data from the battle then so will the analysts at the Admiralty. When they do, all they will have to form their approach to Haven will be the knowledge you took in

Chang and that you have been pirating our freighters. I don't think that is going to make for a very good outcome as far as your hopes of freedom are concerned."

"No," Suzanna responded, "you may be right there. I can dispatch one of my freighters to Earth. It will take it some time to get there but at least they will get your information sooner rather than later."

"Good," James said. "I will put together a report and send it to you later today."

"You are not planning to return to Earth soon then?" Suzanna asked.

"No," James replied. "We need to know more about the Vestarians first."

"What about these aliens, how do they factor into all this? Suzanna queried.

"Honestly, I don't know," James answered. "They are the great unknown. Is the story Maximilian told us true?"

"Yes, as far as I know," Suzanna said. "They came out of nowhere and demanded we give them our military tech. Then when we said no, they attacked us."

"In that case there are two ways it could go. Their attack on your planet will cause panic on Earth. Aliens are one thing, everyone has been aware of the possibility of a first contact situation for decades. But hostile aliens prepared to bombard civilians? It is going to change the face of interstellar politics in ways I could never predict.

"One benefit is that many of the Earth powers will want to see a powerful presence in this area of space. We know the Vestarians use the shift drive and they won't be able to attack Earth or any of our well-developed colonies without coming through this area of space. It might just make the smaller powers get on board with accepting Haven as a British protectorate. We would be able to establish a naval base here and the RSN would bear the brunt of any future conflict.

"On the other hand, that very possibility may turn my government off the whole idea. They may prefer to let the Indians annex your systems and leave them to deal with this hostile alien race.

"The truth is, I just don't know," James finished.

"You are at least trying to help," Suzanna said giving his hand a squeeze. "That counts for something. You don't know how much I appreciate it. Since the reception I have felt completely alone. It seems as if Maximilian and the Earth powers are doing everything they can to crush the dreams of my ancestors and family."

"I have found dreams are often like a good battle plan," James said. "They never survive contact with the enemy. The best we can do is to make sure we are doing the right thing. The rest is up to someone else."

Detecting a hint of sorrow in James' voice Suzanna took a guess, "You are talking about your princess?"

"Yes," James admitted. "I thought we would be married one day. Now she is a Chinese Empress and all I have is the navy."

"But you have made a name for yourself and from the news reports on the Void War you saved a lot of lives. Not to mention what you have accomplished here."

"True," James said. "The navy has a proud tradition and it is my hope to live up to it. But as I said, I can only look after my own actions. I can't determine what happens after that."

This time James squeezed Suzanna's hand. "All you can do is make sure you are doing everything you can for your people. I really think becoming a British protectorate is the best way forward. And I'm not just saying that as a British naval officer."

"Thank you James," Suzanna said, she leaned in and gave him a kiss on the cheek. "Our planet owes you a great deal."

As she leaned back her COM unit gave out a beep. When she looked at it she saw she had a message from her station manager. "Denning is on his way. My manager couldn't stall him."

Before James could say anything the door chimed, alerting them that someone had requested entry. When it didn't open loud voices could be heard from its other side.

Thinking quickly, Suzanna jumped onto James' lap and pulled him into a deep kiss.

"Oh... em... sorry for disturbing you," Denning said bashfully as he came charging into the room, causing James and Suzanna to break apart.

"It's time for your tour," he said with a bit more confidence, "I'll give you a second to freshen up," he added as he turned and stepped out of the room, avoiding the glare of the station manager who stood on the other side of the door.

"I thought I would enjoy that," Suzanna said as she jumped up. "Come on, let's get going before Denning decides he needs to report this to Maximilian."

"Lead on," James said, slightly confused but smiling nonetheless.

Chapter 15 – Making Plans

Before the discovery of FTL communication, naval Captains often found themselves months away from their commanding Admirals and solely responsible for their actions. Those Admirals would then analyze the decisions made with the benefit of hindsight. As a result, the rising star of more than one naval Captain came crashing down in ignominy when their actions met with disapproval.

-Excerpt from Empire Rising, 3002 AD

13th May, 2466 AD, HMS *Endeavour*, Haven system

"And that is going to be my recommendation to the Admiralty," James said as he finished filling in his senior officers about the meeting with Councilor Rodriguez. "I hear a few of you had some fun on the planet while I was away, care to fill me in?"

"Well," Chief Driscoll said. "I got a very interesting tour of one of the government's experimental research facilities. It is where they are working on new versions of the shift drive. I have to say, they are certainly making progress. No doubt a lot of that has to do with the shift drives they captured from those freighters of ours. Even so, their technicians have a few interesting ideas. One in particular has me intrigued. They have been experimenting with a fixed jump station that is able to tear a hole into shift space for other ships to use. Their lead researcher believes that a series of such jump stations would remove the need for freighters to be equipped with shift drives, reducing their build costs. The benefit of having a fixed station open the tear into shift space means much greater velocities can be reached, reducing the travel time between systems.

"All in all it is an impressive idea. I was able to give them a few pointers to help improve the efficiency of the station's jump drive but I still think it is a few years away from leaving the lab."

"That sounds like an interesting idea," James said, "it could certainly reduce the flight time between systems, especially if the concept was married with our more powerful shift drives."

Mentally James filed the concept away for later. A ship's velocity through shift space was determined by the mass of the ship and the energy discharged into the shift drive from the ship's capacitors. It took *Endeavour* thirty minutes to charge her capacitors before she could initiate the shift drive at its lowest power. If she charged her capacitors for longer she could achieve greater speeds through shift space however it was rarely practical. Even the biggest of shift passages had many twists and turns and typically a journey from one system to another would consist of multiple jumps as the shift drive could only catapult a ship into shift space in one direction. To make a course change a ship had to exit shift space, charge her capacitors and then make another jump. In the long run it was usually quicker to just initiate the shift drive when the capacitors were charged enough to open the weakest of tears into shift space rather than wait for the capacitors to charge up more.

"What about you Ferguson, did you manage to find any useful information?" James asked.

"Not really Sir," Ferguson replied. "Farks invited me to his family's plantation in the countryside. I got to see more of the planet but every time I tried to turn the conversation to Haven's history they changed the subject.

"Maximilian joined us for an evening, but even then all Farks and Maximilian did was try to impress me with their wealth. I think that if they thought they could get away with it, they would try and buy *Endeavour* from us. They are desperate for new technology."

"Yes, I have gotten that impression," James said. "I hope you put that notion out of their heads."

"Of course Sir," Ferguson said, but when James met his eye he looked away.

Dismissing the thought that came into his mind as silly, James pressed on with the meeting. "Anyone else find out anything more about Haven's history and how they managed to get their colony ship here so quickly?" he asked.

When no one answered James nodded to Lieutenant Scott to present her findings. "In that case, let's come to the real reason why I gathered you here." James said before she got up. "*Endeavour* is battle ready again. We need to decide what we are going to do next. Sorting out Haven is important but our real priority now is the Vestarians. We need to decide what we are to do about them. To do that Lieutenant Scott has some interesting findings I want her to discuss with us."

As James sat down Scott stood and powered up the holo display. "I have been analyzing the electromagnetic discharge from the Vestarian's shift drives. As I reported earlier their tech is very primitive and inefficient. Their shift drives release a great deal of waste electromagnetic energy when they enter and exit shift space. As a result, it is possible to identify where and when a Vestarian ship initiated its shift drive, weeks after it made the jump. That is how we were able to confirm the Havenites story about the Vestarian attacks.

"Since then I have analyzed some of the wreckage we and the Havenites recovered from the alien ships. We found a partially damaged shift drive yet there was enough of it intact for Chief Driscoll and I to make a theoretical model of how it works.

"As a result, I believe I can predict the direction a Vestarian ship jumps in when it enters shift space. In short, we should be able to track the Vestarian fleet that fled Haven. To calibrate my predicative model we will have to find where the fleet exited shift space after it jumped away. Then I can correlate the shift space speed with the waste energy discharge. Once we have that information we will be able to follow the Vestarian feet wherever they went."

"Really?" Becket asked. "That's great, we can find their homeworld and see just how strong their fleet is."

"Indeed," James said. "There is one caveat though. How long will we be able to detect the waste electromagnetic energy?"

"Up to three months Captain," Scott answered, "after that the energy becomes too dispersed to be able to backtrack it to its point of origin.

"So we have a limited timeframe. If we don't go after this fleet now we will lose the opportunity. I'm inclined to take the chance but I want to hear other opinions," James informed the rest of his senior staff.

"I say go for it," Becket said with her usual enthusiasm, which brought a smile to James' face.

"I agree," Mallory said to James' surprise. "*Endeavour* was built to explore. We've already discovered a lost colony, why not add an alien homeworld?"

Mallory was surprised at himself for speaking up; he knew that the recent battle had impacted him greatly. His experiences on the planet while James had been touring the system had told him that much. Yet he thought it had only been his admiration for James that had grown, now he found himself excited about the prospect of chasing after an alien fleet. *I guess not everyone is as excite*d, Mallory thought to himself as Ferguson weighed in on the conversation

"I know this is a great opportunity," Ferguson said nervously, "but at what point do we overstep our authority? We were sent out to locate Chang. We have done that. We were not trained for a first contact situation. For all we know, following these aliens in a warship could make the situation far worse. I think we should return to Earth and await new orders."

James knew Ferguson had a point but the fact that Ferguson still couldn't look him in the eye troubled him. It was true the British government liked to keep a close rein on her naval commanders. They were meant to fight the Kingdom's enemies, not dictate policy. Yet James also knew his uncle, the First Space Lord. Jonathan Somerville had strong views on how the Admiralty should be run and how Britain should face her enemies. In his view the Captain on the ground had a far better appraisal of a situation than some bureaucrats hundreds of light years away. *Plus*, James thought to himself, *it was Jonathan who got me into all those 18th century naval novels. In the age of sail before the invention of the telegram or radio communications it had been the norm for captains to find themselves on their own on the far side of the world making up policy on the fly. He can hardly blame me when I get inspiration from his books.*

"Your point is taken," James said. "But I don't think we have time to return to Earth. I'm not suggesting we go and attack these aliens' homeworld. All I want to do is locate it. Then we can hightail it back to Earth and let those higher up make the tough decisions.

"Any other objections?" he asked.

When no one spoke up James stood. "My decision is made then. We will break orbit by the end of the day and follow the Vestarians' trail. As you all know I will be appearing before Haven's Planetary Council to receive the People's Recognition R Award and the Haven military's Star Cross. It is going to be broadcast live across the planet.

"To help Councilor Rodriguez's efforts to undermine Maximilian I plan to make a scene. One I think you will all enjoy," James said, smiling.

When everyone looked at him confused he pressed on, "Becket, I need you to prepare a stealth recon drone. I want you to fly it around the planet and locate the stolen freighters. I want to have visual recordings of the freighters ready to release onto the planet's data net after I receive my awards."

"No problem," Becket said.

"Lieutenant Scott, how easy would it be to hack into the planet's datanet?" James queried.

"Very easy Sir," Scott answered. "The only thing that has stopped us so far is that it will be immediately obvious what we have done. If they have good technicians supervising the datanet they will be able to throw us out pretty quickly and make it hard for us to try again."

"Ok then, once I begin my speech I want you and your team to hack into the datanet. According to Rodriguez the council debated whether or not to accept Chang's request for asylum. I want you to see if there are any audio or visual recordings of that council meeting. If you can find any, steal them. We're going to release them to the public too.

"It goes without saying," James added. "If you can find anything about this Gift, get it too."

"Yes Sir," Scott said.

"Everyone else, get *Endeavour* ready to leave," James ordered, dismissing the meeting.

When everyone left James went through the briefing room into his quarters. His steward Fox was already there laying out his dress uniform. "Time to look the part," James said as Fox helped him get ready.

*

Three hours later James was standing on the First Councilor's Podium listening to Maximilian. He was addressing the entire planet, his face and words being beamed throughout the system.

"Ladies and gentlemen of the Council and citizens of the Haven Collective. It is with great joy that I address you this evening for we are gathered here to honor one of the greatest heroes in the history of our colony.

"Captain Somerville of the Royal Space Navy fearlessly led his ship into harm's way in our defense. When he could have turned aside and left us to fend for ourselves he risked all on our behalf. His ship single handedly destroyed more than ten of the dreadful alien warships that tried to rain down death and destruction on everything we and our forefathers have labored to build here. Let us honor this man and his crew, each of us owes them our lives."

Maximilian looked out over the assembled crowd, enjoying their attention. "I come before you now and on your behalf to present Captain Somerville with the People's Recognition Award. Normally this yearly award is given to the citizen who has made an outstanding contribution to the development of our colony, but you, the people, have almost unanimously voted to honor Captain Somerville this year.

"Alongside the People's Recognition Award, Admiral Harris will present Captain Somerville with the Haven Navy's Star Cross. The highest medal for valor and bravery our government can bestow. No man has ever been awarded both but no man has ever deserved them more."

As rehearsed, Maximilian stepped to the side of the podium and allowed James to step forward. As he stepped up a rapturous round of applause broke out from the assembled councilors and those gathered in the chamber. Turning to his right James bent over to allow Maximilian to place the People's Recognition medal over his neck.

Turning to his left James faced Admiral Harris, who stepped up with the Star Cross. As he reached up, James held up his hand, stopping Harris from getting any closer. Instead James turned back to the assembled council.

Suddenly an overwhelming desire to turn and run came over him and to hell with the consequences. He hated public speaking, especially in front of so many important people. His father had forced him to make a number of addresses to important gatherings as he had been growing up and every one of them had been a horrible ordeal. On more than one occasion he had simply run away before he was due to give his speech.

Despite his years in the RSN and the numerous times he had addressed his crew, this felt like something different. But then he thought back to what Suzanna had said about him. He knew he had changed, he wasn't the running away type anymore. And if he was going to return to Earth and fulfil his role as a Duke of England he was going to have to get used to addressing important councils and gatherings. Taking a deep breath, he found Suzanna and fixed his eyes on her to calm himself.

"It is my honor to stand before you all today and receive the People's Recognition award," he began as confidently as he could. "I and my crew would be willing to sacrifice our lives and our ship a hundred times over to protect you and your planet.

That is the Royal Space Navy's tradition. In the days since the battle I have had the opportunity to see your beautiful colony and marvel at all you have accomplished. I take your thanks seriously and you honor me with this award.

"However, I will not accept anything from your government." James said and a deathly silence descended on the chamber. Before anyone could interrupt him James went on. "Your First Councilor along with some of your elected representatives have been engaging in open piracy against freighters belonging to Earth nations. Let that sink in," James stressed as he poured contempt into his next phrase, "your leaders are pirates. They would steal and destroy in order to advance their own goals. I thought your forefathers left Earth to escape such men."

Before anyone could force him off the stage he pressed on with his speech. "Worse, your entire Planetary Council voted to take in and harbor a wanted war criminal. Former Politburo Intelligence Minister Chang Lei is wanted by the UN and the British government for war crimes. He was responsible for starting the Void War, for the bombardment of a British colony, an unprovoked attack on a defenseless colony ship and the death of over ten thousand civilians.

"The very things the Vestarians tried to do to you, Chang did to the British Star Kingdom. Yet your government welcomed him to Haven with open arms. My ship is releasing all the proof you will need to corroborate these claims onto your datanet. You will be able to see for yourselves who really rules you. I for one want nothing to do with such men. I gladly accept the people's thanks. But I will take nothing from your government."

When he stopped speaking it was as if everyone had broken out of a trance. A great commotion broke out in the chamber as everyone began shouting at each other and at James. Maximilian was fuming and as James looked at him and smiled, he thought the First Councilor was about to punch him.

When he didn't move, James turned and stepped away from the podium.

"Wait," a voice called over the others and James recognized it as Suzanna's. She had activated her booth's speakers.

"Where are you going Captain? Haven still needs your protection," she asked.

Wanting to reassure her James turned back. "While your politicians scheme and plot I go to find the alien's homeworld. We defeated them over Haven, that's true. But if we don't end their ability to wage war they will be back. Their actions have already proven they are willing to destroy entire planets to get their way. *Endeavour* won't let that happen."

With that James spun on his heels, and quickly made his way off the podium and out of the council chamber. Just through the doors Major Johnston was waiting with a squad of marines. They weren't armed but anyone would be a fool to try and tangle with them. A shuttle from *Endeavour* was landing outside the council chamber. It was against all their regulations but James didn't want to risk Maximilian getting any ideas. *Endeavour* could blow what remained of the Haven fleet out of space easily but the First Councilor probably wasn't thinking straight at the moment.

As the group set off down the corridor towards the exit an angry voice shouted after them. "What do you think you are doing?"

James turned to face the First Councilor. "Ending your political career," he said. "Next time you want to harbor war criminals and pirate our freighters you had better be prepared to deal with the Royal Space Navy. And this is only the start, the RSN will be back, that I can promise you."

Without waiting for a reply he spun on his heels and left Maximilian in a rage. Outside, the shuttle was hovering next to the stairs that led to the Council Chamber. Its plasma turrets were open and actively tracking the few security guards who were standing outside watching it.

When James appeared, it dropped to the ground and four marines in combat armor jumped out, hefting their plasma rifles threateningly. Jumping onboard James made his way to the front of the shuttle and sat down beside the pilot. "Take us back to the ship," he ordered.

As soon as the shuttle set down in *Endeavour's* hanger bay James opened his COM and contacted the bridge. "I'm back safe and sound, take us out of orbit."

"Yes Sir," Ferguson acknowledged.

James' COM beeped, informing him that he had a personal message from the planet.

Good luck.

James broke into a large smile as he made his way to the bridge. He was pleased Suzanna approved of his performance.

Chapter 16 – Vestar

Tachyons are strange particles, even now we know so very little about them.

-Excerpt from Empire Rising, 3002 AD.

29th June, 2466 AD, HMS *Endeavour,* unnamed system.

James sat in his office peering at the holo map of local space, wondering what to do. *Endeavour* had spent the last six weeks following the trail of the Vestarian fleet. Things had gotten off to a good start. They had found where the fleet had exited shift space after their first jump and Scott had been able to refine her predictive model. They had then set off in hot pursuit of the alien fleet.

Their main problem had been that they were forced to slowly make their way along each shift passage mapping out the dark matter. As they didn't know the length of each jump the alien ships were making they didn't know how far it was safe for them to jump *Endeavour* along the same route. Mapping the dark matter was taking a significant amount of time. Time James had known they didn't have.

They had discovered eight new shift passages and seven new systems. Ordinarily such discoveries would be monumental but now they were just obstacles. Each day spent traversing systems or mapping dark matter had allowed the alien fleet to get further and further away. Each time they reached a point where they detected the tell-tail signs of a Vestarian jump into shift space, the signal was weaker.

Yesterday they had come to a dead end in the shift passage they had been traveling down. That meant they had passed the point where the Vestarian fleet had exited shift space and made a course change, yet they hadn't detected any sign of them. Part of the problem had been Scott's assessment of the Vestarian's shift drive. The first jump away from Haven had been down a particularly long and straight shift passage. This allowed the Vestarians to charge their shift drives to their full capacity to traverse the shift passage quicker. The extra energy released from the jump to shift space had therefore been greater than the subsequent jumps they had been tracking, making them harder to detect.

Now James had a decision to make. He could take *Endeavour* home. There would be no shame in that. He would be coming back with a number of new systems discovered and at least a part of the way to the alien homeworld mapped out. It would give the Admiralty somewhere to start looking with the fleet of exploration ships they would doubtless send this way. Yet he wanted to find the alien system. If for no other reason than he wanted to head home with his mission completed. Heading home now would feel like only doing half the job.

With a sigh James put his head in his hands. He only had one real option. Without a firm lead they could spend years exploring shift passage after shift passage and get nowhere. *There is nothing else for it,* James thought to himself. *Time to head home.*

Just as he reached for his COM unit to contact the bridge it beeped at him. "Captain, I think you will want to come up to the bridge," Ferguson said. "Lieutenant Scott seems to be excited about something."

"On my way," James said, hoping it was going to be good news.

When he stepped onto the bridge there was a hive of activity around the science terminal. One of Lieutenant Scott's ensigns was at the terminal but Scott and two other researchers were leaning over the terminal as they studied its read out.

"What exactly is going on?" James asked when he got close enough to look at the terminal.

Scott jumped in fright at hearing her Captain's voice so close.

"Sorry Captain," she said a few seconds later as her face reddened from embarrassment. "I didn't hear you come onto the bridge."

"That's ok," James said, "you've obviously found something that has caught your attention."

"Yes Sir," Scott said, her face lighting up again. "Tachyons! Our sensors detected a brief tachyon burst that zipped past the ship."

"Tachyons?" James asked.

"They are theoretical particles that astrophysical scientists have long posited exist in our universe." Scott answered. "For over four centuries we have been looking for them though we haven't detected any and we are still at a loss as to how to artificially generate them ourselves."

"That's all very good," James replied. "I'm sure you'll get to publish a very interesting paper from this data but how do they help us on our current mission?"

"Tachyons can travel faster than light Sir," Scott said excitedly. "That means they can be used for FTL communication. The beam of particles that passed by our ship was travelling at over two thousand times the speed of light."

"Amazing," James said impressed. Yet he still wasn't sure what this had to do with finding the Vestarian's homeworld. Yet the implications of artificially generating such particles were staggering. "If we could produce our own Tachyon beam we could send a message from Earth to the Alpha system in just under five hours," James calculated.

"Yes Sir," Scott agreed, "it would revolutionize our society. Almost like the invention of the radio in the early twentieth century. There is more though. I don't think the Tachyon particles we picked up occurred naturally. The beam was too narrowly focused. I believe it was artificially produced by another intelligent race."

"The Vestarians!" James said.

"Perhaps," Scott said, happy that the Captain was following her. For the last few weeks she had been almost depressed. As it had become obvious that her initial calculations regarding their ability to follow the Vestarian fleet hadn't been accurate she had felt the weight of her failure growing. *Endeavour* had been traveling further and further into the unknown and as each day passed their ability to follow the Vestarians dwindled. It had begun to look like the entire venture to follow the Vestarians would prove to be a failure. One that would have been her fault, yet now the tachyons changed that, they had a new lead!

"The Vestarians seem to have a strange mix of primitive and advanced technology," Scott continued, "so it's certainly possible. Though this is an order of magnitude greater than any technology we have seen yet. It's possible that this beam was produced by another race."

"Another intelligent race," James said out loud as his mind ran through the possibilities. "The Vestarians did say they were being attacked by another race. Maybe they are the ones with the advanced technology. That would explain how the Vestarian tech is so diverse. Their ships could be a combination of their own tech and stolen tech from their enemies.

"Either way," James said looking back up at Scott. "Can you trace this beam to its point of origin?"

"Yes Sir," Scott answered. "We were working on that when you came in. Can you put it on the main holo display?" she asked one of her ensigns.

Nodding, the ensign switched the science terminal's display onto the main holo display.

"We can trace both the point of origin and the intended destination of the beam. That's what tipped us off that it was artificial. It is just too accurate to be random," Scott said once the holo displayed a map of local space.

"The beam originated in a system only five light years away. Its destination is a system over one hundred and fifty light years away from us, further out into unknown space. I think we have just found the first two worlds inhabited by an alien race," Scott said excitedly.

"Guessing from the shift passages in this area of space it could take anywhere up to two months to reach that far away planet even if we had all of the space between here and there mapped out," James concluded. "I'd say this nearest planet is the Vestarian homeworld. The other planet could be their enemies. Ferguson what do you think?" James asked his First Lieutenant.

"I agree Sir," Ferguson said. "There was what looked like a fork in the shift passage we are in about a day's journey back that suggested it led in the direction of this new system. I suggest we back track and explore it. If this system was the alien's destination there has to be a shift passage that leads to it somewhere nearby."

"Navigation, plot us a course back to Ferguson's shift passage. Take us there at best speed," James ordered.

"Lieutenant Scott, I want you to continue to analyze the data you got on that Tachyon beam, see if you can decipher any form of communication embedded in the particles."

"Yes Sir," Scott said eagerly.

*

6th July, 2466 AD, HMS *Endeavour*, unknown system.

A week later and *Endeavour's* bridge was crowded with all the senior officers except Mallory, who was in the auxiliary bridge. After locating the fork in the shift passage James had taken his ship towards the planet where the Tachyon beam had originated from. After a couple of dead ends they had finally found a small shift passage that led to the system. In thirty seconds they would be exiting shift space four light hours from the system's mass shadow.

Technically, *Endeavour* could exit right on the edge of the mass shadow created by the planet's star but doing so would give their arrival away to any ships that were patrolling that region. James was taking every precaution so they were going to exit shift space a long way from the inner system and cruise in slowly under stealth.

"Exiting in five, four, three," the navigation officer called out.

As soon as they jumped out everyone who wasn't manning one of the command stations focused on the main sensor plot and the gravimetric plot.

"No ships appearing on the gravimetric plot," Ferguson reported. The gravimetric sensors were able to pick up the gravimetric waves given off by ships that were quickly accelerating or decelerating and could therefore give an almost instantaneous view of what ships were operating within a system.

"The planet is in a binary star system and I'm picking up six planets orbiting the two stars," Sub Lieutenant Malik said from the sensor terminal. "There's one gas giant and one planet in the habitable zone."

"Acknowledged, focus our passive sensors on the habitable

planet," James ordered. "Navigation, angle us towards the habitable planet. I don't want any acceleration though. We don't know if they have any gravimetric sensors or how sensitive they are if they do. Let's just coast in using our velocity from exiting shift space."

"Yes Sir," Sub Lieutenants Malik and Jennings said.

"I'm picking up a lot of residual electromagnetic energy emanating from the edge of the system's mass shadow directly in front of us. It looks like a lot of Vestarian ships have been jumping into shift space in this area recently," Scott reported.

"I guess we're in the right system after all," James said.

*

For the next two hours *Endeavour* cruised up to the mass shadow of the system's star. By then James had a much clearer picture of what was going on in the system. There appeared to be a small asteroid mining complex on the edge of one of the denser asteroid fields in the outer system. Apart from that and the habitable planet, the rest of the system appeared devoid of alien activity. Even the habitable planet was strange. There was one large satellite in orbit and what looked like a number of smaller ones. Yet there was nothing to suggest whoever lived on the planet had the technology to build a fleet of warships. Or even had the kind of space based civilization that needed FTL communications.

On the planet itself there appeared to be a number of major cities that were giving off all kinds of electromagnetic energy, suggesting that whoever lived on the planet, there were certainly lots of them. One city dwarfed all the others and at its center there was a massive structure. Everyone on *Endeavour's* bridge had been mightily impressed. Even Earth's largest structures weren't visible from this far away in space.

"Continue to take us in," James said to the Navigation officer. "We're not going to solve this mystery unless we get a close look at what's going on."

"Lieutenant Scott," James continued. "How are your attempts to understand their COM chatter going?"

"Surprisingly well Sir," Scott answered. "The translation software the aliens gave the Havenites was easily transferable to our main computer. It seems that whoever is on that planet speaks the same language as Haven's attackers for our computer can translate the COM signals we are picking up. Though I haven't found anything useful yet."

"That's ok," James said in an understanding tone. He had already looked at the COM chatter coming from the planet and finding anything useful would be like looking for a needle in a haystack. It seemed that every building on the planet was broadcasting openly without any encryption.

"I want you to put together a team to go through what you can, use your science team and take Lieutenant Becket and a number of the Sub Lieutenants, see if Agent Bell will join you as well. The more we can learn about these aliens the better."

"Yes Sir, I'll get right on it," Scott acknowledged.

*

8th July, 2466 AD, HMS *Endeavour,* in orbit around Vestar.

James finally felt ready to make first contact with the planet below him. He had taken *Endeavour* into high orbit around the planet and for two days they had silently watched the planet go about its day to day business. Scott, Bell and Becket had spent the time trawling through the mountains of communication data and just a few hours ago they had felt ready to present their findings.

It seemed these aliens were the Vestarians, their language matched, the visuals of the aliens on the ground matched bodies recovered from the battle over Haven and they called their planet Vestar.

The largest city was called Amack and the impressive structure they had seen from the edge of the system was the palace of their god-king. At least that was what Bell and Becket had taken to calling the planetary leader. As far as they could tell, the government loosely resembled a military junta from Earth's history. Every city was heavily garrisoned with what looked like military units and there were military outposts and checkpoints throughout the rest of the planet. Their capital was the most heavily defended and the palace where the Supreme Overlord resided was more like a fortress.

From what Scott had picked up from the plant's communications, the Supreme Overlord had been in power for the last forty years and a cult of personality had sprung up around him. Every residence was expected to have a picture of the Overlord and each morning the whole population was to swear allegiance to him. Almost every visual of the various cities

James had seen had contained some statue or poster of the Overlord.

The whole situation still felt surreal to James. Even though they had spent the last two days orbiting the planet watching the aliens, their very existence, not to mention the strangeness of their ways, was still a shock to him. Here was an entire alien civilization. One which did not share the thousands of years of history that every human took for granted in their day to day dealings with each other.

Perhaps the oddest thing of all was the planet's tech base. Militaristically they weren't much beyond where Earth's militaries had been at the beginning of the twenty first century. The satellites in orbit that seemed to serve the sole purpose of monitoring the population were the same. Yet, from what Scott could estimate, agriculturally they were leap years ahead of Earth's production capabilities, which allowed them to maintain a population almost twice the size of Earth's despite having about the same land mass to work with. Their buildings were also impressive, especially the tall thin spires that dominated the capital and stretched almost three kilometers into the sky. James doubted human engineers could produce such thin towers that still had the capability to resist the wind strengths they encountered at such high altitudes, for whilst Vestar resembled Earth in many respects, its weather was far harsher.

Despite these impressive technologies, what stood out was the large satellite orbiting the planet. According to Scott's analysis, it was centuries ahead of even the most impressive technology on the ground. Doubtless it had been the source of the tachyon beam. James had slotted *Endeavour* into orbit at the opposite end of the planet to ensure the satellite didn't detect them.

There was no sign that any of the other satellites in orbit and the ground observation stations they had detected were able to detect *Endeavour* while she remained in stealth. That made the situation all the more surreal. All the evidence before him suggested that this could not be the planet that the alien fleet which had attacked Haven had originated from. Yet, it also suggested that this planet could never produce a satellite as sophisticated as the one they suspected was the source of the tachyon beam. There were a lot of unanswered questions going around James' head.

There is nothing else for it, James said to himself again. *We're only going to get answers by speaking directly to this Supreme Overlord.*

"COMs, open a channel to the planet, run my words through the translation software," James requested.

"Should I direct the channel anywhere specific or to the entire world?" The COMS officer queried.

"No doubt the Overlord will want to hold a private COM conversation once we reveal ourselves but first I want the whole planet to know we are here. That will make it harder for the junta to spin our arrival to their favor. Until we find evidence to the contrary I'm treating this Overlord as a potential hostile," James answered.

"Channel open," the COMs officer announced.

James took a deep breath and began, conscious that this might be the first time this planet had ever heard the words of an alien species. "People of Vestar. My name is James Somerville. I am the Captain of a human exploration ship called the *Endeavour*. My ship followed a fleet of warships that attacked one of our planets to this world. I am here to open diplomatic relations with your people and to ascertain where this fleet of warships came from and why they attacked my people. I would like to formally introduce myself and my people and request that we open diplomatic dialogue between our two races."

Finished, he nodded to the COMs officer to cut the transmission. He had spent hours preparing what he wanted to say and in the end he had decided to keep it short and sweet. He didn't want to come across as too hostile but at the same time he wanted to make it clear that attacking human worlds would never be tolerated. The Admiralty may not be happy with his decision not to mention Britain, not to mention the government, but he had decided he didn't want to let the aliens know that their race consisted of various fragmented nations. It would weaken his position too much if they thought they were only dealing with one faction of another race.

"Sir, the readings from that alien satellite have spiked. It looks like it is powering up," the Sub Lieutenant Malik reported from the sensors station

"It's sending out a tachyon beam," Scott shouted in excitement, "the satellite is transmitting a message, same direction as the one we picked up previously."

"It's beginning to accelerate and change its orbit," Sub Lieutenant Malik chimed in again. "Looks like it is trying to intercept us."

"Can we match its velocity and keep our distance from it?"

"Yes Sir," Navigation answered.

"Then make it so," James said. "I suspect it is guessing our position based on the origin of our COM broadcast. If we can keep the planet between us and it, we should be able to remain invisible. Keep a close eye on it, let me know if it launches any probes our way," he added as he settled down into his command chair to await a response from the Supreme Overlord.

Chapter 17 – The god-king

Once we thought we were alone in the galaxy, now we know that is far from true. Yet when all is said and done, many are surprised to find that so many of the aliens we have encountered share our flaws of pride and self-centeredness.

-Extract from Empire Rising, 3002 AD

30th June, 2466 AD, Amack, Vestar

As James stepped off the shuttle he couldn't help but be overawed at the structure before him. They had landed in the Overlord's palace and as he looked up it seemed as if the white spires in front of him stretched up into space. Behind them he could see even taller spires that were all but blocked out by those in front. Directly in front of him there was a giant set of white steps that led up to the main entrance to the palace structure. They dwarfed those of the Haven Council Chamber by a factor of over a hundred.

No one had come to meet them so, shrugging, he walked towards the steps. Beside him strode Major Johnston, Agent Bell and Lieutenant Scott and to each side they were flanked by six marines in full combat armor. The Overlord had chosen not to reply to James' message personally, instead a text message had been sent back requesting that James and his officers come to the Overlord's palace to discuss their requests in person. There hadn't been anything about coming unarmed so James had decided to bring as much firepower as they could fit into the shuttle. If nothing else, it would show the Overlord that human military technology was far more advanced than their own.

When the last marine stepped onto the stairs a loud crunching noise rumbled from beneath their feet. Everyone looked around in alarm but as the stairs suddenly kicked into life and began to move upwards they relaxed again.

"They are one giant escalator," Bell said, "I'm sure glad we didn't have to walk all the way up them. I thought the Overlord planned his palace this way just to get sadistic pleasure out of making anyone who came to visit him exhaust themselves just walking up the steps."

"Me to," James said, "but let's keep the chatter to a minimum, no doubt there are bugs everywhere recording everything we say. We'll have to keep our thoughts to ourselves."

 As the group ascended the steps in silence they had time to look at the various statues that lined either side of the escalator. James had already seen images of the aliens from *Endeavour's* optical scanners but the statues fascinated him nevertheless. The aliens were quadrupeds but they seemed to stand at almost the same height as the average human. As they continued up the steps each of the alien figures was looking him in the eye and more than one was clearly designed to intimidate visitors. At least that was the effect they had on him, *who knows what those facial expressions mean for the aliens*, James reminded himself.

The statues were painted green to resemble the color of the alien's skin. Analysis of the dead bodies from Haven suggested that the alien's skin actually resembled scales from reptiles back on Earth. As James studied the nearest statue closely he could make out markings in whatever material the statues were made of that looked exactly like the scales from the pet snake he had as a child. The thing that marked the aliens out and their most fascinating feature was their extra set of arms. Four legs he was used to, most earth mammals and reptiles had four legs. But four arms, that was something entirely new and the human like hands with four fingers and a thumb at the end of each arm was more than a little unnerving.

We will look just as strange to them, James reminded himself. *At least if there are some similarities it might make it easier to communicate.*

When the group neared the top of the steps they stopped moving and James and the others ascended the last couple of steps themselves. Before them the giant door into the palace opened as if it had a mind of its own. Inside there didn't appear to be any lights and it looked like they were about to step into a giant black hole.

"Lead the way Captain," Bell said with a smirk on her face.

She is actually enjoying this, James thought as he shook his head and moved forward.

"Greetings Captain," a voice said from the darkness as James crossed the threshold. The ear implants Scott had given them automatically translating the alien's speech. "Welcome to the palace of the Great Supreme Overlord Tal'Nack. I greet you on behalf of his benevolence."

"We thank you for your welcome," James said into the darkness. As his eyes adjusted he made out a shape in the darkness.

Stepping towards it he held out his hand. "It is customary among our people to shake hands when meeting someone for the first time. My full name is James Patrick William Somerville."

"We have no such custom," the alien said as he turned and headed further into the palace. "If you would follow me, we have prepared a room for you to wait in until the Supreme Overlord is ready to see you."

James looked back at Bell and her face clearly said what he was thinking, *that wasn't the best of starts.*

James led the group after the alien. He couldn't help but watch the alien as it walked. Like the statues outside, it was clothed in a tight fitting military uniform which didn't leave much to the imagination. No one knew the specifics of how the aliens reproduced but the rest of the alien's body was very impressive. As it walked its leg muscles bulged under its own weight, suggesting the alien could propel itself at a much greater speed if it wanted to. Its torso was equally covered in muscles and there wasn't an ounce of fat apparent anywhere.

James was sure that if Major Johnston or the other marines accompanying them were ever to don such form fitting uniforms their bodies might portray the same bulging muscles and lack of body fat. Yet seeing it on a potentially hostile alien was unnerving and intimidating.

For five minutes they walked deeper into the palace, following the alien who hadn't given his name. As they went, the amount of light slowly increased until they could see everything clearly. That only served to increase the feeling that everything about the palace was designed to intimidate visitors. Above them were vast open spaces that, even though he tried his hardest, James couldn't see the top of. All around them there were more statues of aliens; some were in diverse military uniforms equipped with strange looking weapons. Others depicted aliens in various stages of hand to hand combat with muscles flaring as they sought to overpower each other.

"You may wait here," their host said when they rounded a corner and entered a small room with a number of seats. They were obviously designed to allow the four legged aliens to sit down but they looked as if humans could use them without too much difficulty.

"You will be summoned by the Supreme Overlord when he is ready for you," the alien said, spinning around and leaving before James could ask him anything further.

"Well this is not how I expected things to go," James said to the group loudly, happy to let any nearby alien bugs pick up his anger at the way they were being treated.

"No," Bell agreed. "But then again, on reflection, maybe this is what we should have expected."

"Explain," Johnston said.

"Well, we know the Overlord wants his citizens to treat him like a god and not just their leader. Is it so strange to think that maybe he thinks that about himself too?" Bell asked.

"If he does, then to him we are just another group of inferior beings to be treated as such. For him to treat us as equals would go against his own self inflated ego," she added.

"What do we do then?" Johnston asked. "How do we negotiate with a god?"

"I'm not sure," James said, "for now though I guess we just wait."

Silence descended on the group as each thought through how one might try to open diplomatic negations with an alien who thought he was a god. *How will he even view another sentient race?* James asked himself.

Having got no further in figuring things out, James was relieved when their host returned an hour later. "The Supreme Overlord will see you now," he said.

Everyone jumped to their feet, glad to be moving, and followed their host down another maze of corridors. It almost seemed as if the palace had been designed to make it difficult for attackers to find their way to the Supreme Overlord.

After five minutes they rounded a corridor to be confronted by a set of massive doors that were even larger than the ones they had used to enter the palace. Pausing in front of the doors their host said, "I must warn you, do not cross the red line in front of the Overlord's throne. Any attempt to cross the line will be taken as an act of aggression and the guards will immediately kill you."

"That's good to know," James said, wondering what other protocols they really should be aware of.

Upon entering the room the group were confronted by a host of attendants who stood on either side of the room. Many of them were dressed in a similar military uniform to the alien who had led them through the palace but quite a few were dressed in much more fancy and colorful attire. James guessed that there were over a thousand aliens present.

At the front of the room stood an extremely large chair that James took to be the Supreme Overlord's throne. It was decorated in fine metals and sparkled with what looked like diamonds and rubies. Worryingly, along the top of the throne were over one hundred Vestarian skulls. Before the throne there were twenty more aliens in military uniform and armed with some form of rifle. Each had his rifle raised and pointed at the newcomers.

Seated on the throne was an alien almost twice the size of any of the others in the room. Like the rest, his muscles bulged in a threatening manner but he was the first alien James had seen with what looked like a layer of fat around his waist and midriff. As he opened his mouth it was clear he had a voice to match his impressive appearance for it boomed across the room. "Ah, our distinguished guests have arrived. They have come a long way from another star system to bring their supplications before me. You may approach," he commanded.

Leading the group forward, James came to a stop well before the red line in front of the throne. "It is a pleasure to be granted this audience with you Overlord," he began.

"As I said in our COM message. We are humans, we come from the planet Earth. A fleet of alien ships attacked one of our colonies. They bombarded the planet before we drove them off. My ship is an exploration ship. We followed the alien fleet to this system. We come in peace offering friendship but we would like an explanation for this attack."

"Attack?" the Overlord chuckled. "Let me assure you human," he continued, slowly working his mouth around his last word. "The Vestarians have not attacked you. If we did, you would not be standing before me. You would already be our slaves forced to submit to our might."

"I'm sorry to contradict you Overlord Tal'Nack," James said in as neutral tone as he could. "The aliens who attacked us looked as you look, they called themselves Vestarians as you do. They came seeking to trade weapons technology and when they didn't get what they wanted, they attacked our planet. After we defeated them their ships fled to this system. If they were not acting under your orders my people can understand that. But we must know the truth of the matter."

Tal'Nack jumped to his feet in anger, "How dare you accuse your god of lying and not ruling this world? Not one Vestarian breathes without my say so. If I say we did not attack you, we did not attack you. That is the end of the matter."

With a wave of one of his hands Tal'Nack sent some form of signal to the guards in front of his throne. In response they formed a semicircle around the human group, pointing their weapons at them. The marines closed in around James and the other officers.

"I will give you one more chance human," Overlord Tal'Nack said. "Tell me of these weapons technologies you speak of."

Deciding to try another approach James gave up on pursuing the attack on Haven. "My people have been exploring space for the last four hundred years. We have many technologies that we have developed, both civilian and military. As a representative of my people we would be happy to open formal communications between our two nations. There are many things we could trade to the benefit of all our people."

"Trade! I don't think you have understood human, we have given you this audience so that you may come before us on behalf of your people and make an offer to the great people of Vestar. We are the chosen people of the galaxy. It is truly a privilege for you to be in our presence."

"Indeed we are thankful for the opportunity to come before you Overlord," James said. "But there can only be trade between two equal partners. We have not come here to give your people anything unless we can come to an agreement. I think you misunderstand our intentions."

At James' last words a ripple of whispers broke out among the watching attendants and James felt he must have said something deeply offensive. This time Tal'Nack didn't jump to his feet but he did lean forward on his throne. "You have miscalculated human, I can command your death anytime I want. You have come to my planet and into my palace and you dare to insult me. Get out of my presence. I will give you this one mercy. Leave now, reconsider your attitude and I may allow you a second audience. If you were anyone else, you would already be dead."

"Quickly, this way," the alien who had lead them into the throne room said in a whisper, clearly not wanting to attract the Overlord's attention.

As the group made their way out of the throne room the large doors shut behind them with a deafening crash. "Well that was short and oh so sweet," Bell said. "Captain, I think you're going to go down in history as the man who pissed off the god-king."

"Yes," James said. "That didn't go quite as I expected. I think we are going to have a problem with these Vestarians. We need to find out where their fleet went and how they constructed it. If they are able, I think they would enslave all of our worlds just so we would show the proper respect to their Overlord."

"Agreed," Johnston said, "I don't like that bastard one bit but if there is one thing starting off in the lower ranks of the marines teaches you it's that you don't piss off someone with more power than you. I hate to say it but if these Vestarians turn out to have us outclassed militarily, we're going to have to do a lot of ass kissing in the coming decades just to survive. "

"Excuse me," a voice called out to them as they followed their host out of the palace. "May I speak with you?" it asked.

Their host stopped and looked at the alien who was now speaking to them. "I'll see them out once I am done with them," the new voice said. Their host bowed and walked off.

"Let me introduce myself," the newcomer said. "I am Rak'la'loren. I serve the Supreme Overlord as his Minister for Technology."

"And do you have any more insults you want to add to those of your Overlord's?" James asked, in no mood to hear more Vestarian snobbery.

"You have to understand, no one accuses Overlord Tal'Nack of making a mistake," Rak'la'loren said. "He is only used to dealing with his ministers and others that come before him seeking his favor. He has never had to deal with someone as an equal before.

"If you are willing. I think together we will be able to come to a number of agreements that we can present to the Supreme Overlord. I think that way you may be able to find his favor."

"We did not come here looking for technology," James said. "We came looking for answers. Can you tell us where the ships that attacked our world came from?"

"Well, I'm afraid I don't know," Rak'la'loren said. "You would have to ask the Minister of Aggression about that. But if you do have a ship in orbit then you will know that we have no military ships nor do we have the industry necessary to construct them."

"Ok, then tell me about that satellite in orbit. We know you did not build it. Where is it from?" James asked, changing direction.

"The satellite," Rak'la'loren said quietly. He looked from side to side in a very human like way suggesting he was nervous. "We don't talk about the satellite in the palace. It would make the Supreme Overlord nervous."

"Why?" James asked, "because its technology proves that whoever built it is vastly superior to your Overlord?"

"That is blasphemous," Rak'la'loren said. "If anyone hears you uttering such things they will report you to the Supreme Overlord and he will have you killed."

"I'd like to see him try," Johnston said. "It sounds like your Overlord needs to be brought down a peg or two."

"Let's get back on track," James said. "If you can't give us our answers we are leaving. We will find them another way. One that does not benefit you or your Overlord."

"I am sorry," Rak'la'loren said. "I simply do not have the authority to give you the information you want. If you would only agree to a number of small trade deals. We have some agricultural technology we would be willing to share. Then from there we could build on our relationship and in time you may get the information you want."

"I am sorry too," James said. "Your Overlord made it clear what he thinks of us. If you cannot give us the information we need then we are wasting our time here. Good day to you Sir. I think we can find our own way out."

With that James turned and confidently strode off in the direction he thought the main doors were in. Once they were out of earshot of Rak'la'loren he said to one of the marines, "Did you map out the palace on our way in?"

"Yes Sir," the marine answered.

"And are we heading in the right direction?"

"Close enough Sir," she answered.

"Then you lead us the rest of the way. Contact the shuttle and tell them to get ready to lift off, we are returning to *Endeavour*.

Chapter 18 – Jil'lal

Jil'lal's lungs were burning as she sprinted down the dark alleyway. She could already feel the lactic acid in her four legs building to the point where they would start to cramp. In desperation she ducked into a smaller alleyway and threw herself against a wall behind a large crate. She tried as hard as she could to control her breathing lest her heavy gulps give her away but the thumping of her two hearts was so loud she was sure there was no hope.

Jil'lal knew she needed to find some water. If they hadn't already the officers from the Ministry of Integration who were pursuing her would soon set their Rakash hounds on her. With six legs and three hearts they were the ultimate predators on Vestar. After generations of careful breeding the ministry had produced a strain of Rakash that was tameable and therefore trainable. Able to run at a constant speed of forty kilometres an hour indefinitely they were equipped with the most sensitive noses on the planet and could hunt and track anything or anyone. The only way to escape was to enter a body of water. The water would throw them off the trail and, with luck, Jil'lal could make her escape before they could pick it up again.

As her breathing calmed she forced herself to think. *Where is the nearest overflow channel? It can't be far.* She was regretting not taking more time to plan her mission. Tak'ar always told her that her impulsiveness would get her in trouble. She loved to jump into situations and rely on her raw skills to get her out. *This may be the time my skills finally let me down*, she thought as the fear she had been keeping locked up threatened to erupt.

Vestar was a violent planet. At least that was what the Kulreans had said when they first discovered it. Savage storms constantly made their way across the planet's surface, dumping huge quantities of water onto the ground as they went. As a result, every city, including the capital, Amack, had overflow channels designed to take the water out of the city and prevent flooding when a storm hit. If only she could find one. She could jump in and let the currents take her far outside the city before she tried to get out and find her way back to the resistance headquarters.

In an effort to remember, she closed her eyes. She pictured the map of the area surrounding the Ministry of Cohesion building she had infiltrated. Then she replayed all the twists and turns she had made as she ran for her life from the building after being discovered. Fairly certain that the alleyway she was in ran east to west she made her decision. If she continued heading west she should run into the channel that flowed past the ministry building.

With a deep breath she pushed herself back to her feet and rushed deeper into the small alleyway. After less than a minute it came to an end with a wall almost six metres high. Smiling, she reached into the pouch strapped to her back and brought out two leather straps with metal prongs on the end. She fastened them to her hands before she jumped up the wall and drove the prongs into the bricks, allowing the metal prongs to hold her weight. She placed her four feet on the lower part of the wall. Slowly at first, she rocked up and down using her hands and feet to propel her. On the fourth way back up she pushed up with all her strength. She was propelled through the air with her final two arms stretched out above her, seeking the top of the wall. With a grunt she clasped her objective and braced herself as the rest of her body crashed into the wall. After pausing for a second to let the effects of hitting the wall wear off, she pulled herself up to the top of the wall.

Ordinarily Vestarians could not lift their own body weight with only two of their arms, they had four for a reason. However, Tak'ar had insisted she bulk up her muscles to the point that she could. 'You never know when you'll need your other two hands for something else' he had always said. As Jil'lal perched on top of the wall she surveyed the alleyway in front of her, thankful for her training. It was wider on this side and in the distance she could see that it widened even further. Thankfully it was night in Amack and the street was deserted. It looked like it would be heaving with people in the day. Not seeing anything to deter her and with no other choice she flung herself off the wall and into the alleyway. Her first two legs hit the ground and cushioned her fall while the other two were already stretching out in front of her, turning her downward momentum into a forward sprint.

Panting heavily, she ran down the widening alley for almost a mile when suddenly, out of nowhere, a fist came swinging out of the shadows and knocked her off her feet.

"Well, well, what do we have here?" a voice said.

"Someone up to no good, that's for sure," replied another.

"So what are you running from little girl," the first voice asked. "Are you being chased by a Talaxar?

A Talaxar was a fictional monster many Vestarian children

feared. Jil'lal thought that if they knew she was likely being chased by Rakash hounds they would be gone in a shot. They weren't likely to believe her though. Why would the ministry send their hounds after a young girl just entering womanhood?

When the second man reached down to turn her over to get a better look at her, Jil'lal fended his hand off. "I'm being chased by the Ministry of Interrogation. I suggest you leave me alone and get out of here," she said. She hoped mentioning the Ministry would send them packing.

Instead the first voice chuckled, "The Ministry of Interrogation! Don't make me laugh. You can wish they were here but there is no one to protect you from us little girl. You made a grave mistake coming down our alley in the middle of the night. Now it's time for you to pay the price."

Both males approached Jil'lal as she continued to lie on the ground. She tensed her muscles and prepared for action. The knock to her face had stunned her but the seconds the men had wasted talking to her had allowed her head to clear. Now her training was kicking in. As the second male reached for her she reacted with lightening quick reflexes. With one hand she grabbed one of her assailant's hands and twisted as hard as she could. Two of her other hands fended off the male's attempts to grab her with his free hands while she struck his twisted wrist with the palm of her fourth hand. The wrist, already under severe tension from being twisted so badly, shattered as her palm struck it and forced it into an angle it simply could not sustain. With a howl the second male jumped back, holding his shattered wrist in two of his hands.

The first male continued to approach her but with a little more caution. His hesitation gave her enough time to scramble to her feet. She backed off, trying to get some space. The first male started after her but as soon as he did Jil'lal changed direction and charged him. He raised his hands to protect himself but that was what Jil'lal was waiting for. As soon as he did she shifted her momentum and threw herself down. As she fell she swept out with two of her legs and struck her attacker off his feet. She used her two free legs to propel herself upwards and brought one of her knees into the falling male's head. As her knee connected she heard a satisfying crunch.

Back on her feet she eyed the second male warily. He was still holding his wrist and did not look like he would pose much of a threat. Satisfied she was safe, she turned and dashed into the dark. Her martial arts skills were another thing to thank Tak'ar for.

*

Twenty minutes later she knew she was getting dangerously fatigued. It had been almost an hour since she had burst out of the Ministry of Cohesion building and she had been running ever since. Suddenly a piercing howl stopped her in her tracks. Rakash hounds! The howl meant one of them had found her trail. Now it was a race. Could she get to the overflow channel in time?

A new spurt of adrenalin raced through her body, giving her the strength she needed to break into a faster sprint. As soon as another alley intersected the one she was running down, she dived into it. With the rakash hounds chasing her the Ministry officers with them would soon realise she was heading in one direction. They would send hover vehicles ahead to get in front of her. She had to make her way to the overflow channel without giving her pursuers an indication of where she was headed.

As she continued ducking and diving into different alleys she heard hover vehicles. Out of nowhere two came zooming over the buildings that lined the alley she was in. She dived into the shadows and waited until they flew overhead and out into the city. They would be using infrared sensors to identify people out in the city at this time of night. With the curfew the government had put in place they could afford to stop anyone they caught outside. Only the bravest of criminals came out at night. It was simply too easy to get caught. Little did her pursuers know that Jil'lal was wearing a specially designed military combat suit. At the moment it was keeping most of her thermal heat locked up inside the suit. Jil'lal was getting hotter and hotter but it kept the thermal sensors from registering her as anything more than a small stromi.

At last she broke into a more open space. Ahead of her she could see the walls that marked the overflow channel. They were over thirty feet high to allow large volumes of water to flow down them without flooding the nearby sections of the city. With a grin Jil'lal reached into her pouch and pulled out her climbing equipment. She loved to climb, it had been the one thing Tak'ar had not had to force her to practice. With her spiked boots on and a climbing axe in each hand she rapidly made her way up the wall. Once on top she looked into the overflow channel below. Thankfully, there was some water flowing down it. There had not been a storm in over a week but there must have been one further upstream. Keeping her climbing boots on and holding tightly onto her axes she jumped in. Jil'lal hated water but she had no choice. It was either this or face the fangs of the rakash hounds.

As she punched through the water, she frantically flailed about until she broke through the surface and gulped in some air. She tried and failed to keep calm as the current took hold of her and moved her away from where she had climbed the wall. She counted to two hundred and then swam to the other side to climb out. Her first attempt to grab onto the channel's wall failed for as she struck her axe into the wall the force of the current ripped it out of her hand. Next time she slammed both axes into the wall and held on as tightly as she could. It worked and she gripped the wall with her boots and climbed. When she got to the top she took off her boots and threw them over the other side followed by her three remaining axes. Then she turned and jumped back into the water. *Let them think I headed on into the city,* she thought as she allowed the current to carry her out of danger.

*

Several hours later the walls of the overflow channel disappeared to be replaced by open countryside. The twin suns of the Vestar system were just rising and Jil'lal was able to take in the beauty of her surroundings. She had been raised in one of Vestar's minor cities but even there the government's restrictions had been enforced severely. She had only been allowed out of her block twice in her life and neither trip had been to the countryside. Since joining the resistance she had travelled much further afield but rarely had the opportunity to just sit back and take in the beauty of her world.

After another hour of floating and dreaming about a world without the Overlord a small town came into view. Once Jil'lal spotted it she swam to the river bank. Pulling herself out of the water, she took off her combat suit and lay down in the light of Vestar's two suns to dry. It would not do if she walked into the town looking like a soaked stromi. Once dry she got up and walked the mile into town. As she walked through the main street she kept an eye out for the local enforcement officers while looking for a building with a data terminal. The first one she found was in an upscale restaurant used by the government officials in the town. The waiter manning the welcome desk eyed her suspiciously, his look only intensifying when she walked straight over to the data terminal. They were only accessible by government officials or government contractors.

His suspicion vanished when she slotted in her access card and the terminal switched on. The waiter probably assumed she was the daughter of some important government official. Recognizing her access codes the terminal gave her a direct link to the planet's datanet. Once connected, she reached into her pouch and pulled out a data chip. Inserting it into the terminal she uploaded its contents.

When she had broken into the Ministry of Cohesion she had hacked into their most heavily guarded files and downloaded as much as she could. Computers had always been her thing, that was why she had been so useful to the Resistance. Yet she had found that even she had her limits. Some of the files had alarms hard wired into them. As soon as she begun to download them they went off and the guards had been alerted to her presence. She only had enough time to see that the files were about the Kulreans before she had been forced to run for it. Whatever they contained she was sure that they were important. If they were important to the government then it probably meant they would be useful to the resistance.

When the terminal beeped to inform her that the data transfer was complete she sat back in relief. The mission was accomplished. After a few seconds congratulating herself Jil'lal stood and walked over to the waiter. He immediately showed her to the best seat in the restaurant and promised to bring out their finest foods. Jil'lal was starving and she needed some time to figure out how she was going to get back to Tak'ar.

After the meal she accessed the terminal to see if there were any messages for her. Sure enough there was one from Tak'ar. He congratulated her and then told her there had been a new development. After opening the link, he had sent her she listened to the audio of James introducing himself to her world.

Aliens, Jil'lal thought with excitement. *Aliens the Overlord has attacked, this could change everything!*

Chapter 19 – New Friends

Today there are strict first contact protocols in place within the Empire. Yet when we first made contact with the Vestarians there were no such regulations. Most modern historians believe that if they existed back then, things would not have turned out as they did for our race.

-Excerpt from Empire Rising, 3002 AD

1st July, 2466 AD, HMS *Endeavour*, in orbit around Vestar

James was on the bridge watching the holo projection of Vestar, going over his audience with the Overlord for the twentieth time when Lieutenant Scott broke into his thoughts. "Sir, we are getting a communication from the surface."

"I thought we were getting continuous COM chatter from the surface alternating between insults and demands for technology?" he asked.

"Yes Sir, but this is different," Scott said. "We have been contacted by a group claiming to be some sort of resistance to the Overlord. They claim to have some of the information we want."

"Let me see it," James said.

"Ok Sir, I'm sending it to your command chair, it was text only," Scott replied.

Captain Somerville, I am contacting you on behalf of the Resistance, we are a group striving to overthrow the Supreme Overlord and return democracy to our world. We have information regarding the Overlord's battle fleet and their weapons technologies we would be willing to trade. We don't have much time. If you want to speak with us, reply to this message and we will send you coordinates to a safe location where we can meet face to face.

James read the message twice and then shouted over to Sub Lieutenant King who was at the COMs station, "Contact Ferguson, Johnston and Bell. Get them to meet me in my office.

"Yes Sir," King said to James' back as he walked out of the bridge.

"Scott, you're with me," James said before he ducked out.

Five minutes later they were all in James' office. After he let them read the message, James spoke up, "I'm going to reply. It may be a trap but I think we need to take the risk. I'll take a shuttle down. Agent Bell, you and Lieutenant Scott can accompany me along with a handful of marines to back us up in case we get into trouble."

"I'm not sure that is a good idea Captain," Ferguson began. "We know almost most nothing about these Vestarians, how can we start to get involved in their internal politics? Surely it is not our place to meddle with how another species governs itself."

"Even when that species threatens us?" James asked with a hint of frustration. He wanted to get on with his plan.

"Yes," Ferguson answered firmly. "We have no orders from the Admiralty regarding how to handle a first contact situation, but if we did I'm sure they would forbid getting involved with rogue organizations within a week of making contact. It is simply not our place. We need to leave these kinds of decisions to our government. If we do any more we may face legal charges. If not from our government then from the UN."

"So what do you propose instead?" James said.

"We can reply and ask for the information they have, that's it. I don't think we can make them any kind of promise of help or aid," Ferguson answered.

"Unacceptable," James said. "I am the commanding officer here in Vestar and I believe we need to do everything in our power to make sure there isn't another attack on human space. Even if that means interfering with the god-king who likely ordered the attack. I don't know how our government will take us contacting this Resistance, but I know I will sleep soundly with my decision.

"Besides," James said more lightly, "I only want to talk with them. It's not like we're about to give them weapons or anything like that. We can just hear them out and then see where things take us."

"I see," Ferguson said diplomatically. It was obvious to everyone in the meeting that he wasn't convinced. "Well in that case at least you must agree that you going isn't very wise. We don't know the politics of this planet. This Resistance could just as easily kill you or take you captive if they thought you were worth trading with the Overlord. The Overlord may have prisoners that they could exchange you for. It's just too risky for you to go. You are needed here."

"He's right Captain," Johnston said. "It's not the Captain's place to be sneaking around an alien planet. You are needed here in case the Overlord tries to contact you. Agent Bell has more than enough experience to command this mission and I can be on standby with two shuttles of marines in combat armor to back her up if need be."

"Lieutenant Scott, what do you think?" James asked, to draw her into the conversation.

"I think the message is genuine Sir," she said. "Everything we know about the Overlord suggests that he wouldn't entertain the idea of admitting the existence of a resistance to us. Even if it was just a fake one to lure us in. I think we need to take the risk. We came here for information after all. That said, Johnston and Ferguson are right, it makes no sense to risk your life when we have so little information to go on."

"You can't argue with that logic," Bell said grinning. "I guess it's just you and me Scott."

"Are you happy to be going in with so little support?" James said conceding their point.

"I've been in far worse situations with far less support," Bell answered. "This will be fun, we may actually get to see more of the planet than just the Overlord's palace."

"Very well. I'll send a reply to the message, Bell and Scott, I want both of you to get ready for a landing mission. Take whatever you need. Major, assign six of your best marines to accompany them to the surface. Dismissed everyone."

*

As Bell stepped off the shuttle she was amazed by the sight that greeted her. In the distance the two suns of Vestar were both setting and as their light filtered through the forest in front of her the rays were reflected off the foliage in a number of dazzling colors.

"Beautiful," Scott whispered from behind her.

"Thank you for coming," a voice said from the edge of the forest and was quickly followed by its owner as a Vestarian made its way to the shuttle. Bell guessed it was a male, probably past his middle age based on other Vestarians she had met at the palace and watched through *Endeavour's* optical sensors. The age was largely a guess though, for they still hadn't figured out exactly how long the Vestarians lived. It seemed that once they reached adulthood they continued to grow albeit at a slower rate. From what they could tell the older Vestarians were taller than their younger counterparts but usually did not have the muscle mass they once did.

"My name is Tak'ar," the alien said. "I lead the Resistance in this part of our world. If you don't mind, could you order your shuttle to take off right away? The longer it waits here the more chance that we will be discovered."

Turning her back to Tak'ar momentarily Bell opened her COM unit. "Ok Sheils, we have our feet on the ground. You can take off now. Just be ready to come back and get us if we need you."

"Yes Mam, I'll be here when you call, have a safe trip," the pilot called back.

As Bell turned back to Tak'ar she was surprised to see he had extended his hand to her. "Welcome to our planet, I believe this is how your people greet each other?"

"Indeed it is," Bell said with a smile as she shook his hand.

"I see you have been informed about our meeting at the palace," she concluded.

"Yes, we managed to steal some details about your meeting. But follow me, this is not the place to talk. There could be a military patrol craft overhead at any minute," Tak'ar said and turned to lead them further into the forest.

For the next twenty minutes they trudged through the thick Vestarian forest. Tak'ar, with his four legs and arms was clearly far better adapted to his environment as he seemed to glide through the forest effortlessly. Bell, Scott and the marines were all panting hard by the time Tak'ar stopped.

"The city of Zekath is just a few kilometers ahead of us," Tak'ar said pointing through a gap in the thick foliage where some of the city's large spires could be seen. "That is the city I was born in and the city where both my parents were executed."

Before Bell could commiserate with Tak'ar he turned back to the cliff they had stopped beside. With two of his arms he pulled back a number of thick vines growing up the cliff and with his other two he knocked out a specific pattern. "Over a hundred years ago the Overlord at the time built a number of military bases adjacent to the main cities to house his troops. This base was never finished so the Resistance has taken it over."

As he spoke, a crack appeared on the cliff that rapidly widened until it was just large enough for a Vestarian to fit through. Tak'ar led the way as Bell and the rest of her team followed him in. For another ten minutes the group followed Tak'ar deeper and deeper into the abandoned military base. Here and there they saw other Vestarians lounging about but for the most part the base seemed empty.

Bell had been trying to remember all the twists and turns they had taken but by the time Tak'ar stopped again she was completely lost. "Now we can talk," Tak'ar said. "I have had refreshments prepared for us in here, I hope they will be suitable for you" he added gesturing through a door into a room with what looked like a Vestarian table in the center.

Bell wasn't so sure but she was confident Scott would be able to determine if the food was safe. As she walked in to the room two Vestarians reclining at the table stood and came over to meet her. "This is my wife, Mul'li'la," Tak'ar said as the older looking Vestarian held out her hand. "She runs this Resistance base."

"And this is one of our best infiltrators, Jil'lal," Tak'ar said as Bell shook the second alien's hand.

"A pleasure to meet both of you," Bell said. "You truly have my respect for trying to stand up to your Overlord. We have seen his palace and some of his military units. It's can't be easy taking on an opponent who wields such overwhelming force."

"No," Mul'li'la said with what looked surprisingly like a human expression of sadness. "We have lost many good friends over the years. But they all died willingly. None of us are prepared to rest until we see the Overlord's rule ended and freedom restored to our people."

"Maybe you could tell us something about the history of your people," Scott asked. "It would help us understand who you are and allow us to follow each other better. We would be happy to share some of our history with you."

"Yes," Tak'ar said. "That would be a good place to start. "Please make yourself comfortable," he added as he gestured to the table.

Once all the humans had found a way to sit somewhat comfortably at the Vestarian table he began. "We count our years as one revolution of our planet around the two suns of our system," Tak'ar explained.

"As do we," Scott said smiling.

"Well," Tak'ar continued, "just over five hundred years ago our planet was divided between many small and large nations."

Bell mentally did the calculation and worked out that Tak'ar was talking about three hundred Earth years ago.

"There was an almost constant state of war between several of the larger nations over territory but for the most part the people lived in peace. The wars largely consisted of border skirmishes.

"There was great celebration when one of the dominant nations launched its first satellite into space but within days an alien ship showed up. They called themselves the Kulreans and they came offering us technology to help us better ourselves. They had one condition though. We had to form one planetary government and put an end to all our wars. A small military force was allowed to keep the peace but we were to abandon every other form of military technology.

"To show the authenticity of their offer, they gave each of the nations a number of agricultural and energy production technologies that were vastly superior to anything we had ever seen. The introduction of these technologies quickly began to change our culture and there was a large movement among the population to form one government and gain access all that the Kulreans had to offer. After a series of democratic votes our nations unified. The Kulreans then built the large satellite you have no doubt seen and slowly began to feed us new technologies that improved our healthcare, our food production and the quality of life of all Vestarians.

"Just over three hundred years ago an omen came, a great fireball that passed through our sky and impacted in the mountainous region of Kal'dar near our capital Amack. Our people have always been a superstitious people and it was thought the fireball from the sky was a warning against the gifts the Kulreans had been giving us.

"A year after the fireball, the leader of the military forces of our unified government announced that he had found the place where the fireball had struck our planet and that he had been given a vision. He said the Kulreans were really our enemies and were trying to enslave us. His forces quickly overtook our capital Amack and he proclaimed himself the Supreme Overlord of our people. When some of the older nations tried to rise up against his rule his armies swooped in against them. They were armed with weapons and air vehicles that were far more advanced than anything the other nations possessed and they quickly defeated the uprising.

"Since then a succession of Supreme Overlords has ruled our planet through fear and military force. Anyone who opposes their rule is imprisoned or executed and if any group tries to stand against them, the military bombs them and their towns or cities out of existence."

"That is awful," Bell said, "in our history we too have faced men and women who have tried to rule through fear and death. Often it came at great cost but we have always managed to defeat them and restore freedom to our people. We can certainly understand why you fight this enemy.

"May I ask," she went on. "How did the Kulreans respond to this military coup?"

"Not well," Mul'li'la interjected. "They demanded that the Overlord immediately relinquish his rule or they would withhold any further technologies from us. The Overlord simply ignored them and continued to cement his power base.

"Since then we have had five Overlords. Each one has further entrenched themselves in Amack so that now the entire city is a fortress. As far as we were able to tell, they have been too scared to attack the Kulrean satellite directly. At least, that is what we have always thought. Information Jil'lal recently acquired has brought many of our assumptions into question."

"What kind of information?" Bell asked.

"Information that implicates the Overlord in the attack on your planet and details about the Overlord's remaining battle fleet. Jil'lal managed to infiltrate the Ministry of Cohesion in Amack and steal a lot of data off one of their central computers," Tak'ar said with obvious pride.

"But before we divulge this data we need to know more about you and your history," Tak'ar continued.

Bell and Scott had anticipated this so Scott proceeded to inform the Vestarians about Earth's history and the recent colonial race between the major space faring powers. She left out details of any of the actual wars but implied that there had been fighting on a number of occasions.

"So your people are a people of war," Tak'ar said.

"I wouldn't say we are a people of war," Bell replied. "At least not all of us. But like your Overlord, there has always been some humans who have sought to use power to force their will on others. Throughout our history there have also been those willing to risk their lives to resist such evil."

"Nevertheless, your people know how to fight. That is good. We can use friends like you," Tak'ar said. "May I ask, is your ship a warship? I presume it has some weapons if it was involved in defeating the Overlord's fleet that attacked your planet."

"Our ship is an exploration ship," Scott said. "I am a science officer, my job is to look for new discoveries in the galaxy. However, *Endeavour* was designed to be able to protect herself and hide if need be."

"That is good," Tak'ar said, "I already know the Overlord is very angry because he cannot locate your ship. If your weapons technologies are as good as your stealth technologies then you will prove to be a useful ally for the Resistance."

"If your information proves that your Overlord attacked our planet then we would be willing to discuss your situation," Bell said carefully. "However, we would need to verify the accuracy of your information and even then you need to know that we will be limited in what we can give you. My Captain only has so much authority. We cannot give you new weapon technologies without permission from our government back on Earth."

"We understand," Tak'ar said. "But there are many things you can do for us without giving us access to your technology and I believe that when you see our information you will be highly motivated to help us. If you can help us restore democracy to our people then in the future humans and Vestarians may become close friends and allies."

"We would like that very much," Bell replied.

"Good," Tak'ar said with a smile. "Then we will share our information with you. We believe your ship will be able to confirm its accuracy. After you have done that then we hope you will lend us what aid you can in our fight against the Overlord. Jil'lal, can you show them what you found please."

As Jil'lal stood she pushed a button on the table they were sitting around and a section of the table parted to reveal a holo projector. Scott studied it closely to compare it to human designed ones and decided they were very similar.

"The data I recovered contained some technical details on a secret construction yard the Overlord has been building for the last fifty years. It is located within a large asteroid in our outer system," Jil'lal said as the holo display showed an image of the Vestar system with a red flashing dot in one of the outer asteroid fields. "The data also indicated that the Overlord has secretly been building a fleet of warships using technology neither the Kulreans nor the resistance knew he had. We believe that the main objective of this fleet is an attack on the Kulrean homeworld. However, our information also included details about a human world called Haven. Supposedly our Overlord made contact with your planet a number of months ago and sought to acquire more weapons technology to ensure his attack on the Kulreans would be successful. When your people would not agree he sent a fifth of his fleet to subdue your world and acquire its technology. The information we have suggests that the Overlord and his analysts believed Haven to be the only world humans lived on. They did not factor in other warships coming to Haven's aid."

"A fifth of his fleet?" Bell asked in concern. "You mean the Overlord still has over two hundred warships under his command?"

"Yes, the data suggests that there are two hundred and twelve ships in the Overlord's fleet apart from those that survived the attack on Haven."

"They must be well hidden," Scott said, "our sensors would eventually be able to detect any other ships in a system unless they were completely powered down. We have been here for over a week and haven't caught a whiff of any other warships."

"Our data indicates that after construction the warships were transferred to other hollowed out asteroids so as to conceal them from the Kulrean satellite. The Overlord wants his attack to come as a surprise," Jil'lal informed her.

"And does your data tell us how the Overlord got the technologies needed to construct and equip such a powerful war fleet?" Bell asked. "I don't mean to be rude but our scans of your planet do not suggest your people have the capabilities to produce so many ships."

"We are not sure," Tak'ar answered for Jil'lal. "To be honest this has been a mystery since the first Overlord took power. As I said before, as if from nowhere his forces were able to seize power using weapons that were far more advanced than anything his opponents had seen before. Most of the military units you see around our world are equipped with state of the art Vestarian tech, but they aren't much more advanced than the weapons we used before the Kulreans contacted us. Yet we know from historical reports and a few brief skirmishes we have had with the Overlord's personal guard that the Overlord has access to a level of technology far beyond that which he equips his usual troops with. It may be possible that the Overlords have had access to these kinds of technologies ever since they took power and have just been limiting their use so that their opponents don't get access to it."

"That's possible," Bell said as she began to wonder exactly what the omen was that had crashed into the plant's surface. *A Kulrean ship maybe*, she thought, *with technology the Overlords have managed to reverse engineer?*

"It does mean that toppling a ruler with the ability to secretly produce his own fleet of warships is going to be much harder," she continued. "There is no way *Endeavour* could take on so many ships."

"That may not be an immediate problem," Jil'lal said. Our data included messages that have been sent to the construction yard ordering the fleet to prepare to leave the Vestar System. They were sent just over two weeks ago and we believe that the fleet has already left for its next target, likely the Kulrean homeworld."

"Well if the Kulreans are as advanced as their satellite in orbit suggests they are, the Overlord's fleet are going to get a nasty surprise," Bell said.

"Yes," Tak'ar said. "But our dealings with them suggests that they are very strong pacifists. It is only a guess but we do not believe that they have a military nor a fleet of their own. There may be nothing to stop the Overlord's ships from attacking their homeworld."

"Oh," Scott said shocked that any species would leave their homeworld undefended. "This could end very badly. The Overlord has already shown that he is willing to bombard alien planets to get his way."

"Yes," Bell agreed. "But that fleet could also be on its way back to Haven. The Overlord may feel like his chances of defeating the Kulreans would be stronger if he could add human technology to his warships."

"I hadn't thought of that," Scott said. "The defenses on Haven couldn't hope to hold off over two hundred of their warships.

"No," Bell said in a serious tone. "Tak'ar, we need to contact our Captain with this information right away."

"I understand," Tak'ar said. "No COMs will be able to penetrate this base though. I will have to take you back up to the surface."

"Then lead on," Bell said as she stood and made her way to the door hoping Tak'ar would pick up on her concern.

Chapter 20 – Boarding Action

In the first Expansion Era it was unheard of for one of the space nations to secretly build up their military forces. Explored space was just too small to hide the mining and construction yards needed to build a large fleet. Now the Empire is so vast that the entire Human Sphere from the First Expansion Era could be lost without even being noticed.

-Excerpt from Empire Rising, 3002 AD

1st July, 2466 AD, HMS *Endeavour*, in orbit around Vestar

James was on the bridge, sitting in his command chair listening to Bell relay the information she and Scott had obtained from the Resistance.

"Good work Agent, this is vital information," James said once she had finished. "I will send a shuttle down to collect you and then we will go straight to this construction yard."

"No," Bell said. "Tak'ar says the Overlord's army units in this area must have detected the shuttle the first time it landed because patrols have more than doubled since we got here. If you send down a shuttle for us now there may be a firefight and you would give away the location of the Resistance's base. You may have to wait until things calm down here to collect us."

"Very well," James said. "We have no time to loose. We need to verify the construction yard's existence and see if we can track this new fleet in case it has headed back to Haven."

"Yes Sir, I understand. Scott and I are prepared to wait here on Vestar. With your permission we would like to provide what help we can to the Resistance while we wait."

"You may give them advice and share tactics," James said. "But don't get involved in any operations yourself and do not trade any technology with them. If this information proves true then the Overlord has attacked and bombarded a human planet. If that is the case, then when we get back I will have no problem relieving the Overlord of as much of his military forces as we can. But until it is confirmed I don't want you taking any direct action against him, understood?"

"Yes Sir," Bell responded, "there is one more piece of information I am sending you. Jil'lal, one of the resistance's technical experts has provided us with detailed information on how their computing systems work. Scott says that if some of her people can get their heads around it in time, they may be able to access the Vestarian computers in the construction yards and get some more data on their attack fleet.

"Excellent," James said. "Tell Scott she has done a good job. You both have. Now I better go."

"Happy hunting Sir," Bell said as she closed the COM channel.

"Julius," James said to the Third Lieutenant who was on the bridge with him, "contact Ferguson, Mallory and Becket and tell them to meet us here."

"Yes Sir," Julius replied.

"Navigation, lay in a course to take us to the asteroid belt Bell's information identified. Take us there under stealth. We don't want to alert the Vestarians that we are coming."

*

Ten hours later *Endeavour* had come to a complete stop beside the large asteroid that housed the Overlord's construction yard. They were within plasma cannon range but hopefully out of range of any x-ray lasers the Vestarians might have hidden on the surface of the asteroid. Scans of the large rock hadn't identified any weapon platforms but James was being extra careful.

"I think I have found it Sir," Julius said.

"Show me," James asked.

On the holo display the image of the large asteroid zoomed into a section and flicked to thermal imaging. Across one section of the asteroid a thin line of heat was clearly visible. "The computer estimates the line to be more than two hundred meters long. That's just wide enough for them to fit their larger warship through. I think we're looking at waste heat from the seal between their external doors." Julius said.

"I agree," James said after taking a few seconds to consider the image. "Send the coordinates to Major Johnston and tell him his mission is a go. Tactical, I want the plasma cannons at full charge, if you get even a hint that a weapons point is charging up take it out immediately."

James turned to Ferguson who was sitting beside him. "You ready to lead the second wave?"

"Yes Sir, I have selected thirty of the crew with the best weapons skills. We'll be ready to back the Major up," Ferguson replied.

"Very well then, go and see to your team. Have them ready to embark as soon as the shuttles return," James ordered.

"Shuttles away," Sub Lieutenant Malik informed James from the sensor station.

*

As Johnston's shuttle took off from *Endeavour's* flight deck he turned to Lieutenant Becket and said, "Let's try to keep you in one piece this time shall we?"

"That would be appreciated Sir," she replied with a smile.

Technically Becket didn't need to accompany him on the first shuttle. She would be Ferguson's second in command once his half of the boarding party landed. Yet Johnston had become used to having her beside him on missions and he had argued that by accompanying him on the first shuttle she would be able to fill Ferguson in on the status of the construction yard when he arrived.

"Missile launch from *Endeavour*," Becket announced as they approached the asteroid.

Everyone in the cockpit of the shuttle and those in the rear who could strain against their harnesses looked out the main forward window and watched as a single missile streaked passed the two shuttles.

When it was fifty meters away from the asteroid it detonated. In space the force from a thermonuclear explosion quickly dissipates but the missile was close enough to ensure a significant amount of its explosive force crashed into the external doors of the construction yard. Even if the doors were made of valstronium, it was hoped that the missile would still blow a hole big enough for the shuttles to fly through.

"We're being hit by multiple target acquisition radars," the pilot announced worriedly.

"I think they know we're coming," Becket said.

"Don't worry, *Endeavour* will handle them," Johnston said. Sure enough, a few seconds later green plasma bolts rained down on the giant asteroid, causing explosions to erupt all across its surface.

"Listen up lads," Johnston said over the COM to his men to take their minds off the danger. "As soon as we enter the construction yard the shuttles are going to scan its interior with ground penetrating radar. One of the aliens in the Resistance provided us with a program that will analyze our scans and identify the likely locations of the construction yard's central computer. Our job is to take those positions and hold them until the tech guys coming across in the second wave can get to them.

"We don't know how good these aliens are in ground combat but we have the element of surprise. Let's use it to our advantage. Don't forget, these are the guys who attacked Haven, unless they surrender show them no mercy."

"The hole that missile blew in the external doors isn't big enough for us to fit through," the shuttle pilot said, bringing Johnston's mind back to the present.

Before he could say anything Becket opened a COM channel to *Endeavour*. "We're going to need that hole widened for us Julius," she said..

"On it," she replied. Moments later four plasma bolts tore into the hole, melting its edges enough for the shuttle to fit through.

"That should do it," the pilot said in relief.

"Here we go," Becket said in excitement as the shuttle eased its way through the hole, closely followed by its sister ship.

As soon as they were through the hole, the pilot gunned the engines and whipped the shuttle into a series of tight evasive maneuvers. They hadn't been sure if the interior docking area of the construction yard would have any weapons defending its entrance. When no weapons fire was detected the pilot slowed the shuttle and waited while its radar mapped out the interior of the asteroid.

"It's vast," Becket said as the first scans began to come in. "It looks like they have hollowed out almost all of the asteroid."

"It sure does," the pilot said. "Look over there, they still have two of their frigates under construction."

Becket looked at where the pilot was pointing. All across the interior of the asteroid there were extremely powerful lights lighting up the whole area. It was easy to make out the two warships amongst all the construction scaffolding. It looked like there were at least six different construction births. Four of them were empty but two contained hulls that looked like they would eventually become alien frigates. Becket was impressed at the swarm of activity going on around both ships.

"Forget about them for now," Johnston reminded them. "Find us a place to put down."

"There," the pilot said pointing to what looked like a landing area for some of the smaller construction ships that worked within the asteroid. "Your Resistance program has identified two areas that might house the central control computer. That landing area is right in between them."

"Take us in," Johnston ordered and opened a COM to the Marine Lieutenant commanding the marines on the other shuttle. "Jeffers, you take position alpha, I'll take beta. No need for anything fancy, just hold the position until the technicians get there."

"Acknowledged," Jeffers said.

"Becket, when we land you find a place to hide and cover the landing site. We will want to land the second wave here once the shuttles return. We'll need to know it is still secure. You can keep an ear on the COM channel and follow our progress so you can update Ferguson when he lands.

"Yes Sir," Becket said a little disappointed she wasn't going to go with the marines. She understood though. Despite all her training she still wasn't as capable in marine combat armor as the marines themselves. The element of surprise was everything on this mission and they couldn't allow her to slow them down.

As the marines rushed out of the shuttle once it touched down, she hung back to stay out of their way. When she did step off, the shuttle lifted off and banked towards the exit. As she looked around she realized that she was already on her own. Both sets of marines had taken off towards their objectives. Behind her the roar of the shuttles' engines let her know she was without backup if anything did happen. Carefully, she looked around and assessed her surroundings.

The shuttles had landed on a large metal structure built into one of the sides of the asteroid. With her magnetic boots holding her to the surface what seemed like the ground was actually one of the sidewalls of the asteroid, at least in relation to the hole they had blasted into the asteroid. Around her a number of small craft with different grappling arms and hooks were parked and beyond that the large flat landing zone was covered in metal crates of various sizes filled with all sorts of components. In the distance there were three hatches that led into the wall of the asteroid that presumably contained more rooms.

Becket carefully made her way into the midst of the crates and chose a spot where she could watch all three hatches. She settled down and listened in on the COM chatter between both groups of marines. It seemed as if they had both made contact with armed aliens but they were still making progress. She winced when she heard that one of the marines had been hit. She hoped whoever it was would be ok. She knew all of the marines through the training she had been receiving from Major Johnston. He regularly got her to spar with them and every one of them had beaten her black and blue at one time or another.

Movement at one of the hatches caught her eye and refocused her mind. A Vestarian head had poked out of the hatch for just a second. *There is it again*, she thought when the head appeared. Slowly, the head appeared for a third time and a full Vestarian slowly walked onto the landing zone. Five more followed it, all armed with a large, intimidating looking weapons that resembled the gauss cannons Becket knew some of Earth's ground militaries used.

As she watched they spread out in twos and began to comb the landing zone. One pair was heading directly towards her. Carefully, she sighted her plasma rifle on the first of the aliens. Taking a deep breath, she then exhaled, slowly letting out half of the breath. As she paused she zeroed in her sights on the center of the alien's torso before pulling the trigger twice. Without even waiting to see the two plasma bolts strike, she redirected her aim and fired two more bolts. This time she watched the alien go down before she ducked behind cover. The others would know her position; it was time to move.

She got up and sprinted to her left at an angle away from the group of aliens. When she was confident she was far enough away, she found a good firing spot and settled in to wait. Sure enough, thirty seconds later two more aliens appeared, carefully moving to flank her previous position.

Before she opened fire on them she checked the timer on her combat armor. The shuttles would be returning in thirty seconds. That would give her an opening. Slowly, she counted to twenty and then opened fire. This time her first shot missed but she adjusted her aim and took the first alien out with her second shot. Her miss had given the second alien time though and he managed to bring up his weapon and open fire. A small explosion erupted beside her as a part of the metal crate she had been using for cover exploded into hundreds of small balls of molten metal. "X-ray lasers," she cursed as she ducked away from the alien's fire.

She was just in time as another explosion erupted where she had been standing. Taking a risk, she charged out from behind the other side of the crate, firing from the hip as she went. Her move and speed caught the alien by surprise and he wasn't able to bring his bulky weapon to bear on Becket before her plasma bolts knocked him down.

Without pausing, she charged in the direction the two aliens had come from. The last two would be either where she had initially seen them keeping an eye on her original position while their friends tried to flank her, or trying to flank her from the opposite side. Either way her route would take her behind them.

Right on time she heard the whine of the shuttles' engines and she looked up to see both of them coming in to land. If she could see them that meant the aliens could see them. Sure enough, there were two small explosions on one of the shuttle's hulls. It veered off, trying to avoid any more hits.

The distraction of the shuttles' appearance gave Becket the time and element of surprise she needed. As she rounded another set of crates she spotted the last two aliens. Both of them had their backs to her and their weapons raised, trying to track the shuttles. Skidding to a halt to get better aim Becket lifted her rifle and quickly dispatched both of them.

"Landing zone is clear," she said over the COM channel to the shuttle pilots.

"Thanks Lieutenant," one of the pilots said. "That was some impressive shooting."

Ignoring the praise Becket switched COM channels and spoke to Johnston, "Ferguson and his men have arrived, have you located the central computer yet Major?"

"Yes, send Ferguson and his men to my position, Lieutenant Jeffers and the rest of the marines are already on their way here. His position turned out to be a storage area."

"Acknowledged," Becket replied before turning and seeking out Ferguson amongst the rabble of crew members who were disembarking from the two shuttles. Becket was glad Johnston wasn't here. He would have had a fit at the unordered way the navy personnel were forming up.

Finally, she spotted Ferguson and made her way over to his position, "The central computer is at position alpha. Johnston is waiting for you there. I'll keep my team here and we will hold the landing zone in case any more aliens show up."

"Ok Lieutenant," Ferguson said, "I'll take the rest of the marines with me."

"They're all yours," Becket said, knowing Ferguson would need them more than her. There were six marines with the second wave of boarders who hadn't fit into the first wave. They were currently standing off to one side of the rabble that was *Endeavour's* crew, carefully scanning the perimeter.

"Marines," Becket shouted over to them, knowing they would find taking orders from her easier than from Ferguson. "The First Lieutenant is taking the tech guys to position alpha to meet up with Major Johnston, you six take point. See that they all get there safely."

"Yes Sir," Sergeant Harkin responded with a marine salute. "That was some fine shooting mam."

"Thank you," Becket said, secretly pleased as she knew Harkin's praise was much harder to come by.

*

"Sir, I'm picking up some energy fluctuations from one of the nearby asteroids," Sub Lieutenant Malik called from the sensor station on *Endeavour's* bridge. "Wait, there is a large door opening on the asteroid. I think it is one of the asteroids where the Vestarians hid their fleet from the Kulrean satellite.

"Tell the landing party they are on their own. Instruct the shuttles to remain in the construction yard if it is safe in there," James ordered. "Then take us into stealth and move us away from the construction yard."

"I'm picking up two alien cruisers coming out of the second asteroid," Malik reported. "They are firing multiple low powered bursts with their x-ray lasers."

"Smart," James said. "They can't have a lock on us, yet one lucky hit and *Endeavour* will light up like one of Vestar's stars on their thermal scanners. Then they will have us"

"Have you got a firing solution yet?" James asked Julius at the tactical station.

"Twenty seconds Captain," Julius said without looking up from the screen she was working at.

"We're hit," Malik shouted.

"Evasive maneuvers now," James ordered, "and bring our ECM to full power. Jackson, no need to stay hidden any longer, engage the nearest ship with the plasma cannons, hit them with everything you've got."

James had been hoping to get off a spread of missiles before the aliens detected them. It would have allowed *Endeavour* to take out one or both without having to deal with their x-ray lasers. That wasn't going to happen now. All three ships were within range of each other's directed energy weapons and in those circumstances anything could happen. It had become a knife fight.

"Direct hit," Jackson said. "Two bolts hit the second vessel, it looks like they took some serious damage. Both ships are going into evasive maneuvers."

"The aliens have switched to full powered beams with their lasers, they have a lock on us," Malik reported.

"Missiles away," Julius shouted.

"Keep up the evasive maneuvers," James began to order Jennings at the navigation station but he was cut off when the ship bucked and everyone on the bridge was thrown against their harnesses.

"We've taken a laser strike to our port bow," Mallory reported over the COM from the auxiliary bridge a few seconds later. "Sections three and four are venting atmosphere, no major damage reported.

"Thank you," James said over the COM.

Even before he finished speaking Julius shouted over him. "Missile detonation, multiple hits!"

Everyone but the navigation officer, who was still throwing *Endeavour* into a series of evasive turns, watched the holo display. It took a few seconds for the feed to clear after the thermonuclear explosions but when it did everyone cheered. Both Vestarian ships were tumbling wrecks.

"Hold on," Malik shouted over the cheering, "sensors are picking multiple incoming missiles. They got off a broadside before we hit them."

"Take them out," James shouted to Julius. He was relieved to hear the flak cannons automatically opening fire as the ships' computer detected the incoming missiles and reacted before anyone on the bridge could.

"Point defense plasma cannons and AM missiles engaging now," Julius shouted.

James watched the plot as it finally firmed up enough to show fourteen missiles incoming. The computer hadn't had time to coordinate the shots from the flak cannons to maximize their effectiveness but they still took out five of the missiles. The range had been so close that even before the final flak cannon round exploded, green plasma bolts and explosions from the AM missiles were lighting up space around the incoming ship killer missiles. Nine quickly became four, then two and finally the last missile disappeared as an AM missile exploded right beside it.

"That was the last one," Julius shouted in relief. "We're safe."

"Good work everyone," James congratulated the bridge. "Let's hope we don't have to do that again any time soon," he added to a few chuckles.

"Take us back to the construction yard," James said to the navigation officer. "Sensors, keep an eye on the surrounding asteroids. Let me know immediately if it looks like another one might have a surprise for us," he added.

"Yes Sir," Malik replied.

Chapter 21 – Consequences

Ever since the First Interstellar Expansion Era it has been a policy of the Empire that if any species attacks a human world, they will bring the full might of the Empire down on them.

-Excerpt from Empire Rising, 3002 AD

2nd July, 2466 AD, HMS *Endeavour*, in orbit around Vestar

"The mission was a success," James said through the COM channel to Agent Bell and Lieutenant Scott. They were sitting around a table in the Resistance base alongside Tak'ar, Mul'li'la and Jil'lal. With James in *Endeavour's* main briefing room sat Ferguson, Mallory, Becket and Major Johnston.

"Jil'lal's decryption program worked wonders," James continued. "We managed to get our hands on some vital information. The Overlord's fleet does consist of two hundred and twelve ships. Ninety four of those are of the design we have classed as cruisers and the rest are their smaller frigates. They left their hiding places just over two weeks ago and set course for the Kulrean homeworld Kulthar.

"Lady Luck was with us for we also managed to get our hands on their flight plan so we now know the shift passages that lead to Kulthar. Their flight plan indicates that they will reach their target in a little over a month. If we left right now we could be there in four weeks. My plan is to take *Endeavour* to Kulthar and warn the Kulreans about the impending attack. They may be pacifists but I'm sure in the face of extinction or enslavement they may reconsider their values.

"However, before we go I plan to confront the Overlord. The information we have gathered from the construction yard confirms that the ships that attacked Haven were built there and that the Overlord ordered the attack. I don't plan to let him off lightly, he will learn that there are consequences for attacking a human world.

"That is why I have requested this meeting Tak'ar. I want to know how we can best hurt the Overlord and help your resistance."

Tak'ar didn't even have to think about his response. "With the truth Captain," he said. "If our people can see the truth, about what the Overlord is really like and what he is up too, I know our numbers will swell."

"And how do we get the truth out there?" James asked.

"That is something we have been working on for the last decade," Mul'li'la answered. "We believe we have found a way to hack into the planetary communication systems and transmit a message to every home on the planet. All we have been waiting for is something that will be convincing enough to lead to a full scale rebellion."

James slowly considered their various options. "We have images of the attack on Haven and recordings from the construction yard. Will they be enough to expose the Overlord?" he asked.

"They will help," Tak'ar said, "but they won't be enough. The Overlord can just dismiss them as fabrications or blame them on his subordinates. We need to expose him directly. I believe you need to confront him personally."

"Right," James said, "I'm not sure he will grant us another audience, not after we attacked his construction yard."

"No," Tak'ar agreed, "you will need to get his attention."

"Hmm," James said, "I think we can come up with a few ideas, let us put together a number of plans and we can run them past you."

"That would be acceptable," Tak'ar said.

"Assuming we can get the Overlord to speak to us, if we can stream the images to you, can you distribute them across your planet?" James asked.

"Yes, Mul'li'la answered, "we have the infrastructure in place. The Overlord's men will be able to shut us out eventually but we will be able to make sure everyone who wants to see will be able to."

"Very well," James said. "What is our next move after that?"

"We need to take out as many of their military bases as possible, can your ship help us with that?" Tak'ar asked.

"We have already identified a number of targets we may be able to hit. We don't want to risk hitting any of your population centers. If you can identify any more military targets that fit those parameters we can add them to our list," James said.

"That will work," Tak'ar said. "We already have resistance cells in place to neutralize a number of the main military bases in the big cities. If you can take out the outlying bases and supply depots it will give us a big advantage.

"Our main problem will be the Overlord himself. We can take out as many of his troops as we like but if he still lives and holds the capital, he can just churn out more troops."

"Then we need to take the palace," James said. "Do you have enough people on the ground for that?"

"No," Tak'ar said bowing his head. "We have enough to launch an assault on the palace, especially if we can rally more to our cause. But I don't think we can overcome the defenses. They are just too strong."

"Captain, may I interject?" Mallory asked.

"Of course," James answered.

"I have been monitoring the defenses of the palace in my spare time and I think that with a big enough distraction, our shuttles could punch through their air defenses and drop a team of marines within the palace. If we could get a team close enough we could capture or kill the Overlord and end his rule," Mallory said.

James was impressed. This was the first time he had seen Mallory take any initiative beyond what his responsibilities required of him. "Thank you Lieutenant," he said, "that could work. I think Major Johnston would have to look over your findings and formulate a plan of attack, but if it is possible, cutting the head off the snake is always the best solution.

"I would be honored to join the attack myself," Tak'ar said.

"It is settled then," James said. "I will seek an audience with the Overlord today, then we will begin our attack on their military outposts tomorrow. If we can take the palace with a surprise attack then that will be our priority. We are on a tight schedule though. If we are going to leave for Kulthar to give the Kulreans enough of a warning, we need to break orbit within the next three days. Can your cells begin their operations that quickly Tak'ar?"

"Yes, we will be ready," the Resistance leader answered.

"Can I make one more suggestion?" Lieutenant Scott said.

"Go on," James prompted. Her analysis of the Vestarians had been spot on so far. Despite the blow her confidence had taken when it had proven more difficult than she had predicted to track the fleet that had attacked Haven, Scott had been growing more and more proficient in her command skills and decision-making. He was sure her suggestion would be useful.

"I think we need to prioritize another target as well. The Overlord has a facility in the Kal'dar Mountains north of the capital called the Omen Initiative. The Resistance has managed to get some information on the facility's location but nothing else. I think this facility is the key to the advanced tech the Overlord's ships are using. I believe an alien ship, possibly a Kulrean one, crashed landed on Vestar two hundred years ago at the site of the Omen Initiative. If there is a ship there it could hold technologies of extreme importance."

"What do you think Tak'ar?" James asked.

"The Omen Initiative is not an important military target, but if there is a Kulrean spaceship there then I think we need to find out. We don't have the manpower to attack it, nor do we have any resistance cells in place to launch a strike but if you can provide assistance then we could add it to our list of targets."

"I don't think we can pass up such an opportunity, Scott and Bell, you two can have the privilege of leading the team that takes on the Omen Initiative."

As everyone else got up to leave Ferguson came over to James and said, "Can I have a private word with you Captain?"

"Certainly," James said. "Why don't we step into my office."

James walked through the adjoining door into his office and shouted to his steward, "Bring us two black coffees please Fox."

James sat down behind his desk and motioned for Ferguson to sit opposite him. "What do you want to discuss?" he asked.

"This attack on the Overlord, it can't go forward like this," Ferguson, said, cutting straight to the point. "Can't you realize what you are talking about? This is an alien race we have just met and you are about to get deeply involved in their politics, attempt to overthrow their government and kill thousands of their military troops.

"This is way beyond our mandate to capture Chang. I believe we are overstepping our bounds. These kinds of decisions need to be taken by our government and the Admiralty, maybe even the UN. Not a single exploration cruiser more than two hundred light years from Earth."

"Not a single Captain two hundred light years from Earth you mean?" James said.

"Yes, I believe you are overstepping your authority," Ferguson said without flinching. "But I'm also thinking of your career. The rest of the crew might agree with this decision but they are letting what happened at Haven cloud their judgment. You will ultimately be held responsible for whatever happens here. They will not. If this goes badly the Admiralty will use you as a scapegoat. Hell, even if it goes well there could still be a public outcry that we attacked the homeworld of the first alien race we met. You could overthrow the Overlord and free the Vestarians and still return home to find yourself court martialed."

"What else would you have me do?" James asked quietly, trying to give Ferguson a fair hearing.

"We should return home, let the Admiralty know everything that has gone on here. Our government will want to send out a diplomatic team to make contact with the Vestarians and the Overlord. Maybe they can achieve some success where we failed," Ferguson suggested.

"And the Kulreans, what about them?" James pushed.

"When we release the details about the planned attack on their homeworld their satellite will be able to transmit the information to their homeworld far faster than we could ever get there," Ferguson responded.

"And what if they don't pick up our broadcast, or they don't believe the information? We don't know how they think. Would you just leave them to their fate?" James said, trying to hide his shock that Ferguson would contemplate not warning the Kulreans.

"Let's be realistic," Ferguson pleaded, becoming aware that the conversation wasn't going well. "The Kulreans appear to be far more advanced than us. If the Overlord's fleet attacked Earth or one of our main colonies the defenders would blow them out of the water. If we go to Kulthar we will likely find that the Overlord's fleet has become a new debris field in their star system. If we are not careful they might even add us to the debris field."

"Again, that's assuming they actually have weapons technology," James said with a hint of exasperation. "Lieutenant Scott's best scans of the satellite in orbit indicate that it doesn't have any offensive or defensive weapons. Everything the Vestarians know about the Kulreans suggests they are committed pacifists. We can't turn a blind eye to their situation. The Royal Navy has a tradition of honor and duty. We always protect the helpless; I don't think that changes just because the helpless are a civilization of aliens we don't even know. Our discoveries over the last few weeks suggest that there could be a whole host of alien civilizations out there. Don't we want humans to be known as the race that will help the weak and bring freedom to the oppressed?"

"I don't disagree with you Captain," Ferguson said, "but I still don't think we have the authority to make the Kulreans our problem. It must be up to the Admiralty to decide. We need to put our interests and safety first."

"Ok," James said in an effort to try another track. "Have you thought about what will happen when we go home? What will the Admiralty decide to do?"

"Well, I presume whatever the government will instruct them to do," Ferguson answered.

"And how will the government decide?" James queried.

"They will likely debate it in parliament and take in public opinion," Ferguson said.

"And the UN, will they not have their say? May they not ban individual nations from contacting the Vestarians and the Kulreans? Or maybe they will try to put together a multinational team to go and meet with the Overlord.

"How long do you think all that would take? Three months for us to get home. Another three months to debate the issues in parliament. Maybe another month or two to put together a fleet to come back to Vestar. In all it would take the Admiralty almost a year to get any ships back on station here. And if the UN got involved that could stretch to years.

"What do you think the Overlord will be doing in that time? He will conquer the Kulreans, repair his fleet and then set his sights on Haven. Even if we were to return home right now, it would take the Admiralty months to put together a fleet to protect Haven. By that time the Overlord's fleet could be back to Vestar, repaired and well on its way to Haven.

"And don't think he would stop there. We have more than a hundred systems that the Overlord's fleet could attack and overwhelm with ease. His fleet could ravage our colonies before we managed to put together a fleet strong enough to counter it. And during that time he would be sitting back here in Vestar safe and sound, terrorizing his people and building another fleet.

"That is why we need to remove him from power now, while his fleet is away and we have the chance. We can then go to Kulthar and warn the Kulreans but if they don't listen there isn't much we can do. My plan is to return home whatever they decide. But we can't return home with the Overlord in power commanding an operational battle fleet. If we can take out the Overlord then even if his fleet conquers Kulthar and returns to Vestar, they will find themselves without a leader.

"Don't you see? I have no other choice. I don't want to be the one who goes down in history as the first human to start an interstellar war. But I couldn't live with myself if we tuck tail and run and allow the Overlord to wipe out the Kulreans or attack another human world."

"I'm sorry Sir, but I can't agree with this decision," Ferguson said, not willing to look James in the eye. "I wanted to speak to you to change your mind but I see that is impossible. I therefore want to make an official record in the logbook that I do not see this plan of action as consistent with our orders from the Admiralty."

"Very well," James said, surprised and disappointed. He just couldn't understand where Ferguson's attitude was coming from. "Do I need to relieve you of your position as well Lieutenant?"

"No Sir," Ferguson said quickly. "I still respect you and want to serve our crew. If you order me to help in this attack I will do my duty. I just want it on record that I think you are overstepping the authority your orders give you and are placing our ship in unnecessary risk."

"You may enter your thoughts in the log then," James said as he struggled to contain his anger. Up until his last comment James had been ok, but by implying that James' brashness was at the expense of his crew, Ferguson had gone too far. Momentarily, he considered removing Ferguson from his position there and then. Yet the Lieutenant had a perfect record, and James was sure he could still trust the Lieutenant to do his duty, even if he disagreed. "Dismissed Lieutenant," James said once he made up his mind.

*

Several hours later James was sitting in his command chair watching a holo display of Vestar, still considering if he had made the right decision about Ferguson.

"It's time Sir," Julius said, breaking into his thoughts.

"Contact the palace, request an audio link with the Overlord," James said to the COMs officer after taking a moment to prepare himself.

"No response," Sub Lieutenant King said.

"Tactical, target one of their satellites with the plasma cannons, destroy it," James ordered.

"Target destroyed," Sub Lieutenant Jackson reported.

"COMs, send the message again," James said.

"They have responded Sir, it's not pleasant, something about the heritage of your mother," Sub Lieutenant King said.

"Ok Jackson, destroy them all," James said with a feral smile.

"Engaging."

"Captain, the Kulrean satellite is sending out a tachyon beam," the sensors officer said.

"That's ok Lieutenant, the more they see the better, maybe it will force them to consider defending themselves."

"I have the Overlord on a COM channel," King said.

"Cease firing," James ordered, "put the Overlord on the main holo display."

"You sniveling piece of alien vermin, how dare you attack one of my satellites. Do you not know who I am? I will destroy your ship and your entire world you puny human," the Overlord boomed across the COM channel. Even though the aliens looked very different to humans James had no trouble telling the Overlord was extremely pissed off.

"Ah, your excellency," James began in a pleasant tone. "I'm glad you have finally agreed to talk with me. Though I must confess, I don't understand why you are so concerned about a few cheap satellites when my ship just destroyed two of your warships and infiltrated your secret construction yard on the edge of the system. I would have thought that was more upsetting to you. Here, let me send you the recordings of what we found hidden in the asteroid field."

"No..." the Overlord began and then bit his tongue as he saw the information had already been transmitted.

"Sir, I'm picking up another tachyon beam from the satellite," King informed him loud enough for the Overlord to hear over the open COM channel.

James smiled. "I think the Kulreans have been monitoring our conversation and have seen something that has caught their interest," he said to the Overlord.

The Overlord had been looking at something off screen but when he looked back at James his eyes were smoldering with hatred. "You don't realize what you have done. You will pay for this."

"On the contrary, I know exactly what I have done. You and your secret fleet attacked and bombarded my people's planet. You have now sent that same fleet to bombard and enslave the Kulreans. It is time you paid for your crimes," James said with deadly intent.

The Overlord shocked James as he burst out laughing, "What are you going to do to me? I have the technology of the ancients protecting my palace. You can bombard my cities all you want. Those weak enough to get themselves killed can easily be replaced. They mean nothing to me. In two months my fleet will return with the technology of the Kulreans to add to that of the ancients and they will drive you from our planet. Then I will personally come and put an end to your world you puny human."

"So be it, you threatened my world again. You leave me no other choice but to ensure you can hurt no one else. We will not see each other again but a new friend of mine will be coming to visit you real soon. You may know his name. Tak'ar."

If the situation hadn't been so grave James would have been tempted to burst out laughing at the change that come over the Overlord's face. His rage was momentarily gone and in its place was a look of utter confusion. "How do you know..." the Overlord began before he cut himself off and the look of pure rage returned.

"Enough of this, do your worst you human vermin," the Overlord shouted and cut the transmission.

James took a moment to compose himself and then opened a COM channel to Tak'ar's base. "Did you get all you need?" he asked.

"Yes," Jil'lal said excitedly, "Mul'li'la is recording a message to go out with the broadcast and we will also be sharing your images of the attack on Haven and the construction yard. It's all being uploaded now and will go live in two minutes."

"Very well, we will begin the second phase of the plan in eight hours as we arranged," James said.

"We thank you for your help," Jil'lal said.

"It is our pleasure. We wish to see our people protected from the threat of attack as much as you wish to see yours freed from tyranny," James replied as he closed the COM channel.

Chapter 22 – The Omen

Today any orbital bombardment is strictly forbidden, but that wasn't always the case.

-Excerpt from Empire Rising

2nd July, 2466 AD, HMS *Endeavour*, in orbit around Vestar

After returning to his quarters for a brief rest James made his way to the bridge an hour before things were meant to kick off. "Have we heard anything from Mul'li'la about how transmitting the Overlord's conversation went?" he asked.

"Yes Sir," Sub Lieutenant King responded. "She has reported that the Resistance is already seeing a surge in support. The Overlord's lackeys have gone into over drive in an effort to put out their own propaganda but so far it doesn't seem to be having any real effect."

"Perfect," James said taking his seat. "And Tak'ar is ready to go?"

"He is still getting his forces into position but they are on schedule," Julius reported.

"Ok, one more hour then," James said and brought up the operational plans to go over them again as he waited.

Exactly an hour later he looked up to see everyone on the bridge staring at him. "Julius," he said to the Third Lieutenant who was manning the tactical station. "Begin operation Overlord."

"Aye Sir," Julius replied.

With a push of a button Julius powered up the flak cannons and locked them onto their targets. After the RSN had carried out a number of raids on Chinese worlds in the Void War it had become apparent that RSN ships needed a more refined weapon for bombarding planetary targets. *Endeavour,* like all RSN warships, was equipped with a limited supply of ground attack missiles. Almost identical to the ship killer missiles she carried, the only difference was that the nuclear warhead was replaced with a solid valstronium core. With the valstronium core added to the mass of the missile, it was capable of creating a five kiloton explosion when accelerated into a planet. The force of the explosion would destroy everything within a mile radius without the residual radiation of a nuclear missile.

The problem with the attacks on the Chinese worlds, as with many of their targets on Vestar, was that often civilian populations surrounded military targets. A valstronium tipped missile would therefore cause far too much damage.

The solution the RSN designers had come up with had been simple. A small modification to the flak cannons allowed them to fire much smaller tungsten spears at ground targets. The flak cannons were essentially electromagnetic cannons that fired explosive shells and the change in their design had only taken a few weeks to test and roll out.

Once they were powered up Julius fired the first two rounds from the flak cannons. On the ground Tak'ar was waiting near the military base that controlled the city of Zekath with a Vestarian camera recording the outcome. Everyone on the bridge saw the two rounds burst through the atmosphere, leaving a trail of fire, and impact right in the center of the military base. As soon as the rounds impacted the visual feed cut off as the light from the explosion overloaded the camera. When the feed came back up one giant fireball was slowly making its way up into the atmosphere. The camera feed was blurry and shaking as whoever was holding it was knocked about by the concussive force of the impacts. Even so, it was clear that the giant military structure that housed the garrison of Zekath was no more. Its two spires slowly toppled onto the ground and the explosions had already blown out the walls, letting the camera see into the compound. A number of the outer most buildings still stood but the vast majority of the compound had been turned to rubble.

As the initial fireball began to pull in on itself Tak'ar stood in front of the camera. "Now is the time to end the Overlord's rule of oppression and murder," he shouted over the din of the secondary explosions. "To freedom," he bellowed as hefted his weapon in the air and charged towards the burning military compound.

Hundreds of resistance fighters jumped to their feet from where they had been hiding and followed Tak'ar. James knew that throughout the city other resistance cells would be carrying out simultaneous attacks on various military outposts and stations. If the majority of them proved successful, the Resistance would have liberated the first city from the Overlord's control in two hundred years.

"They certainly know how to put on a good show," Ferguson said from the command chair beside him.

"That they do," James said, not sure if Ferguson was genuine or was just trying to show he was able to get on board with the operation despite his misgivings. Things had been more than a little frosty since their frank conversation a day ago.

"Alert our targets that they are next, then fire the ten ground attack missiles," James ordered once he was satisfied they didn't need to fire any more tungsten spears at their first target.

The ten valstronium missiles were aimed at important military facilities that were well away from civilian centers. Tak'ar had agents at two of the targets ready to record the missiles' impacts. Everything was being sent back to Mul'li'la to be transmitted around the planet. James was going to give the ten military outposts they were targeting a chance to evacuate, if they heeded his warning they would have ten minutes to get clear.

As the missiles were fired from *Endeavour's* missile tubes James looked over to Ferguson, "there is no going back now. Those missiles will crush the Overlord's main military formations. If we do not see this through now the entire planet will collapse into a long and bloody civil war."

"I understand Sir, I will execute my orders to the best of my ability," Ferguson said, though to James's ears it sounded forced.

*

4th July, 2466 AD, forty kilometers from Amack, Vestar

Two days later Bell, Scott, Becket and Johnston were gathered beside one of *Endeavour's* shuttles just outside one of the Resistance bases near the capital of Amack.

"Good luck ladies," Johnston said to Bell and Scott, "I hope to see you two back here in a few hours, make sure you are both in one piece."

"And may Lady Luck be with you," Bell said, clapping the Major on his shoulder. "Make sure you bring back Becket to us in one piece. We both know she is good at getting herself into trouble," she added, winking at Becket.

"It's time to go," Jil'lal called to Bell and Scott from where she was standing with Tak'ar.

Bell waved to acknowledge and then saluted Becket and Johnston, "Do us proud," she said as she turned and jogged over to Jil'lal with Scott at her side.

"Happy hunting," Bell said to Tak'ar as she passed him.

It seemed as if the Resistance leader had been everywhere over the last two days. After freeing Zekath almost all of the main cities on the southern continent had risen up in rebellion against the Overlord. They had formed their own country before the Kulreans came and there was still a strong sense of national identity. Tak'ar had used it to his advantage. He had been tireless since he had liberated his home city. At Zekath they had captured a number of military transports intact and he had been making great use of them, transporting combatants to aid in the various uprisings. He had also personally taken over the job of directing *Endeavour's* fire from the ground.

Bell was sure that whoever was commanding *Endeavour's* weapons was getting worn out by Tak'ar's constant fire orders. Their ship had been assisting almost all of the uprisings with orbital strikes from her flak cannons and even plasma cannon strikes against individual military formations. The Overlord's military had quickly given up using their own military transports to bring in reinforcements for every time one tried to lift off plasma bolts rained down from the sky and destroyed it.

Now Tak'ar was here, near the capital, ready to play out the final steps in his revolution. Just several hours ago a number of cities near the capital had erupted in riots and attacks against the local military forces. It was hoped that they would distract the Overlord as Tak'ar moved his forces into position to assault the capital and the palace.

That is for Major Johnston and Becket to worry about, Bell told herself, *time to focus on this Omen.*

With one last look at the marines and Vestarians who were gathered around the landing zone waiting for their mission to begin, Bell jumped into her shuttle and strapped herself in.

Endeavour's shuttles were the only ones that had the weapons to fight their way through the defenses of the Omen Installation and the Palace so they would drop off Bell, Scott, Jil'lal and their team before returning and picking up the force that would be assaulting the palace.

It was only a ten minute flight to their target, when they were three minutes out the shuttle pilot called out, "for anyone who is interested, the fireworks are about to begin."

Both Bell and Becket watched in silence but Jil'lal let out a slight gasp. She had seen the images from the other attacks but they didn't compare to real life. Seemingly out of nowhere a single fireball shot down through the sky and impacted the mountainside about ten kilometers in front of them. A colossal mushroom cloud filled with fire shot into the air and the concussion wave could be seen rolling across the mountains and the valleys.

"Such power," Jil'lal said. "Your one ship could force its will on our entire planet."

"If we were willing to use it on civilians," Bell said. "Thankfully all the Earth nations have signed strict agreements limiting the use of orbital bombardment weapons."

"Yes, but what if there are other races out there that don't think as you do? After this is over my people will have to prepare defenses to make sure no one else can ever do this to us."

"That would be wise," Bell agreed.

"The show's not over yet," the pilot called as he dropped the shuttle into a nearby valley and hugged the terrain as they made their final approach.

As the smoke cloud from the impact broke apart, green plasma bolts rained down around the facility, taking out any defensive installations that hadn't been damaged by the orbital strike. The Resistance info indicated that the actual Omen facility was deep under the valley floor, thus the orbital strike had just taken out the structures that were above ground. They had mainly consisted of a military barracks and large anti-air cannons.

"Here we go," the pilot shouted as he lifted the shuttle's nose and rocketed through a gap between two mountains. He banked the shuttle hard to the left, diving into the valley that held the complex. Almost as soon as they entered the valley, small interceptor missiles began to rise from a number of surviving anti-air batteries.

Sensing the target acquisition radar, the shuttle's computer automatically powered up its ECM and began to launch flares while it powered up its two point defense plasma cannons. The pilot reacted almost as quickly as he threw the shuttle into a number of evasive rolls and turns to throw off the tracking radar.

More plasma bolts rained down and destroyed the remaining missile batteries that had just given away their position but Bell's focus was on the incoming missiles. One seemed to lose its track on the shuttle and flew off in another direction. The plasma cannons took out another but a third was still homing in on the shuttle.

The pilot realized that they weren't going to be able to dodge it and five seconds out from impact he leveled off the shuttle and gave the missile a clear target. With the flick of a switch he extended the shuttle's main plasma cannon and fired off a stream of bolts just as the missile leveled off its ascent and prepared to intercept the shuttle. The first two bolts missed but the third and fourth hit the missile and it exploded.

Everyone was thrown about by the explosion and more than one loud thud echoed through the shuttle as debris bounced off the hull.

"Whhhooo, that was fun!" the pilot shouted.

"Shut up," Bell shouted back as she gave him more than a playful punch on the shoulder, "just get us down safely."

As they neared the wreckage of the military facilities a number of alarms went off and a small explosion threw everyone about in their seats.

"Small arms fire," the pilot reported. "There are still some Vestarians alive down there, they must have those laser rifles we saw in the construction yard."

Without further explaining himself the pilot veered the shuttle skywards away from the ground fire. The second shuttle followed suit and together they turned and dived towards the ground with their main plasma cannons extended.

Bell could see that the pilot had shifted his view to the infrared sensor screen and as she watched he methodically took out all the heat blips. He must have updated the targeting parameters of the shuttle's computer for it fired off the shuttle's ground attack missiles at heat sources not directly in the shuttle's line of sight.

After the first strafing run the shuttles split up and circled the landing site, taking out any stragglers. Once the danger was passed, Bell shifted her attention to the wrecked ground facilities. "Over there," she said, pointing towards what looked like two large retractable doors built right into the edge of a cliff that lined the valley floor. "Blow us a hole through them, I bet the research facility is under there."

"Yes Mam," the shuttle pilot said as he swung the shuttle towards his new target and fired a stream of plasma bolts into the doors, blowing a massive hole in them.

"Put us down beside those doors," Bell ordered.

The six marines in combat armor were the first out of the shuttle, plasma rifles raised as they searched out targets. Bell and Scott jumped out after them. Only the marines and Lieutenant Becket had their own combat armor onboard *Endeavour* so they were both wearing military grade battle suits. The suits would give them some protection from projectile rounds but they didn't have the armor of the marine's equipment or provide the enhancements to speed and strength that the marines would enjoy.

Behind Bell and Scott, Jil'lal jumped out of the shuttle followed by ten Resistance fighters. From the other shuttle another twenty resistance fighters disembarked and quickly sprinted over to Jil'lal.

"Lead on Sergeant," Bell said to Harkin once their team had assembled.

Sergeant Harkin took off towards the ruined doors that led into the cliff. Without even looking, the first two marines threw stun grenades through the doors and the rest quickly charged through.

Bell was close behind them but when she got through the doors she was already too late; the marines had dispatched the four Vestarians who had been guarding the entrance.

"Where do we go from here?" Harkin asked as he gestured to the back of the large entryway. It seemed as if the retractable doors opened into a large receiving area where goods and materials could be offloaded. Scattered around the room were a number of crates filled with various materials. At the back of the receiving area on opposite ends of the room were two doors that clearly led in different directions.

"Scott?" Bell asked.

"Already on it," the science officer responded as she brought out a case from her backpack. Opening it and setting it on the ground she pulled out her datapad, after a few seconds of tapping on it, the case seemed to come alive as more than a hundred small objects flew into the air and began to buzz around the chamber.

"These little critters will map out the rest of the structure," she said to the amazed Vestarians. With another tap the micro drones shot off towards the two doors and began to explore the rest of the facility.

"Take cover while we wait for the drones to do their work," Harkin said as he found a good spot from where he could lay down fire on the two doors. "How long will they take?" he asked.

"Depends on the size of the facility," Scott answered. "At least another couple of minutes. Hold on, one of the drones has spotted several Vestarians coming towards the left door."

"Heads up everyone," Harkin called. "Wait for them to clear the doorway."

Thirty seconds later eight Vestarians came rushing through the door, carrying laser rifles and wearing impressive looking battle suits of their own. When they saw their fallen comrades in the middle of the chamber they began to get behind cover.

"Open fire," Harkin shouted, putting action to his words. His first two plasma bolts caught one of the rearmost defenders in the chest before he could reach cover. Plasma bolts and projectiles from the resistance fighters caught all but one of the other defenders.

"Keep him pinned down, we're flanking him," Jal'tak, the leader of the resistance fighters said over the COM units Harkin had provided them with.

As Harkin fired a series of plasma bolts into the crate the defender was hiding behind he couldn't help letting out a whistle at Jal'tak as he sprinted towards the defender, hurdling the last crate in his way he landed right beside the defender and fired a number of rounds from his weapon at point blank range. Harkin could match Jal'tak's movements with the aid of his combat armor but unaided it was clear the Vestarians would outclass even highly trained marines.

"It looks like both doors lead to different facilities," Scott announced once the fighting was over. "They don't seem to connect except for up here."

"Then we split up," Bell said. "Harkin, you and your marines can search the facility on your right. I want you to take five Vestarians with you too. We'll leave six here to guard our exit. We'll take Jal'tak and the rest with us and search the facility through the left door.

"If you find anything that sheds any light on the Overlord's advanced technology alert us and I'll send Scott to you with an escort of Vestarians."

"Understood," Harkin said. "Samuels, you take point," he called out as he trotted off towards the right door.

"After you," Bell said to Jal'tak out of a new found respect for the Vestarian's combat abilities as she made her way to the left door.

"Did you detect any more defenders with your drones?" she asked Scott.

"There are over two hundred more Vestarians within both facilities," Scott answered. "I have uploaded the information to Harkin's combat armor so he has the tactical data too."

"Good job," Bell responded.

The drones made their advancement into the facility far easier than it would have been. The corridors and rooms appeared to be built into the cliff face along a number of veins in the rock that must have been easier to excavate and so had no logical structure. The drones also alerted them to two ambushes the defenders had set up for them.

By the time they cleared the fourth large chamber they came to, Bell guessed that they had taken out all the defenders. Every Vestarian in the chamber they were now in had been an unarmed scientist. None of them had been willing to tell them what work they had been involved in and the resistance fighters had tied them up and left them.

"The next chamber is the largest in either facility," Scott announced once they were ready to proceed again. "Though my drones haven't been able to access it, they have been able to map out its exterior. If we're going to find anything it is likely to be in there."

"Let's keep moving then," Jil'lal said.

After carefully passing through another forty meters of twisting corridors they came to a set of automatic doors that wouldn't open for them. Jil'lal attached one of the portable computers she had brought with her to the door and spent over a minute trying to override its security protocols. "I'm sorry," she said as she disconnected from the door's terminal. "I can't crack it."

"Stand back," Bell said as she reached into her back pack and placed a shaped charge around the door. "Everyone around the corner," she added.

After she set the charge she retreated with everyone else. Thirty seconds later an explosion sent a shockwave down the small corridor forcing everyone to their knees. "That should do it," Jil'lal said.

Bell was the first one up and through the door. "Oh crap," she said as she walked through, forgetting to check for any defenders. The object in the middle of the room was unmistakably a space ship. It was more than twice the size of the shuttle they had landed in.

"What is it?" Jil'lal asked.

"It's not Vestarian," Scott said, "at least it's like nothing we have seen the Overlord build yet."

"That's valstronium armor," Bell said, "and those have to be weapon ports. Can it be a Kulrean ship? I thought they were pacifists?"

Scott had brought out another one of her datapads and was using it to take scans of the ship. "I'm not sure, the satellite didn't have valstronium armor and I'm reading a very different power signature than anything I got from the satellite."

"What are those power cables for?" Jil'lal asked pointing at two large cables that came out from under the ship and led to a large holo projector.

Bell walked over to the projector and hit a few buttons until it powered up.

"Greetings," a pleasant voice said from the projector.

"Who are you?" it said in a sterner tone. "I am detecting unauthorized Vestarians in this chamber. Beginning emergency protocols."

Bolts of electricity danced along the ship's surface and shot into the chamber. In a couple of seconds all the Vestarians in their group had gone down, knocked unconscious by the lightning bolts.

"You two are not Vestarian," the voice said to a stunned Bell and Becket.

"No," Bell said, "what are you?"

"I am the ship's artificial intelligence. I have been designed to interface with authorized Vestarians. Accessing species datafile," the voice said.

"Human," it shouted in what sounded like anger. "Beginning emergency self-destruct protocol."

"Oh crap," Bell said for the second time in a matter of minutes.

"I'm detecting an immense energy surge," Scott shouted. "We need to get out of here now."

Bell looked at the unconscious Vestarians. "We can't leave Jil'lal," she shouted. "Quick you take one side and I'll get the other.

Together they hefted the surprisingly light alien and ran as quickly as they could out of the chamber and along the winding corridors that led out of the facility. As they went Bell activated her COM unit, "Harkin, we triggered some sort of self-destruct mechanism, you need to evac now. We're on our way out."

"Acknowledged," Harkin replied. "We're moving now."

As they burst into another one of the large chambers they had already cleared, alarms began to go off all around them. "Self-destruct initiated," a prerecorded Vestarian voice announced. "Please leave the facility now. Self-destruct initiated..." it continued.

Bell and Scott instinctively picked up speed and tumbled down into a heap on the floor. Scott looked around to see what happened and found one of the scientists they had tied up had managed to trip Bell. Even as Bell shook herself the scientist grabbed her despite the fact that his hands were still tied. Another two scientists shuffled across the floor towards her as well.

"Untie us," they shouted. "Don't leave us here to die."

Bell tried to fight them off but even with their hands tied they managed to get a strong grip on her.

"Ok, ok," she shouted. "Stop fighting. Scott, get Jil'lal out of here. I will be right behind you."

"I'm not leaving you," Scott said as she started towards Bell.

"I said get Jil'lal out," Bell shouted.

Scott was taken aback at Bell's anger. She just wanted to help. Then she remembered something Bell had told her while they were discussing her hopes to captain her own ship someday. Bell had told her that a real leader had to know when to put their own feelings aside and make tough decisions.

Scott guessed that was what Bell was doing now. She was putting her own safety behind that of the scientists they had tied up. Now Scott had to do the same. She didn't want to leave Bell behind, yet she had to look after the unconscious Jil'lal.

"Ok," Scott said to Bell as she lifted Jil'lal over her shoulder. "Just hurry."

Bell didn't hear her. She had already pulled out her combat knife and turned back to the scientists.

Once Scott had Jil'lal in place she took off again. When she reached the entrance she saw Sergeant Harkin and two of his marines were already there, standing by what was left of the large retractable doors.

"The rest of my team are outside, where is Agent Bell?" he asked with concern.

"She is freeing some of the scientists we captured, she should be right behind me," Scott said.

"Come on," Harkin said to the two marines with him as he raced past her back into the facility.

A massive tremor reverberated through the facility, throwing Scott to her knees. Air rushed past her, out the hole in the retractable doors, and a deep rumbling could be heard from within the facility. Scott instinctively hefted Jil'lal over her shoulder and ran to the door. When she reached it she threw Jil'lal to one side and turned back to look for Bell and Sergeant Harkin.

She looked just in time to see a massive fireball erupt from the back of the entrance chamber, wash over Harkin and his marines and then burst over her. For a moment she felt herself lifted up into the air and thrust out of the chamber before an intense heat engulfed her. She screamed as it felt like a thousand knives were being shoved into every part of her body yet as she sucked in a breath to continue to scream all she inhaled was a fire that burnt its way into her lungs. The pain knocked her unconscious and she didn't feel her body crash into the rocks as the explosion finally dumped her onto the ground almost a hundred yards from the entrance.

Chapter 23 – The Palace

One would have thought that as the human race continued to better itself tyrants would have become a thing of the past, sadly this is a problem we have never seemed able to shake. More than one Emperor has been found to have been tainted with the disease. Perhaps unsurprisingly the many sentient species we have come to know all seem to suffer from this problem too.

-Excerpt from Empire Rising, 3002 AD

4th July, 2466 AD, five kilometers from Amack, Vestar

Becket was once again sitting beside Major Johnston on their way into a combat situation. She felt she was finally getting used to these ground missions. After the firefight in the construction yard, the marines had started to treat her with a lot more respect and she had a lot more confidence in herself. That didn't stop her from reliving those moments again and again as she dealt with the fact that she had ended another sentient being's life.

"I've just got a message from the Forward Operating Base," the shuttle pilot informed everyone over the COM channel. "There are reports coming in of an explosion at the Omen Facility. We have been instructed to head straight there after we drop off your assault team. We need to pick up the survivors."

Survivors, Becket said to herself in shock as she tried not to assume the worst. Silently, she said a prayer for Bell and Scott.

"We're not here for a Sunday stroll," Johnston said to his marines. "This is real, we already know the Vestarian soldiers can fight. Don't get distracted. We can worry about our friends later."

As he finished speaking he reached out and touched Becket's arm. She nodded back at him and shook herself. *The best thing I can do now for Bell and Scott is complete this mission and get back to them alive*, she thought.

Looking out the front view screen of the shuttle Becket could see the spires of the city as they approached. As arranged, Tak'ar's people on the ground were rioting and attacking the Overlord's military forces in the outer sections of the city. She could make out the brief flashes of fire from the tungsten spears *Endeavour* was launching at the city along with the green plasma bolts that were pouring down on the city's defenses. They were designed to make it look like the resistance was trying to fight its way through the city to the palace. It was hoped the Overlord would push his forces out into the city to beat back the rebellion and leave the door open for the two shuttles to punch through the palace's defenses and allow their strike team to capture the Overlord.

When they came to within ten kilometers of the city, the two shuttles dived to almost ground level and hugged the terrain. The attack on the Omen Facility had taught the pilots to stay out of sight of the Vestarian ground to air missiles. Images of the palace taken by the team that had met with the Overlord showed that there were over twenty x-ray lasers on heavy mounts protecting the approaches to the palace. They looked like they were designed to take out any approaching ground forces but there was little doubt they could be tasked to hit an incoming shuttle as it slowed down to land. Thankfully they had a plan for that too.

"Targeting data is coming in now," the pilot called, "selecting the best line of approach."

Major Johnston didn't say anything and Becket wasn't surprised. This part of the mission was another ruse. As the shuttles entered the outer sections of the city they split up and began to make a number of strafing runs against positions that were holding out against the resistance fighters. The aim was to convince the defenders that the shuttles were only there to provide back up for the ground forces.

For the next five minutes the shuttles made their way from one target to another, slowly moving closer to the palace. Twice Becket's shuttle came up against mobile ground to air missile platforms and had to duck behind one of the city's large buildings and divert to another target but they escaped unscathed.

"Time to move everyone, we're only three minutes from the palace now," the pilot shouted after taking out a small formation of soldiers with the shuttle's plasma cannon.

"Do it," Johnston replied.

Both shuttles boosted up their engines and veered towards the palace. Each shuttle had released two drones that they had brought for this purpose. When the palace defenders detected the two incoming shuttles the commander ordered the x-ray lasers powered up. The drones were hovering in the area and as soon as the lasers showed up on their heat sensors they fed the information back to the shuttles.

"The drones have detected twenty two lasers," the shuttle pilot informed Johnston and Becket. "We're launching now."

Out one of the side observation ports Becket watched as a compartment on the shuttle's wing opened to reveal a rack of missiles. She knew they contained very sophisticated guidance systems but this time all they would need was their heat sensors to be able to lock onto the data from the drones. She counted six missiles launch from the rack and knew another six had been launched from the other wing of the shuttle. *That will take care of that*, she thought.

"Targets destroyed," the shuttle pilot called out thirty seconds later. "We have another problem though, the drones are detecting at least fifty guards setting up around the stairs up to the palace with handheld lasers. We know from the construction yard they can do us some damage."

"Switch to plan gamma," Johnston said.

"Acknowledged," the pilot responded. He took a couple of seconds to check the feed from the drones and then spoke to the other shuttle pilot, "LZ X2 seems clear, let's put them down there."

Becket didn't hear the other pilot's response but she assumed he agreed for both shuttles banked and rapidly decelerated.

As the shuttles touched down in an open space at the foot of one of the Vestarian's massive towers, Johnston keyed the COM channel to speak to the marines in both shuttles. "This is where we get off, the palace is just one klick to our west. Alpha squad will take point. Lead us off as soon as you form up."

"Yes Sir," Sergeant Jones said from alpha squad.

Becket made sure she stayed close to Johnston as she disembarked and made her way to the palace. The marines approached at a brisk jog that covered the distance in less than a minute with the aid of their combat armor. Becket was impressed to see that Tak'ar and the ten Vestarians he had brought with him were able to keep up. They were panting hard when Sergeant Jones signaled for the group to halt.

"The palace is just round the corner," Jones reported over the COM.

"Spread out into squads," Johnston ordered and waited for the marines to spread out and get into good firing positions. "Wait for the shuttles," he added.

"Go time," Johnston said over the COM channel to the pilots.

"On our way," came the response.

With the aid of her combat armor's enhanced hearing Becket was sure she heard the now familiar hum of the shuttles' engines boosting them into the air. As she listened it came closer and closer until the shuttles came into view. They were already launching more of their ground attack missiles, obviously using the feeds from the drones to take out the defenders. As they flew overhead the pilots peppered the palace defenses with plasma bolts.

"Pick your targets carefully," Johnston said, "we'll only have a few seconds of surprise. Once we reach the bottom of the stairs use your grenades. Move, move, move!"

The four squads of marines leapt from cover and charged the palace. As Becket jumped up she couldn't help but take a moment to take in the palace before them. The stairs alone looked like the wall of a fortress as they loomed over her, going up for more than three hundred feet. At their top she could see a number of makeshift barriers in place with Vestarian guards behind them. Beyond that the tower of the palace blocked everything else from view. It dominated her vision and if she didn't know better it would have been impossible to even guess there were hundreds more towers beyond it. Any one of which would have dwarfed the skyscrapers of Earth.

Lifting her plasma rifle to target the nearest defender she saw Johnston had timed their attack perfectly. As the shuttles banked to retreat many of the defenders stood up from their cover to get a better shot at them. The marines caught them off guard and the first volley of plasma bolts cut down more than twenty of the defenders.

If they had stopped to make the most of their advantage they could have hit more but the marines kept sprinting for the bottom of the stairs and the cover it would provide. As it was a number of the defenders managed to track in on the marines and two went down as lasers blew holes in their combat armor. A resistance fighter joined them before he could make it to the cover of the steps.

When Becket reached the bottom of the giant steps she mimicked the rest of the marines and unhooked one of her high explosive grenades. Without pausing she hurled it up over the stairs. A number of grunts of satisfaction were heard over the COM channel as the grenades exploded amongst the Vestarians who had rushed to the lip of the stairs to get into a position to fire down on the marines.

"Delta squad provide covering fire. Everyone else with me," Johnston said as he leapt up and mounted the stairs three at a time.

Becket jumped up and followed the Major as a barrage of green plasma bolts ripped through the air over their heads. Now and again a Vestarian head could be seen poking above the top of the steps but they disappeared as a plasma bolt hit them or forced them to duck for cover. One managed to get off a shot and another marine hit the ground and rolled back down the stairs. Becket didn't have time to look back and see how badly hurt he was for they were almost at the top.

"Grenades," Johnston called again as he hefted another grenade over the top of the stairs.

The explosions went off just as they crested the top of the stairs and Becket remembered her training just in time to leap into a large jump assisted by the boosters in her armor. The combination of the explosions and the marines suddenly shooting into the air over the last few steps caught the defenders off guard. Three marines were blown back down the stairs by x-ray lasers but the rest opened up on the Vestarians with their plasma rifles, scattering what was left of the defenders.

As Johnston hit the ground a Vestarian jumped out of cover and leveled his laser at the Major but Becket mowed him down before he could pull the trigger. Johnston didn't even notice; he was charging towards the palace doors. A missile from one of the shuttles had battered it in and when Johnston approached he threw two flash bangs through its wreckage.

Pausing only long enough for them to go off, he rushed in followed by five marines with Becket taking up the rear. As she entered the dark of the palace her visor altered its light filters, allowing her to see clearly. With a sigh of relief, she saw that there were no more soldiers defending the entrance.

"The front of the palace is clear," Johnston said over the COM to the marines. "Everyone move up." He switched the COM channel to talk to the shuttle pilots. "We're in, get to the Omen facility," he said.

"Acknowledged," the pilot responded, "we'll be back for you as soon as we pick them up, give the Overlord hell for us."

"You can bet on it," Johnston replied.

"We're going to split up," he said once the rest of the marines and Tak'ar and his men had gathered around him. "The last time we were here our host took us on two different routes into and out of the Overlord's throne room. I'll lead squads alpha and beta and Lieutenant Jeffers and Tak'ar will take his men and the gamma and delta squads. If the Overlord isn't in his throne room we'll fan out and search the rest of the palace, though that may prove impossible."

Becket had to agree, the palace had to be more than a thousand times the size of *Endeavour*, if he wanted to, the Overlord could hide and it could take months to find him.

———

"Don't worry," Tak'ar said. "The Overlord will be there. Even with enemies within the palace he still won't believe he could actually lose. He'll be there."

"Right, well let's get going before any more defenders show up," Johnston ordered.

For five minutes Becket trotted along beside Johnston as their team followed the winding path through the palace that had been uploaded into their combat armor's computer. She came to a sudden halt along with everyone else when the marine who was on point signaled that there was movement up ahead.

Johnston shuffled forward to join the marine. When he peeked around the end of the corridor he immediately ducked back as the wall exploded from a laser hit.

"Becket, contact Lieutenant Jeffers, let him know we have encountered more defenders and to be on the lookout," Johnston ordered. "Sergeant Jones, take your squad and double back, see if you can flank the Vestarians up ahead. Let me know when you are in position."

"Yes Sir," Sergeant Jones said before moving off.

To keep the defenders' attention on him, Johnston poked his plasma rifle around the corner and fired off a couple of quick shots before lobbing a grenade at them.

Two minutes later, after a few more grenades had been thrown, Becket could tell everyone was getting nervous that Sergeant Jones hadn't reported in yet as many of the marines were fidgeting with their guns.

"We're in position," Jones said, breaking the tension. "We encountered another Vestarian patrol, I think they were trying to flank you. We took them out."

"Good work," Johnston said. "Take them when you are ready."

"We're moving in," Jones said.

From down the corridor Becket heard the sound of high explosive grenades going off. Johnston seemed to wait a long time before he led his men around the corner but as usual Becket saw he had timed it perfectly to catch the defenders in a cross fire while their attention was focused on Sergeant Jones' flanking maneuver.

The firepower from both groups overwhelmed the defenders and they were forced to retreat. Johnston and Jones led their marines in pursuit and for the next five minutes a long firefight developed as the defenders fled towards the throne room. One marine took a laser to the leg but the shot must have been fired from beyond the laser's effective range for his armor managed to deflect most of the energy. Another wasn't so lucky and as Becket tended to him she saw that the laser had melted a hole through his armor and burnt off a lot of flesh.

"You'll be alright," she said to him after she upped the pain medication his armor was injecting into his system. As she stood she looked around the open expanse they had fought their way into. *There*, she thought as she saw a corner with a number of Vestarian chairs arranged around it.

"Let me help you to your feet," she said as she hefted the marine. "We'll have to leave you here behind some cover. Don't worry we'll be back for you once we get the Overlord."

"Don't worry about me Lieutenant," the marine said, "I can take care of myself. Just make sure you complete the mission."

"I will," she called to him as she laid him down behind a chair out of sight. With only a quick look back to make sure he wasn't visible from the center of the open area she jogged off to catch up with the rest of the marines.

"I think I got the last of them," Jones said when Becket caught up to the front line, "it looks clear ahead."

"Move out slowly," Johnston cautioned.

As they moved up they didn't encounter any more resistance. "The throne room should be down the next corridor," Johnston said.

"It looks like Lieutenant Jeffers and Tak'ar have beaten us here," Reynolds said from her position on point. Becket understood what she meant as she rounded the corner with Johnston. There were several dead Vestarian guards along with one of Tak'ar's resistance fighters and a dead marine.

"It's Blackfoot," Reynolds said as she rolled over the dead marine.

"Keep going," Johnston said gruffly, not wanting to let Reynold's sorrow penetrate his focus. Ahead it looked like one of the doors to the throne room had been blown open with a shaped charge and the sound of plasma rifle fire could be heard from within.

In a matter of seconds, they were through the door and in the throne room. If Becket had time she would have been even more impressed with the throne room than the outside of the palace. She barely noticed the decorations and carvings though for the room was strewn with dead Vestarians and in the distance she could see the Overlord hiding behind his giant throne. His head was poking out though and he was calling orders to the guards who were standing around him firing volleys of laser beams at their attackers. Lieutenant Jeffer's marines and Tak'ar's Vestarians were weaving their way between the abandoned rows of seats the Overlord's attendants used when he was holding an audience.

"Covering fire," Johnston ordered as he took cover behind one of the back rows of seats and fired into the defenders. The marines got in position and fired a wave of plasma bolts which killed the remaining guards or forced them to take cover. The respite allowed Lieutenant Jeffers and Tak'ar to lead their team in an open charge towards what was left of the defenders.

In a matter of seconds it was over and both Tak'ar and Jeffers were on the central platform aiming their weapons at the Overlord. With the fighting over Johnston stood up and advanced. Becket joined him and together they made their way down the throne room.

"What are they doing?" Becket asked as Tak'ar and his men surrounded the Overlord.

"I'm not sure," Johnston said as he broke into a jog.

When they got close enough their suits were able to pick up what Tak'ar was saying. "In light of the crimes against our people, the embezzlement of billions of credits, the limiting of free speech, the illegal imprisonment of thousands of peaceful protestors, the execution of hundreds of freedom fighters and the reign of terror and fear you have put our entire planet through I sentence you to death by hanging."

"No," Becket shouted as she saw the resistance fighters throw a long rope over one of the beams above the Overlord's throne. "You can't let him do this," she pleaded to Johnston.

With a final burst of speed Johnston was beside the Overlord holding up his hand to Tak'ar. "No Tak'ar, you don't want to do this. This isn't how you want to begin this new era for your people. If you execute him without a trial, you will be just as bad as him. If that happens then he has won."

"Stay out of this Major," Tak'ar said, "you don't know what he did to my parents."

Becket took an involuntary step back at the look of rage in Tak'ar's eyes. She couldn't help but be reminded of the look in Johnston's eyes not so long ago.

"I know what you are feeling," Johnston said. "But this isn't the solution. Trust me."

"You know nothing," Tak'ar spat. "Finish it," he ordered his men.

At his command three resistance fighters pulled on the noose that was already around the Overlord's neck and he was yanked into the air.

Before anyone could even blink Johnston had swung his rifle up and shot the rope with a plasma bolt that burnt through it, dumping the Overlord back on the ground with a grunt. Following his initiative Lieutenant Jeffers and the marines in the immediate vicinity leveled their rifles at Tak'ar and his fighters.

"I'm taking the Overlord into our custody," Johnston said. "He is responsible for an attack on a human colony and the orbital bombardment of civilians. My people will want to see him stand trial for his crimes before he is executed."

Tak'ar looked like he was about to lash out at Johnston but the voice of his wife broke the tension. "Stand down Tak'ar," Mul'li'la said from the middle of the throne room. She was making her way up to the Overlord followed by more than a hundred Vestarian resistance fighters.

"We have fought side by side with the humans today. Each of us has shed blood for the freedom of our people. This is not how this day will end," she added as she mounted the steps to the throne. When she got close enough that only Tak'ar and those around him could hear she placed her hand on his weapon and said, "I know what he did to your parents. But this will not honor their memory. They fought for freedom and justice. The Overlord will get what is coming to him. But he wronged more than just you. Our whole planet needs to see the Overlord pay for his crimes."

Gently, she prized Tak'ar's weapon from his hands and when he let go he turned and walked deeper into the palace. Johnston made to follow him but Mul'li'la held up two of her hands. "Let him go," she said. "He just needs time."

"I understand," Johnston said. "Can I turn the Overlord over to your custody?"

"Yes," Mul'li'la replied. "I will ensure no harm comes to him."

"My government will want him to stand trial on our homeworld before you carry out any sentences against him," Johnston added.

"Don't worry, we won't execute him until your people and mine have had a chance to see him stand trial. He has many crimes for which he will have to pay," Mul'li'la said.

Johnston nodded and turned back to Lieutenant Jeffers and Becket. "Let's get our dead and wounded gathered up. We're done here. The Vestarians will have to figure out where to go from here. The Captain is going to want us back on board *Endeavour* ASAP. We still have to warn the Kulreans."

Chapter 24 – Fortune favors the Brave

Whilst tactics are always changing in space warfare as weapons technologies evolve, one thing has remained the same, the element of surprise can stack the odds in your favor.

- Excerpt from Empire Rising, 3002 AD

5th August, 2466 AD, HMS *Endeavour*, unknown system.

James was sitting in the command chair on *Endeavour's* bridge when the cruiser exited shift space into another unknown system. It was the twelfth they had visited since they had left Vestar a month ago. James had been pushing *Endeavour* and her crew as fast as he could to get to Kulthar ahead of the Overlord's fleet. Despite everyone being worked flat out the mood of the ship had been somber during the flight from Vestar. The initial celebrations that *Endeavour* and her crew had been involved in after the liberation of Vestar had only served to delay the sense of loss that had hit the crew.

Agent Bell, Sergeant Harkin and three marines had been killed when the Omen Facility had self-destructed and another four marines had been killed in the Overlord's palace. Despite the compartmental barriers between the marines and the rest of *Endeavour's* crew it was impossible for friendships not to form and each marine's absence was noted. In addition, James had known that Bell exhibited a larger than life personality but he hadn't realized how much she had touched so many of the crew in her brief time on board *Endeavour*. Everyone was feeling her loss. Lieutenant Scott was also on everyone's mind as she recovered in sickbay. The doctor had been forced to remove both her legs and one of her lungs, as well as set over thirty broken bones and replace over fifty percent of her skin with synthetics. Once they got her back to Earth she could have two replacement legs and a lung grown but that was still a distant prospect. At the moment the doctor had her heavily sedated as he continued to work on her and to keep her from the shock of losing her legs.

Alongside the sense of loss and sadness the crew had developed a steely determination. They all knew that they were going after the remnants of the fleet that had attacked Haven and which now sought to carry out the last orders of the Overlord. Everyone wanted to see the fleet destroyed so as to finish off what Bell and the marines had died to accomplish. James had been using that desire to drive everyone forward.

Now they were in the final system that led to Kulthar. As usual, James had jumped *Endeavour* out of shift space in stealth mode right on the edge of the system's mass shadow. He didn't have time to jump further out and slowly cruise into each system, instead he had opted for jumping out of shift space under stealth and waiting for half an hour to get an initial reading of the system. If everything looked clear, then he had ordered *Endeavour* to charge through the system under full power.

"Anything on the sensors yet?" James asked Sub Lieutenant Malik after waiting for over a minute.

"Just the usual so far, no signs of artificial electromagnetic radiation coming from any of the planets. Though the gravimetric sensors are picking up some anomalous readings. I'm running a systems diagnostic now," Malik replied.

"Anomalous in what way?" Ferguson asked from the second command chair on the bridge. James was happy to see that Ferguson was slowly relaxing back into working with him, yet their relationship was still frosty. Things had been said that couldn't be taken back.

"Small blips from deep within the system, it looks almost like a ship is accelerating for one or two seconds and then powering down again," Malik answered.

"Focus our passive sensors in that direction, let's see if there is anything out there," James ordered.

Five minutes of silence passed as Malik ran the diagnostic on the gravimetric sensors and the computer analyzed the data from the other passive sensors.

"Diagnostic was clear Captain," Malik said. "There is something happening out there."

"Has the computer been able to make anything out from the passive sensors?" James asked Ferguson.

"Small traces of heat energy and other electromagnetic radiation in the delta and gamma range, they are faint but consistent with the kind of energy leakage we've seen from Vestarian ships before," Ferguson answered.

"Navigation, adjust course for these anomalies, we may have found the Overlord's fleet," James ordered.

"Are we going to try and engage them?" Ferguson asked with obvious concern. "I thought we were just going to warn the Kulreans and head back to Earth."

"We're just getting closer for a better look. Let's see what we find before we make any decisions," James answered.

*

Two hours later there could be no doubt. They had found the Vestarian fleet, all two hundred and twelve warships. To everyone's surprise right in the middle of the fleet were four extremely large ships. It appeared as if they were some kind of resupply ships. The fleet had split into four squadrons and each was in the process of having its ships dock with a larger ship to presumably take on supplies.

"Do we know what they are doing yet?" James asked.

Julius was the first to speak up. "I've been communicating with Chief Driscoll," she said. "We've been looking over some of the technical specifications we managed to steal from the construction yard's computers. They included designs for what we thought was an outdated fission reactor. Now we're not so sure. If the Vestarian ships need fissionable materials to run their ships, it's no wonder they need resupply. They have been traveling to Kulthar for the last six weeks. That many shift jumps would eat up a reactor's fuel."

"Didn't Scott say she had detected evidence of an impressive power source on their warships at Haven?" James asked. "Something far beyond a fission reactor?"

"She did," Julius replied. "But we have already seen a very strange mix of technologies from the Vestarians. It's possible the advanced power unit supplies the x-ray lasers and the fission reactors the rest of the ship. Certainly, there is no way a fission reactor could power the lasers we have seen them use so they must have more than one power source."

"The sooner we get Scott debriefed the better. There was definitely something going on in that Omen facility," James said in frustration.

"There are a lot of unanswered questions," Julius agreed.

"Are we going to head to Kulthar now?" Ferguson asked. "We have more than enough evidence to convince them this fleet is about to attack their world."

"Not yet," James said. He had already decided what was about to happen, but he knew Ferguson wouldn't like it. "Focus our passive sensors on the squadron closest to the Kulthar shift passage," he ordered Sub Lieutenant Malik.

"Captain, you can't seriously be planning an attack," Ferguson said, guessing what James' request meant. "There are two hundred warships out there."

James paused to think about how he wanted to answer Ferguson. On face value it looked like suicide to face such a large force. Yet they had the advantage of surprise. James momentarily imagined what Captain Lightfoot would do if he found himself in a similar situation. James almost chuckled to himself, there was no doubt what Lightfoot would do, he would already be charging into battle. After the battle over Haven James knew that he could handle *Endeavour*, and this was to good an opportunity to pass up. *It's time to see what you are made of,* James thought to himself.

"We're certainly not going to take on all two hundred of them," James said in response to Ferguson's question, bringing a nervous chuckle from the rest of the bridge officers. "But this is an opportunity we can't pass up. We don't know what kind of defenses the Kulreans have. Every ship we can destroy now is one less ship they will have to fight over their homeworld. This is to good an opportunity to pass up. Navigation, plot us a course that will take us directly into the middle of that fourth squadron then bring us up to our top speed. Let's see how good our stealth technology holds up against Vestarian technology," James ordered before Ferguson could come up with any more arguments.

Thankfully the First Lieutenant held his tongue but as he sat back further into his command chair James could see out of the corner of his eye that Ferguson's hands were in tight fists. *As long as he doesn't directly challenge me,* James said to himself.

He turned his attention back to the matter at hand. In terms of sub light speed *Endeavour* was one of the fastest ships the RSN had yet built. Her valstronium armor allowed her to reach up to 0.38 the speed of light. Anything more and the electromagnetic radiation of space would boil her crew or a collision with a stray cosmic particle would tear the ship apart.

The bridge descended into silence as everyone watched the enemy fleet getting bigger and bigger on the holo display. When they were an hour out from combat range James ordered the crew to their battlestations.

"I want our first full broadside from the starboard tubes aimed at that resupply ship," James ordered ten minutes out. "Target the cruisers with the other broadside and the frigates with the plasma cannons. At our rate of closure we're only going to get ten minutes to engage them before we pass out of plasma cannon range. Let's make every shot count. Navigation as soon as we open fire begin evasive maneuvers. They are not going to be expecting us so it may take them a while to warm up their lasers but when they do I want to make it as difficult for them to get a lock on us as possible. A few hits from their lasers and we could be done for."

After Sub Lieutenant Jennings acknowledged the order, Lieutenant Julius chimed in. "Captain, I think we should deploy the gaseous shields as soon as we come out of stealth," she said.

"Explain," James said, intrigued.

Gaseous shields were a holdover from the days before valstronium had been discovered. When starships had been made entirely out of nano-carbon composites they needed extra protection from cosmic particles in order to reach speeds anywhere near the speed of light. Without such protection a ship or its crew could be destroyed simply by running into a stray cosmic particle. The gaseous shields worked by venting a charged gaseous mixture into space. Electromagnetic fields projected by the ship would then form the gases into a cone in front of the ship, giving additional protection from cosmic particles.

"It was actually something Lieutenant Scott was working on

before she was injured," Julius said. "From her analysis of the battle over Haven the Vestarian lasers all use the same wavelength. She was working on altering the charge and density of our gaseous shields so that they would give us some protection from the lasers. The Chief Engineer and I have been trying to finish her work. We haven't been able to perfect it but we believe we can reduce the power of any hits by ten to fifteen percent."

"That's a great idea," James said. "Ten to fifteen percent isn't a lot but it is far better than nothing. As soon as we come out of stealth you may power up the gaseous shields."

With five minutes to go James walked over to the tactical station and picked out targets with Julius. They were able to backtrack their sensor data and identify ships that had already been resupplied. They would become the primary targets, for once the resupply ship was destroyed the others would have to move to one of the other three ships to take on more fuel. That would hopefully buy the Kulreans some more time to prepare their defenses.

With a minute to go James sat down in his command chair and watched the timer count down. "Fire," he shouted when they entered range.

Eight missiles shot out of the starboard missile tubes towards the resupply ship in the middle of the enemy formation. They had delayed opening fire until they were within plasma cannon range and six green plasma bolts tore into the nearest Vestarian frigate. It exploded before its commander even knew what was happening.

Two more explosions blossomed among the Vestarian ships as two of their cruisers disappeared. Both of them had been holding station near the resupply ship and with their position so predictable James had ordered that a tungsten spear be fired at them from each of the flak cannons. Normally mass driver type weapons were largely ineffective in long range space warfare for it was all but impossible to predict where a ship would be several minutes in the future. In this case the Vestarians had removed that problem. *Endeavour's* flak cannons had launched the spears seven minutes ago and they had silently closed in on their stationary targets.

The missiles weren't nearly as inconspicuous as the tungsten spears for the high acceleration from their engines made them jump out on the Vestarian's gravimetric sensors. Combined with *Endeavour's* forward velocity, the speed at which they were shot from their missile tubes and their own acceleration, *Endeavour's* first missile salvo approached the enemy resupply ship at 0.7C. As James watched he saw a number of the closest warships try to target the approaching missiles with their point defenses. One was destroyed, yet the missiles were going too fast for the ships to power up their defenses in time to target them accurately. Significantly, no point defense fire was coming from the resupply ship. *It mustn't have any defenses*, James thought, *it's doomed.*

"Target the second starboard broadside at two of the cruisers," James ordered.

Even as he spoke the port missile tubes fired their own missiles at two more cruisers as they came to bear. *Endeavour* was already passing through the middle of the enemy formation.

"I'm detecting energy spikes from some of the nearest warships,"

Malik shouted from the sensor station. "I think they are powering up their lasers."

"Jennings," James called to the navigation officer. "Try and keep us between as many Vestarian ships as you can. Some of those ships may hold their fire if they fear hitting each other."

"Detonation," Julius called as the first missile salvo reached their targets. "Resupply ship destroyed!" he shouted with a whoop when the sensor feed cleared. "There were six warships docked with that ship, they all went up with it."

"Incoming laser fire," Ferguson shouted.

A few seconds later a number of alarms went off around the bridge. "We took two grazing hits," Ferguson said as he looked over his command terminal. "No serious damage, I think the gaseous shields helped."

"Second broadside is away," Julius shouted over the din of the alarms.

"Shut those alarms up," James ordered, as he switched his focus to the holo display to watch the missiles' progress. They were so close to the enemy formation that the missiles took less than thirty seconds to close in on their targets and explode. Three more cruisers disappeared, they didn't have time to launch any AM missiles to defend themselves.

"The warships are beginning to launch their own missiles," Jennings reported but James had already seen the launches on the holo plot. The enemy fire was totally uncoordinated, with each ship firing their missiles as soon as they were ready. Some ships even fired their missiles in ones and twos. James wasn't immediately worried about any of the missiles. *Endeavour* was closing at such a speed that the missiles would have to accelerate for more than twenty minutes before they would even be able to match her velocity. Only then could they begin to close with her.

"We're passing through the middle of their formation," Jennings informed everyone.

James didn't respond. Everyone knew what that meant. Their weapons would be a lot less effective now. Despite the missile tubes being able to fire their missiles out at 0.2C, the missile would still have to accelerate hard to overcome *Endeavour's* momentum which was now pulling them away from their targets. The plasma bolts would also take longer to reach their targets and so would be less accurate.

Julius launched another missile salvo and the Sub Lieutenant assisting her at the tactical station destroyed three more frigates with the plasma cannons.

Several more grazing hits from the enemy lasers meant there were alarms going off constantly. Just when James thought they were going to make it without taking any major hits an immense ripping sound drowned everything else out and *Endeavour* spun wildly, throwing everyone around in their harnesses.

As James regained his senses he remembered feeling his ears pop and he reached up to feel them. When he took his hand away he saw they were covered in blood. "What happened?" he shouted, barely able to hear his own voice.

"W... too... amid..." Mallory's muffled voice said from his

command chair.

"Repeat that," James shouted after turning up the volume on the COM channel to full.

"We took a direct laser hit to our port amidships," Mallory said. "It burnt its way through three decks and almost hit the bridge. Missile tube four isn't responding and over ten percent of the ship is open to space. I fear we have lost a lot of crewmembers.

"We've taken control of navigation here on the auxiliary bridge, we're leveling *Endeavour* out now. You still have control of the tactical station and our point defenses."

"Ok, you've done well," James said. "Plot us a course to the Kulthar shift passage and jump as soon as we cross the mass shadow. We'll take care of the Vestarian missiles."

Satisfied that they were on top of things James let out a sigh of relief. In the time it had taken Mallory to wrestle *Endeavour* under control they had passed out of laser range of the Vestarian fleet. The sensor log indicated that the Vestarians had managed to get one more grazing hit with their lasers but *Endeavour's* wild roll had made it difficult to target her.

The plasma cannons would be in range for another sixty seconds and as soon as *Endeavour* was under control Lieutenant Julius and her Sub Lieutenant opened fire. They destroyed one more light warship before getting out of range. They shifted their focus to the remaining missile tubes and got off another two broadsides.

Once their offensive weapons were useless James and the rest of the bridge crew turned to dealing with the incoming Vestarian missiles. There were now over two hundred of them desperately accelerating towards *Endeavour*. Thanks to *Endeavour's* superior velocity the gap between the missiles and the ship was still growing. The closest missiles eventually managed to match *Endeavour's* velocity and then exceed it allowing them to begin to close in on their target.

"Roll the ship to bring our starboard point defenses to bear on the incoming missiles," James ordered Mallory over the COM channel. "They are in the best condition.

"Julius," James continued, "hold your fire with the flak cannons until there is a particularly dense swarm of incoming missiles. Our AM missiles and point defense plasma cannons should be able to handle the first few waves."

Due to the haphazard way the Vestarians had fired their missiles they were coming towards *Endeavour* in groups of four or five. Given the Vestarians inferior ECM and missile seeker heads, they wouldn't pose too many problems. On the holo projection James could see several larger groups of missiles near the back and he wanted to ensure the flak cannons had enough ammunition to take them out.

"Have you got an updated damage report?" James asked Mallory to take his mind off the incoming missiles.

"Yes Sir," Mallory began. "As I said missile tube four has been destroyed. The laser burnt its way into the ship right through the tube itself. All ten of the gunners were killed in the initial blast. The laser beam burnt its way through decks nine, ten and eleven. There are a further twelve crewmembers missing from those areas. We have sealed off the hull breach and are re-pressurizing those areas but we aren't expecting to find anyone alive I'm afraid."

"What about the shift drive and its capacitors, they are near missile tube four aren't they?" James followed up, trying not to think about the deaths.

"Yes Sir, a couple of the capacitors were destroyed but Chief Driscoll says the shift drive is fully functional and we have enough spare capacitors that we shouldn't need the damaged ones. We'll reach the mass shadow in thirty minutes and we should be able to jump as soon as we get there."

"Very good, thank you Mallory," James said. "Put together a list of the causalities and keep me updated on the search of the damaged areas."

"Aye Sir," Mallory responded.

"Engaging with the point defenses," Ferguson said a minute later as he opened up on the first missiles with the point defense plasma cannons.

By now James had the bridge crew well trained and he had nothing to do but watch as Ferguson and the Sub Lieutenants manning the defense terminal coordinated the point defenses. The first thirty missiles were all easily dispatched as they came in ones and twos. The skillful use of *Endeavour's* point defenses quickly dispatched almost all the rest. Even though they were gaining on *Endeavour* the velocity differential between her and the missiles wasn't very large and the gunners had plenty of time to pick their targets and make sure every missile was taken out.

The second to last group of missiles was the largest at thirty two. They weren't all closely packed together or else they would have posed a real danger to *Endeavour*. As it was, they were still a threat. Ferguson opened up at maximum range with the flak cannons, taking out thirteen. Then the plasma point defense cannons joined the fight. Because of the slow closing speeds Ferguson was able to fire off three rounds of bolts. When the third round took out five missiles, leaving only seven, James allowed himself to relax. The point defense AM's would easily handle the rest.

"That's the last of them Sir," Ferguson reported two minutes later. "We're clear to jump as soon as we reach the mass shadow."

"Good shooting Lieutenant," James said with a big smile. "You see, I knew we could do it!"

"Yes Sir, you · were right," Ferguson conceded somewhat reluctantly.

"Sub Lieutenant Malik," James said turning to the sensor officer. "What has the Vestarian fleet been up to?"

"A few ships from the squadron we hit tried to give chase after we flew through their formation but they turned back when it was clear they couldn't catch us Sir. The rest of the squadron broke up and has now been split between the other three squadrons."

"And what are the other three squadrons doing now?"

"As near as I can tell they are continuing to refuel their ships. Though I think they have picked up their pace. The ships that have already refueled are actively scanning the area around the refueling ships and carrying out patrols."

"They have learnt a costly lesson," James said. "How many ships did we get in the end? I lost track of the full count."

James would review the sensor logs carefully on their way to Kulthar to see if there was anything he could learn about his enemy but he wanted to know the raw numbers now.

"We destroyed ten of their cruisers and sixteen frigates ones along with the resupply ship," Malik reported.

James was taken aback. After the first heavy plasma cannon shots he hadn't been following what the plasma cannons had been up to and he hadn't seen all of the missile salvos hit home, yet twenty seven ships was way beyond what he had hoped of destroying.

More than a few of the bridge crew let out gasps of surprise at Malik's count. Everyone had been too focused on their field of responsibility to fully grasp how well the battle had gone.

"Twenty seven ships," Julius said before letting out a long whistle. "That has to be the most one sided battle in the history of human space warfare."

"Quite possibly," James said. "You have all done me proud," he continued, addressing the entire bridge crew. "But sadly the danger isn't passed yet. There are still one hundred and seventy nine out there. Now we need to find a way to help the Kulreans destroy the rest of them.

Chapter 25 – The Kulreans

We have found many allies among the stars, we have also found many deadly enemies. One thing many of them seem to have in common, they can all be very stubborn.

-Excerpt from Empire Rising, 3002 AD

8th August, 2466 AD, HMS *Endeavour*, Kulthar system

Three days later *Endeavour* limped into the Kulthar system. Mallory and the damage control teams had sealed off the damaged sections to allow the ship to jump into shift space but once there, their ability to repair the ship had been limited. She still had a large gash along her port amidships with a number of her decks open to space.

As soon as they exited shift space the repair crews got to work realigning the valstronium armor to cover the gash and sealing off the damaged sections. The fourth missile tube was beyond repair but the point defenses and damaged hull sections would soon be back to something resembling their original condition.

James' thoughts were elsewhere though for he didn't have a clue how *Endeavour* was going to be received by the Kulreans.

"It's unbelievable," Malik said as the main holo display continued to update with the images from the sensors.

"That's an understatement," James said.

The system was a hive of activity. It looked like there were major industrial nodes in orbit above all the planets in the system. Three of the inner planets were also showing signs of civilization. The one that sat right in the middle of the habitable zone looked like the entire planet was one large city. Between the various planets and what must have been a number of significant mining facilities in the outer asteroid belts there were literally thousands of ships moving back and forth. What was even more impressive was the size of some of them. A number of ships looked like they out massed the entire Royal Space Navy all by themselves.

"I think it's safe to say the Kulreans are a bit more advanced than the Vestarians," Ferguson said.

"Agreed," James responded. "Does it look like they have detected us yet?" he asked Malik.

"No Sir," Malik responded. "Our stealth technology isn't working at full capacity but there is no sign from the movement of the ships in the system that they have noticed anything unusual yet."

"Very well. Jennings, take us out of stealth and towards the second planet at 0.1C. King, transmit our prepared message."

"Yes Sir," both Sub Lieutenants said.

The prearranged message contained a brief introduction to humanity, information about the attack on Haven, the Overlord's fleet orders and a sensor feed of *Endeavour's* battle with the fleet from three days ago. James had also included a personal message pleading with the leaders of the Kulreans to take the threat to their planet seriously.

"Are there any signs of a military presence in the system?" James asked once the message had been sent. It would take several hours for it to reach the Kulrean's homeworld so they had plenty of time to wait.

"Not as yet Sir," Malik replied. "Our passive sensors are only able to get a good read on the closest ships but as yet none of them appear to be armed with any weapons. It's possible some of the orbital installations around the planets are armed with weapons, they are certainly giving off enough power readings to suggest that. However, we won't be able to tell for sure until they activate them."

"I guess they have gravimetric sensors," Julius said. "I think they just spotted us."

James could see Julius was right. Almost as soon as *Endeavour* accelerated, giving away her position, the nearest Kulrean ships veered away from her and deeper into the system.

"No signs of an attempt to open communications from any of the nearby ships?" James asked.

"No Sir," King answered. "They are all quiet."

"One ship has stopped fleeing us," Malik said. "It appears to be holding station with us about thirty light seconds off our starboard bow."

"Interesting," James said. "Try hailing them."

"No response Captain," King said a minute later.

"Well I guess we'll just have to wait until someone from their government wants to speak to us," James said.

*

Four hours passed as *Endeavour* slowly moved deeper and deeper into the Kulthar system. James had spent the time growing more and more amazed at the size and extent of what the Kulreans had built in their home system. Even the smallest of orbital stations looked like they could provide comfortable living space for more than a million humans. Or if they were all used for industrial production, the Kulreans could out produce all of Earth's colonial powers with ease.

"I'm picking up a tachyon beam from the second planet," Malik reported.

"Where is it directed?" James asked.

"Right at us Sir," Malik answered.

"Is it doing us any damage?" James quickly asked.

"Nothing that I can detect," Ferguson answered from his command chair.

"Can you detect any form of communication in the signal King?" James said to the Sub Lieutenant at the communication station.

"There definitely seems to be a pattern in the tachyons," he responded, "but I can't make heads or tails of it."

"Wait," she continued, "we're being hailed by the Kulrean ship that has been shadowing us. It's in English."

"Put it on the holo display," James said.

"Greetings human Captain," a blue face with three eyes said. "I am Superintendent Hallock. I have been given permission by my people to speak to you on their behalf."

James had been trying to prepare himself for meeting another alien race. With the Vestarians at least he had been able to look at the dead bodies from the attack on Haven before he had met any living ones. He knew meeting the Kulreans would be an entirely different kettle of fish.

"Greetings, my name is Captain James Somerville," James said in reply, sure that his shock was as plain as day. The alien actually looked very human. It had a mouth, a nose, two ears and even wispy blue hair that hung down over its back. Yet its blue skin and three eyes gave it a hideous look, like something out of a holo cartoon meant to scare young children.

"I am sure this is very unsettling for you," Hallock said. "Meeting a member of another race face to face for the first time is always difficult. But you did come to our home system. May I ask why you are here uninvited? We Kulreans count such uninvited visits as the height of rudeness."

"My sincerest apologies," James began. "My race does not wish for anything but peaceful friendship with the Kulreans. However, I felt I had to bring my ship here to warn you about a threat to your people.

"If you have looked over the information I sent you in our initial communication you will know that the Vestarians have built a large battle fleet and intend to use it to conquer your people. They attacked one of our worlds so I know firsthand the damage they are willing to cause. When I learnt of their plot to attack your homeworld I felt duty bound to come here and warn you. You will see in the information I sent you that this fleet is just days away. They could actually be right behind us for all we know."

"My people have looked over the information you have sent," Hallock said. "We have had contact with the Vestarians for almost five hundred of their years. Under our guidance they have become somewhat of a peaceful people. We find your information hard to believe. Besides, they do not have the capacity to build a war fleet such as the one you speak of. We have also observed your people, though the last time we visited your planet you humans were traveling around on horse and foot, not in space ships. I must congratulate your ingenuity. We didn't expect to see your race reach the stars so soon.

"Nevertheless," Hallock went on, not allowing James any time to acknowledge the minor compliment. "We did observe your race's behavior. You are a warlike people and we can see nothing has changed. Arming a spaceship with weapons of destruction is not an honorable thing to do. Why should we trust you when you come to us with such stories of war and death? Maybe you are the one who comes here to conquer us?"

"That is not the case Superintendent," James said. "If you wish us to leave we will do so. Yet we must impress on your people the need to prepare for the Vestarians. Their fleet is real. We sent you evidence that they have built a secret construction yard on the outer edge of their system."

"Images can be faked," Hallock said. "The Vestarians are slowly learning the way of peace. We have given them many impressive technologies that have improved their lives. Soon they will come to their senses and embrace the unity we introduced and join us again in friendship."

"I know you have a satellite over Vestar," James said. "Haven't you seen what the Overlord has done to his people? And haven't you seen the recent rebellion that has overthrown him? The Vestarian threat is real."

"I am sorry Captain but I simply cannot accept your view of the facts. From our information the Overlord's aggression against his people only started with this rebellion. Something that I believe your ship instigated. We have seen your ship bombard the Vestarian planet with our own eyes. How can we ever trust someone who uses violence to achieve his aims?"

"I confess, I regret having to bombard the Overlord's military installations and the lives that were ended. Yet that was the lesser of two evils. I did it to protect my people and to free the Vestarian people. Those whom I killed would have done far worse to my people and would have kept the ordinary Vestarians in slavery. Would you have preferred to see the Vestarians continue to be the Overlord's slaves?" James asked.

"You don't understand human," Hallock said, with a distinctly human sigh of exasperation. "My desires do not justify the use of violence. The Overlord was evil, on that we agree. Yet the lives of the normal Vestarians were still better with the technology we introduced than they ever were before we made contact with them. In time they would have come to realize this and fully embraced the friendship we offer. Now you have set them down the path of war and destruction again."

"I did not come here to debate philosophy with you Superintendent. My people wish nothing but friendship with you," James said, trying again. "If you will not heed our warning there is nothing else we can do for you. The history of my people has taught us that sometimes violence is needed so that the strong can protect the weak. I fear that is a lesson your people may learn too late. If you will not listen to me, then maybe you will listen to Jil'lal," James said as he stepped to one side, allowing Jil'lal to take his place.

Upon James' request Tak'ar had sent Jil'lal with *Endeavour* to speak to the Kulreans on behalf of the newly formed Vestarian government. Government was a bit of a stretch as it was just Tak'ar and some of the resistance leaders who were overseeing the cleanup of the devastation the rebellion had caused. Nevertheless, they were planning a planetary vote in just a few months to decide what type of government their people should adopt. After that, another vote was scheduled to decide who would govern the planet. James strongly suspected that whatever the Vestarians decided, Tak'ar would be playing a central role. After the images of his attacks on the Overlord's soldiers had been sent around the planet he had become a living legend.

Importantly for James, he knew that Tak'ar would honor any agreement Jil'lal made with the Kulreans. Tak'ar trusted her implicitly and she had been the natural choice. It had helped that Jil'lal had been demanding to come on board *Endeavour* to see

Scott as soon as she had woken up from the electrical shock that had knocked her out. Sadly, Jil'lal didn't remember anything from the attack on the Omen facility but the survivors had told her of how Scott had carried her out of the burning facility. Since she had come onboard she had spent most of everyday at Scott's side. That hadn't stopped her making fast friends with almost everyone. James just hoped that some of that natural charm could make a difference with Hallock.

"Greetings Superintendent," Jil'lal began. "My name is Jil'lal Lackesh. A number of leading figures of my people wished for me to accompany Captain Somerville on his journey here to your home system. I wish to add my apologies for coming to your home uninvited."

"Your apologies are accepted child," Hallock said with a lot more compassion that he had given James. "Our people hoped there would come a day when your people would be able to visit our homeworld. I'm just sorry that it has happened under these circumstances."

"As am I Superintendent," Jil'lal agreed. "However it was necessary for me to come here and give you this warning. What Captain Somerville has said is true. Our Overlord has secretly built a fleet to conquer your people. I have seen the orders with my own eyes and I was on *Endeavour* just three days ago when they engaged this fleet. They lost over twenty crewmembers trying to prevent it from reaching your planet. The fleet is real and they intend to destroy everything you have built here. Please, listen to our warning. You have to prepare yourselves to stop this attack."

"Your words are well spoken Jil'lal," Hallock said. "Yet you are just one person. We cannot take your word alone on such a matter. For all we know the humans are forcing you to say the things you say."

"They are not," Jil'lal said with a hint of anger creeping into her voice. "I have come here and risked my own life to warn you. For the last three hundred years your people have stood by and watched while the Overlords enslaved my people. Yet despite that I was sent here to warn you. The humans owe you nothing and yet they have bled to bring you this warning. Your people need to listen to us."

"Now, now my dear. We know your people and how they let emotion get in the way of reason but there is no need to spoil this dialogue." Hallock said. "The simple truth is that we will not sanction the use of violence. That means we cannot trust your motives in coming here and even if this fleet were real, we would not resort to the use of violence to stop it. If the Overlord has indeed sent a fleet to attack us, then we will talk to its commander when it arrives."

"Then we have wasted our time coming here," Jil'lal said in frustration. She didn't trust herself to say anything more so she stepped to one side and gestured for James to take over.

"I am truly sorry if our presence here has caused offense. That was never my intention," James began in a conciliatory tone. "If you do not want my help defending your system then we will leave before we cause anymore offense, yet I hope that after you think on our words you will change your mind."

"I think that would be wise," Hallock said. "In the future your government would be welcome to send an unarmed ship with political representatives to open a dialogue between our two peoples. We do not approve of species that use violence. However, that doesn't mean that we cannot communicate with one another. In time we hope your race will come to see the benefit of peace and harmony. Farewell human."

"I will pass on your kind words to my leaders," James said to Hallock. "May your peace and harmony outlast the next few weeks," he added as he closed the COM channel.

"Well that was interesting," James said to the bridge crew. "I guess they don't want our help."

"What do we do now Sir?" Julius asked.

"Turn us around Sub Lieutenant Jennings," James answered. "Now we wait, and watch," he added to Julius.

"We're not just going to leave them to their fate are we?" Julius asked. "We came an awfully long way to watch another alien race conquered and enslaved.

"I'm not too sure the Kulreans have given us any other choice," James said.

"You don't owe the Kulreans anything," Jil'lal said. "You have already lost crew members for them. If they will not listen I'm not sure they are worth anymore of your time."

"I'm not so sure," James said. "You could argue that we didn't owe your people the help we gave them. We could have bombarded the Overlord's palace from space and allowed your planet to fall into civil war as his surviving generals fought among themselves for power. That would have protected our people. Yet we chose to help you restore freedom to your planet. At a personal cost to ourselves."

"You are right," Jil'lal said. "I am used to thinking as a resistance fighter. For us the cause was everything. We had to make sacrifices in order to survive. Anyone who wouldn't help us had to be cast adrift."

"I can understand that," James responded. "But now Tak'ar and Mul'li'la are going to be responsible for all your people. There should be no one left behind. What's more, you need to lead by example. If you want your people to care for each other and other species, you need to show them that you are willing to help them, even when it costs you something. I hope our actions on your planet will prove to be the cement that holds our two races together in friendship. We may yet have the opportunity to do the same here."

"I see," Jil'lal said. "I guess my people still have many things to learn."

"As do I," James replied. "Hopefully we can live long enough to learn them together."

"Jennings, once we get to the mass shadow I want you to jump us five light hours up the shift passage," James ordered, turning away from Jil'lal and leaving her to her thoughts. "Once we jump back out, turn us around and set a course back into the Kulthar system under stealth. We're not going anywhere just yet. Don't exceed 0.25C though, we don't want them detecting us."

"Aye, Sir," Jennings said with approval.

"I'm not sure what we're going to do yet," James said to the bridge. "But I want to be here when the Overlord's fleet arrives. At the very least we will get to see if these Kulreans really are pacifists, maybe they will have a few secret weapons up their sleeve. I'm going to my quarters to think," James finished and then got up. "Ferguson, you have the bridge."

"Yes Sir," the First Lieutenant said.

Chapter 26 – A Change of Heart

It has always been the duty of a Captain of an Empire warship to put himself in harm's way. That has been their tradition from the inception of the Empire.

- Excerpt from Empire Rising, 3002 AD

9th August 2466 AD, HMS *Endeavour*, Kulthar System.

Ten hours later *Endeavour* once again crossed the mass shadow into the Kulthar system. James was in his quarters sleeping fitfully as he dreamt of blue aliens swarming all over his ship trying to strip the weapons off the hull.

On the bridge Ferguson was monitoring the sensor feed when what he had been expecting happened. "I'm detecting ships exiting shift space," Sub Lieutenant Malik called.

"Wait for a full ship count and then inform the Captain," Ferguson called out. "I have something to attend to, you have the bridge," he said to Lieutenant Julius.

When he got off the bridge Ferguson opened his COM unit and contacted Lieutenant Mallory, ""It's time, I'm going to the Captain's quarters now, you secure the bridge," he said.

"Shit," Mallory said as he dropped the coffee he had been drinking. His mind went back to the conversation Ferguson had had with him a few hours ago.

Ferguson had come to him with an ultimatum. He had discovered a number of gambling rings Mallory had set up and had actually found out how many credits he owed a number of the crew. Ferguson had threatened to reveal his illicit actions and have him thrown in the brig if he didn't help.

Mallory had been torn, what the First Lieutenant had been talking about was mutiny. Yet Mallory had thought it had all been theoretical. He hadn't believed the Lieutenant would go through with it so it hadn't been too hard to agree. Besides, he thought, as much as he hated it, what choice had he had? Ferguson was going to end his career.

"Mallory?" Ferguson said.

Mallory shook himself. "Yes, I'm here," he said. "I'll get my men moving now."

Mallory knew why Ferguson had come to him. *Endeavour* had been built with Chester taxes she was supposed to have been sent to Chester to map out the dark matter in the unexplored areas around Chester. The Admiralty had therefore ensured that a lot of the crew were natives of Chester so that they could enjoy shore leave on their home planet. As a result, Mallory had a lot of connections among the crew and many of them owed him or his father a few favors. Ferguson had known that too and now he was making use of them.

Switching COM channels, Mallory contacted two of the crew, "McCullough, Troon, it's time, get your men and meet me on the bridge."

*

Four minutes later James was woken by the beeping of his COM unit. "What is it?" he asked groggily.

"The Overlord's fleet has arrived," Sub Lieutenant King reported, "every ship that we didn't destroy at their refueling point has just jumped into the system."

"What are they doing?" James followed up.

"They are just sitting on the edge of the mass shadow at the moment. I think they are getting their bearings," King answered.

"I'm on my way," James said as he jumped out of his bed and searched for his uniform.

As he stepped out of his quarters and into his adjoining office James was surprised to see Ferguson standing there. He was even more surprised when he saw the pistol in his hands.

"What are you doing Lieutenant?" James said.

"I'm taking you into custody Sir, please raise your hands," Ferguson said.

"This is mutiny, you cannot remove me without due cause," James said carefully. Then it hit him what had prompted Ferguson's move. "You are a coward!"

"That is for the Admiralty to decide," Ferguson said, "but I will not let you kill us all in a vain attempt to save the Kulreans. I know you, that is exactly what you will do. Well not today. Now raise your hands. I don't want to have to shoot you."

As he finished speaking two crew members appeared from the shadows and approached James. They grabbed him and patted him down for weapons.

"You're not going to get away with this," James said. "You can't hold the entire ship."

"I already have," Ferguson said. "We have sealed off the marines' barracks and the crew members not loyal to me are confined to their quarters. My men have taken over engineering and the bridge. You will be joining the other Lieutenants and Chief Driscoll in the brig. It will take us almost three months to get home but you will be more than comfortable. Once we get there, I will turn *Endeavour* over to the Admiralty."

"You're not going to help the Kulreans at all?" James asked, disgusted.

"We will stay in stealth and see what the Overlord's fleet does. But that is all. The Kulreans made it crystal clear that they don't want our help," Ferguson answered.

"But they don't know what they are facing, you are just taking the coward's way out," James spat.

"I'm obeying our orders. You have endangered this crew and this ship for the last time," Ferguson said, finally getting angry. "But enough of this. Take him to the brig. We will no doubt get a chance to present our points of view in a court martial. The Admiralty can decide if it is yours or mine that's right."

As the two crewmen manhandled him out of his offices and into the corridor James saw Second Lieutenant Mallory walking past leading two more crew members, all three had pistols in their hands.

"You too!" James shouted after him. "You are a coward."

Mallory didn't meet James' eye, he just hung his head and walked past the Captain.

When James got to the brig it was already full. Julius, Becket, Chief Driscoll and all twelve of the Sub Lieutenants were there. One or two were carrying nasty bruises on their faces, testifying that they hadn't submitted easily.

"I am sorry everyone," James said once his captors left. "It is my fault we are in this mess. I should have seen it coming. Do not worry, I will ensure your careers are not affected by this either way."

"We're not sorry, or worried Captain," Becket said for everyone else. "We followed you willingly and we would have followed you no matter what you decided to do about the Overlord's fleet. We are just sorry that we cannot help the Kulreans. No race deserves what the Overlord's fleet is going to do to them."

"No," James said as he struggled to get his head around the fact that some of his crew were willing to just watch the destruction of an entire alien civilization.

*

Jil'lal knew something was wrong when the door to her quarters swished open without waiting for her approval. She had been told that no one would be able to come in without her say so. Instinctively she jumped to her feet and turned to face whoever was entering.

A male human she hadn't met before cautiously walked in with some kind of weapon raised. "I'm here to request you accompany..."

Jil'lal didn't let him finish his sentence, she had already jumped into action. Using all four legs she sprung into the air above his weapon and crashed into him. With two of her hands she wrestled with him for his weapon and with her other two she fired short sharp punches into his face.

After the first couple of blows the human let go of his weapon in a vain attempt to cover his face with his hands. Jil'lal whipped the weapon away from him and jumped back.

"Don't say a word," she said.

"Ok, ok," the human said. "Please, don't shoot, I was just following orders," he continued as his fear grew. Jil'lal's attack had reminded him of just how alien she was. Now he wasn't sure how she was going to react to being attacked.

"I'm not going to hurt you. If you do what I want. If you don't..." she left the rest unsaid.

Ignoring the human for a moment she pulled out the datapad Lieutenant Becket had given her. For the first two days of the trip Becket had showed her how to work it but since then she had been teaching herself. With a few minor alterations in the datapad's code she had been able to override the limitations Becket had put on the datapad and use it to interface with the rest of the ship's systems.

She understood the human systems far better than they realized. Tak'ar had said she had been the best computer expert on Vestar. As it turned out, the human systems, though far more advanced, still worked on very similar principles.

With a few quick commands she got the ship's computer to locate the Captain and the senior officers. Unsurprisingly the Captain was in the brig. Jil'lal hadn't spent a great deal of time with Captain Somerville during the trip from Vestar but what she had seen she had liked. She certainly knew he wouldn't have sent an armed guard to arrest her. Along with the Captain, Lieutenants Julius and Becket were in the brig along with all the Sub Lieutenants she had got to know. *Something is definitely up*, she thought to herself.

When she looked for Lieutenants Ferguson and Mallory she saw that they were both on the bridge. *I'm not liking this*, she thought as she saw the armed guards that were on the bridge when she accessed the visual feed. *It looks like Ferguson has taken over.*

"What's going on?" she asked the human as she turned her attention back to him. "Is this some kind of mutiny?"

"No," the human said passionately. "Lieutenant Ferguson has just temporarily relieved Captain Somerville of command until we return to Earth. The Lieutenant felt that the Captain would launch us into a hopeless attack on the Overlord's fleet. We all agreed that it was in the Admiralty's best interest to prevent *Endeavour* being destroyed for no reason."

"You mean in your best interest," Jil'lal said in disgust. "Has your Captain not led you to success and glory in the last year? He is a great war leader like my Tak'ar. It is a shameful thing you have done here."

As she looked at him the human didn't respond nor lift his head to meet her eyes. "So be it," she said.

This time she connected her datapad to the door' controls. She altered a few of the protocols so that any rudimentary scan of the room would tell someone that she was inside. Then she set the door to lock and restricted all COM channels out of the room.

"You will have to wait out the rest of your mutiny in here," she said as she walked out.

In the corridor she paused to listen and look about before she headed on. Her first port of call was sickbay. She needed to see if Lieutenant Scott was still being looked after. She owed the Lieutenant a huge debt for saving her life.

After five minutes of careful sneaking she came to the turbolift that would take her to sickbay. When she entered in her destination nothing happened. Trying again she still found that nothing happened. In frustration she pulled out her datapad and connected it to the turbolift. To her dismay she saw that access to the turbolifts had been restricted to a few select crew members. She could hack into the protocols and add herself to the list but it would surely alert someone to the fact that she was free.

With a sigh she brought up the *Endeavour's* schematics. The exploration cruiser was a big ship and it would take her a while to get to the sickbay on foot. Once she was satisfied she had plotted a safe route that kept her away from the more populated areas of the ship she headed off.

Twenty minutes later she was finally standing outside sickbay. She had formulated a plan for her next course of action but first she had to see Scott. The doors into sickbay were locked from the outside but it didn't take her long to override them. As they swooshed open doctor Anderson looked up in anger. "I said I wanted to be left alone," she began angrily but cut herself short when she saw it was Jil'lal.

"Jil'lal, what are you doing here? I thought they would have confined you to your quarters," Doctor Anderson asked.

"They tried," Jil'lal responded with a feral grin, "but they only sent one man. They should have sent three."

"I see," Anderson said carefully, "I hope you didn't hurt him too badly."

"He's fine," Jil'lal said with a chuckle, "he is the one confined to quarters now. How is Scott?" she asked more seriously. "Are you still able to look after her like this?"

"Yes, the Lieutenant is doing ok, at least as well as she can. Ferguson was here himself to see her. He wanted to assure me that he didn't want Scott's health affected by his removal of the Captain. I am locked into my sickbay. At least until we leave the Kulthar system. But Ferguson assured me that if I needed anything to help Scott all I had to do was contact him."

"That is good," Jil'lal said. "At least Ferguson hasn't lost all of his honor."

"What are you going to do now?" Doctor Anderson asked.

"Release the Captain of course," Jil'lal said. "I don't know what he plans to do about the Overlord's fleet but he has seen us through so far. I think he has earned the right to finish this. Besides, as much as I want to go home the Kulreans don't deserve what is about to happen to them. Even if they have been trying to meddle with my people for the last five hundred years."

"And how will you do that?" Anderson asked.

"One of the marines is locked up in the general crew quarters. I think I can free her and together we should have a chance to fight our way to the Captain," Jil'lal explained.

"In that case I think I have something you could use," Anderson said as she reached into a storage box above her desk. "This is a hypospray injector, it will deliver a very strong sedative that should render a normal sized human unconscious for up to ten hours. All you have to do is press this end to the person's skin and hit this button. They should be out within a couple of seconds. This injector is good for five shots."

"Thank you doctor," Jil'lal said. "If I manage to get the Captain out I will let him know that you helped me."

"Don't worry about that," Anderson said. "The Captain knows whose side I'm on. Just don't get yourself hurt."

"I'll try," Jil'lal said as she turned to leave. "I'll lock the door behind me so that no one knows I was here."

"Thank you," the doctor said.

Once she was outside sickbay she brought up the schematics to *Endeavour* and plotted out her next route. Being in the resistance had taught her a lot of valuable lessons and the first one had been that no one succeeds alone. She needed some back up and she believed she had found the perfect person to help her. Happy that she knew where she was going she trotted off at a brisk pace. She took a longer route where no crew members should be and she was confident that everyone's attention was elsewhere.

Fifteen minutes later she was outside one of the smaller crew sections. Normally this section would house about thirty of *Endeavour's* crew, now it was a prison as Ferguson had managed to trap all thirty in their rooms.

As she peeked around the corner of the corridor that led to the main living area Jil'lal was relieved to see that there was only one guard. *Here we go*, she thought.

She flung a small metallic bolt she had removed from a power coupling down the corridor. It zipped past the guard and struck the floor ten meters past him. He looked towards the noise and raised his plasma rifle.

Before the bolt had hit its target Jil'lal was moving and as soon as the guard began to turn she accelerated into a lightening quick sprint. No human could match her speed and she was on the guard before he had time to turn around and see what the approaching noise was. With two of her hands she fended off the guard's plasma rifle and with the other two she held the injector up to his neck. With a click of the button the injector released its concoction into his system and within a couple of seconds he was slumping against her as she gently lowered him to the ground. *Powerful stuff,* Jil'lal thought as she brought up the schematic again and found Ensign Speer's room.

With her datapad she easily overrode the command that was keeping his door locked and stepped inside. The room was dark and as she crossed the threshold four arms reached out and tried to grab her.

She jumped deeper into the room, in the direction her attackers would least expect. She turned her jump into a roll midair to gain some additional space for her to maneuver. As she came up she raised all four fists, ready to fight off whoever was trying to attack her.

Instead of a follow up attack "Jil'lal?" a voice asked quietly.

"It is me," Jil'lal said. "I have come to release you."

"Oh, thank goodness. We nearly got into a fist fight with you," Private O'Brian said.

"I know," Jil'lal said. "It is good for you that I held back."

"Ha," O'Brian laughed, "I'm sure it is. This is Ensign Speers by the way. We were locked in here together when Ferguson began his mutiny."

O'Brian's cheeks became a little redder when she introduced Speers but Jil'lal didn't understand the cause. Dismissing it as irrelevant she moved on. "Well it is good that you were. The marine barracks is being guarded by ten of Ferguson's men so there is no way I could have freed them. Getting you out was much easier and so here I am. I need your help to free the Captain."

"Well we are willing and able," O'Brian said. "Do you have a plan?"

"Yes, I think I can free the Captain myself. But I will need a distraction to draw some of the guards off. The brig is not far from the main engineering room. I think if you can cause a scene there it will draw off enough of the guards from the brig that I will be able to handle the rest of them," Jil'lal said as she handed the unconscious guard's plasma rifle to O'Brian.

"I think I can handle that," O'Brian said, she hefted the plasma riffle with a big smile. "I can send Speers with you if you want."

"No," Jil'lal said. "I can move faster alone. Besides, your distraction will be more believable if there are two of you."

"Why don't we just release the rest of the crew members in this section? That would give us more than enough people to take engineering and release the Captain," Speers said.

"I thought of that," Jil'lal said, "but I wasn't sure who I could trust."

"She's right," O'Brian said. "Ferguson would have locked up anyone who he wasn't completely sure he could rely on. Yet that doesn't mean there aren't more crew members sympathetic to his view. If we let them all out one of them might turn us in before we can accomplish anything. If you are confident you can get the Captain out, then I think we need to do this alone."

"Ok," Speers said. "I understand. I guess it's just the three of us then."

"Just the three of us," Jil'lal agreed.

She then brought out her datapad and checked the time. "Do you think you can get to engineering in thirty minutes? We are locked out of all the turbo lifts so you will have to get there on foot."

"That should be doable," O'Brian replied.

"Then thirty minutes it is," Jil'lal said. "Try to make as much noise as you can. If Ferguson thinks some crew members loyal to the Captain are trying to take over engineering he will likely send all the nearby troops to help out. If you can thin out the guards stationed at the brig, then I can make my move."

"Good luck," O'Brian said. "Say hi to the Captain for me and Speers."

"I will," Jil'lal said. "Just don't get yourselves killed. You only need to cause a distraction, not actually take over engineering."

"We know," O'Brian said, "now get going or our distraction will be for nothing."

Jil'lal nodded at O'Brian and Speers and headed off to her target. Ten minutes later she was heading down a long narrow corridor that would take her to the brig. Suddenly she stopped. In the distance she heard the familiar sound of human laughter. It was getting closer. As she listened for a few more seconds she was sure she could make out the soft thud of at least two sets of footsteps.

She glanced back the way she had come. It was over forty meters to the other end of the corridor. Whoever was coming would round the corner ahead of her and see her before she managed to get away. Without thinking she whipped out her datapad and connected it to the nearest door to override the lock on it. The door was registered as a secondary storage room and it had some additional security she had to overcome. It only took her a couple of seconds and as soon as the doors opened she burst in and turned to shut them behind her.

A noise from her rear caused her to spin around in alarm, "Hold it right there," a voice said as a stunner was aimed at her.

*

Mallory sat in the bridge watching the Vestarian fleet, the Captain's words ringing in his ears, *Coward*. He had been called a coward before, on more than one occasion. Yet now that one word cut him to his core. He knew it was because he had come to love his Captain. Somerville epitomized everything that Mallory had dreamed of being as a little boy, he led by example, was a master tactician and seemed fearless in the face of danger, and to top it off he didn't even realize he had those qualities. And now Mallory found himself betraying his childhood dreams

Am I doing the right thing? He asked himself for the hundredth time since he had sat down. Ferguson had made a strong case. At least that was what he had told himself when the First Lieutenant threatened his career.

There was no doubt that James would try and take on the Vestarian fleet, and he might get the ship damaged or destroyed in the process. Ferguson had said that was the height of irresponsibility, especially when the Captain had no orders about what to do about alien threats. They were supposed to be out hunting down Chang. Not tearing across the galaxy attacking alien planets and fleets.

Yet is it irresponsibility or bravery? Is it needlessly endangering RSN lives or is it leading RSN crew members to fight for the very ideals the RSN stands for? And is Ferguson doing what he thinks the Admiralty wants him to do or is he only trying to save his own skin? Mallory couldn't decide.

To distract himself Mallory looked back at the Vestarian fleet. They were forming up into an attack formation and heading towards one of the less populated Kulrean worlds. The image brought back another memory. James sitting in the command chair Ferguson now occupied. They were over Haven and had just fired off their last broadside at the alien fleet. To the crew it had looked like the battle was over. They had failed to stop the Vestarians. *Endeavour* was about to shoot past the planet and leave the Haven fleet to make one final stand before they were destroyed.

Then James had broken through the gloom that had set in on the bridge. He had ordered *Endeavour* to fly into Haven's atmosphere to slingshot her around the planet. Mallory had been on the auxiliary bridge at the time but he had been watching the Captain on a holo display.

The look in his eyes had been infectious, Mallory remembered. *He knew he could still win and he made everyone else believe it.* Mallory knew that those moments had been what had really changed him. The battle as a whole had set him on a new path but it had been James and his confidence that had awoken something inside him. *I want to be like that,* Mallory acknowledged to himself. *Then what am I doing?*

"Everything ok Lieutenant?" Ferguson said, "you seem to be staring off into space."

Mallory almost jumped out of his command chair. "Eh, yes Sir," he answered as he made up his mind. "I just remembered I need to go and check on a few of our men. If you don't need me here I better do that now."

"Ok," Ferguson said, "but don't be too long, we need to keep a close eye on the Vestarians."

"Yes Sir," Mallory replied.

Once he got out of the bridge he made his way down to one of the storage rooms near the brig. On his way he tried to come up with a story that would explain his actions. In the end he settled on staying as close to the truth as he could. He had been forced to join Ferguson's mutiny; now that Ferguson was distracted he was doing what he had planned to do all along, double-crossing Ferguson.

When he got to the storage room he entered his command code and went inside. He made his way to one the locked containers and pulled out the electrical stun guns Major Johnston had brought on board *Endeavour.*

He spun around when the door to the storage room whooshed open. He grabbed a stunner and aimed it at the intruder, "Hold it right there," he said.

"Lieutenant Mallory," Jil'lal replied with a low growl when she saw who it was. "What are you doing here?"

"I could ask you the same thing," Mallory said. "Aren't you supposed to be locked up in your quarters?"

"I am supposed to be yes," Jil'lal said as she took a step closer to the Lieutenant hoping to get within striking range.

"Don't come any closer," Mallory said, picking up a strange looking weapon from a rack beside him as he took a step back. "I have seen images of your people fighting in the Overlord's palace. You're not to come any closer."

Jil'lal let out another low growl, she needed to take care of Mallory quickly or else her window to free the Captain would close.

"Now tell me this," Mallory said. "What are you doing out of your quarters, are you trying to free the Captain?"

"Maybe, or maybe I just thought I would go for a stroll. What is it to you?" Jil'lal said.

"Here, take these," Mallory said with a smile as he tossed two pairs of handcuffs towards her.

"You are a fool if you think you can get these on me human," Jil'lal said.

"Ha," Mallory said, "I know better than that. I'm hoping you will put them on yourself. You see I am in here getting the weapons I need to free the Captain. I think we can work together."

"Free the Captain?" Jil'lal asked, "but you are the reason why he is locked up in the first place."

"Not exactly," Mallory said. "Ferguson came to me with his plan just minutes before he made his move against the Captain. He had already recruited a number of the crew members from Chester who are, or at least were, loyal to me. I had no choice, if I had refused him he would have locked me up then and there. The only way I could help the Captain was by going along with his plan. Now that the Overlord's fleet are here and attacking the Kulreans Ferguson is distracted enough that we can make our move and release the Captain."

"Even if I believe you," Jil'lal said carefully, "what am I supposed to do with these?" she asked as she held up the handcuffs.

"You put them on of course," Mallory said with the same smile as before. "How else are we going to walk into the brig? I don't think the guards would believe that you captured me and were escorting me to the brig."

Chapter 27 - Jailbreak

Mutiny is the worst crime a crew of an Empire warship can commit. The penalty is death.

-Excerpt from Empire Rising, 3002 AD

10th August 2466 AD, HMS *Endeavour*, Kulthar System.

"Ok," Jil'lal said after taking a few moments to consider her options. She really didn't have much choice. Mallory had her caught. If he was just bluffing in an effort to get her to come peacefully he could shoot her at the first sign she was trying to get away. On the other hand, if he was telling the truth then this was her best chance to get into the brig.

"I'll do it," she added. *But I'm not telling you about O'Brian and Speers.*

"Well get those cuffs on then," Mallory said. "No time to waste."

Jil'lal gave him another growl but she picked up the cuffs and put them on.

"Lead on," Mallory said as he hefted his gun and pointed it at her. Before she turned to head out of the storage room he picked up a few more of the strange looking weapons and stuffed them into a backpack he had brought with him.

Jil'lal took a deep breath and pushed the button to open the storage room door with cuffed hands. As it swished open she stepped out and headed for the brig. To her relief the guards she had heard earlier had already passed by.

When they got near the brig Mallory poked his head around the corner of the corridor they were in. There were four guards standing outside the brig guarding the entrance. Before he could formulate a plan a small vibration rumbled through the floor plating that caused Jil'lal to jump.

"What was that?" Mallory asked.

Before Jil'lal could say anything alarms began to go off and Ferguson's voice came over the ship intercom. "All non-essential personnel report to engineering. All non-essential personnel report to engineering. We believe some of the crew are trying to retake control of *Endeavour's* power generators."

"Does that have something to do with you?" Mallory asked

"Maybe," Jil'lal said.

"Well let's make use of the distraction," Mallory replied as he poked his head around the corner again. Two of the guards were already heading off in the direction of the engine room. "Time to go."

As Jil'lal rounded the corner that led to the brig the two remaining guards raised their weapons.

"Hold your fire," Mallory shouted as he rounded the corner. "I'm escorting a prisoner to the brig. She escaped from her quarters."

"You made us jump out of our skin there Lieutenant," one of the guards said. "It's not every day an angry looking alien comes running around the corner at you."

"Ha, I guess not," Mallory chuckled. "I think we will all be a little happier once she is safely locked up. She was roaming around the ship on her own."

"Do you know what that explosion was?" the other guard asked.

"I don't know anything more than what Lieutenant Ferguson just said," Mallory answered. "I was on my way here when the alarms went off. I'm heading to engineering as soon as you get this alien locked up."

"This way then," the first guard said as he opened the doors to the brig.

When they stepped through the guard called out, "it's ok Hanson, we've just got another prisoner for you."

Hanson had been sitting behind a monitoring station but he had jumped to his feet as the doors had opened. Behind him there were three cells that formed a semi-circle around the monitoring station. One of them was full of *Endeavour's* command crew.

"Ah, Lieutenant. Do you want to put her in a cell of her own?" Hanson asked.

"No, she'll be fine with the rest of them. At least until Ferguson decides what to do with them," Mallory answered.

"Alright," Hanson said as he leaned over the monitoring station and input his authorization code. "Stand back," he called to the prisoners. "You know what happens if you stand too close to the doors when they open."

James and the Lieutenants jumped back before the electric shock that was designed to stop anyone rushing out of the cells when their doors opened could hit any of them.

"In you go," Hanson said as he pointed his plasma rifle at Jil'lal.

Before she could move Mallory turned his electrical stunner on Hanson and hit him with an electrical bolt square in the chest. He turned to take out the guard who had followed them into the brig but Jil'lal was already launching herself at him. She knocked him to the ground, sending his weapon skidding across the floor. With one strong punch she knocked him unconscious.

"Time to get out of here Captain," Mallory shouted as he opened his backpack and handed out more stunners to the Lieutenants as they came tumbling out of the cell.

"Why the sudden change of heart?" James asked Mallory after he had picked up Hanson's plasma rifle and leveled it at the Second Lieutenant.

"There was no change of heart Captain," Mallory said earnestly. "I was always on your side. Ferguson came to me just thirty minutes before he made his move against you. He had already convinced a number of the crew members from Chester to join his cause. He wanted me to persuade the rest. If I had refused, he would have knocked me out and stuffed me into my quarters. The only way I could see to help you was to go along with his plan and wait for a chance to free you. I bumped into Jil'lal as she was planning the same thing and so we decided to join forces."

"Why did you decide to help me at all?" James asked. "I've watched you closely since I took command. You don't look out for anyone but yourself. Don't forget I have read your record and the appraisals your previous Commanders have given you. Why didn't you just keep your head down and go with Ferguson's plan?"

Mallory hung his head in obvious shame. "You're right captain. In the past I've always looked out for number one. But I've changed," he said as he raised his eyes to meet James'. They were burning with a newfound passion.

"Ferguson's plan showed me just how much. I didn't think you could keep us alive over Haven, never mind save the planet. Then you managed to stop the Overlord cold and destroy over twenty of his ships. I believe in you Sir. You can make a difference here for the Kulreans and you deserve a chance to show us all what you can do."

James was taken aback. He knew mediocre officers could come good. That was what had happened to him after all. But he had been so busy concentrating on his own problems he hadn't noticed the change that must have been coming over Mallory. "I thank you for your trust," he said. "I hear-by promote you to First Lieutenant. If we can wrestle back control of *Endeavour* and help the Kulreans I will be in your debt."

"I am just doing my duty Sir," Mallory said as he saluted James.

"We all are," Becket said as she lifted the other plasma rifle off the floor and saluted James. The other officers followed her example and James felt a lump rise in his throat. He saluted them back and gritted his teeth for what was to come.

"Let's get back control of our ship and see what we can do about the rest of the Overlord's fleet," he said to his officers.

"We're with you Sir," Julius said with a grin.

"Ok then, Mallory, you and Chief Driscoll will take the Sub Lieutenants and make your way to the marine barracks. I'm guessing they will be heavily guarded but if we are going to get control of our ship we will need the marines' help. Julius, Becket and I are going to make our way to the bridge. We'll free as many of our people from their quarters as we can on the way to add to the general confusion."

"I have already freed Private O'Brian and Ensign Speers," Jil'lal said, "they were going to cause a distraction in the engine room so that I could sneak in here and free you. That was before I met Lieutenant Mallory."

"Good work," James said. "You go with Mallory and see if you can meet up with them on the way. Maybe they will have some ideas about how to take back engineering. If they were causing some problems for the mutineers who are in control, there they might have reinforced that area."

"Yes Sir, we won't let you down," Mallory said.

"Ok then, let's move," James responded. "Becket, you take point, don't hesitate to fire. We need to regain control of this ship quickly and the mutineers have already forfeited any right to leniency."

"Aye Sir," she said as she started towards the bridge.

Mallory made sure everyone in his group was equipped with stunners and headed out. "Can you get us a safe route to the marine barracks?" he asked Jil'lal.

"Of course," she answered as she pulled out her datapad. After a few seconds she set off towards their destination.

When they got close Jil'lal accessed the sensor feed for the area around the marine barracks. "There appear to be eight guards," she told Mallory.

"Ok, we'll do our trick from the brig again," he said. "If you don't mind donning your handcuffs again that is?"

"No, it's ok, I trust you now," Jil'lal said.

"Right, the rest of you wait here," Mallory said to the Sub Lieutenants. "As soon as you hear me open fire you can rush round the corner and open up on the defenders. As quick as I am, I won't be able to take them all out before they can zero in on me."

"Yes Sir," Sub Lieutenant Jennings said. "We'll have your back."

"Give me a stunner," Jil'lal said. "I can hide it between my arms and help you shoot them."

Mallory didn't hesitate to reach into his backpack and throw one over to her. "They're not very accurate so watch where you aim it," was all he said.

When Jil'lal had the cuffs on again she set off around the corridor. The marine barracks was a separate section of the ship from the rest of the crew quarters. The marines kept to themselves for disciplinary reasons. It also meant they had their own gym, pool and sparring facilities. There were two main entrances into the marine barracks and Jil'lal had led Mallory to the one that was the lightest guarded.

Again as she rounded the corner the guards jumped in surprise. They relaxed slightly when Mallory came into view but two of them kept their rifles trained on her.

"Don't worry boys, she's with me," Mallory said. "I need a couple of volunteers to escort her to the brig. I caught her wandering around out here."

"We were ordered not to leave the barracks," one of the guards said.

"And I'm the Second Lieutenant," Mallory almost shouted. "Who do you think is in charge around here?"

The guard began to mumble something in response but Mallory was already in motion. As he had shouted at them the crew members had instinctively lowered their eyes and that was all the opening he needed.

"Now," he shouted for the Sub Lieutenants' benefit as he opened fire with his stunner. Jil'lal already had hers up and multiple electric bolts hit the guards. Four of them went down immediately. A fifth was hit as a number of bolts came crashing down the corridor from the Sub Lieutenants.

The sixth and last guard had been shielded from most of the bolts by her comrades and she was able to bring up her plasma rifle and sight on Mallory. At the last second a bolt from Jil'lal hit her, throwing her aim off but not before she fired.

The bolt almost missed Mallory but the edge of its superheated plasma grazed the Lieutenant's side, sending him to the floor with a groan of agony.

Sub Lieutenant Jennings was at his side in a matter of seconds. "Are you alright Lieutenant?" she asked.

"Yes, I think so," Mallory said through gritted teeth. "It's just a flesh wound. A damn painful one I might say though."

As Jennings helped him to his feet he let out another groan but he tried to ignore the pain and carry on. "Get these doors open. I bet Major Johnston is itching to get into action."

Mallory wasn't surprised to see the Major already standing on the other side of the doors when they opened. "We heard some shooting outside the door," he offered as an explanation for his presence.

"Do you have any weapons?" Mallory asked through gritted teeth.

"No, Ferguson has locked us out of all our equipment," Johnston answered.

"Well you can take these guard's plasma rifles and our stunners. You'll be better with them than us." Mallory said, handing over his weapon to a nearby marine. "The Captain has tasked us with retaking engineering. From there we can shut off power to the rest of the ship. He is hoping it won't come to that though. The Captain is making his way to the bridge now to confront Ferguson and end this farce."

"Ok," Johnston said. "Mind if I take over?"

"Sure," Mallory said. "Though I have an idea about engineering. Some of the men in there are from Chester, they are loyal to me. I think I can convince them to change sides. If they will put down their arms there shouldn't be too many of Ferguson's men left to put up a fight."

"And what made you change sides?" Johnston asked coldly.

"I was always on the Captain's side," Mallory said. "How do you think he got out of the brig? I needed to play the mutineer to get Ferguson's trust that's all."

"Right," Johnston said, quickly changing his tone, "smart thinking."

"Follow me," he said loud enough for the rest of the group to hear, "I'm taking point."

On their way to engineering they encountered two patrols but Johnston quickly dispatched them with his plasma rifle. All four crew members went down with plasma bolts to their legs. Mallory winced when he saw the burns on some of them, guessing his side would look similar. Still, he gritted his teeth and carried on through the pain.

When they got to engineering the access door they were at wouldn't open. Mallory told everyone else to stand out of sight and keyed the intercom. "Mallory to engineering. Open up, I'm here for an inspection."

"Hold on a minute Sir," a voice replied.

Thirty seconds later the door slid open. Mallory headed through, closely followed by a number of marines.

Engineering was a massive room. The ceiling was more than forty feet high and the room was filled with all kinds of pipes and conduits that diverted energy from the fusion reactors to the various sections of the ship. He purposefully strode into the middle of the room, trying not to limp from the spreading pain in his side. The marines behind him spread out around the outer edges, taking up positions where they would have clear fields of fire.

"My fellow men of Chester," Mallory called out loud enough for all the crew in engineering to hear him. "I know most of you joined this mutiny on my say so, either because you trusted me or because you owed me something. Well I'm here to tell you I only did so to win Ferguson's trust, not because I believed in his concerns. I'm here to return control of the ship to the Captain. If you throw down your weapons now there will be no consequences for you."

"What are you doing?" an Ensign loyal to Ferguson shouted as he raised his COM unit in one hand and a plasma rifle in the other.

Before he could get off a call the bridge, Johnston hit him with a plasma bolt in the chest, killing him instantly. "We have you surrounded," Johnston called. "This is your last chance."

The mutineers threw down their weapons. Marines appeared from nowhere to snap them up for themselves and herd the mutineers into a large group in the center of the room.

Satisfied that the crew wouldn't put up any more resistance Mallory sunk to his knees. The pain was becoming unbearable. Within seconds both Jennings and Jil'lal were at his side.

"You're not ok Sir," Jennings said as she pulled back the burned sections of his uniform. "We need to get the Lieutenant to sickbay," she shouted to Major Johnston when she saw the extent of his burns.

"Ok, you take him," Johnston said. "I'll send two marines with you as an escort."

"I'm coming too," Jil'lal said as she helped Mallory to his feet.

*

James, Julius and Becket had released over forty of *Endeavour's* crew and sent them to make a nuisance of themselves across the ship and release everyone else. Now they had made it to the bridge. Thankfully, Ferguson hadn't got around to blocking out James' command codes and as he tried the main doors they acknowledged his orders to open.

"Here we go," James said, "try not to damage the bridge but whatever happens, I want Ferguson in custody."

When the doors opened Becket rushed in at full speed. She

spotted one of the bridge crew holding a plasma rifle. Before he even knew that someone was attacking the bridge she had dispatched him with a single shot to the chest. Two more of the mutineers manning the bridge tried to bring up their weapons but Becket shot one of them and leveled her weapon on the other. "Don't," she said. "It's over."

Julius was already at the feet of one of the dead mutineers, picking up his weapon and scanning the rest of the bridge for any more troublemakers. "Everyone else stay where they are," she said.

James ignored everything around him and walked to the middle of the bridge to where Ferguson was standing looking at the main holo display "I can't believe they did it. They did it, they really did it, I can't believe they did it," he mumbled over and over to himself.

James was horrified when he paused to see what Ferguson was looking at. The holo display was showing one of the Kulrean worlds. *Endeavour's* sensor scans of the planet when they had first arrived in the system had estimated that there were over forty large cities on the planet. Now they all burned. Mushroom clouds were rushing into the air over each city and mountains of debris were raining down onto the planet as what was left of the giant orbital structures was sucked into the planet's gravity. It looked like the Overlord's fleet had destroyed everything the Kulreans had built. There was complete devastation. The loss of life was far beyond anything James could imagine.

"I can't believe it," Ferguson said again, pulling James' attention back to the bridge. In that instant James had a moment of compassion for the man. He had genuinely thought he was doing the right thing. Now the destruction had broken him. Deep down Ferguson must have come to realize the Admiralty would never approve of someone who ran away and let a hostile fleet do this to a defenseless planet.

Pushing down his compassion, James approached Ferguson and lifted the butt of his rifle. For a split second there was a flash of recognition on Ferguson's face as James came into view but it was gone as soon as James brought the rifle butt down on Ferguson's forehead. He hit the deck unconscious.

"Take him to the brig," James ordered. "And get these traitors out of here."

He spun and made his way to his command chair. With a few quick commands he released the remaining crew then opened a COM channel to engineering.

"Chief?" he asked.

A few seconds later Driscoll replied, "this is the Chief. We have regained control of engineering Captain. Everything seems to be in working order. I assume you are back in control of the bridge?"

"Yes Chief, Ferguson is no longer a problem," James said. "How soon can you give us full power to the engines? I think we're going to have to hurry." James didn't know where the Overlord's fleet was but he knew they would be up to no good.

"Ferguson had the reactors powered down," Driscoll began. "It will take me at least ten minutes to warm them up but once I get them started you can get *Endeavour* under way."

"Ok, get on it Chief. Inform me as soon as we are ready to get moving," James requested. "Send Mallory and the Sub Lieutenants to the bridge if you don't need them anymore."

"They're already on their way Sir," Driscoll said. "All of them but Mallory that is. He took a plasma bolt to his side, Jil'lal and Jennings are taking him to sickbay now. I don't think his injuries are life threatening so he should be fine."

"Thank you Chief," James said, closing the COM channel.

Ten minutes later he was satisfied that he was now fully in control of his ship. Major Johnston and his marines had regained access to their equipment and they were now apprehending the last of the mutineers.

When the Major contacted him to inform him the last of them were caught, James ordered the Major to release any of them who were willing to man their battlestations. The Major protested but did as he was ordered. James opened a ship wide COM channel.

"All crew members, this is the Captain speaking," he began. "I am now in complete control of *Endeavour*. I'm afraid we have no time to spare. The Overlord's fleet has already attacked and destroyed one of the Kulrean's worlds. We need to act now. I'm ordering everyone to their battlestations. I'm sending the live feeds of what the Overlord's fleet has done to every command terminal on the ship. You need to see for yourselves what we are fighting against. I don't know what we can do to help but if we can do anything to prevent this from happening again then we need to act.

"I'm also releasing all the non-senior officers who were involved in the mutiny. *Endeavour* s going to need every crew member she has in the next few hours.

"For those of you who did mutiny, if you do your duty now I promise it will go a long way towards alleviating any consequences you might face in the future. To the rest of you, fight well. This day could have repercussions that ripple through the coming centuries. We cannot let another race simply be wiped out."

Just as he finished speaking the first of the Sub Lieutenants entered the bridge and took their seats alongside Becket and Julius. "I want a full scan of the system with our active sensors. It will give away our position but we need to know what's happening out there."

"Aye Sir," Malik said from the sensor command terminal.

"Julius, I want you to get to the auxiliary bridge. If anything happens to me do your best to help the Kulreans," James ordered.

"Yes Sir," Julius said. "I won't let you down."

A couple of minutes later Lieutenant Mallory walked in. "What are you doing here Lieutenant? Aren't you supposed to be in sickbay?" James asked.

"I was there. The doctor gave me some pain meds and I checked myself out. I wouldn't miss this for the world," Mallory said.

"Then take your seat beside me," James said, "It's a pleasure to have you along for the ride. I'm just waiting on a system wide scan to see what's going on."

Chapter 28 - Reality

Our Scientists have made great leaps in their ability to produce extremely realistic holo entertainment suites. Individuals have been known to seal themselves off in their own self-contained fantasy worlds for years, yet in the end no one can truly escape reality.

-Excerpt from Empire Rising, 3002 AD

10th August 2466 AD, HMS *Endeavour*, Kulthar System.

"Situation report," James asked Malik once he felt he had given the Sub Lieutenant enough time to analyze the sensor data.

"There are almost no signs of life left on Kulpath," Malik reported. "I think the attack was another attempt by the Vestarians to test the waters. Their main battle fleet is now on a direct course for Kulthar itself. The Kulrean capital planet is on the other side of the system's star so they will reach their target in five hours."

"How many ships do they have left?" James asked.

"Eighty four cruisers and ninety five frigates, the same number we left behind after we hit them when they were refueling."

"Damn," Mallory said, "it looks like the Kulreans really don't have any weapons."

"I guess not," James said. "And what is happening over Kulthar?"

"It looks like all hell has broken loose," Malik said. "There are literally thousands of ships flying around the planet. From this range it's hard to make anything more than that out. Even some of the larger stations that were in orbit look like they are trying to accelerate away, though I don't think they will be able to get very far in five hours."

James took several minutes to study the holo display. The entire system looked like an ant nest he had disturbed as a child. Ships were scurrying about in every direction, seemingly without any kind of order. He imagined the entire social order of the Kulrean civilization was breaking apart for they had nothing in place to handle such an attack. *Ants*, James said to himself, *they have their own way to defend themselves don't they? Even against bigger and more powerful opponents. It might just work!*

"Chief," James called over a COM channel, "do you have the reactors up and running yet?"

"Yes Sir," Driscoll answered, "I have just begun feeding power to the engines. You should be free to maneuver now."

"Navigation, plot us a course to Kulthar. Take us around the opposite end of the star to the Overlord's fleet. As soon as you have the power for it, take us up to eighty percent of our top speed."

"Yes Sir," Jennings said.

"How long will that take us to get there?" James asked.

"We can be in orbit around Kulthar in two hours," Jennings answered after plotting the course.

Good, James thought, *maybe that will give us enough time to convince them*. Thankfully *Endeavour's* sub light impulse drives were far more powerful than whatever technology the Overlord's fleet used and they had a significant acceleration and top speed advantage. "Engage the engines," he commanded.

"I think the Overlord's fleet has spotted us," Malik said twenty minutes later. "There are about thirty ships breaking off their main formation."

"So I see," James said. "It looks like they are trying to intercept us before we reach the system's star. Jennings wait until they have reversed their velocity in relation to the main fleet then bring us up to our full speed."

"You don't want to engage them?" Mallory asked

"No, I think that is what their commander wants. If we engage those ships they might be able to destroy us, certainly we will take some heavy damage. Meanwhile, the rest of the fleet will be free to attack Kulthar.

"We can simply go to our max speed and zip past them. The Vestarian commander will then have to decide if he wants to leave these ships behind or slow his main fleet to allow these ships catch up."

"You wanted the enemy commander to send some ships after us? That's why you started off going slower than we could," Mallory asked.

"Yes," James said, "I bet after our attack on the resupply ships the enemy commander is very concerned about us. Probably more scared than he needs to be. We can use that."

Ten minutes later Jennings boosted *Endeavour* up to her top speed. The thirty alien ships trying to intercept her initially boosted their own speed by a marginal amount. Yet it soon became clear they wouldn't be able to stop *Endeavour* from swinging around the star in front of their main battle fleet. Giving up, they reversed their course and fell in behind the main battle fleet, though now they were almost an hour behind.

"That evens the odds a little," James said, happy that they had won a minor victory.

*

"Contact Kulthar," James said when they were close enough that two way communication would be manageable.

"Captain Somerville," Hallock said when his face appeared on the holo display five minutes later. "I'm afraid you have been proven correct. Kulpath burns, that war fleet killed over a billion of our people."

"You have my deepest sympathies," James said. "I had hoped the Vestarian fleet had only come to conquer your people, not exterminate them. I am here to offer my help again. We may yet still save some of your people."

"We are evacuating the system now," Hallock said. "I'm trying to get as many of my people out of here as possible. We will not resort to violence however. We have already talked about this. My people may be dying all around me but if we try to save ourselves by killing others then we will already have lost who we are."

"You may not have to resort to violence," James said and proceeded to outline his plan to Hallock.

"Absolutely not," Hallock said. "What you are purposing is as close to Kulreans killing as makes no difference."

"But what about your people?" James said in frustration. "They are dying out there even as we speak. You need to let them decide. Surely some of your people would be willing to fight to protect their young."

"Our leaders have decided. This has been the Kulrean way for the last two thousand years. We will not change who we are," Hallock said.

"Suit yourself," James shouted in frustration, "but sooner or later your people are going to have to face up to reality. Even if you run away now the Vestarians will not simply go away."

James didn't listen to Hallock's reply; instead he focused on his own frustration. The alien was leaving him with no other option. It was just like his encounter with the Swedish colony ship all over again. He was now faced with certain death if he stood against the Overlord's fleet. Yet how could he run away? Cowardice was not the RSN way, and he would bring shame on all of mankind if he just left a defenceless civilization to destruction.

James' thoughts turned to the final battle with the Chinese in the V17 system. There he hadn't hesitated following Rear Admiral Jensen into a mad dash against overwhelming forces. Yet that had been a heat of the moment decision. Now he had plenty of time to think over what he would do.

Deep down he knew there was nothing to think about. He had changed. He wasn't the man from before the Void War. Like Christine, he had learnt the price of duty. Now it was time to put those lessons to use. After the battle over Haven and the recent raid on the refuelling Vestarian ships he had complete confidence in his own abilities. *Endeavour* was going to give as good an account of herself as he could possibly manage.

"It's time to show these aliens what a King's ship can really do," James said to the bridge and Superintendent Hallock. His decision was made. When he looked around the bridge he saw that all the officers were nodding at him. They were with him.

"Good luck Superintendent," James said, turning back to the holo projection of the alien.

"What do you mean, where are you going to go?" Hallock asked.

"You'll see," James said before he cut the COM channel, he was too angry at the alien's refusal to help his people to give him anymore time.

"COMs, send a replay of my conversation with the Superintendent to the rest of the system. Instruct the Kulrean people that if they want to help *Endeavour* defeat the fleet attacking their system they should follow the plan I gave Hallock," James ordered.

"On it," Sub Lieutenant King responded.

"Jennings, take us away from Kulthar and back towards the approaching fleet. We have the advantage in missile range so we're going to use it. Becket, coordinate with Julius on the auxiliary bridge and Chief Driscoll. I want them to transfer all our anti-ship missiles from the port tubes to the starboard ones."

"Acknowledged," Jennings and Becket said one after the other.

"What's your plan Sir?" Mallory asked.

"We need to thin out their numbers as much as possible," James answered. "We have the advantage in missile range and they won't deviate from closing with Kulthar. That means they will be flying right into the face of our missiles. If we can group up enough missiles we can punch through their point defenses and start to destroy the ships on the edges of their formation. Unless the Kulreans decide to join us there isn't too much else we can do."

"I understand, given the circumstances I guess that is the best plan we have for now," Mallory said.

"Indeed," James replied.

"Tactical," James said, turning to Lieutenant Becket. "We're going to make a charge towards the Overlord's fleet. As soon as we line them up I want you to flush missiles out of our launch tubes. I want you to vary the speed at which you flush them out so that they will reach the point that they can engage their engines at the same time. The calculations will be too imprecise to get exact but get them as close together as you can. We'll fire off two super volleys and then decelerate away from the Overlord's fleet, turn around, and then do it again if they will let us."

"Yes Sir, I'll set up the firing solutions," Becket answered.

Ordinarily attacking fleets would come in on semi random attack vectors to make it difficult for the defenders to fire ballistic projectiles at them. Some of the human powers had experimented with mass drivers but they had proved to be too inaccurate over long ranges. Missiles were far better weapons.

Endeavour's missile tubes had the capacity to fire their missiles on ballistic trajectories to extend the range of the missiles but usually it was too difficult to predict where an enemy fleet would be. Instead the tubes were used to impart some initial velocity to the missiles and once they cleared the tubes the missiles would engage their own engines and home in on their targets.

The Overlord's fleet was coming in on an unchanging vector. That was going to allow Becket to launch a series of volleys of ballistic missiles, each one with slightly more initial speed. Once the missiles got into attack range they could power up their engines and engage together.

"I think we will be able to get off two super volleys of forty missiles," Becket said.

"Begin flushing the tubes as soon as you are ready, then I want you to line up the flak cannons. Fire off as many tungsten spears as you can. Time them to impact just as the first volley of missiles will be switching on their engines and seeker heads."

"Got it," Becket responded.

For almost fifty minutes *Endeavour* flew straight into the teeth of the approaching battle fleet, flushing missiles as soon as the missile crews could reload the tubes. Just before she entered the maximum range of the Vestarian missiles Jennings began to slow and reverse *Endeavour's* course.

"Impact in thirty seconds," Becket called out.

James focused his attention on the gravimetric plot. The distances were too great for the rest of the sensors to give him a real time update on how successful his attacks would be. Just when Becket predicted a number of Vestarian ships disappeared off the plot. Over a hundred tungsten spears had been fired at the center of the fleet, it looked like ten had hit their targets.

At the same time forty new contacts appeared on the gravimetric plot as the missiles engaged their engines. They weren't lined up in a perfect volley so the Vestarians would have a chance to pick many of them off with their point defenses. On the other hand, the Vestarian fleet was charging straight towards the approaching missiles and the closing speed was more than half the speed of light. James knew from Jil'lal that their computers weren't nearly as advanced as human ones and he hoped their firing computers would struggle to hit such fast moving targets.

"It will take the missiles five minutes to hit their targets," Becket announced.

"Enemy fleet is beginning evasive maneuvers," Mallory said. "I think our second volley will still be able to hit them but we won't be able to repeat our trick."

"Bring us about," James ordered. "Jennings, match their course and speed. Becket resume firing as soon as we come into range, we'll just have to keep hammering them with single broadsides.

"How are we doing on missiles?" James asked Julius over the COM to the auxiliary bridge.

"We have moved all of our missiles over to the starboard tubes already," Julius answered. "Becket should have another forty to play with. After that we will have to resort to the missiles we took on at Haven. They have about half the range of our missiles but they still pack a punch and their ECM isn't too bad."

"Ok," James said, "Keep moving them over."

As he switched his focus back to the gravimetric plot he saw that the first wave of missiles had entered the Vestarians' point defense range. The forty missiles had been reduced to thirty four. They were further reduced to less than twenty when they all disappeared as they detonated amongst their targets.

When the plot cleared up Becket let out a whoop. "We got at least fifteen of them!" she shouted.

James was impressed. The Overlord's fleet had numbered one hundred and seventy nine when it had entered the Kulrean system. Thirty were now lagging well behind the main fleet which had now been reduced to one hundred and twenty four. They were making a real dent. *It's all for nothing unless the Kulreans are prepared to stand up to them though*, James thought to himself.

"Second super volley has ignited its engines," Becket announced, "they should all be able to get into range."

James turned to the gravimetric plot to follow the progress of the missiles. Before they reached their targets the plot updated to show eight more contacts as Becket fired off another volley of missiles.

"I think we got nine of them this time," Malik said after their second super volley hit the approaching fleet.

For the next half an hour *Endeavour* flew in front of the charging fleet as if she was leading them straight to Kulthar. The only indication that she wasn't intent on the same death and destruction were the regular broadsides of eight missiles that she threw out at the Vestarians. Occasionally one of the missiles from the broadsides would get through and take out one of the alien warships but with only eight targets the Vestarian point defenses were able to do a much better job.

"That was the last of our missiles," Becket reported. "If we want to keep hitting them we'll have to switch to the Haven missiles."

Everyone looked towards James to see what he would say. They all knew what it meant. The Haven missiles still had a slight range advantage over what they knew the Vestarians could do, yet because the Vestarian fleet was flying straight towards them their missiles would also have the momentum imparted to them from their motherships. That meant the Vestarians had the greater effective range. For *Endeavour* to be able to get into range to use the Haven missiles she would have to enter into the range of the Vestarian ships.

"We have no choice," James told everyone on the bridge, "take us into range and open fire."

The only saving grace for *Endeavour* was that the enemy ships could only fire their forward facing bow tubes. James hadn't yet seen how many bow missile tubes the Vestarian ships had but he was sure it wouldn't be as many as they carried on their broadsides.

"First Haven volley is away," Becket said.

"The Overlord's ships are opening fire," Malik announced.

"Here we go," Mallory said as new contacts began to appear on the gravimetric plot.

"I'm counting eighty missiles Captain," Malik informed the bridge. "I think it was only the frigates that opened fire. I don't understand why the cruisers didn't fire too."

"Maybe they don't have any bow missile tubes," James thought out loud. "Their x-ray lasers and the power plants they need to supply them probably take up a great deal of space."

"We may yet survive this," Mallory shouted with a grin.

"Malik, prepare four of our recon drones for launch. Program them to give off signals to make them mimic *Endeavour*. We're going to throw up a flak screen, fire off a volley from our point defense plasma cannons and then take *Endeavour* into stealth mode. With any luck all the remaining missiles will lock onto the drones," James ordered.

Because of the reduced range James didn't have to wait long for the Vestarian missiles to reach *Endeavour's* outer point defense ring. Under Mallory's supervision the flak cannons created a wall of flying shrapnel in front of the missile swarm. Thirty of the eighty missiles were destroyed.

Next was the point defense plasma cannons. As James had ordered they fired one burst of plasma bolts, taking out a further five missiles. Silence descended on the bridge as *Endeavour* shut down all her non-essential systems and powered down her engines and reactors.

At the same time Malik activated the four recon drones that would mimic the electromagnetic profile of *Endeavour* that the Vestarian missiles were homing in on. The remaining forty five missiles split up into five groups. Forty one missiles split over four groups dived towards the decoys but five continued on towards *Endeavour*.

"They are still detecting something to home in on," James shouted. "Evasive maneuvers now Jennings!"

Jennings was ready to act but with *Endeavour's* reactors powered down to stealth levels she was severely limited in what she could do. As the sound of AM missiles being automatically launched by the ship's computer filled the silence on the bridge Jennings desperately tried to throw *Endeavour* into a series of spins and turns.

Three missiles lost their lock on the ship because it was still only giving off a small amount of waste electromagnetic energy. The other two stayed true and though they failed to get direct hits, both exploded less than twenty meters away from the ship's hull.

Everyone on the bridge was thrown about in their seats and a number of alarms went off. "Damage report," James ordered.

"We took two proximity hits," Julius said over the COM. "No sign of any internal damage though everyone is a bit shaken up. Wait... I just got a report from Chief Driscoll. He says one of the reactors is fluctuating dangerously. He is going to have to take it offline."

"How are our point defenses?" James asked.

"One flak cannon is down, we have also lost contact with about twenty percent of our point defense plasma cannons. I think the two proximity hits just burnt them right off the hull," Julius replied.

"Damn," James said.

"I don't know if we can take another volley like that one," Mallory said, concerned.

"No," James concluded. "But what would you have me do? Could you live with yourself if we ran away just to watch what happened at Kulpath repeated at Kulthar?"

"No," Mallory said.

"No indeed, and every ship we destroy now will give the Kulreans more of a chance to flee," James added.

"Close us to plasma cannon range," he ordered Sub Lieutenant Jennings.

"Aye Sir," she replied quietly, everyone on the bridge knew what the order meant.

"We took out another two Vestarian warships with our first broadside of Haven missiles," Becket reported. "They are having a hard time targeting our missiles at this reduced range. I think I can get a couple more before we enter plasma cannon range."

"Do it," James said.

Endeavour's crew and her automated systems were obviously far better than the Vestarians for as Jennings closed the range further, Becket got off another broadside and managed to destroy three more warships before the Vestarians replied.

"Seventy missiles inbound," Malik reported when the Vestarians finally managed to reload their missile tubes. "Hold on, twenty of their cruisers are turning, they are bringing their port missile tubes to bear on us! I now count two hundred and seventy missiles in bound in two staggered volleys."

"Will we get into plasma cannon range before the hit us?" Mallory asked Jennings.

"No Sir," she answered deflated.

"Then this is it," Mallory said. "It's been a pleasure serving with you Sir."

"And with all of you," James said to the bridge. "But we are not dead yet. Becket, see if you can get off another broadside. Jennings boost us past our top speed. If a stray cosmic particle penetrates our armor and kills us all it hardly matters now. Mallory, as soon as we get into plasma cannon range I want to hit a cruiser with each of our cannons. We can still go down fighting!"

None of the Lieutenants replied, they simply threw themselves into obeying James' last orders. Sure enough Becket got off another broadside of missiles but moments after their engines ignited thrusting them towards their targets the Vestarian missiles arrived. The point defenses took out almost forty of them but over two hundred tore in towards the British warship.

Jennings' evasive maneuvers managed to avoid the first few missiles but then three got proximity hits at once and the explosive force threatened to tear *Endeavour* apart. Moments later a fourth got a direct hit, it impacted the ship right in *Endeavour's* nose, penetrating through half the valstronium armor before it exploded.

On the bridge everyone was already being thrown about from the force of the proximity hits when the fourth missile exploded. The concussive force momentarily overloaded the inertial dampeners and James was hurled about so violently that he blacked out. The rest of the bridge officers didn't fare much better and when the explosion from the fourth missile threw *Endeavour* into wild spin no one was in a position to correct it.

An eternity seemed to pass as James slowly regained consciousness. "We're still alive?" he asked out loud, hoping someone else was more aware of what was going on than him.

"Yes," Mallory said groggily, "I'm not quite sure how though."

"We're currently spinning out of control," Julius said over the COM, "one of my Sub Lieutenants is correcting now."

"We're being hailed by a Kulrean ship," Sub Lieutenant King reported.

James took a moment to sort himself out and then said, "Put it on my personal holo display."

"Hello Captain," a Kulrean said, James wasn't sure but he thought this was a different Kulrean than Superintendent Hallock.

"My name is, Pemel, we're here to give you an escort. My ships should be able to take a few hits from these Vestarians,"

The feed from the Kulrean ship dropped for a few seconds and then reappeared. Pemel looked startled but still alive. "Oh my, that was close, we just took a hit from one of their missiles. They blew a great hole in the side of my ship. But I'm still here, is your ship still functional? It looks to be in a bad way."

"We're still able to put up a fight but we can't destroy all the Vestarian ships alone." James replied still not sure how he was alive. "Your ships need to attack the Vestarians,"

"Don't worry, we're on it. I'm just the escort," Pemel assured him.

When James looked at the sensors he had to blink a couple of times to make sure he was seeing things clearly. It looked as if all the space between *Endeavour* and Kulthar was alive and moving towards the Overlord's fleet.

They can't all be automated can they?" James asked Pemel.

"No, as soon as we got your signal we began automating our ships like you instructed Superintendent Hallock but we didn't have enough time. When we saw the sacrifice you and your crew were prepared to make we decided to come to your aide. Your actions today have taught us something new for the first time in more than two millennia. For thousands of years our people have believed the most honorable way to live has been to eschew all violence and use of weapons. Now, today, we have seen a different type of honor. You and you crew were willing to give your lives for my people. That is something we can emulate. Many of us will die today. But far fewer of us will die because of you."

Even as he was listening to Pemel, James was watching the holo display. Literally thousands of Kulrean ships shot past *Endeavour,* travelling far faster that he would have believed possible. When he played back the last couple of minutes of the battle he saw that hundreds of Kulrean ships had thrown themselves in between *Endeavour* and the missile volley he thought was going to end his ship. He couldn't find many of them on the sensors now.

"Follow them in," James ordered as a wave of emotion washed over him. "Use the plasma cannons Mallory."

As *Endeavour* went to full speed the battle was already turning. Hundreds of missiles and lasers reached out from the Overlord's fleet to wipe Kulrean ships off the plot. Yet for every one that was destroyed three took its place. Soon they got close enough to make kamikaze runs against the Vestarian ships. James had recommended that the Superintendent automate his ships and fly them into the Overlord's fleet but as Pemel said there hadn't been time. Many of those ships contained living crews.

At first it looked like the Overlord's fleet would be able to fend them off. X-ray lasers, anti-ship missiles and AM missiles filled the space around the Overlord's fleet, destroying anything that got close to them.

"They got one," Malik called out as a Vestarian cruiser disappeared when a Kulrean ship finally managed to penetrate the Vestarian's defensive fire and ram it.

"We're in range," Becket shouted, "opening fire."

Endeavour's plasma cannons picked off warships in ones and twos but within seconds there were hardly any targets for Becket to pick out. Hundreds of smaller Kulrean ships broke through the mountain of fire and swarmed the Overlords fleet like ants protecting their nests. Hundreds, perhaps even thousands, of Kulrean ships were destroyed but as soon as the main body of the Kulrean fleet got close to the Overlord's ships both groups simply vanished off the plot.

"They are all gone," Malik said, stunned, once the sensors were able to make out anything from the debris field that had appeared around them. There were hundreds of broken ships tumbling about in front of *Endeavour* but there was no sign of any Vestarian ships.

James wasn't surprised, the drive technology the Kulreans had was almost unbelievable. There was no way the Vestarian ships could have avoided them once the Kulreans got through their defensive fire and close enough to ram.

"I'm getting a signal from the remaining thirty Vestarian ships," Malik said. "They wish to surrender to us."

"No chance," James said in anger. "Tell them if they don't want to face the same fate as their sister ships they must surrender to Pemel."

"They have acknowledged," Malik said.

"Get Pemel on the COM," James said.

"It's over," James said to him once his face appeared on the holo display. "The remaining ships have surrendered. You have saved your people and your planet. It was a brave sacrifice your ships made."

"No Captain, you have saved us. My people will owe you an eternal debt of gratitude," the Kulrean replied.

"It was our pleasure," James said bowing his head, "now, let us see to our dead and wounded," he continued before his emotions got the better of him.

"Certainly," Pemel agreed.

After the COM channel shut down James let out a long breath. He had been sure that had been the end. Once before he had thought he had faced certain death. Then he had been filled with many regrets. This time he had known his death would have served a purpose. He had been doing his duty. *I hope I am doing your memory proud*, James said to Admiral Jensen in his mind.

Duty never ends, was his next thought as he turned his mind to

Endeavour and the dead and wounded he had to care for.

Chapter 29 – Homeward Bound

Captain Somerville's discovery and intervention into the Vestarian and Kulrean civilizations sent shockwaves throughout the human nations. Many people and groups would become very fearful and suspicious of the aliens. Yet without them, the Empire might never had been formed.

- Excerpt from Empire Rising, 3002 AD

24th August, 2466 AD. HMS *Endeavour*, in orbit around Kulthar.

Two weeks after the battle for Kulthar, James was sitting in *Endeavour's* conference room with Pemel and three other representatives from the newly formed Kulthar Union. Their old way of governance had fallen apart when Pemel had abandoned the Kulrean's insistence of pacifism.

The Kulreans had abided by an ancient code of laws that their forefathers had written thousands of years ago. Everyone was simply expected to follow them and the Superintendents were just there to deal with the extraordinary. Apart from their occasional intrusion into the running of the Kulrean civilization, life within the Kulthar system had gone on in the same way for centuries. The only real change had been when they had made contact with the Vestarians and decided to try and spread their ideals there as well.

Now things had been thrown into turmoil. There were new

factions springing up throughout the system as the Kulreans woke up to the possibility of life without their ancestors' rules. Pemel and those who had followed him had taken charge for the present. His leadership had saved their entire civilization and the people were giving him a lot of leeway. It also helped that he ran one of the largest shipping companies in the system. His years of experience hashing out business deals had prepared him well for handling an ever-growing number of political groups who were all vying for his attention.

In the conference room with James and Pemel were Lieutenants Mallory, Julius and Becket along with Jil'lal. James knew this had been a historic meeting, it was the first time members of each race had met each other face to face. Although nothing would be decided from the hours of talks they had just gone through it would still go down in history.

"Let me give you our people's thanks one last time," Pemel said. "To you Captain Somerville, your crew and to you Jil'lal. We know this fleet that attacked us does not represent your entire race and we hope to open peaceful negations with your people once again. Negotiations that don't just happen through a satellite in orbit."

"I do not deserve your thanks," Jil'lal said. "I was just an observer in the end. But I know I speak for my people when I give you our sincerest apologies. We hope that you will allow us to do whatever we can to make up for what the Overlord's warships did to your people and your system."

"Forgiveness will take time. My people are still in shock at what has happened. However, your presence here has already gone a long way to showing us that the Overlord's fleet does not represent the true Vestarian people. I am sure in time our people will be able to become friends. The last two weeks have shown that we can work well together," Pemel said.

James nodded at that. The last two weeks had been hectic. After spending a few hours doing essential repairs, James had placed a couple of marines or armed crew members on the bridge of each of the Vestarian ships that had surrendered. Then he had taken *Endeavour* to Kulpath and joined the rescue operations. In total more than twenty million survivors had been lifted off the broken planet. *Endeavour* had played a very small role in achieving such a great feat but they had done all they could. Jil'lal had even managed to talk a number of the Vestarian captains into helping relieve the humanitarian crises.

Now there was nothing left for them but to return home and report on everything that had happened. All the lives that could be saved had been and the Kulreans were going about the business of resettling the survivors and considering their futures.

James knew *Endeavour* would need at least a few weeks or even a month or two in a repair yard before she was mission ready again and they had now lost over forty five crew members on this mission. James hadn't got to know all of them personally but their loss still weighed heavily on him. It was time to go home, see to *Endeavour's* repairs and inform the families of their loss.

Pemel had taken the names of all the crew who had died fighting the Overlord, at Haven, Vestar and Kulthar and a monument was being erected for them on the Kulrean homeworld. Pemel had also promised to visit Earth to open formal communications between their two peoples. Though Pemel still seemed reluctant to trade technologies that could be used for warfare, he was willing to trade a great deal of the other advances the Kulreans had made in the last thousand years.

"I guess there is nothing to say now but farewell," James said. "I look forward to welcoming you to Earth when you arrive."

"And I look forward to seeing your homeworld," Pemel said. "Our exploration ships visited it more than a thousand years ago and I'm sure it has changed a lot."

"Indeed it has," James said, "I hope you will be impressed."

"I don't doubt it," Pemel responded. "I don't know yet when I will be able to leave but the FTL communicator I gave you will allow us to stay in contact once you place it in orbit around your planet. I will let you know exactly when we will arrive through it," he added.

"Farewell my friend," he said as he shook James' hand just as James had taught him to.

"Farewell," James said again.

*

20th September, 2466 AD. HMS *Endeavour*, in orbit around Vestar.

Three days after arriving at Vestar James stood on the bridge of

Endeavour looking down at the planet. They had returned to drop Jil'lal off at and update Tak'ar and his new government about the events from Kulthar.

When they had opened communication with the planet they had found that Tak'ar was fully up to date on everything. The Kulreans had opened up full communication with the Vestarians through their FTL satellite and the news *Endeavour* had brought hadn't been a surprise to anyone. On the other hand, what James and his crew had found on Vestar had been a real shock.

In just two short months Tak'ar and the Resistance leaders had managed to completely reform their government. A planetary wide government was now in place, one that vaguely resembled the federal system of the old United States constitutional government.

Tak'ar had turned all the old nations of Vestar into their own federal states. Each state could elect its own local senate and senate director while the entire planet elected one parliament led by the parliamentary President. James suspected that Tak'ar had spent more than a few hours reviewing the histories of Earth that Scott had supplied him with for the setup seemed to take some of the best bits of Earth's lessons in democracy and apply them to the Vestarian people.

The one thing that hadn't been a surprise was that Tak'ar had been elected as the first Parliamentary President. As such, his schedule had been very busy, yet he had made ample time for James over the last three days. Tak'ar, Mul'li'la, Jil'lal and most of James' bridge crew all had a private meal on board *Endeavour* the night they had returned. The next day Tak'ar had insisted on holding the Vestarian's first state dinner to officially welcome

James and *Endeavour* to Vestar. Between both meals Tak'ar had also spent a lot of time picking James' and the officers' brains regarding the different democracies on Earth and how they worked. Freedom was something completely new to the people of Vestar and Tak'ar was trying to make as few mistakes as possible.

One of his first acts as the new Parliamentary President had been to seize the Overlord's secret construction yard. The Vestarian's space industry was small but they did have some shuttles that could make the journey to the construction yard. Tak'ar had taken it over and was in the process of re-tooling it so that the first Vestarian defense fleet could be constructed.

When James had first heard what Tak'ar had done he had been concerned. It would take years for the Vestarians to build a fleet that could be a threat to even the smallest of the Earth powers. Yet the very fact the Vestarians were still building warships would concern everyone back on Earth. Not to mention the Kulreans.

Tak'ar had been ahead of him though for after informing James about the new construction project, he had handed James a data chip. It contained all the technical details on the Overlord's fleet. Including the technical details on how to build the x-ray lasers and the powerful energy reactors that supplied them. Tak'ar wanted it to be a symbol of his peaceful intent. Both James and Tak'ar knew that with the technical details of the Vestarian warships it would be much easier for a human nation to defend themselves from any future Vestarian aggression, not to mention allow an Earth power to invade Vestar. It was a great risk Tak'ar was taking, but the gesture was appreciated.

Neither the Overlord nor any of his scientists appeared to know exactly how the lasers and energy reactor worked. There were no theoretical descriptions within the designs, just technical instructions on how to build them. It seemed that whatever had been going on in the Omen facility, the Overlord had somehow gained access to technology far beyond what the Vestarians understood. Even James wasn't sure how the technologies worked but he was certain there would be scientists back on Earth who would. Once they figured it out it would no doubt bring about a revolution in energy production.

Already a vast number of scientists from different nations were working on alternative energy reactors to the fission ones used throughout the Human Sphere. James was sure the technical plans he now held would advance much of that research by decades or more.

He wasn't sure the x-ray lasers would be just as revolutionary. After Chief Driscoll had looked over their designs he had dismissed them. They got most of their added range and intensity from the colossal power that the energy reactor fed them.

James had enjoyed his few days on Vestar. It had been vastly different from his first visit. The populace was repairing the damage *Endeavour* had caused in her orbital bombardments and James had been delighted to be given a tour of the Overlord's palace. It was being turned into a museum on the history of the Vestarian people. Even though museums weren't James's thing, he had enjoyed the tour, if only for the fact that he had received a far warmer welcome than his first visit to the palace.

Now it was time to leave Vestar just as they had Kulthar and

James was keen to get back to Earth and inform the Admiralty about what was going on.

"Signal the new parliamentary building," James ordered Sub Lieutenant King, "let them know that we are breaking orbit."

"Message sent Sir," King answered, "they are replying. They wish us well on our voyage and hope to see *Endeavour* back in orbit in the near future."

"Very good," James said, "Jennings take us out of orbit."

*

15th October, 2466 AD, HMS *Endeavour*, Haven System.

"We will be coming out of shift space in thirty seconds," Sub lieutenant Malik reported.

James didn't answer, his mind was elsewhere, thinking about what kind of reception they were likely to receive from the Haven government. He hadn't exactly left on friendly terms with Maximilian. But the First Councilor may have fallen from his position. James' revelation to the population of Haven that their government had been involved in harboring a war criminal and international piracy was sure to have caused him some problems. Plus, James knew Suzanna would have spent the last several months actively working against Maximilian. He didn't know exactly how much clout Suzanna had with the other councilors but he knew she would be doing her best. The real question was, could he risk seeing her again? If she was trying to overthrow the First Councilor and establish a government that would be favorable towards British intervention in Haven, then any contact with him might give her opponents ammunition to use against her. She would be called a traitor.

James was so deep in thought that he didn't notice *Endeavour's* transition out of shift space. "Nothing unusual in the system," Malik said after the sensors had enough time to make out what was going on around Haven. His words pulled James' mind back to the matter at hand.

"Take us in towards the colony then," James ordered after pausing to look over the main holo display of the system to make sure he hadn't missed anything.

Four hours later James was still sitting on the bridge. He had expected to receive some form of message from Haven but so far nothing had come. James guessed Maximilian or whoever was in charge was waiting until *Endeavour* was close enough to open up two-way communication in real time. That suited James fine for it meant he could get in the first word.

"Transmit our report to the entire system," he ordered Sub Lieutenant King who was manning the COMs terminal.

"Aye Sir," King responded, "the transmission has been sent. Still no sign of any COMs activity from the planet."

The report was a simplified version of the report he had prepared for the Admiralty. It detailed how the Overlord was responsible for the attack on Haven, *Endeavour's* role in overthrowing him and James' efforts to stop the attack on the Kulreans. The report also included messages from Tak'ar and Pemel communicating their desire to begin a close friendship with humanity. James hoped the report would ease the fears of the Haven populace.

"How is the colony looking?" Mallory asked to break the silence that had developed as everyone waited for a reply.

"It looks like they are recovering well," Malik said. "There appear to be a number of new orbital stations under construction. I'm also detecting an increased amount of activity in the outer asteroid belts. The Havenites must be working like devils out there to mine all the resources they need to rebuild their infrastructure."

"Give us a run-down of what military ships they have operating," James requested.

"Certainly Sir," Malik answered. "Admiral Harris's flagship appears to be in a repair yard though it seems the rest of the ships that survived the battle of Haven have been returned to service. I'm detecting one destroyer and eight frigates patrolling the approaches to the colony."

"They certainly work fast," Mallory said.

"Yes," James said, "though a destroyer and a few frigates aren't going to deter some of the Earth powers from thinking they can claim Haven for themselves. I suspect Haven has a very interesting future ahead of itself."

"I would bet on that," Mallory said.

"At least, when I was a betting man I would have," he added when James gave him a stern look. On their journey back from

Kulthar James had made an effort to take Mallory under his wing. He knew he had neglected the Second Lieutenant during the initial stages of their mission, in large part because James had written him off. As a result, James had missed Mallory's transformation.

Now he was determined to do all he could to help Mallory continue to develop into a competent and accomplished King's officer. Part of that process had been a frank one to one discussion about Mallory's past failings, gambling being one of them. Thankfully Mallory had acknowledged the error of his ways. As James had suspected, Mallory had developed his gambling habit as a young man disillusioned with the wealth of his family. Gambling had been a way to bring risk and excitement into his otherwise comfortable life.

Now Mallory had something else to find fulfillment in; his duty as a naval officer. James had been impressed and James' own upbringing as the second son of one of the wealthiest Duke's in the British Star Kingdom had allowed him to understand Mallory better than most. They were becoming firm friends.

James had also learnt an important personnel lesson, *never underestimate the potential of a junior officer.* Having said that, the betrayal of the former First Lieutenant had taught him a different lesson; *always follow your gut.* Ever since his decision to follow the fleet that had attacked Haven, James had suspected something was wrong with Ferguson. He had just dismissed it as the First Lieutenant seeking to look out for the ship's best interests, something that was part of his job. Now it was clear that Ferguson had only been looking out for himself and his cowardice had been driving many of his actions.

As those thoughts were going around James' head, *Endeavour* continued towards the colony for another thirty minutes before any attempt to open communications was received from the planet. "I have the First Councilor on a COM channel for you Captain," King reported when the silence was finally broken.

"Put it on the main screen, make sure you are recording it," James requested.

"Captain," Maximilian said when his face appeared on the holo display, "I'm surprised you decided to show your face here again. Let me tell you now, you are not welcome on our planet. Do not try to enter orbit. If you do, I will be forced to order our navy to escort you out of the system."

"It's nice to see you too First Councilor," James began. "I must say I am surprised. I was expecting a warmer welcome. We have come here to let you and your people know that the Vestarian threat has been taken care of. I would have thought you would have been more pleased to hear that."

"Don't play nice with me," Maximilian spat. "I don't care about what you did to the Vestarians, you tried to interfere in our politics, for that our council has voted to permanently ban you from our system."

"How nice of you," James said. "I guess pirates can run the government on Haven while the crew of the ship that saved the entire planet from destruction is shunned. Didn't you read the report on what happened to Kulpath? That could have been Haven if it wasn't for us."

"To hell with you and those aliens," Maximilian shouted,

outraged by James' reference to his piracy. "I have warned you once. Your actions have earned you a ban from our colony. Let that be a warning to your government and the others on Earth. We at Haven will not stand for any interference in our internal politics or sovereignty. If you come any closer, I will order my ships to open fire."

"So be it," James said. "I came to offer my country's friendship. The discovery of the Vestarians and the Kulreans will mean this area of space will become the center of attention for all the Earth powers. One way or another, you are going to need some friends in the future. If this is the route you want to take, then it will be on your own head. I wish your colony all the best. Even if it is led by a pirate," James finished.

Before Maximilian could say anymore he cut the feed. "Transmit our recording of the conversation to the entire planet," he ordered King, "then turn *Endeavour* around and get us out of here, lay in a course for Earth."

Two hours later *Endeavour* was well on her way out of the Haven system. Since they had turned around they had been bombarded by messages from the surface. All sorts of people who had the ability to send COM messages to the ship had been trying to contact James and *Endeavour's* crew.

James had listened to the first ones that had come in and sent back text messages to them, but when the numbers had grown he had been forced to pull other officers in to help him. Many of the messages had been offering the senders' thanks for what *Endeavour* had done. Others had been asking about the future and British policy towards Haven. More than one had been hostile and insulting. James had ordered those ignored. For the rest he had instructed his officers to reply curtly and civilly, informing the people of Haven that *Endeavour* had been doing their duty and that the British government would be willing to provide Haven with whatever protection they needed against alien attacks or attempts by other Earth powers to interfere in Haven's sovereignty. However, his officers were also to make it clear that Britain would not deal with pirates and war criminals.

James wasn't sure if all the messages would have any effect but he knew they would anger Maximilian and anything that would put the First Councilor off his game was worth doing.

"We're getting another COM message," King reported.

"Just add it to the list for us to look at," Mallory instructed him.

"This one is different Sir," King said. "It's coming in via a laser link."

"A laser link?" James asked, his interest piqued. "We can't be close enough the planet to still receive a laser link?"

"No Sir," King answered. "It's coming from one of the gas mining stations. We are passing as close to it now as we will come."

Suzanna, James thought. He had guessed she would be on Haven trying to win the support she needed to overthrow Maximilian, he hadn't expected her to be on her gas mining station.

"Send the message to my office, I will listen to it there," James ordered as he stood up and left the bridge.

When he sat in his office chair he activated the holo display on his desk and brought up Suzanna's message. "Hello James," she said with a smile. "I hope this message gets to you. My engineers have boosted the power of our laser COM link as much as possible, though they still aren't sure your ship will pick it up.

"I couldn't risk Maximilian or anyone from his faction finding out that we have been in communication, so if you get this please reply by laser link as well. If they think we have been collaborating they will use it to turn popular opinion against me.

"Let me begin by thanking you and you crew for all you have done for us since you left. Maximilian won't admit it but our colony has been full of fear for the last several months. Every day we have woken up not knowing if the Vestarians would return. You have brought us some very good news. News I know cost you and your crew a great deal to bring, so I thank you again.

"Now, down to business," Suzanna said with a smile and a wink, "I have spent the time you have been away trying to undermine the First Councilor's position. A number of councilors have come to my side. They agree that if we are to fall under the influence of one of the Earth powers then Britain is by far the best choice, especially if we can enter into some form of protectorate arrangement.

"However, my efforts have only met with limited success. Maximilian's influence reaches far deeper into the council than I ever imagined. He has many of the councilors dancing to his tune. As a result, I have been forced to flee to my gas mining station. I fear that if I return to Haven Maximilian will find some charge to arrest me on. I believe I am safe enough here, if he tried to send his military ships to arrest me everyone would see that he has over stepped his authority. The First Councilor is meant to be an independent keeper of the peace, not the ruler of our colony.

"I am not out of the fight though," Suzanna continued. "I can still communicate with my allies on Haven, and I have begun to release weekly broadcasts to the general populace. I think I have far more support there than in the council chambers. Yet things are moving slowly. Every day Maximilian stays in power he is able to cement his position. If our plans are to work your government needs to move fast. I know you are going back to Earth now. You need to bring a message back for me. Tell your government to hurry, if they act fast they could send a diplomatic envoy with the offer for Haven to become a British protectorate. If a formal offer is made, Maximilian would be forced to hold a general referendum on the issue. If the entire colony gets a chance to decide our future, I believe we may choose to join you.

"If that doesn't happen I fear Maximilian will alienate us from every Earth power. As you have said, if we make an enemy of the Earth powers then sooner or later one of them will attempt to take control of our colony. I would rather see our people freely vote to join you than be forced to join one of the colonial empires at gunpoint.

"So please, hurry home and take my message to your government, I know I can trust you," Suzanna said, she paused and looked at the ground. "I'm sorry we couldn't meet in person this time, I have thought of you often since you left, it warmed my heart to see that you returned safely. Hopefully we will get to meet again soon, I enjoyed how our last diplomatic talks ended," she finished with a smile.

James listened to the message twice before he composed his own reply. In it he thanked Suzanna for her kind words and assured her he would do everything he could to persuade his government to see Haven as a potential ally.

He took a moment to think about how he wanted to end his message. He wasn't sure how he felt about Suzanna. She was stunningly beautiful and he had enjoyed their conversations a great deal. Yet every time he tried to say something affectionate to her, images of Christine popped into his mind. He knew he still loved Christine, yet he had thought time would diminish his feelings. She was married now and he knew there was nothing for him to do but move on. Yet he couldn't bring himself to say something that would betray his feelings for Christine. Finally, he gave up and just said how much he was looking forward to a time when they would be able to meet each other again face to face.

With the message done he stood up and walked back into the bridge. "Send the message I just composed back to the gas mining station. Use a laser link. I don't want Maximilian to know about the communication."

"Yes Sir," Sub Lieutenant King answered.

"Navigation, have you a course plotted out to take us back to Earth?" James queried.

"Yes Sir," Jennings answered. "It will take us approximately seventy days. I've plotted a course that will take us through French colonial space and then to the alpha system rather than returning through British space. I thought you would want the quickest route home."

"Indeed I do," James said, "the sooner the better."

Chapter 30 – Homecoming

For almost five hundred and fifty years Earth has been the capital of the Empire, that isn't likely to change any time soon.

- Excerpt from Empire Rising

26th December, 2466 AD. HMS *Endeavour*, in orbit around Earth.

Seventy days later James stepped into his uncle's office onboard the RSN construction yard HMS *Vulcan*, he was dressed in his best naval uniform. He had sent his report on *Endeavour's* maiden voyage to the Admiralty as soon as his ship had jumped into the Sol system. Now he was about to find out just what his superiors thought of his actions.

"Well you have certainly stirred up a storm my boy," Jonathan Somerville, Admiral of the Red and First Space Lord of the Admiralty said to his nephew by way of greeting.

"Chang presumably dead, a lost colony found, a mutiny, not one but two alien races discovered and the complete extinction of one race averted. Your report takes some reading. If I didn't have corroborating reports from your Lieutenants, I would say you had made it all up. You certainly like to lead an exciting life."

"It seems I do Sir," James said with a smile. "But let me remind you, you are the one who sends me on all these exploration missions. I can't help stumbling into what is already there."

"Ha," Admiral Somerville said, "don't try and blame this on me. I didn't tell you to go and discover that we are not alone in the galaxy. You did that all by yourself."

"Technically the Vestarians discovered Haven," James replied.

"Technicalities," Admiral Somerville said, waving his hand at his nephew, "I don't think that is how it's going to play out in the news reports.

"And don't get me started on the Havenites," he complained. "They have been causing me headaches in parliament ever since *Innocence* returned. And that Haven freighter you sent with your suggestions didn't help. Parliament has been split right down the middle about what to do about them. The UN has been worse. Every minor power is trying to have their say in the debate.

"And now you bring me all this. There is going to be an uproar in parliament. I'm sure some people will be singing your praises but the rest will be wanting you lynched for all you have done."

"The Havenites deserve our protection," James said, unconcerned about the political fallout from his actions. "They really have accomplished some amazing things. The Vestarians might not be a threat anymore but there are other human powers who will seek to steal all that the Havenites have accomplished. And we don't know what else is out there. It will take the Havenites years to build up their defenses again."

"We will see," Admiral Somerville said, "but that is for your betters to decide."

"Now," he continued as he reached into one of his office drawers and pulled out two cigars, "that was your official chastisement."

He unwrapped one and handed the other to James, "let me personally say well done. I couldn't be more proud of you. You handled yourself admirably,"

"Thank you Sir," James said, taken aback at his uncle's change of tone.

"Oh don't get me wrong," he said as he lit his cigar. "You have made my life a living hell, but I wouldn't have it any other way.

"I'm going to have to organize a court martial to deal with Ferguson, that's going to bring a lot of negative press. And even though these aliens are going to bring new technologies and trade opportunities, I'm going to have to completely redeploy my fleets to protect the new trade routes as they open up. Never mind all the work dealing with Haven will bring. Yet if we can convince the Havenites to join us, our colonial empire will almost rival the Americans. If we could achieve that it would be no trivial feat.

"Yet that is all ahead of us. You have had all the fun putting us on that road. Now I'm the one who has to see it finished, so don't blame me if I seem a bit grumpy."

"You are the Lord of the Admiralty," James said as he began to relax. He had known his uncle liked him but he wasn't entirely sure how the senior Somerville would react to everything he had done. "Yours is the honor and the duty."

"Honor, duty, burden, joy killing weight of pressure, it's all the same really," Admiral Somerville said, "you'll find out some day boy."

Before James could say anything more his uncle leaned in, "tell me this boy, just how close did you and this Councilwoman get? She seems to be a real looker," he asked with a gleam in his eye.

James had suspected this was coming. He knew his uncle was keen to get him married off. It wasn't good that a Duke of England was unmarried and without any children. It was the duty of every British citizen to help expand the British population and feed the Kingdom's ever growing need for personnel. Plus, his uncle wanted him to put the whole Christine affair behind him.

"Not very," James partially lied, "we really didn't spend that much time together. Just a few minutes at the First Councilors ball and then less than an hour at her gas mining station."

"Humm," his uncle responded, "that's not the impression her last message gives."

"So what about my ship?" James asked to change the topic. "She will need to go into a repair yard to get properly repaired. Is there one available? It shouldn't take too long. Maybe a month or so but that's all."

"I've been thinking about that," Admiral Somerville said. "The Chester colony has just completed a new repair yard. The same money that built *Endeavour* paid for it. I think the people of Chester would enjoy seeing what their taxes have been spent on."

"But that will take me away from Earth when the Kulreans

arrive," James protested. "They will want me to meet them here."

"Not exactly," Admiral Somerville said. "If you can time it right, you should be able to get your repairs done and meet the Kulreans in the Alpha system. We can arrange it with them through their FTL communication satellite. I'm sure they will enjoy having you escort them to Earth.

"And more importantly, it will keep you out of the spotlight for a while. I think our planet will have enough to think about for the next few weeks without having to deal with all the protests that some MPs or concerned citizens will raise against you.

"Besides," Admiral Somerville continued, "most of our construction yards and repair yards are still working on refitting our larger warships. If you wait around here it could be months before *Endeavour* gets seen to. This will be the quickest way to get your ship back into pristine condition."

"I guess that would suit me fine," James said, not sure that he really had another option. He certainly didn't want to have to deal with all the news reporters who would no doubt make it their life's goal to hunt him down.

"Good, good, then it is settled," Admiral Somerville said with an air of authority. "You will have to remain here for a week at least to go through some more serious debriefs, but as soon as I can I'll write you some new orders and send you on your way.

"Now," he continued after taking a long puff on his cigar, "tell me about the family Dukedom, I hear you and your friend Clements have been making some big moves into the interstellar trade business."

"Well I don't know how much I can tell you," James began. He had given over control of his finances to a friend from the naval academy, Andrea Clements. Andrea had turned out to be an investment whiz kid and with James' help she had started her own investment company. His Dukedom had been her first client. She had sent him an updated report on the Dukedom's finances as soon as *Endeavour* had entered the Sol system but James hadn't given it more than a cursory glance. Still, he proceeded to tell his uncle as much as he could remember, making sure he gave Andrea all the warm recommendations she deserved.

James was pleased to see the pleasure it brought his uncle to hear that the Dukedom was once again turning a profit and looking after its employees. It hadn't dawned on James before just how much his father's mismanagement of the Dukedom had hurt his uncle.

After covering the family finances James wasn't surprised to see the old style paper book his uncle magically produced as a gift for him. "A late Christmas present," his uncle said with a smile.

More inspiration, James thought as he returned his uncle's smile.

The next hour was filled with more questions as Admiral Somerville took time to go over James' story once again. James knew his uncle was a renowned warship Captain but that had been in the past. Now he was stuck in an office, not the bridge of a warship. It wasn't too surprising to find that his uncle wanted to hear all about James' experiences and decisions. It was the only way the Admiral could relive his past accomplishments.

When his uncle finally dismissed him James felt exhausted. He was happy to return to *Endeavour* and crash into his bed. Getting reacquainted with Earth would have to wait.

*

A couple of days later James found himself standing in the last place on Earth he wanted to return to, the UN Interplanetary Committee. The Committee dealt with all international disputes between Earth's colonial powers.

News of his actions against the Indian mining station had reached Earth long before *Endeavour* had returned. His uncle had told him that the Indians had lodged a complaint with the British government but they had left it at that. Clearly they had changed their minds for within a day of returning to Earth he had received a summons to appear before the Council, the Indian government had requested that he stand trial for charges of piracy. This hearing was to see if the Council would allow the charges to continue to a UN trial.

"And so in summary," James said to the panel of thirteen diplomats that represented each of the main colonial powers, "that is why I took the actions I did. We had strong reason to believe that the Varun Shipping Company had aided Chang's escape from Chinese space and would try to prevent any attempt I made to apprehend him. If I hadn't destroyed the Varun mining station's point defenses, they would likely have shot down my landing shuttles and killed many of my crew. As you know, article eighty-nine point seven of the UN Interplanetary Act states that anyone who aids a war criminal in their activities becomes implicit in their crimes. I was therefore acting within the stipulations of this panel's declaration of Chang Lei as a war criminal. As soon as Varun took Chang in they forfeited their right to the legal protection this council provides to all interstellar organizations.

"Having said that, I would still like to apologize to the Indian government for my actions, in an ideal world I would not have had to board the mining station at all. In light of that I would like to offer to personally cover the costs of repairing the mining station. I hope that will go some way in making up for the anger my actions have caused among the Indian government."

James wasn't sure it would change anything but it was an offer his uncle had suggested he make. The repairs would likely run into the tens of millions of credits but James could easily afford that. In the end, it was a rather cheap way to win the favor of some of the independent panelists.

When James sat down a representative of the Admiralty stood to address the panel. James' uncle hadn't come himself as he didn't want to be seen to be involved in the proceedings but he had assured James he would send his best legal representative. "My name is Oliver Arian, I am a legal officer in the RSN. The Admiralty of the Royal Navy has asked me to present some information to this Committee on Captain Somerville's behalf."

"You may present your evidence," the leader of the Committee said.

"Thank you," Oliver began. "Well, you have all heard Captain Somerville's testimony. I would like to add the official orders Captain Somerville had been given by the Admiralty into the record."

As he stood Oliver lifted a datapad and tapped it a few times to send the information to all the panelists. "As you can see, his actions were perfectly consistent with the orders he received. He was expressly instructed to consider all those who colluded with Chang as potential hostiles and war criminals as recognized by this Council.

"To be frank then, this hearing is quite simply a farce. Captain Somerville was acting as a Captain of the Royal Space Navy when he boarded the Varun mining station. If the Indian government wants to make an official complaint about what happened in the Kerala system then their complaint should be against the British government, not an individual captain.

"What's more, as Captain Somerville has already pointed out, the evidence that Chang was on the mining station and that Station Commander Chowdhury knew about his presence is overwhelming. By any reasonable determination Chowdhury and the station itself should be considered collaborators in Chang's crimes. Therefore, the Indian government's decision to bring this request and their claim to be the hurt party here necessarily implies that they were complicit in Chowdhury and the other Varun official's crimes. If this trial is to go ahead then my government will be bringing charges of war crimes against the Indian government.

"That's preposterous," the Indian diplomat on the committee shouted.

"Preposterous it may be," Oliver agreed. "Yet if the Indian government wants to claim that their rights were personally infringed upon by James' actions, then they are implicitly acknowledging that they were responsible for harboring a war criminal.

"It is the estimation of my government that this is not actually the case. It is a sad fact that the Varun Shipping Company was pulled into this ordeal by a few corrupt trading managers. We accept Varun's and the Indian government's claim that Varun as a company had nothing to do with Chang's escape."

James knew that wasn't strictly true. RSNI had uncovered more than enough information to indict most of Varun's top board members for helping Chang but the British government had decided to keep that information under wraps to help bring the whole situation to an end sooner. There were bigger fish to fry.

"Yet, if this complaint goes ahead it will make a lie of what Varun and the Indian government has said up to this date. The Indian government and Varun can only bring this charge of piracy if they are the complainants, yet if they are the complainants then this committee must also denounce them as war criminals for their collusion with Chang."

James had to suppress a smile. Oliver had the committee over a barrel. Many of the representatives of the space faring powers who were opposed to the British Star Kingdom's expansion would jump at the chance to embarrass the British through finding James guilty. Yet if they allowed the trial to go ahead then they would be forced to accuse the Indians of war crimes. As many of Britain's opponents were friendly or even open allies with the Indians they wouldn't want to do anything to upset them.

"As you just heard from Captain Somerville," Oliver continued. "The evidence is inescapable, Chang had been present on the mining station and a Varun freighter, under the direction of Varun employees, transported him there. Given these facts there is no grounds to approve a trial against Captain Somerville. He was simply acting in accord with this Council's laws and statutes, as well as following the lawful orders of his government.

"Captain Somerville has also personally apologized for the damage he caused to the mining station and has offered to cover the entire expense of repairing the station.

"I, on behalf of the British government, would therefore ask this Committee to dismiss this request to approve a trial into Captain Somerville's actions and allow Captain Somerville to settle the matter privately with the Varun Shipping Company," Oliver said and sat down.

"We will break for a recess to make our decision," the leader of the Committee said when it was obvious that none of the other members had any questions for Oliver.

"Don't worry," Oliver said to James as the committee shuffled out. "They won't dare let this go any further, the Indians are just taking out their frustrations on us."

James found it hard to be so confident as it was his career being discussed. Yet when the panel returned half an hour later they announced that the case was to be dismissed. James let out a long breath in relief. He knew from past experience that the Committee was unpredictable. The fact that each of the major space faring powers had their own appointee on the committee meant that almost every meeting was an extension of the national rivalries that dominated human politics. Still, the committee meant that many of the disputes were played out here between the representatives rather than out in space between the different colonial navies.

As James was making his way out of the council room Oliver walked over to him. "You see, no problem," he said with a smile.

"Easy for you to say," James said, "even if it was just all for show, your career wasn't on the line."

"I guess not," Oliver said, "but I had you covered. By the way, your uncle asked me to let you know that he wants you to report to the Admiralty buildings in London once this hearing is over."

"Very well," James said. "I guess I better organize some transport."

"No rest for the wicked," Oliver said before he walked away, leaving James to his thoughts.

Chapter 31 – The King

What the Vestarians found in the Omen facility was only the beginning, if the human nations had known what the alien ship meant they could have averted disaster, but how could they know what was to come?

-Excerpt from Empire Rising, 3002 AD

28th December, 2466 AD. Earth.

Thankfully, the UN Interplanetary Committee met in New York and there were always plenty of shuttles traveling to London. Just forty minutes after he left the UN meeting James' shuttle touched down in one of the landing zones outside Admiralty House in Whitehall London.

The old Admiralty building had lain unused during the twentieth and twenty-first centuries. But with Britain's first steps towards a permanent naval presence in space, the buildings had been reopened and refurbished. Now most of the structure was deep underground. The old seventeenth century surface building was just for show.

As James traveled down in the turbolift to his uncle's groundside offices he hoped he was about to get his new orders to leave for Chester. He was already more than fed up with UN politics, the news reporters who had been hounding him and the constant images of Christine that were dominating the news.

When James stepped into his uncle's office he was surprised to see that they wouldn't be alone, there were two men standing with his uncle. "Ah, James," his uncle said, "I think you have already met my two guests."

As the two men turned to meet him James had to get a firm grip on his emotions. Prime Minister Fairfax he liked, or at least agreed with on most political issues. The King of the British Star Kingdom was another matter. During James' relationship with his daughter, King Edward XI had done everything in his power to get rid of James.

To his surprise, King Edward was the first to speak. "Congratulations Captain, your recent accomplishments have done your country proud and greatly enhanced your reputation," he said as he held out his hand.

James was completely taken aback, last time they had met the King had intentionally ignored him. Yet here he was singing his praises. James had to kick himself into action as silence descended on the room. Everyone was waiting for him to move, no one left the King waiting with his hand outstretched.

"Thank you your Highness," James said as he took the King's hand. "It is my pleasure to serve, it is my crew who deserve the real praise."

"Indeed they do," Prime Minister Fairfax said, jumping in, "and I'm sure all this publicity isn't hurting your chances with the ladies either," he added with a chuckle.

"I don't know about that," James said, "but it has certainly made getting any privacy all but impossible. I'm eager to get back to my ship."

"All in good time my boy," James' uncle said, joining the conversation. "We have brought you here to pick your brains. Both the Prime Minister and the King have read your report in great detail. Still, they want to hear your account in your own words."

"I understand Sir," James replied, "where would you like me to begin?"

"Come and have a seat," Admiral Somerville said to the group, "then we can begin."

When everyone was sitting around Admiral Somerville's desk James recounted his story. A number of times Fairfax and King Edward interjected with a question or two, especially when it came to the two alien races, but for the most part, the three older men let James speak freely.

When he was done James took the opportunity to offer his own opinion on the situation. "And so it would be my recommendation that we do everything we can to peacefully incorporate the Haven colony and the surrounding systems into our colonial empire. If we, or any of the other powers try to force them into something against their will, I believe it will quickly become a serious incident. We would have to provide an occupation force to police and garrison the planet. We all know that such endeavors almost never end in success."

"What is your evaluation of the general populace then?" King Edward asked.

"They are fiercely independent and highly competent. To have accomplished all that they have in the last two hundred years has only been possible because each member of their society is fully committed to their ideal of a free and productive society. I think they have made amazing progress, in large part because they wanted to meet the Earth nations as equals. I fear that if we or any of the other powers were to turn that passion and ingenuity against us, actually controlling their population would prove impossible. Or at least so costly that it wouldn't be worthwhile," James answered earnestly.

"So you think the general population would take up arms against any attempts to control them? Fairfax asked, "hence your idea of a protectorate."

"Yes," James said, "if Councilwoman Rodriguez and the others can be convinced then I believe that we could convince the rest of the population. I don't know all the ins and outs of interstellar politics but it seems like it would give everyone the best deal. The Havenites would get to keep their sovereignty largely intact, they would also have control over their closest systems; giving them plenty of room to expand. We, on the other hand, would have direct access to their systems with our military and exploration ships. If Haven became a protectorate it would open up an entirely new area of space for us to explore and expand into. Just as importantly, so far the only known way to Vestar and Kulthar is through the Haven system. We would therefore be able to control what will most likely become the most important trade route in the Human Sphere."

"Well, you make a strong case," Fairfax approvingly. "Now tell me, what do you think of this Council Woman Rodriguez? Can she lead the Haven people towards joining us?"

James took a moment to consider his answer; he didn't want any of his feelings to cloud his reasoning. "She is a very competent woman," he began. "And she is deeply concerned about the future of her people. Yet First Councilor Maximilian has a firm grip on the colony. The people look up to him as the heir of the founder of their colony. Even after we revealed his involvement in harboring Chang and the piracy of our freighters, he managed to hold onto power.

"I'm not saying she cannot convince the people of Haven to join us, however, it will be a very hard task. The population are deeply untrusting towards any Earth nation and Maximilian has been using that to keep himself in power.

"I believe Rodriguez would make a good and faithful alley, yet without some form of help I do not think she can carry the people away from Maximilian. At least, she won't be able to convince them before it is too late. Maximilian is determined to keep Haven independent at all costs. Even if we were to ignore the colony and its strategic importance, Maximilian is going to get himself into trouble with one of the other major powers."

"Thank you for your honesty," King Edward said. "We will take everything you have said under consideration. You'll be pleased to know that your uncle has largely agreed with your assessment. However, there will be a lot of work involved in just getting the Houses of Parliament to agree to any kind of intervention in Haven. We are still sorely over stretched after our war with the Chinese and our expansion into the Void.

"I will tell you this much, the Prime Minister and I are convinced we need to make a play for Haven. Just what that will look like yet we don't know. We do plan to send an envoy to Haven as soon as possible. Our diplomat will be fully briefed on our desires and he will be actively assessing the possibility of offering protectorate status to Haven, among other possibilities. There is one thing I think we can all agree on however, we can't let the Indians or anyone else get their hands on the colony and the shift passages to our new friends."

"Agreed," Admiral Somerville said. "I'm glad my nephew has been of some help to your thinking."

"I am happy to have been of some service," James said, pleased at his uncle's praise. "I just hope we can sort things out peacefully."

"Indeed," Fairfax said, "I suspect that will not be up to us however."

"No," the King agreed, "but that is for you to worry about Admiral," he added as he stood. "I would advise that you do everything you can to get the fleet back to full strength."

Admiral Somerville sighed, "Isn't that what you say to me every time we meet your Majesty?"

"It may well be," Edward replied, "but that doesn't make it bad advice. Now, I really must be going, I have three more meetings today."

"Of course your Majesty, Prime Minister, I hope this meeting has been helpful," Admiral Somerville replied.

"Yes," Fairfax said, "it is always good to see the personality behind the report. Your thoughts will be taken on board

Captain," he added as he shook James' and his uncle's hands.

King Edward followed suit and the two men left Admiral Somerville's offices.

"What has come over the King?" James asked his uncle as soon as the two other men left. "He hated me before."

"Politics," Admiral Somerville said, laughing. "When you were chasing his daughter you were a political obstacle to be overcome. Now you are one of his richest Dukes and an up and coming naval officer. King Edward can't afford to keep you in his bad books."

"I see," James said. He didn't tell his uncle but he was certain it would take a lot longer for his ill feelings towards the king to disappear. He still blamed the man for ruining James' chance at love and a family, even if he knew why Christine had made the decisions she had.

"So, about *Endeavour*," Admiral Somerville said as he reached into a drawer in his desk.

"Yes?" James said eagerly.

"I have your new orders," Admiral Somerville replied coyly. "Are you ready to depart?"

"Certainly," James said, "I think I have had enough of London for another few years."

"Ha," James' uncle said, "I remember a young lad who loved wasting his time and fortune frolicking around London, throwing his money at any pretty girl who would look at him."

"Yes," James said contemplatively as he remembered his misspent youth. "That was a long time ago, a lot has happened since then."

"It certainly has," Admiral Somerville said thinking of his brother. "Your father's actions were hard on us all. I still feel guilty that I didn't notice any sign he was in trouble before things got so bad."

"There is no blame to be laid at your door," James said forcefully. "My father brought all his troubles on himself. I miss him in a way, and I pity him for how things turned out. But the only one to blame for his misfortune was himself. I'm just happy that Andrea has managed to turn the Dukedom's fortunes around and compensate all those who lost their jobs and livelihoods because of him."

"Yes," Admiral Somerville said, "I don't think you have realized it yet but your decision to pay out such generous compensatory packages and to hire back so many of those who lost their jobs has proven very popular among the masses. Your discovery of the Void and now Haven and these alien races is making you a household name."

"Hardly," James said dismissively, "it just made me a target for a bunch of annoying news reporters. The sooner I'm back on board *Endeavour* the better."

"Yes, well, back to your orders then," Admiral Somerville said as he handed James the data chip he had taken out of his desk drawer. "I'm sending you to Chester as we discussed. You can return to your ship and depart as soon as your crew return from leave. I have already assigned a number of new crew members to replace the losses you suffered."

"That's great," James said excitedly. "I'll get her fixed up and back to the Alpha system as soon as possible. I'm looking forward to Pemel's arrival. It's certainly going to cause a stir. He can be the one who has to deal with all the reporters when he arrives."

"Yes, you would enjoy watching that," Admiral Somerville said. "Well, that is all I wanted to say to you. I'll see you in a couple of months Captain," he added as he stood and shook James' hand.

"Farewell uncle," James said as he walked out of the office.

*

An hour later James walked into the recovery ward of the Royal Marsden Rehabilitation Hospital in West Sussex. Lieutenant Scott had been transferred there as soon as *Endeavour* had reached Earth. James wanted to make sure she was being looked after properly before he left for Chester. Jil'lal had made him promise that he would personally make sure she received the best treatment. A quick COM message to Andrea had ensured that the best rehabilitation center in Britain had taken Scott immediately.

"How is she doing doctor?" James asked the woman in charge of Scott's care.

"Remarkably well," the doctor said. "We have taken her out of the induced coma and are beginning the first stages of helping her cope with what she went through. Her new legs and fingers should be grown and ready for transplant in about a week."

"I thought *Endeavour's* doctor said she needed to stay in the coma until her new legs were attached?" James queried.

"No, not exactly." The doctor began. "Recent studies have found that if the patient is made aware of the loss before the operation then they appreciate the new limbs more. If they just wake up with a new leg or arm they instinctively know something is wrong and yet they can't figure it out, for on the outside it looks like everything is exactly the same. Helping them realize the loss they have gone through helps them cope with the new arms or legs. The real problem comes if they have gotten used to not having a limb. Then attaching a new one can be much harder to adjust to."

"I see," James said. "Can I talk to her?"

"Certainly, actually she has been asking for you," the doctor said as she turned and lead James into Scott's room.

"Hello Captain," Scott said with a smile from her bed as soon as he walked in. For anyone who had known her before it was obvious that she had lost much of her beauty. The Marsden might be able to get rid of a lot of the scar tissue but she would never be the same. Her smile however, was exactly as James remembered it.

"Hello Lieutenant," James said, taking her hand. "It's good to see you finally awake, we've missed you."

"It seems I've missed a lot," Scott said. "Though no one around here knows exactly what happened after the explosion, I was hoping you could you fill me in?"

"Well, of course," James said before he dived in to telling Scott about capturing the Overlord and stopping his fleet.

"It seems you are all heroes," Scott said.

"Not any more than you are," James replied. "You saved Jil'lal, she was at your side daily until we dropped her off on Vestar."

"I'm glad she is ok, and that reminds me," Scott said. "That's why I wanted to speak to you. The explosion. It wasn't a booby trap or anything like that. It was an alien ship like we thought."

"A Kulrean ship?" James asked, curious.

"I don't think so," Scott said. "It was armed to the teeth and it spoke to me."

"Spoke to you," James said in surprise.

"Yes, it seemed to have some sort of artificial intelligence that communicated with us. It was even able to identify us as humans," Scott said.

"Identify you?" James repeated. "Then if it wasn't Kulrean or Vestarian you mean there is another alien race out there. One that knows we exist."

"Yes, I believe so. And if the Vestarians obtained their advanced technology from them then they must be far more powerful than we are," Scott concluded.

"What did the RSN intelligence agents make of all this?" James asked.

Scott hung her head, "I didn't pass my psych evaluation. They say I have post-traumatic stress and survivor's guilt. I'm not sure they believed me about talking alien ships."

James wasn't surprised. Humans had abandoned the development of artificial intelligence more than two hundred years ago. The research had got to the point where the AI's were basically self-aware. However, try as many times as they could, the researchers could never instill a sense of morality into the machines. The results had been truly terrifying. The AI's had come to see humans as the cause of all humanity's problems. Their logical solution had been the enslavement of humans to the direction of AI's. If they had been allowed out of the laboratories they would have tried to take control, all for the good of mankind. As a result, AI research had been banned.

The common consensus had been that any alien race they would encounter would have come to the same conclusions. AI's were just too powerful to actually allow them to exist. James hadn't spoken to Pemel about any Kulrean AI's but he made a note to bring it up when he got to Earth.

"I believe you," James said as he turned his attention back to Scott. "This is something we will have to take very seriously. But for now you need to get better. If you make a full recovery then the rest of the navy is much more likely to take you seriously."

"I know," Scott said, squeezing his hand. "I'm going to do my best. It helps that you believe me."

Epilogue

29th December, 2466AD, New Delhi

"Our request for a trial was denied then?" Prime Minister Slaman Devgan asked.

Yes, but it served its purpose," Sha Roshan the Minister for External Affairs said. "The British think we have put the matter to rest."

"So they suspect nothing?" Devgan followed up.

"I wouldn't say they suspect nothing," Roshan answered. "They will know that we must be considering our options towards Haven. Yet I believe they will think we are taking our time, weighing our options."

"Then we must press ahead with our plans," Devgan said confidently. "Admiral Kapoor, how are your preparations coming together?"

"A messenger freighter has just returned from our colonies," Admiral Kapoor began. "Our fleet is prepared and ready to move. They are just waiting for a large enough ground force to be gathered. The latest report estimates that we will have gathered fifty thousand troops by the end of next month. By then, the fleet will be ready to move.

"I have placed Admiral Kumar in charge of the main attack force.

Admiral Khan will remain behind with one battlecruiser to block any British attempt to send ships to Haven. Once we secure the colony Admiral Kumar can release more ships to Khan to beef up our defenses. The only way the British can get to Haven is through our colonial space. If we move fast, the British won't be able to stop us. The majority of their large warships are still undergoing refits after their war with the Chinese."

"It is settled then," the Prime Minister said, "send your messenger freighter back to the colonies today with the go order. As soon as enough ground forces have been gathered Admiral Kumar is to make her move."

The End

You can follow James, Gupta and all the others in the next book in the Empire Rising series – Return to Haven!

If you enjoyed the book don't forget to leave a review with some stars. As this is my first self-published series every review helps to get my work noticed.

https://www.facebook.com/Author.D.J.Holmes

d.j.holmess@hotmail.com

Comments welcome!

Made in United States
Orlando, FL
06 March 2023

30763644R00293